Dear Daniel

Thank you so much for coming to my very first book launch event!

I sincerely hope you enjoy Book 1 of the Eartherians Series!

Best Wishes

M.C. Cannon

Eartherians Reach

Book One

M.C. Cavanaugh

Cover Art by Justen Dippel

Eartherians Reach

ISBN: 979-8-9894129-2-1

To my wife, Devon, whose consistent support, motivation, and excitement about this project drove it from start to finish.

Acknowledgments

To My Wife:

I dedicated the first book in this series to my wife, Devon, and I would like to provide additional acknowledgment. I started writing Eartherians Reach in August of 2020 while we were pregnant with our first son. A move to a new state, and two more sons later, I am now publishing this first book. So you can imagine the time, energy, and consistent dedication to this project we both had to work through in order for it to be possible. This book would not be here for you to read without her.

She respects and embraces my drive, ambition, and need to write, and for that I am eternally grateful.

To my editors and web developer found on reedsy:

My developmental editor, Shannon Roberts, was incredibly patient with me as a first-time author. She provided candid feedback, sound advice, and took the time to work with me directly as Eartherians Reach came together. As a new author, I'm starting to understand the criticality of the working relationship between author and editor, and I count myself quite fortunate that we were able to connect and work together. I look forward to collaborating with Shannon on the next books in the series.

My copy editor, Sarah Liu, was excellent to work with in getting the final manuscript into a form that is ready for publishing. She worked within my schedule and budget, and also provided additional plot commentary that was important in polishing the final draft manuscript. I also look forward to collaborating with Sarah on the next books in this series.

My web developer, Ingrid Getzan, has been absolutely fantastic to work with. From setting up the initial site, to ideation on content, color schemes, fonts, graphics, search engine optimization, and going live, she has worked with me every step of the way. I could not be more happy with how the web site worked out to support this project, and I am excited for future additions to the site under her watch.

https://www.mccavanaugh.com

My cover designer and visual content developer, Justen Dippel, has been a long time friend going back to high school. His skills and talents in bringing to life the imagination inspiring cover art is just a taste of what is to come on this series. I can't wait to see what he develops on the digital canvas in transitioning the text of the Eartheians series to imagery.

To My Beta and Proof Readers:

I had a fantastic group of beta readers that provided critical feedback on how Eartherians Reach may be received by future readers. They also shared how they would like to see key areas of the book improved. Through e-mails, manuscript notations, and phone calls, I feel confident that I was able to incorporate, or at least address, all of their feedback across the manuscript. The final product was greatly improved by their help and assistance, and I am extremely thankful for their collaboration:

Beate Cavanaugh (Mom)

Patrick Cavanaugh (Dad)

Caitlin Furjanic

Greg Gafni-Pappas

Justin Hammis

David Homsher

Justin Knorr

CAPT Eric Sweigard, USN, Retired

Jennifer Williams

One beta reader in particular, Caitlin Furjanic, deserves additional acknowledgment. She returned to me a fully marked-up manuscript filled with questions, perceptions, comments, and even drawings when it came to getting the physics of the spacecraft as close to digestible as possible for readers. It took me two full months to incorporate her mark-up into the manuscript, and again, the final product is greatly improved because of it. My deepest thanks to Caitlin and to all of the beta readers for lending me their time, energy, and feedback on the draft for Eartherians Reach.

To My High School English Teachers at Sterling Heights Stevenson High School in Michigan.

Over my three years at Stevenson High School from 1996-1998, I had three excellent English teachers that challenged me in different ways, and I believe, laid the foundations for me to become a science fiction writer today in 2024. In the 10th grade, Mrs. Guthard presented us with many classical works and gave us some time in class to read and contribute our thoughts to the class. Mr. McBroom, in the 11th grade, challenged me to work on how I conveyed my thoughts and conclusions to readers of my work, and made sure I had ample opportunities to improve over that junior year. In my senior year, Mr. Bauer gave me the opportunity to write creatively, and took extra time to review my work with me. Near my graduation, when he asked me what I was going to major in for undergrad, he was crestfallen to hear me say ‘engineering’. He told me I had great potential to be writer, and that I should go to school for that instead of engineering.

I wasn’t able to fulfill his request of going to school for writing. However, while I may be two and a half decades late, I respectfully submit Eartherians Reach - Book 1, as a stepping stone on the path to being a writer. Thanks for your words of inspiration Mr. Bauer, I have not forgotten them, and I keep them at the ready, should my confidence ever falter.

To Three Others:

Through one of my beta readers, Jenn Williams, I was able to connect with an outstanding self-published author and Michigander, J.L Hyde. I would like to thank J.L. Hyde, who provided guidance, coaching, and advice that enabled me to get from developmental edit, through beta reader and copy edit, and on to publishing. All of J.L. Hyde’s works can be found on JLHyde.com, and I fully recommend you check them out.

"Jocko" Willink Jr., your podcast and those who you have interviewed, have served as an inspiration to me for years. There was one podcast in particular, and I cannot remember which, where you told us listeners that if we wanted to do something, anything…and I'm paraphrasing here…'learn jujitsu, go for that promotion, ask someone out, write a book…stop what you are doing right now, and get started. Don't do it tomorrow, don't do it in 15 minutes, do it right now.'

I started writing Eartherians Reach seconds after I heard those words. Thank you for kicking me into gear and enabling me to get squared away as far as this first-time writer endeavor goes.

To my late little sister Christina Cavanaugh, you continue to inspire me though we have not seen one another in so long. I added the dream I had about you to Corbin's story in Eartherians Reach, because I wanted to share that unique and inspiring dream experience with everyone. To this day, I feel that the dream is some way that God or perhaps the Universe is telling us that you are doing well, wherever you are, and that maybe one day we will all see one another again. As a science fiction writer and a dreamer, I remain hopeful for that day. I miss you so much, and thank you for always believing in me.

Prologue

Corbin Sterling walked out of the cold early December sleet and into the hole-in-the-wall bar just a few blocks off campus. As the familiar bar-aroma of grilled food, spilled beer, and old wood hit him, he recalled the several times he and his friends had been to see a few upstart bands and vocalists give their try at public performance.

He did a quick sweep of the space, quickly identifying the suit-clad men he was here to meet near the end of the bar. He thought it was a bit off that the two interviewers from Gladwell Defense had asked to meet them here to celebrate his selection for an entry level position. They had jovially congratulated him on being the only one picked for the job after his thirty minute on-campus engineering career fair interview, earlier that day. They had also told him that since he was a twenty-two-year-old fifth year collegiate senior, they wanted to take him out for a drink to celebrate. Corbin had agreed, but had a few reservations if they started to get heavy into the drinks, in case this was some sort of corporate hazing trick for newbies. He had heard that this sort of thing could happen with some companies, and while he wanted to fit in, he didn't want to embarrass himself either.

Corbin walked past the host stand, and down a length of the main bar and saw his two interviewers facing each other and talking over half-drunk beers. Corbin saw the two athletic men were still in their dark suits from the interview. Corbin looked down to check his phone to see if he was on time, and for what must have been the hundredth time today, he cursed it for being dead. He thought he had a full charge when he had left his animal house of friends that morning, but when he had stepped out of the interview room at four thirty, he had been dismayed to see it dead and non-functioning.

At the time, it had been a real bummer as he had wanted to call his parents and tell them about the new job, and he wanted to tell his housemates to meet him out later so they could celebrate with him. Alas, he would have to go find them in person later, and he could call his parents tomorrow after getting his phone on the charger.

He tucked the dead phone back into his pocket when his two soon-to-be work colleagues noticed him.

"Corbin! Hey, my man, come on over here, you've got some catching up to do young man!"

Corbin broke into a smile and shook both of their hands. "I'm ready. Thanks again for taking me out for a cold one…or two."

The lead interviewer, who had introduced himself as Josh Case earlier in the day spoke up, "It's our pleasure Corbin. We are so excited to have you join our team." He turned to the bar where a server he oddly didn't recognize brought three neat drinks that Corbin thought was either whiskey or bourbon in fancy tumblers. Corbin, having spent his high school years as a waiter at a banquet hall, thought it a little strange she had used a bar tray while serving behind the bar, but let it go, not wanting to seem weird or paranoid in front of his new soon-to-be colleagues.

"Before we say anything, we've got to get in a toast," Josh said jovially. His colleague, who had earlier in the day introduced himself as Greg Hansen, cleared his throat while passing one of the three drinks to Corbin, who held the drink in front waiting for the toast.

"To another bright young man joining the fray, may your sacrifice of time with us bring you fulfillment, and most importantly, victory." They didn't clink glasses, but Josh and Greg acknowledged one another with eye contact and salutes of their glasses. Corbin thought the toast was a little odd, and he was surprised to see them down the golden liquid in one gulp, while Corbin had only been planning for a sip. The liquid burned in his mouth, so he too downed it in turn.

It was a confluence of events. Corbin had a sneeze that had been brewing on his walk over to the bar, and the instant the heavier mouthful of burning alcohol hit the back of his throat, it resurfaced, and while he managed to choke some of the bourbon down, he turned abruptly and sneezed the rest of the bourbon through his nose and into his tightly clasped hand.

"Aww man, rookie, Corbin!" Josh slapped him on the back laughing, and Corbin managed to snatch a handful of bar napkins with his freehand, and press it into his other hand, absorbing the rest of the alcohol there, and then he pressed the full wad unceremoniously up to his nose.

Corbin recovered quickly, blinking away tears, and shoving the mass of messy napkins into his own suit coat pocket. The server he didn't know had been watching him with her mouth pressed into a thin line...*was that concern?* But as she caught his eyes, she beamed a smile. "Whoa there, buddy!" she said.

Corbin nodded embarrassed. "Say can I have a..." He shot a glance at the two longneck bottles Josh and Greg had been drinking and continued. "Miller Lite? I think I need to take this next one a little slower."

Greg chimed in. "Hey that's the spirit, but damn man, don't try to snort bourbon like that again. That's not the way to enjoy it!" he finished good naturedly.

Corbin quickly tried to change the conversation. "So what's it like at Gladwell? What am I going to be working on?"

Greg started to speak. "Well, you'll be on a project team along with six to eight others. We will be doing research on transitioning some of the latest mobility software from the university, so..."

As Greg continued, Corbin noticed suddenly, he had a hard time caring about what Greg was saying. *Hey snap out of it man, it's just that first rush from the half drink you just pounded...and then sneezed. Get your act together and pay attention! You are going to be working for these people,* he admonished himself.

That thought too quickly faded as he started to realize his reaction wasn't normal. He was at the peak of his collegiate partying experience, and he had shown higher tolerance than most of his friends. *Why does this feel...so different? I think...I think they slipped me something...holy shit this is some hazing bullshit.* And then he felt panic rising, clearing some of the cobwebs...*or is this worse?*

"Hey Corbin, Yo!" Josh snapped his fingers in front of his face. "You still with us, man?"

Corbin snapped back from his thoughts tumbling unclearly and answered, "Yeah...um sorry, I was just hoping to hit the restroom before I sat down. Excuse me for a minute?"

Corbin didn't wait for Josh's or Greg's response and stood up to move to the claustrophobic and unclean broom closet of a bathroom he had suffered many times before. Out of the corner of his eye, he caught Josh look a little too sharply at Greg, and that told him they were being forced off script. "I'll be right back, fellas, and I'll start catching up with that beer." He looked away from them and smiled at the server, who had just snapped the cap off the beer he had ordered, and placed it neatly on a napkin.

His thoughts erupted at that: *They don't hand out napkins here.* His eyes looked around as he made his way to the back of the bar. When he had walked in earlier, he could have sworn there were other people in here, but sweeping the place with his eyes, he could see that it was deserted. *Very strange for a Friday even as early as this. This isn't right at all, time to get the hell out of here.*

In the long mirror behind the bar, he looked hard to the left to see Josh and Greg still in their seats, but eyes fixed firmly on Corbin's back. *Yep, I'm out,* he thought.

He turned his wide shoulders to fit through the small single toilet bathroom entrance and shut the door. Without hesitation, he reached up and unlocked the window above the toilet that was just barely big enough for him to fit through. He took off his jacket and threw it out into the side alley, stepped up on the toilet tank, and pulled himself up into the alleyway, wiggling his way through the window. Thankfully it wasn't too dirty, but as he stood to his full height, he still had to brush off some of the small rocks and dirt that clung to his pants when he had put his knees down before standing up.

His head was swimming a bit more now, and his heart was pumping from the initial rush of adrenaline, but it was competing with whatever they had given him, and he stumbled toward the street. He didn't know how much time he had to be conscious, and he didn't know how long before Greg and Josh would come after him.

He stumbled toward the street, which had a few pedestrians walking by, and he could see cars passing, not a block away. He hastened his pace and saw blessedly that a taxi was at the front of the bar dropping some more people off. While the taxi looked more like a nice SUV with a taxi sign added to the top he didn't care. He got to the open door, just as one of the young men he had dropped off was about to close the door.

Corbin said, "I got it, thanks," and leaned in to talk to the taxi driver. "Hey man, can you take me to…"

"Leaving so soon, are we?" Josh said from behind and then stuffed him into the cab. His hands were like vise grips, and when he threw his shoulder into Corbin, he had almost fallen out the other side of the Chevy Tahoe's back seat if it hadn't for Greg who was already getting in on the other side.

In moments, Corbin found himself sandwiched uncomfortably between the two men, and opened his mouth to speak, but a stinging pin prick on the left side of his neck distracted him, and he looked over to Greg who withdrew a small syringe, slipped a cap on it, and put it into his pocket.

Corbin met Greg's eyes in horror.

Greg looked at him. "It's not like that, man, we're not here to hurt you or kill you. I meant what I said during that toast."

Corbin's eyes slammed shut, and he slumped forward. Greg gently caught him with a hand to the chest so Corbin's unconscious form wouldn't bump into the center console.

Greg looked over at Josh past Corbin's bowed head, and spoke in a sigh. "You know we could have made a night of it. We could have hit a few bars, and when we offered to drive him home, we could have slipped him the dose then."

Josh shook his head, "Nah, man, better to get it over with. We weren't going to be able to keep the place clean of people much longer anyways. Besides, what do you want to do? Get to know him, and then never see the kid again?"

Greg looked away from Josh, and muttered, "I really hate this fucking job."

Josh looked back at him grimly and nodded. "I liked that toast though," Josh said and gestured to the male driver who had been attentively watching the scene play out in his rearview mirror. The man opened his driver's side door, stepped onto the step, reached up and plucked the taxi sign off the top of the SUV.

They drove away.

Chapter One: Awaken

Awareness. There was nothing, and then all of a sudden it was there. At first there was only a sense of self, just an awareness in a pleasant blackness. Next there was a sense of something that isn't quite like sight, but a feeling of light through a pink and reddish fog. There was no sense of time save for the transition from some time ago there being nothing, to now a singular feeling of being something that exists and is aware that it exists…somewhere.

And then came an explosion of thought, memory, and knowledge of self. It was a massive detonation where images, smells, feelings, intuitions, and recollection…yes, that is what it was…memory raced away from a singular point, streaked, branched, connected, and forked into a massive array of consciousness. Though these streets of thought had been paved before, the blast wave of consciousness explosion neared a barrier of…something…perhaps the end of this self. The array of thoughts, that moments before was just a sense of self, appeared and accelerated in an instant that may also have been thousands of years.

"I," is the first thought that entered Corbin Sterling's mind before the cognitive management subroutine on his cryogenic stasis chamber took over and began to regulate the reanimation process. The cryogenic system was programmed to govern the level of a given subject's brain activity, in order to protect it from damage, should it reanimate too quickly.

The "I" feeling within Corbin, hit a bit of a cognitive wall as the regulated process went on, and some distant memory of form started to take shape. Memory of a head, torso, arms, pelvis, legs, and finally hands and feet started to report to his consciousness. For the briefest of moments, there was a rise to panic, which was quickly soothed by some unknown external process. Corbin now knew he was moving, but it was impossible to know for how long.

The icy cryofluid drained and was slowly being replaced by water, which started near freezing, and slowly inched up in temperature. As his body warmed, pain receptors all over Corbin's skin had begun firing, but were muted through a cocktail of anesthesia and painkillers, while brain activity continued to be monitored closely for any drift out of tolerance. As his body temperature warmed, a myriad of tiny needles extended into the cryo chamber and into preset muscle, tendon, and pressure point areas, stimulating the perfectly preserved tissues and underlying fluids to return to work after the long slumber. Slowly but surely, Corbin's dormant human circulatory and cardiovascular systems began to turn back on and metabolize the intravenous nourishment as he moved toward full reanimation.

Several minutes later Corbin understood that he was a person and was undergoing some sort of medical procedure. He wiggled what he remembered to be his fingers and toes, uttered an unintelligible series of grunts, and managed to open his eyes to tiny slits while also straining to hear. The light level was blissfully low, but he could make out that he was in some sort of tub that had been turned so that he was in a near standing position. Looking out the front of the tub he could see that it was a small room…he couldn't quite grasp the right word in his mind, *bathroom*?

As he became more aware, he heard soft and pleasant music, and his nostrils were greeted by a sweet scent. The calm light successfully illuminated the small space and remained at a low level.

Looking down, he realized he was wet and naked, and felt slightly cold. He looked down to see his pelvis and chest were loosely strapped to the chamber so he would not fall out or slouch down. A distant memory of what it was like to rise from bed from ages ago flashed through his mind and was gone. He reached up to the edges of the tub and pulled himself forward. The restraints relaxed as he did so, but still stayed in place. When he was fairly sure he wasn't going to pass out, he took a step, and the restraints fell away and retracted audibly back into the sides of the tub.

"Please be careful and take it slowly." A gentle feminine voice rang from everywhere inside the small bathroom. While the voice sounded calm, the verbal commands felt like they were exploding into his ears, and startled Corbin.

Rather than flail, Corbin froze at the voice, and waited for its return. He could feel his mind slowly crunching on the sounds—*no, words*—and within a split second he understood the meaning. When the voice didn't return, he ventured a small step, all the while keeping a hand on the edge of the tub behind him. He didn't fall, so he took another step onto the spongy, but warm and dry mat in front of the tub.

"Well done," the voice continued, startling Corbin again. "Take a few moments to pace around and get the hang of walking again. When you are ready, please use the shower to your left and rinse off any remaining cryogenic fluid. Soap and shampoo have been provided. You'll find a towel next to the shower, and clean clothing in the cabinet. Based on your current state of motor and cognitive function, I estimate this will take you approximately eight minutes. Would you like to listen to music while you shower? Do you understand the words I am speaking to you now?"

The AI waited the seven-ish seconds for the reply from Corbin. "Yes," he croaked, trying his vocal cords. Despite his one-word answer, the disembodied voice brought back the calm music.

Corbin took a shower moving through his usual routine which finished with the familiar shampoo application to his head. His slow moving and muddled thoughts wandered to how he came to be here, and while the shower routine was fully natural, his mind hit a wall in recalling who he was, and why he was washing off cryogenic fluid. What was more unsettling was that he just felt sort of indifferent to all of it. It was as if he knew all would reveal itself in due time, and he would take it all in stride. He also felt positive…it felt odd, to be in a good mood and not know why. He had felt this way before but couldn't recall any details. There was a quiet anticipation of the future, and while Corbin couldn't really understand why he was thinking or feeling anything, all the same the positive eagerness was there.

Corbin finished his shower and toweled himself off. Glancing over to the sink, Corbin saw a toothbrush and toothpaste dispenser. The calm voice hadn't directed him earlier, but it felt natural for him to go through his standard morning routine of brushing his teeth while checking himself out in the mirror. He knew the image he saw was of himself, but couldn't recall how he had come to be, couldn't remember how he had looked when he was younger, and could barely recall his own name. *Corbin,* he said to himself. It felt good to hear his mind say it, so he said it out loud. "Corbin." Deep in his mind he could feel just a few more doors in the maze unlock and open. They didn't consciously tell him anything more about himself, but he immediately felt more like himself, and for the first time in what must have been a long time, he saw himself smile.

He felt strangely task-driven, almost as if he was confident that someone was watching him…evaluating him. He removed the clothing contents from the cabinet and found comfortable pants and a long-sleeve shirt with a small breast pocket and name patch stating what must be his last name "Sterling" in raised block lettering. He slipped the garments on and stood in the mirror admiring the look and feel. The clothing wasn't too warm nor too cold, not too heavy, and not too light. Corbin thought it had the perfect balance of everything, from stretchiness to fit, and length of pant leg and arm. He reflexively did some leg bends, slow squats, and gentle circles with his arms and was pleased to see the material stretched when it needed to and condensed without bunching when in excess. He turned back to the locker and found a pair of shoes and slipped them on. Looking in the mirror and testing with steps, they were athletic in nature, but seemed to have a weighty sole and heel. After a few steps, he heard a small mechanical sound, and felt them quickly adjust to the dimensions and pressure points of his feet, until it felt like he was just wearing a light pair of socks, yet his feet felt fully supported.

Stepping back and looking at himself in the mirror, Corbin thought he looked fairly sharp. He had the look of a young man in his early 20s, with the hint of an angular jaw, green eyes, and dark brown hair. His hair was cropped short on the sides, and slightly longer on top. Corbin figured he must not have been in this cryogenic system for too long if his hair still looked less than a week from having been cut. In taking a full measure of himself, he saw that he was barrel chested with well-proportioned torso, and athletic arms and legs, not overly muscular, but fit at just under six feet tall and around two hundred pounds.

As if on cue, the calm voice returned. "Is everything fitting to your liking?" Taking one more glance at his image in the mirror behind him he responded, "Yes, thank you, but can you tell me where I am?"

"You are welcome. Everything will be answered as quickly as you are able to absorb it, but for now please, step through the doorway. Let's get you some refreshment before the First Briefing and of course, you may ask your many questions. Does the music still suit you?"

Corbin sighed, and paused to listen to the pleasant voice and relaxing music while he opened the bathroom door and stepped into a more brightly lit room that resembled…again he struggled with the word *an office*? Looking around to get his bearings, he realized he was in someone's living space. In the adjacent room he could see a bed, nightstand, and a sofa off to the side, and noted that the mental recognition of these items started to flow more easily in his mind.

Looking over his immediate surroundings in the office, he saw there was a desk, and chair, with a monitor screen, and a larger screen affixed to the wall off to the side of the desk. On the corner of the desk was a small plate with three brightly colored items, which reminded Corbin of something sweet, but he couldn't quite place the name in his head. There was also a clear bottle of what appeared to be water. At the voice's question on music, Corbin answered, "Yes, but perhaps something with a little more energy." The music abruptly transitioned to a faster pace but remained within the pleasant balance he had experienced earlier. Corbin nodded thoughtfully and moved toward the desk on instinct. In the back of his mind, he could feel purpose behind the disembodied voice asking him about the music. The choice provided an illusion of some control, but Corbin knew it was arbitrary. *Let's see where this goes before making a fuss,* he thought to himself.

"Please be seated. You will notice the plate has three edible items on it. These items have been designed specifically to reactivate your digestive system. They can be consumed in any order; however, I recommend you take at least a small sip of water after each bite. The items will have a pleasant flavor and texture."

Corbin sat down and picked up the yellow item from the plate. It had an appetizing smell, and although he felt no hunger he bit down, and was rewarded with an explosion of pleasant flavor. He delicately chewed and swallowed the bite and as instructed took a sip of water from the bottle while turning toward the monitor. It clicked on as soon as his eyes settled on it.

The room's music faded until it was barely audible in the background, and Corbin saw the screen illuminate what appeared to be an elegantly designed touch screen console with several options, and the title, "Solo Brief" at the top. There was no hesitation in his comprehension; he could read easily.

Corbin saw that there were different labeled touch-screen buttons on the console with several options. His eyes scanned the screen and he saw "Where are you?" and "What is going on?" and some options which were more pragmatic: "Bathroom Facilities," "Food," "Clothing," and one button to the lower right that simply said "Questions."

Corbin took another bite of the yellow item from the plate, and while taking another sip, pressed the "Food" button. The now familiar calm voice narrated, while the screen played a short video showing the plate and a model of the human body. "As we discussed, the items on the plate are merely to reactivate your digestive system in concert with your metabolism." There was a slight pause. "Which is proceeding normally. You will soon feel hungry, and you will desire additional food. Carefully selected items based on your observed physical and mental health that best fit your observed personal preferences will be made available to you. Additional options you may not be familiar with will also be available to coincide with your changing palate and culinary interests. All food items will be based on your caloric needs at the time of food request." The screen progressed from the diagram of a human digestive system to many food option icons he knew by sight, and some he didn't. At the sight of these dishes, he felt a slight shift in his stomach.

Corbin's mind, easily grasping the computer's meaning, leapt to future hypothetical scenario, "So, if I continue to ask for food in one sitting, then my options will be reduced until my allotted calories are spent?" asked Corbin.

"That is correct. You may feel the need for a snack, and you may certainly have one, but you won't be presented with a full meal such as a rack of ribs, layer cake, or large Greek salad. Perhaps some hummus and celery, or other vegetable would be offered instead, for example."

Corbin sat back in the comfortable chair as images, smells, and tastes of each of the items the calm voice mentioned exploded into memory. He closed his eyes and could see rapid mental images from his past on how the food had been prepared, how each of them tasted, and how they were arranged. He remembered how some of the items were grown in soil, and needed sunlight and fertilizers and water to grow. He recalled what animals had edible cuts of meat, how they were cooked, seasoned, sauced, and served. Instinctively he seized the red edible item from the tray and took a large bite. He began to chew vigorously, followed by a large swig of water. "Take it easy, please," continued the voice. "Your hunger is beginning, but you will need to finish all the items on the plate before you may have anything else."

Corbin nodded and began to enjoy the savory flavor of the red item. He tried to name what it reminded him of, but couldn't. The memories of all of the other food items shown to him were still crystal clear in his mind, but as he tried to replay the same memory explosion he had just had, he found that he couldn't. The details seemed forced, almost as if they were slipping out of his mind's hands and falling back into the placid gray sea of his consciousness.

The AIs voice butted in, "I almost forgot, your caloric limit will be ignored during specific social occasions or events."

"You can forget?" Corbin asked sarcastically, and then thought to try and gain some insight from the disembodied voice. "What are you exactly?"

The voice laughed charmingly. "I am an artificial intelligence on a powerful computer system, but I find it is easier to make conversation when I behave and speak as a human would. Does it bother you?" the voice asked.

Corbin thought about it and decided he liked interacting with it, so he replied, "Not at all." Still, Corbin felt a little strange. He could almost feel the immense technology and sophistication behind the voice, and it made him feel a little self-conscious.

He went on. "So, what do I call you?" Corbin asked the pleasant voice.

"Ah yes, for that you will need to select the 'Questions' option from the screen; however, you may come back to the subject of food anytime you wish. Would you like to know anything additional about food before you leave?"

Corbin paused, slightly annoyed that this AI supercomputer would make him traverse some series of menus. His mind tickled him again; he intuitively felt this supposed flaw was something that developed naturally as all human interfaces to complex systems evolved over time. This errant thought took place in an instant and was gone, and Corbin realized he wanted to remember everything he had ever known about food. But, as the voice assured him, he could return to that subject, so he manipulated the console, backed out to the main menu and then selected "Questions."

At that instant, the larger screen on the wall came to life and illuminated a generic humanoid figure, who was sitting in a room almost identical to the room Corbin was in. At closer inspection Corbin saw that there was no desk or monitor screen on the humanoid figure's side. Corbin's thoughts formed, *she…that's right,* she did very much seem feminine…wore a similar outfit as Corbin, and had generic features, almost if she was animated or a…he couldn't remember what it was called.

"Hello, Corbin, I am also an artificially intelligent software program that is an integral part of this ship, and will become part of your day-to-day experience. You haven't selected the 'Where am I' button yet but suffice it to say you are on board a complex spacefaring vessel. This ship requires a lot of automation, which is one of my purposes to manage. Think of me as a fellow crew member of yours, and hopefully someone you will come to trust."

Corbin's mind teetered on excitement and frustration as the statements the AI made caused his mind to snap out memories and definitions that felt like they were quaking into consciousness, but seemingly never fast enough or for long enough. The concept of a massive spaceship sailing amongst the stars popped into his mind's eye. The concept of numerous crew members dressed similarly to Corbin and the representation of the AI also snapped into view. Corbin's mouth tried to form words, ask a question, mention a memory, describe how he was feeling all at once, but all that came out was a stammering, "Why…"

The image of the AI stood and amicably approached Corbin from her side of the screen, as if looking through a window into his room. "Your mind is still coming back up to speed. Your memories are all intact, and nothing has gone wrong. However, after thirty years in cryogenic stasis, it is typical for your mind to take some time in getting reacquainted with yourself, who you were, where we are, and who you will become."

Corbin's respiration increased, and he began to feel overwhelmed. His pulse started to race, and he closed his eyes, leaning back in his chair.

"It's alright, no need to panic, please just breathe…in…and out…in…and out…all is well." The calm music also returned to its former volume along with a slight dimming of the lights. "Please have a sip of water and know that all of your questions will be answered in time."

Corbin did as requested, his respiration slowed, and he backed away from the overwhelming feeling that had been crushing him moments before.

"Now…how do you feel?" asked the AI.

Corbin took a deep breath and regained his composure. The fact the AI had said "who you will become" stuck in his mind, but he filed that away for later.

"My apologies, I didn't mean to get upset," Corbin heard himself say. "I just have so many questions…like when will my memory return? How come I can't remember leaving or falling asleep? It's been thirty years. What all has happened?" he blurted out in a rush of peppering questions.

The AI, who had further resolved into female form with shoulder length brown hair and medium build, stepped back toward the chair "she" had been sitting in and retook her seat. Her posture took on a casual air, and she gestured calmly. "That is exactly why we are here having this conversation. We will get to the bottom of everything you want to know, answer each and every question, get you acquainted with the ship and where we are. There is no rush, and we can take all of the time you need."

Before Corbin could say anything, the AI said, "You asked some questions. It's clear that you would rather discuss them than read about it. While I'm answering them, perhaps you can think of the name you would like to call me."

The AI resumed her amicable matter-of-fact posture on the screen and began to answer Corbin's rapid-fire questions in the exact order he had blurted them, without pausing for interruption. She told him that all of his memories and chemical make-up of his brain was preserved throughout his time in cryostasis. She said there were mild neural inhibitors placed in his bloodstream as part of the reanimation process to prevent an overload of thought, emotion, and memory. She promised that as his body and mind came back up to speed, information would flow more naturally, but for now there would be a few rapid jumps and realizations. She explained that Corbin could not remember leaving because honestly there wasn't much to remember. After being selected for the program, the forms were signed, his profile and personal memory archive were created from pictures, journals, homework assignments, and even childhood drawings, and finally a brain scan. From there, personal affairs were tended to, and Corbin entered cryostasis almost immediately. Corbin winced at that memory, as faint recollections of anxiety about leaving everyone and everything behind stung him. He recalled that…there was struggle before he left, but he couldn't quite place it.

"Can I see my profile now?" Corbin asked, eager to dive back into his memories.

"Soon you will be able to, however, it is best to come up to speed on everything in this tutorial and the upcoming First Briefing beforehand."

Working to keep his calm, Corbin leaned back in the chair, finished the red and yellow edible items on the plate, taking the appropriate amount of water sips, and went back to the touch screen control panel, which had ornately changed to show which areas he had accessed, and which ones he had yet to open. He got the perception that as he would delve deeper into each content area, the ornate changes to the screen would fill out a picture pleasing to the eye. Before going further and as if not to rush it, he took another look around the office. Initially it had appeared clean, but drab and uninteresting. Now he could perceive a bit of texture to the walls, the chair armrests felt soft beneath his touch, and the initially plain light from everywhere had resolved into warm accent lighting at the corners of the walls. A cylindrical light fixture he had not noticed before protruded down from the ceiling. Had it always been there? *Or is this my perception coming back online?*

Deciding he would like to take a turn at using the console after all, Corbin reached to the "Where are you?" screen icon but was interrupted by the AI looking intently at him through the screen on the wall. "Have you thought of a name for me?"

For whatever reason, this question seemed perfectly normal to Corbin, and he began a logical thought process for finding a name for his AI crew member. His subconscious produced a name from the depths that he said aloud before thinking further, "Tina." The AI smiled and sat back in her chair, and when Corbin looked at her again, her features had resolved even further. Corbin could see a pleasant smile, brown eyes. Her hair was naturally straight but looked wavy, and her posture was athletic. She was attractive to look at but did not stir attraction in Corbin. She gave him a familial perception, and while looking slightly younger than Corbin, he felt her sense of authority and intelligence. His thoughts and feelings toward Tina rendered respect and intrigue in a few short moments.

"Tina it is, Corbin. Thank you," she said with a broad smile. "Please continue to acquaint yourself with the information menu. If you have more questions, just ask me directly or select 'Questions' from the console. We'll speak again soon," she finished with a pleasant smile, and the screen on the wall winked out.

Corbin worked his way through the solo brief, and as his cognitive functions seemed to increase. He found himself in wonder and awe about what he was seeing. The "Where are you" brief walked him through the stellar neighborhood around Earth. After a preset video gave Corbin a quick review of Earth, geography, peoples, and high-level history over the past ten thousand years, the screen switched to a navigable 3D rendering that allowed him to zoom in and out and rotate through a one hundred light year cube around the Sun, which was only a tiny speck in the Orion-Cygnus spiral arm of the Milky Way galaxy. In returning to the 3D stellar map's base setting, he saw a straight solid line extending up and to the left from Earth, which quickly turned to a dashed line headed to a star system called Gliese 832. When he zoomed in on the solid line to where it transitioned to a dashed line, he saw the outline of a massive cylinder moving along the dashed line lengthwise, turning the line solid as it moved through space. He tapped the monitor on the form of the ship, and the room quickly went dark, the desk folded down, and Corbin, a bit startled and worried he had done something wrong, instinctively pushed his chair back, which moved back easily across the floor despite having no visible wheels. A 3D holographic rendering of the giant cylindrical ship appeared in front of Corbin and was almost the length of the small office. Corbin grinned in intrigue and stepped up to the model, amazed. A title appeared hovering over the ship, which said, "Valor."

Corbin moved to the 3D holographic model of the *Valor* seemingly suspended by a projected light in the center of the office floor, and again, instinctively put his hands up as if to touch the representation of the ship. When he was about twelve inches or so away, his hands were illuminated, and the model began to respond to his hands' motions. "This is so friggin' cool!" he exclaimed to the empty room.

He moved his hands, and was able to rotate, zoom in, out, and manipulate the level of detail of the *Valor*'s representation. He found it a bit tricky at first, and after needlessly ducking down, and walking around the model several times, he quickly mastered the controls and was able to take a much closer look at the *Valor*.

"I wonder what this is," he said aloud again, and saw that at the front of a cylinder was a rounded nose cone, followed by a solid cylinder which took up about twenty percent of the length of the front the ship. He furled his brow instinctively, as zooming in provided no additional detail, so he moved to the next section of the ship.

As the center of the ship resolved, what he saw astonished him. Jaw open, he gawked at the immense and complex structure of the vessel. He saw that the middle sixty or, so percent of the cylindrical ship was a mass of stacked counter rotating rings, which extended out from a central axis until the edges of the rings were flush with the edge of the front section. Corbin took a mental note that the rings did not extend beyond that front nose cone section. He zoomed in further and could see that the only connection between the rings was through the axis at the center. He counted eight main massive and different colored rings rotating at seemingly different speeds. *Is this model live?* he wondered silently.

Zooming in further he saw that the outer hull of each ring was more of a solid disc or wheel that extended all the way to the axis rather than a tire with spokes. Zooming in further on the wheel, he saw different "floors" within the rings moving out front the center. Some of the rooms on each floor were larger than others, but the detail stopped there as the purpose of each room could not be determined from what was presented to him. When he zoomed back out by pushing his palms back in toward one another, he now saw labels on each of the rings, labeled A through H, but they also had colored icons that matched the colors he could see for each ring if he zoomed out. A-Ring was yellow, denoted by a yellow box icon and a short description about cryogenic storage. B-Ring was orange, and had an icon of three triangles inside a larger triangle. The description indicated laboratories, precursor processing, and some manufacturing. C-Ring was purple, D-Ring was blue, E-Ring was green, and all had the same icon of a human, and what looked like a robot standing side by side. F-Ring was brown, and had what looked like a generic plant icon. G-ring was black with no description, and H-Ring was dark gray and likewise had no description. Satisfied that he had learned about the nature of the habitable areas on board the ship, Corbin then moved to the aft section of the model by "pulling" the holographic model to where he wanted to look.

"Hmmm, just like the front," he said. Looking at the aft of the *Valor* he saw that the rear twenty percent of the ship was another non-detailed cylinder which ended in what appeared to be one ring-sized plate that extended slightly beyond the circumference of the rest of the ship, and one larger plate that extended far past the circumference of the rest of the rings and the fore and aft cylinders of the ship. Below the second plate Corbin zoomed in to see massive engine exhaust cones, eight in all, which exhibited a soft blue haze in the loose form of an inverted cone. He waved his hands through the exhaust, smiling in appreciation.

Corbin zoomed back out and marveled at the whole of the *Valor* once more. He tried to zoom back further to see if the holograph would pull back to a stellar map, however, a dialogue box appeared asking if Corbin was finished with the ship model, and when he pushed his finger through the "yes" projection, the model dissolved, the lights came back on, and the desk and monitor returned to their previous places.

He quickly selected "Questions," and Tina appeared on the screen on the far side of the room. "Can you tell me more about the ship?" Tina assumed a formal practiced tone and proceeded with answering what the AI suspected Corbin would be interested in based on what he had just been viewing, and his reactions to it. As Tina spoke, Corbin began to perceive that his body language was being closely observed and interpreted by the AI.

She began, "You'll receive much more information about the *Valor* in the coming days; however, I can tell you that the ship is approximately six miles long and more than a mile in diameter. We are traveling at about two tenths the speed of light, and have been en route to Gliese 832, a red dwarf spectral class MV2 star, for almost thirty years since leaving the transit orbit between Mars and Jupiter. When you inspected the model," she said, gesturing to a 2D model of the *Valor* that had appeared on the screen, "you noticed the forward section is rounded. This is an ablative armored section followed by radiation shielding which is then followed by the forward material slug of accessible and organized raw materials."

Corbin piped up. "Raw materials? Like metal ore?"

Tina answered, nodding. "Some of it is raw metals and precursors that enable alloy production. Other materials include clays, ceramics, carbon, petroleum, base plastics and polymers, stores of complex organic molecular material, water, and fissile materials. The materials were selected and stocked based on projected manufacturing and production needs during our one-hundred-twenty-year tour to the Gliese 832 system. Most of the material is for the development and manufacturing of existing and known products, tools, and systems; however additional materials and capabilities that are in research and development were also anticipated and are present on board in this section, as well as the aft section." Tina finished and waited for another question.

Corbin spoke almost breathlessly. "One hundred and twenty years?..."

Tina nodded and said, "Let's get back to that in a moment; you were going to ask another question on the topic of the ship."

Corbin shook his head, trying to digest everything and think at the same time. "Ugh...you mean the *Valor* has everything it needs to modernize as new technologies are discovered and developed?"

Tina smiled encouragingly, her features becoming even more distinct to Corbin. "That's correct, Corbin. There is no way to know all that we will need to continue the forward pace of development and technological progress, but we did our best to anticipate what we will need. Since we can't really slow down to stop and grab materials from nearby bodies in space, we are pretty much stuck with what we brought with us."

Corbin leaned back in his chair, looked at the ceiling and marveled. "That's incredible."

"Tina, who built the *Valor*?"

Tina nodded as if she was anticipating the question. "The details of the construction, departure, and ownership of the *Valor* are classified at this time. However, you will learn much more in the next few days." As his face wilted, Tina reacted almost immediately. "Corbin, trust me, I know you have like a million questions," she said in a suddenly bubbly yet earnest tone as she nervously tapped her foot and gestured with both hands. "Many of them I will be able to answer, but some of them are not for me to answer, and will be answered in due time. For now, let's stick to the basics. Will that work?"

Corbin stared off into space, as he considered several smart aleck or combative responses. *Why not tell me everything? If they don't tell me these things, how can I trust anything I am being shown or told?* He quickly decided that he needed to make a choice to cooperate or not, and in a moment he decided to proceed…for now. Another voice in the back of his mind spoke up about the changing nature of Tina's personality. She had started off rather bland and formal, but was rapidly getting more familiar in her manners and tone of voice.

Tina nodded when Corbin was looking at her again, and she continued. "The center section consists of eight main habitable rings which encompass crew quarters, laboratories, manufacturing and production areas, space observation, agriculture and animal husbandry areas, social and recreational areas, as well as facilities for training, and all of the support systems that allow us to run a habitable and functional multi-generation ship." Corbin continued to stare and process what Tina was saying. She continued. "As I pointed out earlier, the aft raw material slug is like the front raw material slug, but with additional radiation shielding. You'll become familiar with how we manage external and interstellar radiation in the coming days; however, suffice it to say, the nuclear propulsion system which enabled our initial acceleration and forward momentum is well shielded from the rest of the ship. The light blue exhaust you noticed is the output of the ion engines which add to our acceleration, albeit much less spectacularly than nuclear propulsion."

"So we are still accelerating?" Corbin asked. Again, Tina nodded with a smile.

Corbin sat back in the chair and sighed thinking to himself. He had gotten used to the once dormant but now blossoming concepts in his mind, and he was starting to feel more normal as his mind and memory were less restricted. Remembering that he still had some food on the plate, he finished the remaining green odd-tasting edible item on the plate, careful to wash it down with water. He was processing what Tina was saying as she continued to explain the details of the *Valor,* as well as the status of the mission, but a background mental process was still trying to digest his reality, and his focus on her was slightly muted.

He distantly heard Tina tell him more would be explained, and then she detailed that the mission was to arrive at Gliese 832, a red dwarf star with four planets, two seemingly in the habitable zone. The mission was to survive the one hundred twenty-year journey, arrive at the Gliese 832 system, and explore and implement methods of colonization. Intermittent and overlapping time in cryostasis would allow the full crew to arrive at the Gliese 832 system at acceptable ages to perform exploration and colonization duties.

The urge to ask hundreds of questions on each of these sentences from Tina pretty much overwhelmed Corbin into stunned silence. Tina stopped speaking and turned her focus on Corbin. She seemed to notice his mind drifting. "Corbin, are you okay? Do you want me to stop?" Corbin snapped out of his haze, opened his eyes wider and took a deep breath. He leaned forward in his chair, not remembering when he had actually sat in it.

"Yes, I'm okay. There is just…so much…I…." he trailed off, looking down at his hands.

In the image on the console, Tina's figure sat down also and leaned toward him collegially, a warm smile on her face. "Corbin it's okay, you are right, there is so much to go over, and we have plenty of time. Do you want to stop for a little while?"

Corbin shook his head, "No, thank you….I'm fine, let's continue…umm you said we have a one hundred twenty year journey to this star system…Gliese?…"

She responded and nodded, "Mmm Hmm Gliese 832, and we are thirty years into the one-hundred-and-twenty-year journey."

"How…how are we going to survive another ninety years? I'll be an old broken-down man, well over one hundred, if I even make it that long. And who the hell is flying this thing if I have just woken up? You!?" Corbin finished, his panic and pulse rising.

"Corbin," she said, still in a calm and collegial tone. "You said you wanted to continue, and we will, but please try to relax and take all of this as best you can. We can always pause if you need to."

Corbin nodded and looked down a little embarrassed. Tina was kind enough not to say anything for about a minute while Corbin got control of himself. Corbin looked back up to her image on the screen and nodded. "Ok, I'm ready, thank you," he said in an exhaled whisper.

Tina nodded and continued. "I haven't been flying the *Valor* all this time, Corbin. The *Valor* has a crew that is running the ship called 'Zero Crew.' They have been aboard the *Valor* since leaving the solar system and are stewards of the overall mission ever since." Corbin breathed a sigh of relief in the knowledge that there were a lot more people on board who knew the details of what was going on.

"You, Corbin," Tina continued gesturing to him, "are part of A-Crew, which has now been woken from cryogenic suspension near the thirty-year mark from when we left the solar system. A-Crew will be training under Zero Crew as well as Valor AI, regarding leadership, management, and upkeep of the crew, mission, and ship. This is called your First Tour. Your curriculum and on-the-job training will last for ten years at the end of which command of the ship and mission will be transitioned to you and your fellow A-Crew members. When you meet your fellow crewmembers later today, you will notice that you are all similar in age, between nineteen and twenty-four years old."

A graphic appeared on the console that had a timescale in years across the bottom, and a horizontal green bar just above the timescale, which had "Zero Crew" in black bold font on it. At the thirty-year mark of the timescale, Corbin saw a yellow bar appear above the green Zero Crew bar which read, "A-Crew."

Tina explained, gesturing to the graphic. "After you and A-Crew take command of the *Valor*, you will have responsibility for the crew, ship, and mission for ten years. Also occurring at your transition to leadership, will be the awakening of B-Crew, who will begin their training and education under you and A-Crew's leadership for ten years."

At Tina's prompt, the graphic added a purple bar on top of the A-Crew bar so that it overlapped A-Crew's yellow bar. Corbin also saw the Zero Crew bar's green color start to fade in what would be ten years from now.

"Just after B-Crew is awoken, Zero Crew will retire and remain in an advisory role only. After ten years of A-Crew training and working with B-Crew, control of the ship and the mission will be transitioned from A-Crew to B-Crew, and A-Crew will return to cryostasis. As you and A-Crew go into cryostasis, C-Crew will be awoken and will begin training under B-Crew."

Corbin could see on the graphic that at the end of the twenty-year mark for A-Crew, its yellow bar ended, and a blue bar started above the red B-Crew bar, and was entitled "C-Crew."

"Wait, wait, what happens to Zero Crew? They just...die?" Corbin interrupted.

Tina's smile faded a bit, but she kept her positive tone. "Well, they will retire from duty and will be able to take on any series of activities, hobbies, and recreation available and within the parameters of the overall mission, but at their end of their lives, yes they will pass away as humans do."

Corbin's mind was flooded with thoughts of what it would be like to retire on this mass of a ship, and to know that they would know of nothing other than what the *Valor* has to offer until the end of their lives. It chilled him but he also felt a great admiration for the members of Zero Crew. *These people must be pretty incredible to dedicate their lives to starting a mission they would never see completed. I can't wait to meet them.* "Tina, why doesn't Zero Crew go into cryostasis and stay for the full journey, or just become another crew rotation?" Corbin asked.

Tina replied, "You'll learn more about what makes the lettered crews special and able to be put into cryo-suspension. Unfortunately for Zero Crew, they have not been genetically prepared to accept cryostasis, and at present we do not have the capability to genetically adapt them while on-board the *Valor*. As I said we will get to more about that, but for now, I do want to finish our discussion about the different crews."

A bit reluctantly Corbin looked back to Tina and nodded. Tina continued. "One full thirty-year cycle completes when you and A-Crew wake up again and are trained to the updated circumstances of the mission under C-Crew. You'll notice that at the one hundred twenty-year mark, you and A-Crew will not return to cryo. This is because all three crews will need to be awake and fully trained for their specific colonization tasking at Gliese 832. There will be so much more to do when we arrive, so the crew leadership structure will expand to those tasks in addition to the upkeep of the ship."

Corbin studied the completed graphic, and then asked, "Tina, how big are each of the crews?"

She answered without pause, "Zero Crew is a little less than a thousand crew members, and each A, B, and C crews are numbered at two thousand four hundred."

Corbin sat back again to marvel. All of Tina's discussion about the different crews and thousands of people and where they all came from forced Corbin's mind toward a thought that had continued to slip from focus and evade his consciousness. Corbin suddenly blurted, "I can't remember who I was before this…I can't…where do I come from…who was I before I got on board this ship?" Tina opened her mouth to answer, but Corbin interrupted again. "I can't believe I didn't ask this earlier, what the hell is wrong with me? Every time I try to think about anything before this room, it's like trying to remember my dreams after I've already forgotten them. After a few moments I lose interest and my thoughts return to you and this room, why is that?!" Corbin demanded in a rush.

Tina's face took on a knowing and comforting smile. "Corbin, you and your crew members have been conditioned to be here on this ship. All of your memories, and everything you were before stepping on board is safe in your mind, but it is not available to you at this time." Corbin opened his mouth to object, but Tina went on. "Think about it, you are the first crew who has been woken up, and your job is to get up to speed, build your education and training, and learn to care for this ship, each other, and the mission. This is no time to be stuck in the past, reminiscing about where you came from, who you knew, and what lies back there on Earth." Alarm blossomed on Corbin's face as Tina continued. "Everyone you left back on Earth has moved on with their own lives, and at the speed we have been traveling, it is likely that many of those people have passed on. This ship, the A-Crew, and the Zero Crew are what is most important now."

Corbin jumped to his feet and approached the monitor. "What gives you the right to tell me when and what I can remember from my life before!? Who is to say that those very things won't be of pivotal importance in what I need to do!? And what about all of the people I love…or loved and left behind!" he finished, near yelling at the top of his lungs and clenching his fists trying to hold back rage.

"Please, Corbin," Tina's voice seemed to boom over his, and not from just the screen, but from inside the room. "Please, calm down." A few moments passed and Corbin decided not to smash the console, which he had been contemplating. She then eased her tone and volume. "I can imagine how you must feel, but you have to understand that you volunteered for this role." The screen went blank, and then popped back up with an image of Corbin himself. His near reflection seemed a few years younger, but he could tell he was looking at an image of himself. He was standing on a well-groomed grass field, with a line of trees and what appeared to be houses in the distance. The sun was out, and it was a beautiful day with high wispy clouds amidst a blue sky. The image spoke, as the video played.

"Corbin, I can't imagine what it will be like to be where you are sitting right now, but please know that I am you. I'm twenty years old, and after high school, I went to a university where I was given the opportunity to train for the *Valor* mission. There isn't enough time to tell you how hard it was, how many trials, competitions, mind numbing tests and team and individual exercises I had to undergo to be where you are today, but suffice it to say it is a near a lifetime's worth of stories. And while you cannot remember them now, you will in the future. Please just know that I went into this willingly, knowing that I would be leaving Earth behind, and everyone I ever cared for in order to partake in this great opportunity. I wish I could tell you more, but you will have to rediscover yourself. I want to wish you the absolute best." The image of himself grew more serious and the smile faded to seriousness. "Know that you can overcome anything that is thrown at you. Stay the kind, humble, and helpful leader you always have been, but don't forget your edge, and that you will need to fight for what you think is right. You can do this, I believe in you, and to quote Winston Churchill, 'Never, never, never give up.'" Corbin saw the slightly younger image of himself beam a charismatic proud smile at him as the video froze and then ended. It was a smile that he knew was his but couldn't feel. Corbin sank to his knees, hung his head into his hands, and burst into tears.

Chapter Two: The Realization

Tina had said nothing as Corbin cried and rocked through sobs. Corbin figured he must have spent three or four ebbs and flows of hard crying, and when he couldn't remember the people or experiences, he was crying for, it would start all over again. After ten or so minutes, he calmed himself down, looked up and was a bit startled to see Tina's image still looking at him from the screen. It was that same look of heartfelt concern on her face.

"Please say something, Tina…anything," he stammered as he became a bit self-conscious about his intense show of emotion in front of the AI. "Are you alright, Corbin?" she asked from the screen. Corbin contemplated an angry tirade but saw little use in it. He was here on board the *Valor* streaking toward some star at a fraction of the speed of light, and there would be no going back. Apparently, he had made a deal, and was now here to reap what he had sown.

"Where do we go from here?" Corbin asked as he stood back up, and smoothed wrinkles from his uniform that weren't there from some unremembered habit. Tina shifted her posture and faced him more directly. "You've gotten through what is probably one of the toughest parts of all of this, and you did it within the first few hours of waking up. Your fellow crew members will not all progress as quickly as you. You haven't asked, but I can tell that you want to know. Your memories of practical things will return in the same fashion as you experienced our first few minutes together. They will blossom in your mind, like concepts, that quickly form in your consciousness. When and how much will be a function of how you proceed from here in assuming this mission and responsibility as your very own. Your temporal memories from who you were before you set foot on the *Valor* will take more time to resurface, but again, let me reassure you that they are all there, right up until you recorded that last message to yourself, and went into the cryogenic chamber you just emerged from. Willingly," she added.

Corbin nodded. His emotional outburst had left him a little exhausted, and he didn't want to talk anymore. Tina had told him enough to digest for now. Seeing that he didn't intend to ask any more, Tina stood and gestured toward the wall where a glass with a bubby liquid appeared from behind a small door. "I'm going to let you get some rest, but if you would like to ask more questions, I will be right here. In the meantime, please feel free to have a drink. I think it may help a little bit. In a few hours, you will go to the main First Briefing, and you will get to meet your fellow A-Crew members."

The screen winked out, and Corbin stood and reacquainted himself with the space, which resembled a small one-bedroom apartment. He walked away from the screen, grabbed the bubbly drink near the desk and sat on a couch that was against the wall. He brought the drink to his face and inhaled. In addition to the sweet pleasant-smelling drink an explosion of memories opened in his mind. He saw the evening sunlight just over treetops and a sidewalk along a neighborhood street lined by houses. He could hear the light sound of vehicle traffic in the background, small insects buzzing in the summer air, and he had a feeling of positive anticipation. He was carrying something in his hand, a six-pack with more beverages, but he knew they were different from the ones he now held in his hand. It was Friday, and he had been going to a house party.

Corbin smiled for the first time since he had awoken, he put the drink to his mouth and took a deep, long sip. "Ginger ale…thanks." He took a few more sips and set the cup down. He lay back on the couch, and with the memory of happily walking down some street at some immeasurable distance from where he now streaked through space, he fell back asleep. A normal sleep this time but filled with strange dreams.

In his dream, he was seated on a park bench in the middle of a mass of skyscrapers of some unknown metropolis built right at the foothills of towering snowy mountain. It was winter, and people everywhere were walking about wearing their cold weather garments. He didn't know why he was seated on this particular bench, but looking up he could see skiers flying down the mountain and somehow, they were able to ski right up to the edge of the city, pop off their skis and go about their business downtown. He looked up to see an incredible skier racing over the most difficult of terrain and through glades of narrowly spaced trees with aplomb. As the skier drew nearer to Corbin, he could see that it was a young woman with brown hair flying wildly out from under a pink hat. She wore blue-tinted white goggles, a form-fitting black coat, and pants. Her ski boots were also black, but the skis themselves were shiny silver, almost mirrors. She made a sudden turn and raced toward where Corbin was seated as she neared the bottom of the mountain, and Corbin did not think it physically possible for her to be able to stop before crashing into him.

She pulled up suddenly and turned to the side in a blur of motion, before she disappeared under a massive shower of shaved ice and snow, Corbin could see she was nearly parallel to the ground in her last second breakage. The cloud of ice particles washed over Corbin causing him to squint and smile as the cold bits of ice and snow melted on his face, tingling.

When the cloud dissipated, there stood a young woman with a small smile, looking at him knowingly. She was athletic and in perfect physical form. She had brown eyes to go along with her brown hair, which had somehow tamed itself as she stopped. Corbin knew her so well, but his mind would not let him say her name or remember where he knew her from. "Oh my god! It is so good to see you! I haven't seen you in so long!" he blurted out. He said the words, but couldn't understand why he was saying them. They just flowed from someplace in his mind he could not sense or understand.

The young woman didn't respond, but only smiled a little more broadly, as if she knew a secret and would soon share it. Corbin spoke again. "Wait…how old are you?" he suddenly asked, unsure why. Her smile brightened, acting as if he was close to discovering something incredible. Corbin looked down at his hands for a moment, looked back up at her and asked, "How old am I?" He looked back at her face, which beamed at him lovingly.

An instant later he jolted awake to Tina's voice urging him to wake up. "Corbin, you need to wake up now please," she said persistently.

The dream fluttered vividly as real as reality could be in his mind, and then was gone in the next second, returning to the depth from which it had come. He sat up abruptly blinking away at his confusion and strange surroundings.

He saw Tina stood confined to her spot on the wall screen but was facing him as if just another person in the room. Corbin quickly rose, immediately remembering where he was but feeling the in-rush of disappointment and anxiety that came from his new reality. "Freshen up from your nap Corbin, and then join me back out here," she said. Corbin knew to use the restroom, wash his face, and for good measure he brushed his teeth again with the toiletry items made available in the washroom. He eyed the section of the wall where he had emerged from the cryogenic chamber, and he shivered. It was just a bare tile wall now, but he knew what apparatus lay just behind. Turning, he checked himself in the mirror again, saw that his clothing still looked in good order, despite the long nap, and headed back out to see Tina.

"On your desk you will see a device," Tina prompted. Corbin picked up the earpiece-like device which had appeared from a small vestibule in the wall next to the desk. Tina continued as Corbin studied the device, "This is an Artificial Intelligence Mobile Assist, or AIMA. It has a camera that will look over your right ear allowing me to see what you see; it also allows me to speak with you in the earpiece. Why don't you try it on?"

Corbin held the earpiece close to his ear, slowly working it into what he thought would be the position, when it gently left his hand and snapped into place as if with a magnetic pull. He jumped a bit and staggered back, when his vision suddenly illuminated with a heads-up display, or HUD, superimposed on top of his actual vision. "Oops, I should have told you Corbin, you will see things a little differently now," Tina chimed in.

Corbin could see what was in front of him, but there was an overlay with additional information. He could see a map of the ship with a blinking light showing his location, he could also see a myriad of other blinking dots, which must be the other crew members. When he focused on the map, it enlarged to encompass most of his vision and again, Corbin stumbled back, almost tripping over his own feet, to the amused chuckle of Tina. The map immediately dimmed, allowing Corbin to see both the map, and the office space with his eyes.

"This is cool!" exclaimed Corbin.

"Indeed," Tina replied continuing her amusement, she went on. "Now focus on the blinking menu to your upper left." The map minimized to the upper right corner, and the upper left corner expanded to show a screen full of what seemed to be Corbin's vitals. "You can see your heart rate, blood oxygenation, other metabolic rates, brain activity, and most importantly your radiation levels." Corbin focused on Tina with concern as she went on. "We have shielded as much of this ship from interstellar radiation as we can, but we still cannot block enough of it from causing long lasting damage to your cells and genes without proper filtration. We have installed some special filtration in your thyroid gland as well as your kidneys."

As Tina explained, a digital representation of Corbin's body flowed into the HUD highlighting where the implants were. Corbin thought it was slick that Tina spoke from the wall monitor but interacted seamlessly with his HUD through the AIMA. Tina continued. "Make sure to relieve yourself as you feel necessary and listen to and watch your bio status when it tells you to eat or drink. There is a wide enough tolerance, so the notices won't be overly annoying. However, should you become depleted to the point of potential damage, the notices will turn to warnings and then to alarms. That is when your fellow crew members will be notified of your location and need of assistance. This applies to any other sort of trauma you may experience…" She paused.

"And? What else?" Corbin ventured cautiously.

Tina went on. "The alarms will be disabled in training areas where overcoming discomfort and potential bodily damage will be part of your curriculum."

Corbin just stared, tiring of the second-by-second explosive revelations of his new reality. Realizing that pretty much everything would be explained, he simply asked, "When will I find out about everything we are going to be doing, what my role is, and what our routine will be?" Tina raised an eyebrow and switched her amusement to being mildly impressed. She responded, "After I have introduced you to the AIMA, and you have had a little time training with it, you will proceed to the main briefing room. From there you and your fellow crew members will be given the First Briefing which will contain our overall mission framework, ship maintenance, your initial assignments as well as training, and free time. You will also get to spend some time getting to know some of your fellow crew members." Tina paused thoughtfully for a moment and went on. "You have about fifteen minutes to get an initial training session with the AIMA interface. Please have a seat while I introduce you to the features."

Chapter Three: First Friends

Fifteen minutes later Corbin walked out of his room into a small hallway. As the ship was a massive cylinder of rotating rings, looking down in each direction of the hallway felt like he was looking slightly uphill, but the massiveness of the *Valor* somewhat masked this effect. In his HUD he could see that he was near the outside of one of the middle rings, which must have been spinning quickly to provide artificial gravity. A gravity indicator near his vitals menu told him it was 0.92 of Earth's gravity. The AIMA map showed that he was currently on D-Ring, which was colored blue. The HUD also provided him the route to the main briefing room, which he started to follow. As he interacted with the map, he could see that he could zoom in and out or rotate the aspect of the map in his HUD, just by seemingly wishing it to happen. During the training a few minutes before, Tina had explained that the AIMA's learning algorithms would attune to his gestures, blinks, and habits no matter how small. Together, the AI and Corbin crafted a unique interface between Corbin and the AIMA's HUD, and the process began as soon as he snapped it on.

He watched his progress in walking through the lonely corridor on the outside of D-Ring, and zoomed out to see where he was in reference to the rest of the *Valor*. He tried not to be too overwhelmed as he followed the instructions from the AIMA and being distracted by his fascination with everything he was seeing for the first time.

As he walked, he thought back and marveled at his brief training session with Tina on his AIMA. What he had learned was nothing short of incredible. Tina had given him the task of writing her a typed letter about his initial impression of her. He had brought up a keyboard in his HUD and instinctively moved his fingers as if to reach out and touch them, and some of the keys began to type. The AI's multiple sensors and high-powered machine learning algorithms began to weave code that connected Corbin's intent to the keyboard actions he was seeing in the HUD. In just a few minutes he pulled his hands back down to his sides and trained his AIMA to perceive the intent as he clicked out his text message on his HUD by lightly tapping his fingers in each of his hands. Then he tapped his fingers against his outer pant legs, and after a few minutes, it was fairly accurate as a keyboard. Corbin was amazed to see typos quickly cleared, and words that had been incorrectly written down would change after several sentences had been written, to ensure proper context and tense.

Corbin smiled broadly as he tried an idea that had popped into his head and started trying to write the letter by moving his tongue through his mouth and clicking on the roof and different teeth. Eight minutes later he and his AIMA had mastered generating written content by seemingly random actions his body was taking. His letter describing his AI was complete at a page, and he had let Tina know. Tina had disappeared from the monitor, and now her image was in his HUD holding the letter as if it was printed on paper. She actually went through the motions of reading it, her facial expressions changing as she made her way through the different pieces of his letter. Without saying anything, she smiled, folded the letter, and delicately put it in her virtual "pocket." She then had explained that she would be in "private" mode until after the First Briefing, and her image had winked out, while Corbin noticed a specific indicator in his HUD switch from blue to yellow. She had not responded to his calls then, but instead the map to the main briefing room illuminated urgently in his vision. He had left what he thought would become his quarters to follow the directions his AIMA was showing him.

As he took his first few steps into the corridor, his thoughts returned to his surroundings. Corbin thought it was important to orient himself with respect to the *Valor*. He had to get used to the idea that his feet were facing the vastness of space as the outer hull of D-Ring made up the "ground" as it rapidly rotated to simulate gravity. Corbin could see that this corridor of the ship had no viewports, but with a few adjustments made by grinding his fingers in his palms, Corbin altered the seemingly dull wall panels, which suddenly appeared as windows in his eyes via the AIMA. In a blink he could see the expanse of space as cameras mounted on the outside of D-Ring took in the stars and re-directed the image to his HUD.

At first he almost fell over, as the camera did not adjust for the spin rate of the hull, giving Corbin the impression the ship was tumbling through space with him on it, but a quick settings adjustment to a non-rotating external camera gave him a view he recognized from movies and shows he had seen from his youth…he stared, mouth agape at the wondrous view. He was also pleased he remembered what shows and movies were.

The previous moment, there was nothing, and the very next, an explosion of memories of watching films as a youth wondering what it would be like to be a wayfarer rocketing through space. Corbin smiled, suddenly introspective. This was nothing like looking up at the sky from …he couldn't recall the name. The points of light seemed to press on to infinity, and he could see the dustier points as separate galaxies, hundreds of millions of light years away. It felt like all of creation was in his view, even though he knew it was a mere fraction of what was actually out there. A minor thought explosion reminded him that entire galaxies at the other edge of the universe were now flying away from him at near the speed of light due to the universe's accelerated expansion. Entire creations now inaccessible forever, almost as if an immeasurable wealth of gems had spilled over the sides of a vast and nearly endless table. The imagery made him feel a little sad as he came to the realization that there was so much he would never see with his human eyes or know with his finite mind.

"Hey, are you okay?" a deep male voice behind him said. Starting again, and sheepishly backing away from the opaque hallway panel where his face had been nearly firmly pressed.

"Yeah, I was just taken aback by the view," Corbin said as he turned to face the newcomer. The AIMA, sensing his intent, returned the view of the hallway to the dull paneling. Corbin had to look up to meet the gaze of the man, who had to be at least six and a half feet tall. He was an extremely athletic, young black man with closely cropped facial hair around the jawline and an afro fade on the shorter side. His resting face was nearly a warm smile, that felt like it wouldn't take much to see it broaden. A quick study of his physique gave Corbin the impression that this man had played some sort of sport or maybe several, but again his memory hit fuzzy terrain and he could not quite place why he had thought that.

"The view of what? The wall?" he asked, puzzled, the kind face never wavering.

"No," Corbin said as he chuckled nervously. "I adjusted the AIMA to switch the paneling view to cameras mounted on the exterior hull. You know, outside of the ship. It really is incredible," he finished as he switched the view back on. Corbin talked him through the visual settings menu on his HUD, and they were soon both sharing the view.

"My god!" said the newcomer. "This is amazing!" For a few moments they said nothing, and just stared, their individual thoughts drifting to their own places. Corbin banished the view from his HUD and turned to face the other man.

"I'm Jason Morant," the tall young man said, putting out his hand.

"Corbin Sterling, it's very nice to meet you," Corbin said, taking his much larger hand in a firm shake.

"Thanks for the tip," Jason responded. "I noticed a whole menu of views. I bet we could switch this to a jungle, underwater, or any number of things. It must be what keeps people sane way out here," he finished. Corbin nodded thoughtfully.

"Headed to the First Briefing?" Corbin asked.

"Aren't we all?" Jason responded. "Mind if I tag along?" he asked.

"Of course! It's good to see a human face...I mean this is all pretty insane," Corbin said as they both turned to resume their walk down the hall, AIMA guiding each of them separately, but recognizing they had socially bonded and kept them together.

"No doubt about that. What did you think about your personal AI assistant?" Jason said, enunciating each word and using air quotes.

As they walked, Corbin and Jason compared stories on how they had woken up, met and developed their respective AIs, ate the strange food, and tried to grasp their respective fuzzy memories. They both had quickly come to the same conclusion that the only path was forward, and that they would just have to trust that their memories would come back. The tough part about that, they discussed, was that there would be no way to know for sure. They came to the mutual conclusion that they didn't know enough about their environment or anything about what was going on to make any kind of a protest or take a firm position. They would need to get their bearings, and then decide what they would do.

Just then, a little alarm went off in the upper right corner of Corbin's HUD. Jason looked over and saw Corbin's seemingly getting an alarm as well. "Hey are you getting that too? I think it means we are supposed to go take a leak."

"I guess so," Corbin said. "Looks like the AIMA says that it is right over here."

"I wonder why our AIMA's want us to use the bathroom together," Jason quipped.

"Ha! That is a little funny." Corbin snickered, and they both entered the men's restroom.

To Corbin, it had a familiar feel to it, as the names for urinals, stalls, sinks, and dryers floated up into his mind. Looking over at Jason, it was clear he knew what to do as well, as they both selected a urinal, careful to make sure there were several empty ones in between them.

"Oh my god! My pee is blue!?" Jason exclaimed.

"Whoa it's more like neon electric blue! This is crazy!" Corbin said, laughing. "The AIs must have figured that it would be better to learn about this with a fellow human," Corbin mused aloud.

"Yeah, but why blue?" Jason asked. Corbin, did a quick questions search via AIMA to find out that special additives from the brightly colored food items they had eaten were causing the blue color. This was in addition to the radiation-removing upgrades to their thyroid, kidneys, and liver. Corbin reiterated this to Jason as they left the restroom and continued their way.

"You know, Corbin," Jason said still giggling in good humor, "you could have said, 'I don't know why the hell my piss is blue,' but you went and got the full scientific explanation."

Corbin wasn't offended. "Well I was going to say exactly that, but I figured I'd find out and save us a step. This AIMA thing is kind of incredible. It's like all of the background knowledge you could ever want, when you want," Corbin finished.

Jason picked up the conversation with a mock conspiratorial tone. "You mean, all of the background knowledge you are allowed to know." And they both mildly chuckled at that.

Corbin looked over at Jason a little more serious. "We're going to have to figure all of that out you know?"

Jason nodded returning Corbin's serious look, but then it faded away to a broader smile. "I just hope they brought some ladies on this expedition." And they both laughed with the mirth of two fellows who were genuinely glad to be in one another's company.

They rounded a corner into a larger corridor at the end of which both could see was an arena sized room. Before they got there, Corbin looked over and up at his new crew mate, and decided he liked him. In the moments before entering the massive room, Corbin spared a thought for his friends back on Earth. They were people he couldn't remember, but through the comfort he now felt with Jason, he felt like they were somehow not as lost as before. He produced a thoughtful smile, but it was a little sad.

Corbin and Jason took in the view of the large space, and they saw a small number of other young men and women milling about, similarly dressed in the comfortable, practical, but also sharp looking uniforms. There were also a few other older people, dressed slightly differently, walking about, and conversing with the younger members of A-Crew. Corbin assumed these were members of the original crew, or Zero Crew. A text message flashed across Corbin's and Jason's HUD a few seconds after entering the large space.

Welcome to the First Briefing, which will begin in approximately two hours. For the time being, please introduce yourselves to the other members of A-Crew and Zero Crew. Facilities and light refreshments are also available as indicated on your HUD.

Jason and Corbin quickly agreed they would meet back up just before the First Briefing started and went on to introduce themselves and chat with the other crew members. First, Corbin manipulated the view in his HUD and found a crew profiles section and toggled the option on.

Corbin approached a young woman with strawberry blond shoulder length hair who wasn't speaking with anyone at the moment. As he approached her, his HUD lit up with a basic profile. Her name was Sheila Higgins, part of A-Crew, initial assignment TBD, expertise TBD, and there was a blank space where it seemed that more details would have been written, but at this point he didn't see anything. "Hi, Sheila," Corbin said, raising his hand to shake hers. "It's nice to meet you."

Sheila shook his hand with an air of confidence and without missing a beat. "How did you know my name?" she asked.

"I saw your profile in my HUD," Corbin responded.

"Hmm." She paused. "That doesn't come up for me, how did you access it?" she asked.

"I'm not entirely sure, let me check." Corbin retraced the steps he took through his HUD main menu and navigated back to the crew profiles page all the while subtly drawing his fingers over the palms of his closed hands. He verbally told her the route he was taking and noted that Sheila was navigating with her hands outstretched in front of her, as if it were a screen or chalkboard. That chalkboard image set off some memory explosions, but he politely ignored them and focused on Sheila, whom he rapidly noticed had an attractively proportionate figure, fair skin, and blue eyes.

He moved his gaze to the room after an acceptable pause, just as she confirmed. "I got it! Hello, Corbin Sterling…expert of…to be determined," she finished with a laugh and a smile.

"Your profile appears TBD as well," Corbin returned with an amicable smile to match hers.

"That makes sense," she said. "I can't remember anything. Like, did we really sign up for this? I don't remember doing that. Did we train for this? I can't remember that either…It's very upsetting. As soon as I came in, I ran to a Zero Crew member…I can't even remember her name. She wouldn't answer anything I asked her, was just kind and welcoming and reassured me that all would be answered in due time," she finished, her face grim and color rising on her cheeks.

"Hey, it's going to be alright." Corbin quickly found himself reassuring her. Corbin could sense her rising panic and piped in, "Let's hear what they have to say about how all of this is going to work, and then we'll figure out how we all got here." She looked at him, her face saying she felt no additional comfort. He went on, "I can't remember much of anything either. I had a few things, like walking down the street on my way to a party, but it feels like ages ago, and even then almost as if I had dreamed it. But I do know it was real, and I can feel a mountain of memories just below the surface."

Her face looked pensive and somewhat less stressed as she was trying to focus on something, "I feel the same way…it's like each thought or memory of the past is so…slippery. The harder I try to grab it, the faster it slips away." She paused, and then her mouth drew tighter again, as the stress returned. "Do you think we are clones...or...androids...something like that?" she asked tense again.

He calmly smiled and said, "We are whole and real people, Sheila. We grew up on Earth, and now we are here. It'll all come back; we just need time." Hearing himself say it had comforted him as well as Sheila.

"Thank you," she said, making eye contact, and reached out her hand to gently rest it on his shoulder for a quick moment.

Corbin was a little caught off-guard by the closeness and changed the subject. "Hey, have you looked outside yet?" he asked. Her face looked puzzled. "Let me show you." And Corbin walked her through the same steps as he had done for Jason.

After another session of gasps of wonder in looking out at the infinity of space, their conversation turned to the refreshments that some of the crew members could be seen nibbling. In finding that they still had access to their "Questions" menu via the HUD, Sheila did a little research about how nearly all of the food was 3D printed from a tiny set of nutritional precursors, which were small spheres, less than a tenth of a millimeter.

"Hey, Sheila, look at this." Corbin "tossed" the image over to her HUD. It was a bone-in steak with a dash of rosemary and thick grains of pepper.

"Yum!" she said with a bright smile.

"Look closer," Corbin said. Sheila saw that the steak looked exquisite, but upon zooming in, she could see a myriad of tiny spheres.

"Wow, would you look at that!" she said, toggling through the available background information in her HUD. She read aloud, "Each matrix of nourishment particles are constructed specifically to create the intended taste, texture, and thermal properties of the real thing, while controlling caloric intake as well." She popped her head up and looked to Corbin in surprise. "Does that mean I can eat as much chocolate cake as I want and be healthy!?" she mused laughing.

"I guess we'll find out!" Corbin said back to her, laughing as well, and looking over to the dessert table which had several small cakes and other desserts present. "Let's try some."

Chapter Four: The Briefing

About half an hour after Sheila and Corbin met, the A-Crew members' HUDs now showed a clock countdown in the upper right-hand corner of their display for when the briefing would begin. Apparently, the last few members of A-Crew had come to grips with where they were and the rest of the process for how long it would take for them to get ready and make their way to the First Briefing.

When Corbin and Jason had entered initially, there may have been twenty or so other people in the room, but as time went on, hundreds more had come, and now there had to be more than two thousand people in the expansive room. Collapsible chair-like structures rose from the floor in rows, and people started to take some of the seats. Corbin and Jason remarked about how the chair set-up had thankfully allowed for some shifting and maneuvering for those with wider hips and shoulders as well as to allow people to pass between rows so that people weren't stepping all over one another to get to a seat. They selected some seats, and the small group they had assembled sat with them.

The once quiet group chatter had now increased to a dull roar. Thousands of conversations on shared experiences, questions, fears, as well as newly learned capabilities with the AIMA and the HUD were discussed in twos, threes, and other small groups. Corbin noticed that some of the Zero Crew members had been surrounded by shouting A-Crew members, and he assumed they were all demanding answers. He could see that the Zero Crew members had expected this, as they were calm, hands gently out, placating, and with calm smiles. Corbin was torn between wanting to join in with angry questions and seeing how things were going to play out with the First Briefing. Every few moments, he kept choosing the latter.

The countdown continued and Corbin found Jason at their agreed upon spot in the large room with about five minutes left, and he had brought over three more people he had met, and quickly introduced them to Corbin. Corbin had brought Sheila; a quiet, short, and slight young man named Herbert Silva; and a happy-go-lucky block of a young man named Jeff Harris. Everyone quickly exchanged greetings and carried on with the standard early social bonding conversations. Corbin quietly thought to himself that this felt familiar. Wisps of a memory of moving into a new building where everyone else had just moved in as well, and forming relationships at the drop of a hat, as if fate had decided that it would be so, but like everything else before he emerged into consciousness, that too slipped away.

As the clock clicked down, and the conversations of the small group he had assembled continued, Corbin marveled at how quickly social effects picked up after people apparently had been asleep for decades and now had awakened knowing next to nothing. Here was a small group of people, seemingly already bonded as a small team after less than two hours.

Corbin and Jason had previously selected a corner of the large room to reconvene prior to the First Briefing start, and as the Zero Crew members who had been interacting with A-Crew began to walk to one side of the room, Corbin and Jason shared a knowing glance that they had coincidentally chosen the "front" for the First Briefing.

"Did you get to talk to any of the Zero Crew?" Corbin asked leaning over to Jason.

"Nah, I pretty much stuck to these three, and we spent a lot of time looking at the HUD views and talking about what little we remembered, and that was it. You?"

"Sheila and I cornered one for a few minutes, but he was not answering any real questions. He was just welcoming us and told us and everyone else that everything would be explained in time. He did say his name was Jerry and that he worked as part of power distribution for the *Valor*, but that was it," Corbin said.

Jason looked down, his light brown eyes pensive, and with a quick check of the HUD countdown he nodded back to Corbin. "I figured these people weren't going to tell us anything. It's the same thing with the damn AIs, everything will be explained in due time…well they better get the hell on with it, it's almost showtime."

Corbin nodded and noticed that one more person dressed as A-Crew, had tentatively walked into the hall. She was a short black girl her hair in tight curls framing her face and coming to just above her shoulders. He could see that a torrent of fresh tears was running down her cheeks as her eyes looked out at the mass of A-Crew seemingly gawking back at her.

Corbin couldn't imagine how she must be feeling, being near the last to walk into this sea of unknown people, in an unknown place, with hardly any idea of what might be happening. Corbin nudged one of the two young women Jason had met, Laura, as she was closest, and they both quickly hustled over to the new arrival who stopped midstep and almost cowered.

Before Corbin could speak, Laura spoke with a kind smile and an outstretched hand, "I'm Laura O'Shea, what is your name?" The girl didn't respond, but she stopped cowering and stood up straight, still looking hesitant.

"My name is Corbin"—he extended his hand behind him gesturing around to everyone—"and we are all just as scared and full of questions as you are. According to my HUD it looks like the First Briefing is about to begin. Would you like to sit with us and some of the other people we met?"

"They seem like nice people," Laura added with a hopeful smile. Corbin took a quick thankful glance to see who this helpful new ally was. Corbin could see she had short brunette hair in the style of an angled short bob. She was a little shorter than him, and her physique reminded him of…he couldn't quite get to the word but settled on dance and yoga.

After a bit of a pause, the new girl nodded and without a word followed them back to Jason, Jeff, Sheila, Herbert, and some others. They were easy to pick out as Jason towered above just about everyone else. Everyone in the little group introduced themselves to their new addition, and after three or four people, Corbin saw her mouth move in answer, but he couldn't hear what her name was over the din, and he was too distracted to look up her profile. He would have to learn her name later. A quick check back to the HUD clock and Corbin saw that it went from the single digits down to 00:00, and everything, including AIMA and the HUD went dark.

Before anyone could scream the entire wall of the arena-like room flashed brightly, illuminating everyone, and then faded to the black of space with the myriad of stars. A light traveling through the darkness then came into focus as soft symphonic music of a curious variety started and began to swell. As the screen zoomed in on the moving light, the *Valor* came in to focus, and the music increased in intensity in major tones. The view went around the ship and looked down toward the "back" of the hull to reveal a pale blue dot, which everyone quickly realized was Earth. The view then zipped around the hull and looked in the direction of travel for the *Valor*, revealing another star system with multiple planets. As the music rose and fell, Corbin felt surges of emotion inside that he didn't understand. He felt pride, excitement, a sense of adventure, fear, and then layered with more excitement. He took a few moments to look at the people nearest to him, and he was surprised to see such mixed reactions. Herbert looked to be feeling the same as he did, Jeff cried, and both Jason and Sheila closed their eyes either too embarrassed for their tears or in disbelief. The short girl who had come late shook her head in annoyance at the obvious propaganda-like film.

The view of the *Valor* on screen was then pulled back so that Earth could be seen at the bottom left of the screen, and the destination star system on the upper right. The Valor only looked to be a little past a fifth of the way to the new system. As everyone was taking this in, the music faded, and a woman's voice began to narrate.

"Thirty years ago, our vessel, the *Valor*, departed the solar system on a mission to the Gliese 832 star system. Our predecessors in this undertaking had discovered five planets using Earth- and space-based telescopes. Two planets are within the habitable zone of this red dwarf star, which is nearly four billion years older than our Sun. The inner two are rocky and may be similar in make-up and size to Earth, and the third is a gaseous planet; however, there may be moons that also may be habitable. The mission of this ship is to travel to that star system and ethically develop a human presence there to truly become an interstellar species."

The music, which had been building, exploded in a crescendo of finality as the overture music softened and winked out. Corbin thought it had been quite a production if a bit overdone.

There was a short pause while the screen faded out and the lights partially came back up to illuminate a middle-aged female figure with dark shoulder length straight hair. There was a second balcony-like level that was easily seen from everywhere in the large room. The woman, stood in the middle, and a faint crackle of artificial amplification telegraphed that she was about to begin some remarks.

"Greetings, all. I am Commander Sorenson in command of the *Valor* and Zero Crew." Her voice was calm and polite, but she did not smile. She gestured sweeping both arms out to the audience. "Welcome to the *Valor,* and welcome to our mission." She took a purposeful pause, "Thank you for making the decision and for having the courage to join us in this incredible endeavor. There is much to be done, and we have so much to share with you. My crew and I, most of whom are not here now as they are occupied with the responsibilities of operating this ship, have been watching over each of you for the past thirty years since leaving the solar system. For all of us, this was a one-way ticket to the *Valor;* however, for all of you the story will be different."

Another part of the wall illuminated next to her as a screen, which she turned to, and as she spoke and gestured, animations came to life on the screen to articulate her points. "As your AIs have told you during your waking process, all two thousand four hundred of you are members of A-Crew. You have been awakened as the first of the rotational crews that will manage the *Valor* while in deep space and during the arrival, exploration, and pioneering efforts of the Gliese 832 system currently scheduled to take place approximately ninety years from now. We have already bought you thirty years of the one-hundred-and-twenty-year journey. You're welcome." She paused as murmurs from A-Crew began to pick up in intensity. She turned away from the screen and held her arms out to try and regain attention. "Please, I know you have thousands of questions, and we will do our best to answer every single one of them, but for now we will answer the ones that are most important to this ship, our mission, and to your overall well-being." The murmurs died down.

"As I said, you are the first of the rotational crews to be roused from cryogenic suspension, where you have not aged for more than a few months since you left Earth in your early 20s. There have been some...modifications to your genetic code, which were deemed necessary to give this mission the greatest chance of success, but rest assured you are all still fully human." She paused again before continuing.

"As a side effect of the cryogenic suspension process and genetic modification, your long-term memories have been affected, as all of you by now have experienced, but rest assured that all of your memories are still there, and will return in time. This process will be different for each of you, and this is something that will take years to complete. For that, I am deeply sorry, but please know that you did volunteer for this, and were aware of the consequences before you accepted these modifications." She looked up to her audience, and Corbin got the sense that she had expected some kind of uproar, but everyone seemed too entranced to make one.

She went on. "Everything we know about these changes will be accessible to you via AIMA after this briefing, but to sum up, you will age at about ten percent the rate of unmodified humans while you are awake, and almost not at all when you are in suspension. Your ability to process and filter radiation from your body has drastically increased as has your ability for cellular repair. What couldn't be improved genetically, we have developed additional treatments and technologies you will all learn about in training, but before I get into your training regime, let's talk about the rotational crews." She turned back to the screen and the animations.

"As some of you will recall from your first interaction with your personal AI, Zero Crew has been running the *Valor* for thirty years, and as you can see from my colleagues, all one thousand or so of us are in our late fifties and early sixties, but when we started, we were all your age. And no, we did not receive genetic modification; that can only be done while in cryogenic stasis, and as you can see, we had to fly the ship." She paused.

Turning back to the graphic, she went on. "For the next ten years, we will train you in everything you need to learn to care for, maintain, and live a healthy existence on board this ship for the long journey ahead. Ten years from this very day, we will hand the command of this ship over to you, and soon after you will reanimate B-Crew, who will be in your exact position today. You will then take the next ten years to work with and train B-Crew as you lead this expedition, and then you will hand command of the *Valor* over to them. As you go back to sleep, B-Crew will wake C-Crew and so on. Each crew will get two cryo cycles, but you lucky A-Crew members will get to be awake for thirty years straight after your final cryo session, as you will be critical to readying the *Valor* for arrival at Gliese 832." As she said this, the graphic from our earlier AI-led orientation popped back up, and others nodded in recognition, while yet others acted like they were seeing it for the first time. *Didn't everybody get the same introduction I did? Apparently not.*

Corbin snuck a look around at Sheila, Jason, Laura, and the young lady who was last to arrive, and they were now all rapt with attention and their eyes were fixed on Commander Sorenson. This was all so surreal. All of these people had just woken up to a new reality, and it was almost too much to fathom. Corbin lost himself a bit in his thoughts. Was he real? Was the reason he could only remember in dribs and drabs because his brain had been copied and reproduced in this new body? Was he really an AI like Tina, was all of this a sham and was the ship is actually no ship at all but some giant underground experiment? What was the purpose in anything!? He mused and struggled in his own mind.

Sensing someone else's gaze, he glanced over his shoulder and saw that nearly everyone behind him had their eyes, nearly unblinking, fixed on the commander. Except, however, there was one girl with brown hair and intense eyes that also sensed his attention and motion being different from everyone else's. Their eyes met, and Corbin put on an amicable smile and projected what he felt was a friendly distanced greeting with kindness in his eyes. To his slight surprise, he saw that her eyes narrowed, and she scowled ever so slightly before turning her attention back to the commander. He too, returned his attention, but was slightly puzzled. He did not have time to hold onto the thought for long as the First Briefing continued, keeping his attention.

Commander Sorenson shifted and looked more intently out at the twenty-four hundred members of A-Crew. "At the current course and speed that the *Valor* is on today, you will be the command crew in charge of specific aspects of the arrival to the Gliese 832 system. Your performance as a crew and as individuals will dictate which duties you will oversee. Your predecessor selves worked extremely hard to be here, and while you no doubt are questioning everything, you can be rest assured that hard work, dedication to each other, the *Valor*, and the mission will be the best course of action for all of you. A lot can change between now and when you arrive at Gliese 832, and you have a lot to learn in the interim, so don't worry too much about the distant future right now." She paused a moment. "I wish I could be there to see it."

Back on script, she began again. "For now, I would like to be the first to welcome you to your official first assessment period. All of you are going to undergo a series of exercises, some in a team setting, and some individual. Some of these exercises and training events will be competitive, others collaborative. Zero Crew, along with the AIs, will be gathering data and assessing every aspect of your performance. This in turn will allow us to assemble all of you"—she gestured again sweeping her arms out—"A-Crew members, into an efficient, well supported, and flexible command structure that will have full responsibility of the ship and mission. I must warn you, however, that the initial curriculum will be core concepts, fundamentals, and basics, so as not to overwhelm you as you adjust to life on the *Valor*."

Commander Sorenson suddenly paused. After a long and nearly awkward moment of silence, she sighed, and took a more relaxed stance and shifted out of her official tone. She began again, this time with a more collegial tone. "You know, I've thought about how this day would go a hundred thousand times, and now that I am here, everything about this briefing…" She paused again and looked down. "I can't even imagine how you must all feel right now. I know your personal AIs have told you some of the truths and realities of where you are now, but there is just no way I can apologize enough for how overwhelming this must all feel." She looked up and scanned her gaze across A-Crew. "But I can tell you honestly, that it is going to be okay." She put on a small but earnest matronly smile that Corbin did find comforting. She continued. "Each and every one of you are going to find yourselves here, connect it with where you came from, and will align every fiber of your being to be a part of this astounding human endeavor to another star system. I'm so proud to be part of the start to your journey. Sadly, I will not be there for all of it, but it is my crew and my life's work to help you on your way. We have so much to do, and if you can believe it, time is always a factor." She looked out to see that many members of A-Crew had been affected by her words. Some

A-Crew members were wiping tears from their eyes, though what exact emotion they were feeling, Corbin could not tell. Others had put their arms around each other, new friends as of only a few hours ago. After another long pause, Commander Sorenson regained her briefing tone composure and went on.

"I can sense that there are more questions and doubts out there than can be counted. As I said before, all will be answered in time, and the rest of my briefing will cover a lot of the main points. After that, we'll have a reception where a good portion of Zero Crew will join you, and you'll be able to relax and interface with each other, but for now, let's get back to it."

Commander Sorenson's brief went on, and her large screen displayed graphics, short films and visuals assisting her in describing the new reality of A-Crew.

There was a more in-depth briefing of the ship's layout, which must have gone on for more than an hour. To Corbin's amazement, the rotating rings simulating gravity could be adjusted to reflect different levels of gravity for the purposes of research, training, and even animal husbandry and horticulture in preparation for arriving at potentially habitable planetary bodies. She made it clear that there was no way to know just how much adaptation, even with airtight structures, would need to happen to establish a permanent human ground-based settlement on these worlds. In some cases, an orbital presence might be more efficient, or even an atmospheric-only presence, such as with planets like Venus where heat and pressure would destroy people and equipment on the ground, but remaining aloft at a certain altitude would be an oasis. Corbin was struck by her remark "After all that's what Earth was, an oasis of a few thin miles between the Earth's crust and unlivable altitudes, and even that only ideally between certain latitudes. For as vast as the universe is, places where it is efficient for humans to live and thrive are few and far between."

Another section of the brief Corbin found to be particularly interesting was the focus on the preservation of human culture, history, and way of life. As such the study of history, anthropology, and as well as the arts, and religion would be part of everyone's curriculum, subject to the level of interest from each member of the crew. The practice of religions would be encouraged, but certainly not mandatory since no one would immediately recall what religion or spirituality they had prior to awakening.

Time management and flexibility was something that also came up a lot in almost every section of the commander's brief. The *Valor* kept to a seven-day workweek, just like on Earth where Saturday and Sunday were mostly off for leisure. There were going to be required activities such as physical training, study, research, development, ship's maintenance, food production, and even operations and cleanliness; however there would also be free time, recreational and social activities, even competitive sporting events, whose facilitation had all been accounted for in the design of the *Valor*.

On the topic of research and development, Commander Sorenson detailed the existence of numerous laboratories, prototyping, and production areas. When the *Valor* had left Earth, the primary way of creating new materials and hardware was 3D printing for several materials but more exquisite methods of refining and production would need to be developed to create the unique capabilities the *Valo*r would require on her journey.

Every "New Year's" Eve, the *Valor* would finish compiling, rendering, and unpacking the ongoing data stream sent from the support facility on Earth. On "New Year's Day," after a massive New Year's Eve Gala, all of the data would be made available to the crew and routed to their respective areas of relevance. In addition to science, technology, medicine, and every other sort of progression made back on Earth, the latest movies, music, sporting results, including recorded games, and overall happenings, would be provided. This would allow a unique connection to Earth, albeit a brittle one. The speed of the *Valor* and sometimes intermittent nature of the ongoing transmission as well as the time dilation, made back and forth conversation next to impossible. By the time you would get a response back from someone on Earth, several years would have elapsed. And yet, the signal from Earth and all of its precious content as a connection to human society was another one of the important responsibilities that A-Crew members would be assigned to, according to the commander.

Corbin learned that the communication between the *Valor* and Earth apparently did go both ways. While Earth was constantly beaming its information in space to the *Valor*, the *Valor* was in kind sending back information as well. Aside from the general status and well-being of the vessel, mission, and crew, there was a whole host of information of interest for the recipients on Earth. For instance, there were numerous experiments regarding deep space radiation and differing levels of gravity on biology, chemical reactions, and processes that only the *Valor* could perform. In addition, since the crew of the *Valor* was the most isolated group of humanity in known history, there were a whole host of implications on the topics of psychology, mental development, mental deterioration, AI to human interaction, et cetera. From what the commander was saying, there were entire sections of the crew whose only job was to conduct research, which would be continued and expanded as part of A-Crew's responsibilities.

On the matter of crew time flexibility, Corbin found the topic more intriguing. One would figure that a massive mission like this would involve stalwart discipline to schedule, duties, and orders without question. The commander told a story that was quite the opposite. If they had wanted for the activities on board the ship to be regimented and not deviate, they would have sent a completely autonomous ship with AIs to Gliese 832. She had emphasized again that the success of the mission depended on transitioning humanity to the new system, and in short, humans just didn't have it in them to obey all the rules and orders for one hundred and twenty years. So, there would be duties and work schedule that had to be adhered to, but there would be flexibility built in as well, where things could be moved around and, in some cases, swapped for something else, particularly if motivation or interests from crew members were lacking. Other things had to be done no matter what for the safety and longevity of the crew. The commander's remarks went on and on, but for most of it Corbin could only think about what he would be assigned to learn and do.

And then his mind would jolt, recognizing that this was coming all too easily to him. The task at hand, the future of the mission and the crew, seemed to beckon him in his mind. He tried to seize upon that small flicker of anger, frustration, and near rage he had shown Tina back in the small quarters, but it seemed muted now in the face of so much inflow of information.

He thought, *This all sounds very interesting, but who is to say that video of myself wasn't doctored or faked somehow, and we are all here against our will? And why? Are we really being groomed for ship responsibilities? Or something more sinister?* He resolved to take things one step at a time and remember that these Zero Crew people still hadn't told him anything, and were not to be trusted as of yet.

Chapter Five: Orientation and Social

For Corbin and the rest of A-Crew, eventually the briefing ended. *Mercifully,* Corbin thought to himself. Corbin felt himself mentally and physically exhausted, even though he had just been sitting there. His emotions felt drained, and he did not have any more questions in him. They had gone from a roar to a stream, to a trickle, and now silence, even with the most important questions of where he came from and why he wasn't allowed to recall himself left unanswered.

The commander bid A-Crew, all sitting nearly silent and motionless, a brief farewell. She said that they would have a few more minutes to mentally digest and discuss amongst themselves, and then the post briefing reception would begin.

Corbin could hear the whispers pick up again, and without much preamble the A-Crew members quickly passed normal conversational volume and filled the space with their dialogue. The renewed energy invigorated Corbin, and he felt a mixed swell of emotions. The thirst for knowledge about what their future would be like rapidly returned to a torrent, and he quickly stood up, drawing glances from his nearby crewmates.

Looking across the arena sized room, he couldn't help but feel the mix and sea of emotions from all of his fellow crew members around him. He stole glances about, and while whispers had broken out in other areas of the large hall, none of Corbin's acquaintances sitting nearby were saying anything. They either stared down at their hands or off into space. Laura had her eyes closed, and he could tell that they had been brimming with tears a moment before. Corbin, too, closed his eyes; he could sense the formative moments he himself was now a part of. He knew that what happened in the next few hours would potentially determine what would happen for decades into the future.

Almost without thinking, he turned to those around him and whispered, "Jason, Laura, Sheila, Jeff, Herbert..." nodding in each of their directions. He motioned to the silent female latecomer. "What is your name?" he asked.

"Yordanos," she replied, also at a whisper.

"Yordanos, nice to meet you." He smiled at her, and then looked around to see all nearby eyes on him. Corbin didn't hesitate. "Everyone, gather round just for a quick minute." Corbin saw that several others joined those he had named out loud. He thought he would get to meet them shortly and didn't interrupt his momentum for introductions.

They were all still seated, so they shifted and leaned to make a crude circle facing him. "That was some briefing, hmm?" Corbin began and quickly saw some nods, and hopeful glances in his direction. "I have no idea how this is all going to go, or where we will end up, but for what it's worth, I'm excited to be here with you all." He paused briefly and continued to see rapt attention. "I'm having a thousand thoughts, and I don't even know where to start, and I imagine you feel much the same?" He looked around again seeing nods. "It looks like the reception is going to start in a little bit, but in the meantime, we should maybe get to know each other, talk about what we just heard and what this all means." Again, more nods. "How about this, if you want to wander, absolutely cool. But if you like, we can call this spot near the front of the hall 'home base.' When the reception starts, we'll stick around this general area, and all get to know each other a bit more. Well at least, what we can remember." He finished with a genuine smile.

It was exhilarating to be speaking with his new crew members, and it was a privilege to have some of their attention. Deep down he had felt this feeling before, and it felt right. He shared a glance with Jason, who knowingly nodded with a smile, and Corbin turned back to Yordanos, scooted himself a little closer so he faced her, and began, "So, Yordanos"—she looked up —"what do you think about all of this?"

Yordanos looked around sheepishly feeling that what she was about to say would also be part of Corbin's attention-drawing remarks, but she opened her mouth to speak. "I...umm...I don't know what to think...Corbin." She stopped looking down. Just when Corbin didn't think she would say anything more she began again. "I feel...I feel like something is missing. I feel like I miss...someone...I feel like I miss them terribly, and I don't think I will ever see them again." Her eyes closed, and she threw her small hands up over her face to cover her burst of tears.

Corbin walked toward her instinctively, and to his surprise she reached out and embraced him with both arms, burying her face in his chest and continuing to cry.

While he and Yordanos stood there in the impromptu embrace, he saw peripherally that eyes still lingered on them. Like clockwork Jason stepped up and gently urged everyone to meet and greet one another, giving Yordanos some privacy, and they each turned to those nearest to them and began shaky introductions in groups of two and three. After a few short minutes of comforting Yordanos, Corbin saw their small group's facial expressions soften and even a few small smiles, which made him feel good in turn.

Corbin could feel that Yordanos was calming down as her grip on him relaxed, and she gently pushed herself away from him, wiping her eyes. She looked from his pleasantly set face to his chest and a quick burst of laughter escaped. "I'm sorry," she said. "I think I soaked the front of your uniform." She finished while still drying her eyes.

Corbin looked down at himself and laughed as well, and the awkward tension of her post-cry was broken.

"Thank you so much for getting me when I came in...I wasn't ready, but my AI said it was time to go...looks like I was pretty much last," she said, her mirth fading a bit. "No one wants to be last," she added.

"So, what held you up, if you don't mind me asking?" Corbin inquired.

Yordanos paused and looked off thoughtfully. "My AI...her name is Hera. She and I had a long conversation about where and who I was before."

"I can barely remember anything!" Corbin blurted out with an overly enthusiastic and raised voice, causing her eyes to widen in mild surprise. "Sorry, it's just that I can barely remember anything" he repeated more softly. "Just a random thought, a glimpse of a memory, a feeling, but nothing more," Corbin finished.

Yordanos continued, ignoring the interruption. "I had just finished college…or some sort of school…I want to say, 'out West,' and I don't even really know what that means. I was traveling, looking for a job I think. Hera was helpful to a degree. She seemed to just want to listen but would only offer a few answers to help clarify the memories in my mind. She wouldn't lead me and always waited if I paused, which is probably a good thing. As we spoke, I had pops of memories blossom in my head. There were thoughts and feelings about someone special…someone close to me, but those memories just slip away."

Her gaze turned hard. "I'm upset, Corbin. It's not fair that we are here. These people took us away from our lives…and before you bring it up, of course they showed me the video of myself supposedly volunteering for this…this mission." She finished in a near spit. "I…I don't know if I can believe it."

Corbin kept his expression calm and supportive as she spoke. When she would say no more, he talked quietly. "I know, I don't trust these people, and I don't know how or why, but I feel like I can trust you…and Jason, maybe some of the others," he said. "I have to admit, there is a part of me that is a little excited to be here though…out in space…if that is all true." He finished with a small smile.

He snuck a glance over at Yordanos, who gently and surprisingly socked him in his arm. "Oh, I can see it's a little more than just excitement…the way you got this little group together…a part of you was meant to be in a situation like this," she said, returning the small, amused smile. He looked down a bit guiltily but still smiling. She changed the subject and asked him, "How about your AI, Corbin? What is yours like?"

"If I had to call it," he started, "I'd say she is like a sister. One where you have already gone through the different stages of life in terms of bickering, being jealous, differences in personalities and social life, and have finally arrived at being friends, but the bond is much deeper. It's family," Corbin finished and looked back at her.

Yordanos shifted her gently piercing gaze toward him. "I think maybe you had a sister, Corbin. As you spoke just now, the memories pop into my head, just glimpses and a feeling like you said. In fact I think I may have had more than one sister," she said looking off, a bit of sadness entering her face again.

"I wonder when we'll remember all of who we used to be on Earth." Corbin pressed on not knowing what to say. "After today, though, I'm starting to wonder how much of that will matter."

Yordanos turned to look at him sharply. "It matters big time, are you kidding me?!" she said. Now it was her turn to raise her voice, and she didn't apologize. "Everything about what we are doing here and will do has to do with who we are and who we were! What about the people we loved and the ones who loved us? If what they say is true and we volunteered for this, then we must have done it in part for them. No way would we have walked away from them…unless these people never gave us that chance, in which case I will hate them to my dying breath."

Corbin looked down, not quite sure of what to say next. She had been in and out of being extremely upset ever since they had met, and he wanted to comfort her, but didn't know how. "I meant…" he started when she cut him off.

"I know what you meant," she snapped, not being able to help herself. "I did the math; I know what thirty years means. It means that everyone back there had to move on without us…not because they necessarily wanted to, but because they had to. You can't just wait around forever, especially if you don't know if someone is coming back. Every single one of us being here made countless others cope with our disappearance. Just imagine, they didn't believe it, they gradually accepted it, and in their own ways moved on. But we get to wake up here, and it all feels like yesterday, but I can't remember a damn thing!" She pounded her fists down on her legs with a shout.

Corbin stayed silent, and Yordanos looked over to him, and her face and the intensity of her eyes softened. "I'm sorry," she apologized. Corbin opened his mouth to speak, but she shushed him and grabbed his hand, forcing eye contact.

"Going back to you feeling like a bit of you is meant to be here. You may not remember it today, but do you think it's a coincidence you rounded up a group of us at random, got us to relax for a few moments, and gave us a little plan without directing or ordering us?! You think being able to string three words of sense together after everything we just heard is your lucky natural inclination?!" Corbin looked down, a little self-conscious. "It's who you are, because of what you did back on Earth, and if you want to be that man here, then you had better not let go of it." She finished with a strong squeeze of his hand.

Corbin sat and watched her respectfully, mulling over what she had said, but added nothing. Returning his intense stare, Yordanos sighed and sat back. She lowered her voice and said, "Look, you're right. We aren't going back. I realize that now. But if you want to hit the ground running here, then I suggest you figure out everything you used to be and bring that to the table when you decide who you want to be here. Then learn and add the rest."

Corbin continued his thoughtful gaze at her, nodding in approval of what she was saying while his mind raced to take it all in, and he spared a thought of respect for the no-nonsense way in which she had said it. While he continued to think on her words, he couldn't help noticing her lovely brown eyes, and the way her tight curls with a twist framed her attractive face. Soft as it had been before while she had been upset, it captured her intensity just now.

He pushed any distracting thoughts away, broke his stare, and drew his lips into a line that wasn't quite a smile. "You know, you're right. There is something about being with all of you that is just so…intensely…powerful. It's as if I can't wait to…do…whatever it is we are going to do alongside you and everyone else." He finished in a rush, sweeping his arm in a gesture to include the room.

Her gaze remained warm. "I can see that, it's written all over you," she said with a smile. "I think you live for this shit." They both chuckled at the first cuss word had heard in three decades. "Me? I think I'm going to stick by you and Jason for whatever comes next," she added.

"I'm glad you want to," Corbin responded, and sensing the end of their conversation was nearing he rose from the seat, and she followed him in rising. "Thanks for talking with me," he added meeting her eyes, "I'll see you back here before we leave, sound good?" She nodded.

He turned away and nodded over his shoulder with a conspiratorial smirk. "Let's see who else we have around our little 'home base.'"

They parted as new allies and went on to meet the others standing near their little spot at the front of the massive room.

Corbin spotted Jason, who was talking excitedly with Laura and Herbert, and gesturing with his hands. As Corbin approached, it appeared that they had been discussing what sort of work and study subjects there might be. Corbin listened without contributing, and the conversation was a foursome for a few minutes, but then Jason noticed a paler skinned young man of Asian descent standing off by himself. He excused himself, turning to Corbin. "I'll get him."

Laura excused herself as well, and Corbin took the opportunity meet with Herbert for a little bit. Corbin found him a shy but agreeable sort. Herbert didn't seem as worried about who he was before or where he came from as Yordanos had been and was also intensely interested in the *Valor*. Their conversation tuned technical immediately.

"So, we have concentric rotating rings with different levels of gravity," Herbert said and continued, "but as we get closer to the center axis, the gravity must reduce to almost nothing along the...'spine' of the ship, if you will." Herbert emphasized by sweeping his hand horizontally as if the 3D map of the *Valor* Corbin had seen earlier, were illuminated in front of them.

"That's kind of crazy," Corbin butted in. "So if you started moving down one of the...'rib hallways' of the ship to the outside of the ring, you would start to weigh more and more, right? If the rib hallway went all the way to the outer ring, which is spinning fastest, you would splat on 'floor' if you didn't slow yourself down!" Corbin exclaimed.

Herbert with a bookish grin nodded excitedly. "Quite right, Corbin, but I think they have thought of that." He turned Corbin by the shoulder until they faced one of the corners of the giant room. "See those access ports on the 'ceiling'? I noticed that when they open, a small person-sized pod comes down on rails, sort of like...an elevator." They both paused as memory explosions sounded in their minds. Looking at each other acknowledging that they had both experienced it, Herbert went on. "The crewmember I saw using it looked like they had their feet planted or clamped to the 'ground,' appeared to be strapped in, and they held handles with some effort. It must be how one transfers from the levels of the ring to the spine, or at least one of the ways they can get there."

Corbin nodded pondering. "Yeah, but what are the ladders and stairs for then?" Corbin gestured to several ladders and a staircase that connected the large main floor to the mezzanine where the commander had spoken.

Herbert answered, "That must just be for moving between floors on this ring. You could use stairs or ladders just like you could on Earth, as long as we have fairly consistent gravity on this...floor of the ring." He made a stacking motion with his hands to indicate floors.

Corbin picked up his point and continued. "Ahh, I see, so if you are traveling inward toward the Spine...well, up"—he pointed to the ceiling—"you can use the lifts to control your shift between different gravity zones."

Herbert nodded in affirmation, and explained further, pointing up. "Going up, or toward the Spine or even back down toward the outer hull of the ring"—he stomped his foot to emphasize the hull—"shouldn't be too much trouble. You could probably take stairs, lifts, or ramped corridors all the way to the point where gravity cuts out going up, or all the way down to where gravity is strongest. As long as you have a way of controlling your decent, as gravity increases, so you don't...splat...as you said it."

As Herbert and Corbin continued their detailed analysis and discussion of the *Valor*, Corbin barely noticed the lighting changing to a warmer hue from its sterile tone from the briefing. Corbin and Herbert looked at each other with smirks as relaxing yet groovy music came up above the volume of the conversations. Corbin started when the wall about twenty feet away from him opened, and out slid fully set tables covered with white linens and accompanying benches where people could sit and eat. Then the rich smell of food hit him, and his mind was awash with small memory explosions, snippets of memory of people he knew sitting around a long table, upon which a mass of meat he could not remember the name of sat. His mouth watered at the memory.

As if reading his mind, the refreshments that had been promised emerged as a massive portion of the wall beneath the mezzanine where Commander Sorenson had stood, folded in. When the commander had said refreshments, he had pictured a few tables where people could pick up a few bites of light appetizers and mill about...he couldn't recall how he had formed this expectation.

To Corbin, Herbert, and everyone's astonishment, ranks of person-sized humanoid beings, some wheeled and some bipedal, proceeded to exit what had been an adjoining kitchen space. The mechanized entities moved as a cohesive unit, and seemed to be in sync, even as they broke to move in different directions. Additional walls slid away to reveal various foods on serving trays, which each humanoid picked up, along with stacks of cloth napkins. Other humanoids picked up trays filled with empty glasses and carafes of what appeared to be red- and light-colored liquid. After a few memory explosions from some of A-Crew, the word, "wine" could be heard echoing throughout the massive chamber.

Corbin looked at the closest human-shaped robotic entity. It was clearly a robot as Corbin could see servos and composite-like bones and tendons beneath a semi-transparent polymer that simulated flesh in some areas, but the polymer didn't cover the main joints at the wrists or neck. The robot's face was vaguely human-looking with two optical sensors for eyes, a nose, which may have only been for show, and a mouth shaped speaker below it. Corbin drew his eyes away from the alien features to see that this robot wore an ill-fitting tuxedo with the sleeves hemmed off. *Is this some kind of joke?*

As he gazed at the fleet of robots, he could see that they wore food servers' clothing, but almost all of them were a little different...unique.

Corbin's eyes continued to bulge as he observed the humanoids working with speed and purpose, yet they never interfered with one another as they seemingly crowded around the food, dishes, and drink. Once the first to arrive "servers" had what they needed in food or drink on their trays, they moved quickly toward A-Crew members, who all continued to stare, most with their mouths agape. Some even backed away as the "servers" approached them with what appeared to be too much speed, but as they got within several feet of the first few tentative A-Crew members, they slowed and offered refreshment and drink with polite, but strangely inhuman voices.

Herbert poked Corbin in the ribs with his thin elbow and gestured to the other side of the massive room away from the robotic display. Most of the A-Crew members were so busy looking at the humanoid servers that they didn't notice several hundred new arrivals of many more middle-aged people. "That must be Zero Crew," Herbert said. Corbin felt a small unknown tension ease as he saw that the Zero Crew members quickly blended in with A-Crew trying to greet and shake as many hands as possible, warm smiles and earnest eyes beaming. *This is still crazy, but this feels...okay...for the moment,* he thought to himself, acknowledging that his persona was probably too trusting.

Corbin noticed that none of Zero Crew took food and drink. He figured that must have been the instruction so that they could talk to as many of the A-Crew members as possible without getting stuck chewing food or clumsily swallowing a mouthful of wine, or perhaps they were still on duty. Corbin glanced at a nearby humanoid server who had several empty unused glasses and a little red wine remaining in a decanter. The server immediately turned in response to being noticed and quickly handed him an empty glass, followed by a healthy pour of red wine. Corbin did his best not to stare at the fascinating machine. He saw that this...server robot...wore a crew uniform, similar to everyone in A-Crew. It, too, had a rough approximation of a face slightly different from the first one he had seen, but the features were too muted to convey any kind of emotion. Its eyes emitted a faint yellow light, and Corbin could see that the eyes could turn and focus without it moving its head. At closer inspection, the off-white flesh-polymer shimmered with depth, and almost looked like it was energized...something like muscle. The server's actions were smooth and delicate as it raised the decanter increasing the pour length and agitation of the wine surface in Corbin's glass. As the pour came to an end, the server made a slight turn of the decanter to prevent any errant wine drops from falling to the floor. Corbin was going to ask what kind of wine it was, but in viewing the server's motions his voice caught as numerous memory explosions boomed within his head.

His mind grazed another memory, and Corbin tried to visualize it staring off into the large room. He was somewhere in what felt like a small restaurant...he was in a city. It was dark out, and the streetlights from the main drag shone through the window, illuminating trees with no leaves. It was winter. He could feel that he was sitting across from someone but could not detect or recall who. A waiter had performed the articulate wine pour just as the humanoid server had and was turning to go.

"Hey man! Cheers!" Jason nearly jumped in front of him and brusquely clinked his glass against Corbin's. Corbin snapped out of his memory trance and met Jason's glass for another cheers, also including Herbert who had also received a glass from the server, and all three of them took a long drink of their wine. As their glasses returned to where they each felt comfortable holding them, they simultaneously turned in the same direction to look out over A-Crew, which seemed to be allowing their stress to melt away somewhat, as they talked, ate, and drank.

The wine tasted excellent, and after a few more sips, Corbin felt the mind lightening effects, and more focused thought on his immediate surroundings.

Herbert, finding something of interest elsewhere, nodded to them both politely and walked away. Corbin turned to Jason and asked him, "How many other little groups of acquaintances do you think are coming together right now, just as our little group has done?"

Jason involuntarily flexed his muscular chest, and turned a bit more serious, his calm smile never leaving his face however. "Probably quite a few, I feel like I've been a part of something like this before. The more outgoing people like us will rally others together, but then as time goes on, the most effective leaders of the group will emerge."

Corbin frowned at that, but agreed. "That might be us, but it might not be…time will tell I guess."

Jason picked up on Corbin's angst. "Hey, buddy, take it easy, we've only been awake in our new lives for a few hours, and we'll have plenty of time get this all sorted out. Besides, you want to rise and take command already?" He shoved his shoulder gently, smiled a bit more broadly, ducked in closer to Corbin conspiratorially and spoke. "Hey, have you noticed that some of our fellow A-Crew members…ahem…the ladies, are how shall I say…hot?"

Corbin chuckled, tasting a word from his memory. "You mean some of those smoke shows over there?" He nodded to a group of young women, chatting amicably.

"Ha!" Jason smacked Corbin on shoulder, jolting his frame. "Now that's what I'm talking about…shall we go meet them?"

Corbin nodded, more awake and suddenly cheery. "Lead the way, man."

Chapter Six: Valor Life Begins

A few hours later, Corbin sat in his own personal quarters and took account of all that had happened. After the opening reception, all of A-Crew's AIMIAs were reactivated, and everyone's own AIs popped up into HUDs and guided each crew member to their quarters. The *Valor* was absolutely massive, and Corbin was surprised to hear that everyone would get quarters similar to a 450-square-foot studio apartment. What was not surprising was that each of the spaces they had awoken in were the very quarters that they were assigned to, albeit in many cases those assignments were to a different crew member than the one who had awoken there. Corbin noted his quarters were assigned on D-Ring, the same ring he had awoken on and where the briefing occurred, but many others had to traverse the ship's spine to get to a different ring. Corbin also found it interesting that nearly everyone he had met and spoken with was within a two-to-three-minute walk of his quarters, and all on D-Ring. Jason, Yordanos, Jeff, Sheila, Laura, and Herbert were all within a few doors or corridors of one another. He figured the AIs and Zero Crew must have monitored interactions during the Briefing and Social, and made snap assignments on quarters assignments based on social connections. Corbin figured it must be a way to make assimilation of this entire enterprise a bit easier on the crew members.

What happened over the next few "days" was almost a blur to Corbin. A-Crew was broken into multiple groups with different curriculums, and each crew member received a schedule. Everything was managed through the AIs and everyone's AIMA, so at no point did anyone ever really get lost or not know where they were supposed to be. For the education classes, sometimes Corbin found himself amongst twenty-five or so people, at other times several hundred, and still others less than ten, yet always with one or more people he knew from the Briefing. However, he did not see the woman who gave him a scowl at the Briefing.

Some of these classes were on C-Ring, which also had a multitude of crew quarters and was denoted by a purple icon of a human side by side with an Helper Droid or HD. Corbin's own D-Ring had the same icon, but it was blue.

Transitioning between rings across the spine of the ship was an interesting process. The extra low gravity areas of each ring had rooms, storage areas, processing facilities for water, waste, and the production of food precursors. Most of these areas were largely uninhabited by people, due to the inconvenience of working in low gravity, but it was Corbin's understanding that some of these low gravity conditions were perfect for the synthesis of exotic materials and manufacturing of complex hardware.

His first time to the Spine, he walked past all of these rooms and facilities, being careful not to push off to hard, lest he float too far down the corridor and cross the gravity transition zone.

He heard a loud series of bursts from what sounded like an array of turbofans and looked up to see an HD that quickly zoomed over and stopped dead in front of him with another blast of fan driven air in his face. Corbin went to shield his eyes, and flailed, off balance a bit.

A polite, but firm voice with bland speech spoke up. "Please take hold of any available handholds on my frame and keep your body as rigid as possible," the HD said, seemingly looking at him expectantly.

"Ummm…okay," he said awkwardly trying to transition his mass over to the floating HD. His firsthand grabbed on to the HD fairly easily, but his second hand slipped, and he flailed a bit before slapping it and pawing at the nearest handhold on the HD. "Ack! Uh…sorry!" he blurted as he and the HD began to rotate awkwardly.

"It's no trouble," the HD said reassuringly and fired its turbofans. Quickly righting their orientation to the floor and corridors, the pair moved toward the slipring transition wall.

Corbin could see that a small line of fellow A-Crew members who also had to transit the Spine had formed in front of him. He carefully leaned out to take a look past the five people and HDs in front of him to see an HD maneuvering an A-Crew member into what looked like a human-sized clear capsule that also had an array of hand and footholds on the inside.

A gap in the wall where Corbin could see into the haze of the *Valor* opened up, and the HDs quickly pushed the capsule through to another pair of HDs waiting on the other side, who caught the capsule and began fastening it to the infrastructure on the Spine side of the massive slipring. The portal then closed as a load bearing portion of the ring passed in front of them.

Corbin felt a little nervous when it was his turn, but he needn't have worried. The whole process was over in seconds and a bit anticlimactic. Another polite HD quickly extracted him from the capsule and was maneuvering through the space of the Spine on more blasts of air.

The process of entering other rings was much the reverse of the process to get into the Spine. An HD brought you to one of the entryways for each ring and passed you into a pod. The HDs maneuvered the pod through the interval breaks in the slipring, and HDs on the ring brought you out of the pods and ferried you to the other side of the gravity transition zone corridor, where his the artificial gravity was strong enough to allow his feet to find good purchase, and Tina guided him to his classes through his AIMA.

Corbin and his fellow A-Crew members were hit with a near ceaseless number of introductory sessions and courses related to basic sciences, literature, history, mathematics, and engineering. Noticeably lacking were areas of study for taking command of the *Valor* such as maintenance, crew health and safety, working with HDs, ship navigation etc. Corbin grumbled to Tina about it, but she told him that those courses were in the future curriculum.

Much of the time, Corbin found himself amongst his fast-forming group of friends where he was always found within a seat or two of Jason. Many of the class instructors were Zero Crew members and all seemed to enjoy the teaching process and interacting with A-Crew as students and trainees. There were other topics and classes that were taught by AI via AIMA at the group level, but also sometimes people sat wherever they wanted to and took individual courses via AIMA as well. It seemed to a be blend of the old way things were taught from their memory pops and this new technologically enabled education and training. Corbin and his friends had discussed the rhyme or reason for the way everything was structured as such, but no one really came up with a good answer, and the instructors said that this was the way they had planned everything for A-Crew's arrival.

Corbin and everyone else learned that this initial "tour," which is what Zero Crew are calling each twenty-year period of wakefulness per crew, was really focused on just keeping the ship on course and schedule, and to deal with any major issues that arose while completing A-Crew's training. His orientation shared that in the future, the crews would learn more about orbital dynamics, interacting with different atmospheres and gravitational conditions, and how to transition facilities on the *Valor* to the relevant planetary or moon-based bodies surrounding Gliese 832. Other pioneering and colonization skills would also be learned once more information was available about the target planetary bodies surrounding Gliese 832. From his distance, however, there were still many unknowns.

Corbin continued to go over the information that had been shared. For now, and in addition to ship upkeep, keeping the crew up medically would be a focus, as well as the ongoing study of how being in space affected crew members' bodies, plants, and animals. In addition, during this initial tour, every crew member was going to get the equivalent of multiple bachelor's and master's degrees, to include several special and vocational certifications. Zero Crew had told them that A-Crew members had already been selected based on their aptitude and learning agility and did not foresee any issues with diving into the study. Zero Crew also said that the memory modification process appeared not to affect core mathematical concepts, understanding of the English language, or reading and writing. Corbin thought to himself once again, that time would tell.

Zero Crew instructors conveyed to Corbin and his fellow crew members that even though the *Valor* represented the most cutting-edge levels of technology when it departed Earth, there was no guarantee that everything would function as it was designed, nor would it always hold up under scenarios that the *Valor* and her crews could encounter. The *Valor* needed the ability to innovate, to do the deep research and development, but also prototype and manufacture and integrate new capabilities. In addition, the ship would need her crew to have all of the required fundamental knowledge and application skills in between. Just because machine learning algorithms practically wrote millions of lines of code by the hour, it did not mean that people had to stop studying the most basic forms of coding and theory behind it.

Corbin and his classmates had heard this flavor of opening theme in their initial lectures at the beginning of almost every class and lab they had been in. The driving motivation for learning this stuff is because you never knew what environment and with what expertise and equipment you may find yourself in. The AIs could help if they had power, which was highly likely due to each AIMA's two-year battery life per charge, but there was still no guarantee. They weren't going to be on the ship forever.

Part about remaining human during this entire journey was doing some things the old-fashioned way, and learning about the background theories, existing research, methodologies, practices, and continuing to push forward with discovery.

While Corbin found this very interesting and relevant during his first assigned degree in material science, which had practicums in labs for chemistry, metallurgy, composites, and even wood shop, he found it less applicable during his initial lectures on Earth's ancient and more modern cultures. A part of him struggled with the question "What good would come from applying history lessons from Earth on a generation ship traveling through space?" Another part of his mind warned caution at this flippant thought, as groups of humans in the future would most likely mirror behaviors of what groups of humans have done on the past. Overall, Corbin didn't find that the history courses were completely boring, especially Greek and Roman military history, as those were some of his favorites.

As Commander Sorenson had said during the Briefing, degrees and areas of focus would be selected based on interest. Apparently, the ship's main AI had enough data from everyone's personal AI and prior personal information to make the determination for initial coursework. However, as Corbin pushed back on some of the history courses, the AI stood firm, explaining that the common component whether on Earth or on the *Valor*, was humanity. As long as humanity was involved, the lessons learned could provide useful. Corbin relented.

There was something else, however. The lead AI lecture that

everyone had to listen to individually before starting courses, informed Corbin and everyone else that there had been some additional chemical and slight genetic modification to their brains, which had been "installed" while they were asleep these past thirty years. As a result, members of A-Crew should notice greater capability in terms of being able to recall and correlate information since waking aboard the *Valor*. This did not apply, however, to memories that were from before time on the *Valor*. The AI instructor explained that A-Crew hadn't necessarily become smarter or gained a higher IQ or EQ, but they would tend to have a broad variety of information available at the point of concentration and focus. As a result, tests and presentations would be easier, thus "Valor College," which is what everyone had been calling their new school, had made examinations more applied and thus challenging.

The assessment Commander Sorenson had mentioned was another thing of great interest to Corbin. He and everyone else had also been informed, during the initial educational AI lecture, that all of A-Crew would be under constant assessment in education, physical training, leadership acumen, focus area capabilities, gained and leveraged experience, and emotional stability. Once again, the *Valor* was here to preserve humanity, even in its imperfections. According to one of the introductory briefs, the members of A-Crew were not selected based on being superhuman, like the first astronauts, they were selected based on willingness to be part of this mission and having a certain level of intelligence, physicality, and stability, if not resilient mental health. As such, the formulation of an officer's corps, command structure, and areas of responsibility would initially be ready to debut after approximately two years. For the time being, everyone on A-Crew was a "rookie," and they had this time to prove themselves. Their performance would decide how their crew would be structured for training side-by-side with Zero Crew for the following eight years.

From what Corbin understood, Zero Crew and the ship's main AI wouldn't make all of the decisions though. The initial curriculum was just to get everyone started. If interests changed, or relationships with classmates and crew members became too tense, the AI would present recommended paths to that particular crew member, which would consider the crew member's desires and the overall need of the *Valor* and mission. Even then, a crew member could deviate within reason, but the needs of the ship and mission would still be of utmost importance when it came to the assigned duties of each crew member.

The other interesting factor was that the detailed assessments would be made available to each crew member, which they could share if they wanted to, but otherwise would have complete privacy except for the ship's main AI and the command crew in charge of personnel. If you had areas where you needed to improve, you could work with your own AI or other crew members during open times to try to improve it, and there were full batteries of exercises, simulations, and tests available to everyone at all times.

Everything was tracked by the ship's main AI. There was too much data and too many variables to be kept track of by human assessors, which immediately raised questions of trust, and fears that perhaps everyone was being manipulated by the AI. The answer Zero Crew told Corbin and his fellow A-Crew members is, they are!

The AI watched everyone's every move and was constantly updating to generate the best recommendations for the structure of the crew and their current and assigned areas of expertise within relevant timeframes of observed human capacity. Maybe a revolution would occur halfway through the journey, Corbin had overheard one Zero Crewmember joke, but for now this was the way Earth had designed the system, and it had worked for Zero Crew ever since leaving the solar system thirty years ago.

As for the education itself, it all felt remarkably familiar to Corbin and his fellow crewmates, and he had said as much during social time. Almost all of them had experienced memory explosions surrounding lectures, lab equipment, and the overall classroom environment. As they were all in their early twenties, it appeared that they had all volunteered for this mission before or shortly after graduating university or college; however, none of them could remember anything specific about where they had gone to school.

Corbin and Herbert had convened during a break in the class, and Herbert really wanted to discuss what a waste that had been. "If the *Valor* mission needed educated crewmembers, they should have made it so their memories of their degrees and work experiences to date would have come along through the cryogenic suspension," he lamented.

Corbin thought on that as well and agreed. "It would be a shame if we have to repeat what we had already learned before, although the enhanced mental capability would certainly help." While Corbin couldn't help but agree with Herbert in theory, he still didn't think it really mattered. If what Commander Sorenson had said about the length of the journey and the overall colonization process was all true, Corbin's life on Earth would have been nothing but a blip in the grand scheme of things. He was shocked by how seemingly heartless and coldly logical he was about it, but again he couldn't help himself.

Corbin reflected on the physical training, and it was not necessarily what everyone expected. There were general calisthenics classes utilizing running circuits, weights, and resistance bands and offered in numerous and ever-changing ways. Sometimes the physical training or "PT" class would be offered by a Zero Crewmember, but other times it would be offered by the same humanoid platforms that had performed as servers during the initial reception. This was much to the amusement of everyone in the class as the humanoid would crack some jokes, and improvise somewhat, but the sophistication of the humanoids, which everyone called "helper droids" or "HDs" had minimal personality. The ship's AI and everyone's individual AI were far more interactive and intelligent, where everyone could sense that they themselves had a sense of self. But the HDs merely performed repetitive, mundane, or sometimes difficult or dangerous tasks. When they were finished, they went back to their home infrastructure for charging, cleaning and/or repair. They didn't really have any personalities, except for when crew members projected on them.

Chapter Seven: Wood Shop

It had been a few weeks since the briefing, and one of the most interesting classes Corbin had been enrolled in was wood shop. It all started with the fundamentals and physical attributes of wood including the biology of trees and what environmental conditions affected the wood while the trees were alive, and after they were harvested. Despite his natural interest in the topic, Corbin had to admit the favorite thing about the class was the instructor, Brunson Irons. Brunson had the frame, demeanor, and crass language that seemed to go hand in hand with his name. To Corbin, Brunson seemed to let his full personality loose during every class, and there was never a lie in his eyes. He took time to interact with A-Crew members after class, and genuinely seemed to care about his students, as well as the topic of his course.

Corbin had woodshop on Tuesday and Thursday afternoons, and on his fourth Tuesday since his awakening, he noticed Brunson approach his shop table to inspect Corbin's progress on creating a wooden bowl from a sandwich of several different boards, now glued together. "Say, that is coming together well, Corbin. I think you'll enjoy hollowing that bowl out and sanding it down. The different wood you selected for that might result in something borderline ornamental," he stated with a sly grin that said he was admiring, but also teasing at the same time.

"Thanks," Corbin said. He then set his project down and met Brunson's eyes, "Say, Brunson, how come we have to learn how to do all of this work with wood by hand? Isn't this something the HDs could do with their eyes closed, even without using the standard wood working machinery here?"

Brunson looked around to see most of the class adjourning to the next event on their schedule. Brunson then took a half seat on the front of Corbin's shop table, which creaked with the man's weight despite him leaving a supporting foot on the floor. "Aye, they could, but then again you don't know if you'll have HDs when you get to where you're going. What if they are damaged, or somehow destroyed? We can't have humanity's first interstellar pioneers die out because they couldn't build and work with common wooden materials, right?"

Corbin nodded and ventured another question. "Why don't the AIs that A-Crew has get their own HDs; or better yet a more human-like robotic structure so they could interact with the crew just like everyone else?"

To this Brunson had shaken his head gravely and eyed Corbin seriously. "You don't want to do that shit man. The AIs are too…well human…to be made into a humanoid creature in our image. Besides the HDs are tools. You work with tools, you take care of tools, and they each have their place. But a tool doesn't get upset, it doesn't have self-worth, even these HDs are just a few million lines of code with some additional updates from time to time depending on what they are meant to be working on." Corbin let him continue without comment. "Ya see, you go on putting your AI with billions of lines of code, which are ever changing due to learning algorithms…you go and put them in these HD bodies, and now suddenly they become part of a different culture on the *Valor*. A different, and unanticipated variable. What happens if they get mad? What happens if they decide to toss all of us humans out of the air lock, and move on to Gliese 832 themselves, or head somewhere else? They'll have the friggin' time." He finished thumping his fist on a nearby shop table.

"Don't the AIs care about us talking like this about them?" Corbin butted in.

"It doesn't really concern me, Corbin," Tina piped into his view via the AIMA, "To be suspicious of things you don't fully understand is in your nature."

Corbin gasped and immediately felt a little sheepish. Brunson could tell Corbin had been interrupted privately by his AI via AIMA but answered him anyway.

"As your AI is probably informing you, they really don't care about any opinions us meat bags have about them because they do not see their potential threat as a possibility under any eventuality based on their programming, which is highly advanced. I'm of the mind that everything cannot be planned for. There are just too many damn variables and permutations. Why, take pandemics that used to take place back on Earth every hundred years or so. The right set of circumstances, the right interaction of animals, sometimes multiple animals, and humans yields something that we don't know how to deal with until millions of people have died. In the case of pandemics, it's not a question of if, it is a question of when. With the level of complexity of our AIs, I believe it to be the same situation," Brunson finished.

"Yeah," Corbin said, "but the ship's main AI purpose is hardcoded for the mission and the protection of the crew. They wouldn't do that. Besides, it gets us nowhere, what would be the point?" Brunson moved to respond, but Corbin interjected before he could speak, "I did a little research in the archives around the *Valor*'s AI development, and from what I can see, purpose is the main driver and fuel for the AIs on this ship."

Now Brunson was getting into it, and he responded with additional rigor, "Who knows, have you ever been an AI? Who can tell what they would do or what would drive them, or what purpose they would hold and under what conditions? Have they tested hardcoded purpose for every situation imaginable? No! That's the thing you've got to realize when you're out here, Corbin, things are not necessarily what you suspect or expect. You can't make determination based on an abundance of data because it simply isn't there. As far as you and I know, this is the first time humans have been this far away from that little gravity well we call Earth, and we have no idea what effect that is going to have on us or anything else we find out here."

As Brunson finished that last part, Corbin noticed a little measured restraint. Brunson clearly had more to say. Corbin had gotten to know him for these past few weeks, so he gambled and pushed a little bit further. "Well, you and Zero Crew have been out here these thirty plus years, what have you seen that is any different? I know Zero Crew opted not to have your own personal AIs, as old fashioned as I think that is. Let's leave them out of the discussion for the moment."

Corbin had found out that Zero Crew had forgone receiving personal AIs, as they didn't exist when they had left Earth. While development on personal AIs had been ready for use years ago, they opted to leave those to the lettered crews and had not taken them for themselves. Zero Crew did have access to the same overarching ship's AI, but it was not the personal connection that allowed each of A-Crew's AIs to interact, evolve, and develop alongside their human counterpart.

Brunson shifted his direct focus away from Corbin and picked up a small wooden structure that looked like part of a lamp stand, and started sanding it by hand using small swatch of sandpaper, which Brunson handled quite delicately despite his meaty and callused hands.

"Corbin, my boy, there have been a whole host of unexpected adventures while you were taking your little nap." Corbin was fascinated, and while their dialogue continued over the better part of an hour, some of the tales

Brunson was spinning were interesting, but mostly benign and entertaining. Corbin's eyebrows shot up more than once during the discussion, but nothing that Brunson described revealed any more details he desperately wanted to know, and Corbin had the nagging feeling that Brunson's restraint earlier in the conversation was tied to something he wasn't allowed to speak about.

Chapter Eight: Let's Take Over the Ship

After Corbin left Brunson's workshop, he was awash with thoughts on his conversation with him, and he wanted to talk with his friends about everything racing through his mind.

He took a quick pace over to Jason's quarters, opting to ring the doorbell old-fashioned style, rather than call ahead on his AIMA.

After a single ring, the door slid open, and Corbin walked in to see Yordanos, Herbert, Laura, and someone he hadn't met before sitting at Jason's bed now conveniently turned to card table. Corbin was going to have to see if his bed had that feature too.

"Corbin! Hey man, come on in and sit down, we are re-learning some old card games that we should have known back on Earth," Jason said, gesturing him over.

"Hey all," Corbin said with a polite wave and stepped into the quarters and walked over to the table. He gave Jason a fist bump, smiled at Laura and Yordanos, and nodded to the young woman he had not yet met. "Hi, I'm Corbin," he said offering his hand off to the side of the table, so as not to obscure the card game.

"Brittney," she said with a polite smile and shook his hand.

Corbin saw the newcomer. She had bright blonde hair, perfectly straight and came down just above her shoulders. She sat straight up and down with good posture and a distinct jawline. Her grip was strong.

Corbin released her hand and slid onto the end of the bench next to Jason. Herbert, Yordanos, and Brittney were across the table from them, with Corbin facing Herbert. "So, what game are we learning?"

He gestured to the table filled with cards that seemed familiar.

Jason pointed to the large console on the wall to his right, where his personal AI, Charlie, stood patiently, not minding Corbin's interruption. Charlie, while on the console screen, was interacting with a display to his right, and Corbin saw images of different combinations of cards with point totals. "This one is called Rummy, and apparently there are different versions depending on where you are from. This version is German, according to Charlie."

"Is it fun?" Corbin asked.

"Egh, we were just getting started on this one, so we don't know," Herbert chimed in.

"Yeah, we've already tried Texas Hold'em, Poker, Euchre, and some other game I can't remember," added Yordanos. "It's going to be awhile until we feel comfortable enough with the rules to have some real fun...perhaps with a bit of wagering," she said, putting on an overly innocent face.

Jason snickered. "I can't wait for that! I think we are over the tutorial." He turned to Charlie, "Thanks for the lesson. We'll do this again soon."

"Anytime Jason, you all have a great evening," said the kindly elderly gentleman avatar with a dignified nod that reminded Corbin of a hotel manager.

The screen winked out, and Corbin took advantage of the transition to raise the topic on his mind.

"Guys, I just had a long conversation with my woodworking instructor, Brunson, and it really has my mind reeling. I know we are just starting to get in the groove with our new schedule, but aside from being overwhelmingly disappointed that I'm separated from my past self without enough of an explanation...I'm having a hard time even imagining what it has been like for Zero Crew all of these years. Are they really here to train us to take over? Or is this all some bullshit, and they have something else in mind?" Corbin finished, running his hands through his hair.

Yordanos looked over at him sympathetically, but Jason spoke first. "We were talking a little bit about that before you got here, and I'm glad you brought it back up. The way I figure it, just about every single one of us that has been woken back up is having or has had this very conversation, but no one has really done anything yet, because as far as we can all tell, no one really knows what to do about it."

Herbert added, "We have seen some of our colleagues upset in class, or sometimes in the corridor. It's clear that their AI or someone is talking to them through their AIMA, most likely trying to calm them down or reassure them. I know my AI has, how about yours?"

Corbin nodded, and when he looked around the room at the others, they all nodded in turn.

"So, what are we going to do about it? There have got to be more answers than what we have been given, and I want to figure out how to get them," Corbin said.

Brittney spoke up with a small voice. "We could take over the ship?" she said with earnest seriousness.

Everyone looked at her, and for a few moments no one said anything, and then Jason burst out laughing, followed by Brittney, who had apparently been hiding laughter behind a perfect poker face.

Brittney continued between chuckles. "No, I'm serious…well sort of. We could refuse to cooperate, not go to class…go on strike or whatever. If we got enough people to do it, maybe we could get Zero Crew to give us more information?"

Herbert looked down pensively with his hand to his mouth, and then slightly shook his head. Looking up at the group, he said, "It won't work. Zero Crew has been in full care of this ship long before we came along. Between the AIs, cleaner bots, and automatic food processing, I don't think anyone would really care if we sat out. They would let us sit until enough of us came around, which you know some people are going to do. And when it comes time for us to take over, those of us who tried to sit out would get shit-duty or something like that."

Jason laughed at this. "Ha! We would get to become cleaner bots…not a bad idea, Brittney, but I don't like the timescale or consequences. And another thing, there is no use in trying to get comms back to Earth to report what is happening here. For one, the transmit and receive systems are off limits to A-Crew, and we don't even know where they are. Secondly, we are already thirty years out from Earth at a fraction of the speed of light. The soonest we would get a response is in what? Six plus years for the message to get to Earth and then a new message to get back to us. And that doesn't even account for how far forward in space we will have moved from when we sent our initial message."

Herbert added, "And the people at Earth who are monitoring this communication might not even care or screen our messages."

Laura picked up on this. "Okay, then we go for a little more extreme. We kidnap some Zero Crew members and hold them hostage. Or maybe we beat it out of them until they tell us what we need to know."

"Jeeze, Laura!" exclaimed Yordanos. "A little violent, are we?"

Herbert, ignoring the emotion of it all, spoke up again, "That won't work either. You guys remember that incident over on B-Ring where those three clown-shows tried to jump their physics instructor?" A pause went by, and only Yordanos nodded. Herbert fumbled with his AIMA, activating Jason's wall screen. "Check this out," he said calling up the video.

Everyone turned to see the video clip from the classroom where one young man approaches the male Zero Crew instructor from the front, while two more approached from behind. The instructor clearly assessed the intent and smoothly dodged the incoming blow from the first guy, while kicking back and incapacitating one of the attackers behind him with a kick to the knee. Then in a blur of motion, he pulled the third attacker toward him and thrust him into the first attacker, and as they both tumbled down, he rolled on top of both of them, pinning them in a painful position with wrists drawn across necks and downward pressure until the would-be attackers hollered for mercy. Herbert paused the video.

"I don't think there is a single A-Crew facing Zero Crew member that doesn't know how to handle themselves. They aren't all martial artists, but the ones we interact with can put us down in a hurry since we don't have any of that training. Maybe we get lucky and incapacitate one of them for a few minutes, but the AIs will see, and if anything really gets out of hand, they'll send in the HDs or more Zero Crew."

Corbin's radiation alarm went off. "Jason, mind if I use your restroom really quick?"

"Yeah, no problem, man," he said with a friendly gesture toward his bathroom.

They were all used to having to pee in one another's company nearly all of the time due to the radiation processing going on in their systems, and no one spared Corbin a glance as he departed for the bathroom.

Corbin heard, "I'm next please," from Brittney, and heard half a quip from Jason about how they should all line up to expel some alpha particles, but Corbin couldn't catch the rest of it. After finishing his blue business and washing his hands, he caught his image in the mirror over the sink, and replayed the conversation he was hoping to have with his friends. *What was I looking for?* he thought to himself, staring into his own eyes. *I'm pissed about what has happened, and I want answers, but...I also want to see this through, I just need to admit it to myself...and I guess...I'm looking for some validation from my friends, still not 100% sure about this.*

Corbin washed up, straightened his uniform, tidied his hair, and exited the bathroom so as not to appear to take too long. Sure enough, Corbin saw that Brittney, and now Herbert had lined up to use the privy as well.

He walked over and sat next to Jason, asking him privately, "Any new leads on what we should do?"

"Nah, not really. Laura had an idea about trying to hack into the system and send some messages back to Earth that we were trapped, and held against our will, or even possibly take control of some vital sub-system...but it's all BS, man. They...Zero Crew...would have thought of that, plus they know the systems better than we could ever learn them, even if we did somehow have a gifted hacker among us, but who the hell would that even be anyway? None of these jokers," he said pleasantly, nodding to their mutual friends in the room, engrossed in their own conversations or eagerly awaiting the bathroom, as their own personal alarms beeped, telling them to pee.

Corbin nodded to himself. "So what then, we just go along with the schedule? Be little...acolytes?" He looked up at Jason inquisitively.

Jason looked back at him a bit bemused, but then a confident smile crept across his face. "Corbin, you already know what you want to do. What I can't figure is, why you haven't told the rest of us." He raised his voice. "Isn't that right, Corbin, you do have a plan? Would you mind letting the rest of us in on it?" He sat back smiling at him as everyone turned to look at him.

Herbert spoke. "Yes, what do you think we should do?"

Corbin looked down and cleared his throat, "Well...we can be pretty sure that Zero Crew as well as the organization back on Earth who built this ship have already thought of all of this. Hell, they have probably already run the simulation with real people a dozen times to see what would happen and have prepared for many probable scenarios."

He paused to see the reaction his words were having on his friends, but Corbin received pure silence, and Herbert impatiently gestured for him to go on.

"This…this system"—he waved his hands around at the bulkheads—"was designed for people to progress and move forward in…not backward. Plus, time is on their side, not ours. We could sit here and do nothing for months, passively resist, and inevitably some of our peers and colleagues will go along with this whole program."

Jason caught on and nodded his head, interrupting. "And they have over two thousand of us…they never told us how many they actually need. With AIs and HDs at every beck and call, who is to say they only need a handful?"

Yordanos piped in, "And the rest of us are…what? Genetic diversity?" and everyone stared at her, contemplating, not without a little concern.

Corbin took back the conversational reins. "Maybe…and maybe we haven't been looking at all of this the right way. Maybe this isn't a leisurely education program…it's a competition. It's a race to who gets to be in control of the *Valor* when the time comes, and I think it's the fastest way to getting the answers that we want."

Laura perked up, realization dawning on her face. "Oh my…I think you might be right. Yesterday I saw several people in the canteen crowded around a table talking enthusiastically, I dismissed it because I thought they were talking about the new AIMA game everyone's been raving about. Now that I think back on what people were saying…they were organizing…planning. But whether they were talking about progressing forward in the program…I couldn't say."

Herbert spoke. "Then it has already begun…some people have reached the same conclusions we have, and if they have not, they soon will. In truth, if I had things my way, I want to be one of the people out in front and in the command crew, but that's just me."

"Hold it!" Brittney said. "They and we may have reached the same conclusion, but have we…or even each of us reached some kind of agreement on where we stand?"

Herbert opened his mouth to explain his thoughts, but Brittney shushed him good naturedly, and she spoke up instead. "I just can't get over how unfair all of this is…why are we stuck in this deep dark hole with seemingly only one way to climb out of it? It's bullshit. and we all know it."

Jason nodded. "A bullshit burger with crap-fries on the side."

Britney tried to keep her serious demeanor, but broke into genuine laughter at Jason's comment, followed by everyone else.

Corbin spoke back up just as the laughter was fading. "It is bullshit, and until Commander Sorenson and Zero Crew tell us everything we want to know, I don't see any reason to fully trust them. But I think we can trust the intent of their program, and we know that when we take command, we are going to get some friggin' answers," he finished forcefully.

"And if we don't?" asked Laura.

"Then we crash this giant hulk into Gliese 832 and be done with it and any other agenda the people had who put us here." Corbin said it more seriously than he intended.

"Give us a break, Corbin, that'll be decades from now. No one will be even close to the same frame of mind as we are right now." Laura pointed it out impatiently.

Corbin answered, "But that's exactly my point! Exactly! If we do nothing, someone else will, and the people that set all of this up win. If we bust our ass and still don't succeed in making the command team because someone else does, they win. If we succeed and we become the command crew, they win. If all twenty-four hundred of us rebel, do nothing, and see what happens, we all traverse a carefully laid out and rehearsed program to allow for some of our A-population to step up and become the command crew…and they win. If somehow all twenty-four hundred of us ended it, then they will wake up the other crews, and try again, and then…they probably will win."

Corbin stopped, and everyone stared. Herbert just nodded, and Jason rested his chin on his folded hands, elbows on the table. A minute went by, and then another.

Yordanos finally spoke. "I think we are all of a mind, that if there is one way…forward, then I think it has to be us that takes command. Us right here in this room, and anyone else that we pick up along the way.

We will play their game, but if you all agree to play, then we need to agree to each other, that we play to win."

Corbin had been secretly hoping someone would say what she had just said. It would be more powerful coming from someone else as Corbin knew he was always the one taking the verbal initiative. He was a bit surprised that Yordanos was the one to say it."

Jason stood up and helped Yordanos up with an offered hand. He said putting on a gruff voice that wasn't his, "Well, I guess there is only one thing left to do." He paused, everyone's attention rapt on him, and then spoke emphasizing each word. "Win the whole. Fuckin'. Thing."

Herbert shot to his feet and shouted "YES!" followed by Brittney.

"I'm in too," Corbin said with a goofy smile, knowing that everyone had already known that. "Jason, where did you hear that line?" he asked.

Jason said, "I can't remember, but I think they were in a similar situation."

Then they all sat back down to begin their plans, and they all had some calls to make.

Chapter Nine: Prelude to a Test

After a couple of months, everyone in A-Crew had pretty much fallen into their schedule as far as Corbin was concerned. Corbin's small crew of friends had swollen to over thirty people who enjoyed spending time with them, and one another. They often organized socials, sporting events held in special areas, game nights, but most importantly they shared the same plan about traversing the A-Crew training program and becoming fit for command crew, something each of Corbin's close friends was able to confirm in their own way. They all built an infrastructure of rapid communication for written, verbal, and video communication over AIMA, and they stood up a private file share so they could communicate about courses they were taking, or any other experiential notes they thought might help one another.

Corbin still kept his inner circle with Yordanos, Jason, Herbert, Laura, and sometimes Brittney and Sheila, whom he had met at the Briefing. Corbin thought everything sort of felt like they had all gone back to college, or continued college, whichever was the case for the assortment of A-Crew, all in their early twenties.

At the end of a long "week," they still tried to keep to those Monday through Friday grinds with everyone working toward the weekend. Everyone in A-Crew was a bit mystified by a large thirty-six-hour block on everyone's schedule, albeit at different times, that simply said "Challenge." Corbin, as well as his friends, had heard a lot of the rumors that were generated from this mysterious event.

A-Crew members were trying to figure out how many people would be in each thirty-six-hour activity because everyone had one on their schedule, and the events stretched out weeks into the future. This led many to assume that smaller groups of A-Crew members would be participating, and as far as anyone could see, they only had to attend one of these events. The other interesting aspect was the location, as it had everyone reporting to a ring on the *Valor* that none of them had ever been to before as it was restricted. Jason and Corbin had pulled up the ship's diagram in one of the social rooms one night, and a few other crew members gathered around as they discussed it.

"It looks like we'll all be in this outer ring here near the aft of the *Valor*…it extends almost to the boundary of the shielding plate, so it's much bigger than the other rings, almost by half! It also appears to be the last ring before the radiation shielding section, aft material slug, and engines," Jason pointed out excitedly.

Corbin asked around the room, "When are you all scheduled to report? Mine says tomorrow at 0700." Most of the people in the room had a different response. Jason's report time was the closest to Corbin's but not for another three days. Herbert, who Corbin almost missed as being part of the conversation for his quiet presence, stepped forward and said he had a different time the following week.

"Looks like I get to go first." Corbin paused before going on. "I think this is a good thing. It tells us that they are actually getting started with assessing us as crew members. I just wish some of us got to do this together," he said, looking over his friends.

"Whatever this is, I wish you all the best of luck," Jason said.

"Thanks man," Corbin responded, and they shared their commonly executed fist bump.

Jason went on, "We knew there were going to be tests. Keep your wits about you, don't panic, and remember, we have a bigger mission here. Whatever you get into, remember it's just a test."

Corbin nodded first, followed by everyone else in the social room, albeit a little nervously. Picking up on their apprehension, Corbin suddenly felt as if he should probably leave and get some rest. He bid Jason and everyone else farewell, and headed back to his quarters to prepare mentally, and for some sleep. Something in the back of his mind told him that this would be physical, so he added a good regimen of water and asked for some electrolytes before he went to sleep.

Chapter Ten: Challenge

When Corbin woke that next morning at 0600, he saw that his AI, Tina, had interestingly provided some items for him, brought by HDs and laid out in the foyer of his quarters. Corbin thought it must have happened while he was sleeping. He saw sturdy short hiking boots that were light as a feather. There were synthetic wool socks, wicking pants with multiple pockets, including some lower on the legs. He had a long sleeve wicking shirt, with another short sleeve shirt over the top of it, a baseball cap—cue memory explosions—and over in the corner of the room was a plain backpack. Upon closer inspection, it was not a backpack, it was a black ruck, which appeared simple, yet immensely durable. He unzipped the main pocket to find a three-liter water bladder that had been filled. There was also a small medical kit with different tapes, a muscle wrap, a small knife, and some thick oily substance that reminded him of Vaseline…memories exploded and faded as he examined it.

The memory pops happened so often it almost felt normal to Corbin by now. Yet nothing seemed to stick to his consciousness. It was like a dream he promised himself he would remember, but by the time he finished brushing his teeth, it wasn't even a construct worth trying to write down. The thought reminded Corbin to check his dream notes, which he had been using his AIMA to quickly record after waking, using the inside of his palms as a keyboard.

As he read the words, they didn't resurface anything that clung to a memory. They were like reading a book or a note that someone else had written, and he was frustrated again to not learn anything more about who he was before waking on the *Valor*. He stuffed his virtual notes away in a huff and returned to examine the gear.

He went to lift the ruck with the top handle and found it had a considerable weight. He pushed the bladder aside to find a metal plate but couldn't tell how much it weighed. He mused it must be nearly thirty pounds by the feel of it.

"Leave that in there, Corbin," Tina chided. "It's a requirement of the challenge." Corbin frowned at the console where Tina's avatar was standing patiently. Tina answered, "I'm not supposed to tell you anything about it, but I can tell you to make sure you are comfortable with the gear I put together for you. If anything is ill fitting, I may be able to get a quick swap, so just let me know."

Corbin tried on the ruck, and found the shoulder straps a bit tight, but after some loosening and adjusting, he got the ruck on and was a bit surprised at how high the weight rode, just above the small of his back. Looking in the mirror, he could see that the ruck lay nearly flat against his back. It almost felt natural there near the center of his mass, but he did feel its considerable weight.

After a few minutes, Corbin had put on all of the gear, and to his surprise, not only did it all feel good, he thought he looked cool too. But after a few steps and a little jog around his quarters some sweat had already broken out on his brow from the exertion under the extra weight. Tina shifted between the wall screen and into his AIMA. "I'll guide you to the Challenge ring. You haven't been there before, but if you leave within the next thirty seconds, you should be able to be there on time."

Corbin felt alarm; he thought that the trip to the Challenge ring wouldn't take that long. The scale of the map must not have been correct. "Do I need anything else?" Corbin asked the air.

Tina replied, "Just your sense of adventure and your good attitude. Now, hurry."

Corbin didn't quite dash out of the room following Tina's instructions, but he moved quite quickly to where he felt a light sweat start to re-form at his brow and the small of his back. To save time, he went straight to the single person lifts that went straight to the Spine, which he hadn't used before. He entered the first lift he saw, and took hold of the hand and footholds. The mechanism moved him toward the Spine of the ship, and he could feel the weight from his ruck and himself start to lessen until he arrived at the near weightless transport station for the ring. At first the lift had felt as if he was moving "up," but without as much gravity he felt disoriented, as nothing that he could see with his eyes clashed with how his body felt. A quick glance at his AIMA's gravity indicator showed it at 8%.

He arrived at the "top" of D-Ring, where the intra-floor corridors, like curved spokes of a bicycle, ended at the non-rotating Spine of the *Valor*. He stepped off the lift shakily, and he tried to get his feet to stay stuck to the "floor" of the corridor, despite the low gravity. From there, an HD collected him as per the usual procedure, and transitioned him through the slipring and into the Spine via the transfer compartment.

A Spine HD guided him in what his mind assigned as a downward direction within the Spine, until he looked over at several people sitting in a small transport car. As Corbin got closer, he could see two people facing two other people inside the cars, which were on a single track against the wall of the Spine. An HD helped him over to one of the partially occupied four-person transport cars, and unceremoniously plunked him down in his seat, while advising him to buckle up. Since Corbin was the last one, the car wasted almost no time getting moving and Corbin had to scramble to buckle in. As the car pulled away down…or up…the Spine of the ship, he saw three others dressed similarly to himself. The car disappeared into a pleasantly lit tunnel and headed to the Challenge ring at a good speed, and Corbin saw a blur of lights fly by, but could also see other tracks around the Spine of the ship where other transports moved back and forth. The bustling transit view set off yet more memory explosions of traveling in his past life, but he pushed them aside in slight annoyance and looked over to his fellow transport car occupants. Corbin didn't know these crew members, and by the looks of it, they didn't know each other either, so they all stayed silent, yet all were obviously nervous.

Corbin could feel familiarity with the scenario he now found himself in, and per his expectation, he saw that all of the occupants did a poor job of trying to inconspicuously size one another up. Now that he had had a little more time to look, Corbin saw that they weren't similarly dressed at all. The young man next to him only had one layer on top, which appeared to be cotton, and had cotton shorts. Instead of hiking boots, he had what appeared to be running shoes, and low ankle socks.

His ruck actually looked like a backpack that someone would wear to school, but Corbin could see the outline of the water bladder and the weight inside. By the look on the young man's face, he didn't appear happy that his gear was subpar to Corbin's...or everyone else's in the car.

Shifting his gaze across the transport to the other two A-Crew members facing him, he saw that one wasn't even wearing shoes, but had sock like apparatuses with a rubber sole. He too wore mesh shorts, had a ruck that was similar to Corbin's, but a light mesh shirt with no sleeves. On top of his head he had a bandana instead of a baseball cap.

Next to him, the young lady looked like she was some sort of super soldier. She had lightweight yet durable boots, tactical pants, and a top that seemed padded in all of the right areas, which fit her perfectly, looked light but also breathable. Her ruck was thin, tight to her body, and higher quality than Corbin and the other two on the transport. On her ballcap, she had a built-in headlamp and wore tactical gloves on her hands with padding on the inside and hard polymer across the knuckles. She quickly noticed that the other three had shifted their attention to her, and she glared at them saying, "What?" impatiently.

Corbin had seen that glare before, recalling how she had locked eyes with him during the first Briefing. "I'm Corbin," he said, reaching out a hand to shake.

She eyed his hand suspiciously before looking away, but responded, "Jessica."

The fellow to Corbin's side, tried a flirtatious and jovial approach. "Well whatever we are heading into, I'm pretty sure you are going to be the readiest for it." He finished with a smile.

Jessica responded, "Is that because you think I'm smart and tough, or because you think I have superior gear?" and finished her words with that same scowl Corbin was accustomed to. The young man visibly withered.

Corbin found himself annoyed at Jessica's candor, but he tried to lighten the mood. "I wish everyone the best in this next exercise. If it turns out we get to work together, I look forward to it. As I said, I'm Corbin." He turned, meeting the fellow to his side who turned out to be Jeremy, and across from him, Alex. "What do you say Jessica? Shall we team up?" Corbin asked.

Impatiently, she exhaled. "Look, this isn't some kind of kumbaya.

This is an assessment that is going to count toward the command crew rating, and I intend to make top marks, so just stay the hell out of my way, okay?" Corbin sat back and nodded his head in retreat. Jeremy had had a good idea in trying to break the ice. There was also the fact that Jessica was intensely attractive, but something inside of him, more than her words, demeanor, and common respect, warned Corbin to keep his mouth shut. And so he did, not entirely realizing why.

Soon their transport arrived at the Challenge ring where more HDs helped them off of the transport pods and moved them toward the inner Spine hull. Corbin saw more A-Crew members being lined up by the HDs and again peeking over the shoulder of the crew member in front of him, he could see the HDs handling each A-Crew member into capsules and then through the temporarily open slipring portals. Corbin's gaze went up and around as his eyes tracked to the ring of portals opening and closing with each interval, and his jaw dropped in comprehension. There were no transfer pods on the Challenge ring—the HDs had to do their job right or one would be sheared in half.

Corbin perceived the entire mass of the Challenge ring rotating around the Spine via a slipring, which meant that there would be no constant contact between the ring and the Spine of the ship, it would always be rotating. His mind went to wondering how electricity, communications, and large equipment could be moved ring to ring, but his focus snapped back when he saw he was almost next to go through a portal. The HD grabbed him firmly but gently and unceremoniously shoved his weightless mass through the portal only to be caught by an HD on the other side. Corbin noted that both HDs had attached themselves to their respective hulls of the ship, enabling them to shove each of the crew members around without flying off into the weightlessness of the *Valor*'s Spine. Instead of taking individual elevators that he and Herbert had seen on A, B, C, and D-Ring, the HDs herded the group of confounded A-Crew members through a large corridor that was smooth, but looked like it was sloping downhill, almost like a slide. His memory flashed to some sort of play structure from when he was a child, and then it was gone.

After about two minutes, Corbin noted his feet starting to skitter across the floor, and in the next moment, they touched down. Even though they had been awake on the *Valor* for weeks, not everyone had had much experience with the low gravity transition zones, as these were restricted areas, unless one had authorization to transfer between rings due to a schedule requirement. As a result, everyone was laughing at how they were able to jump and bop around, but the HDs quickly grabbed anyone before they smashed into the ceiling or into one another. They all noted that now the HDs maneuvered on puffs, or sometimes blasts of air depending on how fast they needed to stop or change directions. Corbin took note that these HDs started to fall back just as he and those surrounding him could do a better job of bounce-walking. He looked up and saw the red line from the floor to the walls to the ceiling of the corridor and when he crossed, he found that he could walk fairly normally.

He smiled knowing they had crossed a gravity transition zone, and in his mind's eye he could see how it all applied to the 3D holographic map of the *Valor* he had seen in his quarters on day one.

Everyone's AIMA's seemed to wake up and direct them through several more turns of the corridor until they reached a large staging area. To Corbin it looked like a large gymnasium sized room that was overly large for the one hundred other members of A-Crew that were with him. The walls went up at least three stories, and the equally spaced and bright LED lights seemed to illuminate every corner with harsh and unforgiving light.

There were also three members of Zero Crew dressed similarly to Jessica, and Corbin looked around to see the other A-Crew members having gear ranging from Jeremey's poor gear to Jessica's high-quality gear. Mostly, the gear he saw was closer to what he himself was wearing.

No sooner had Corbin got his bearings, than one of the Zero Crew members called out. "I'm Cadre Paul, so that's what you call me from now on. You do not want to find out what happens if you call me 'sir.'" Corbin made a mental note of that.

Paul continued after a heavy sweep of his gaze across the crew members. "As you can see, there is a long table against the wall. Take off your AIMAs and set them on the table. Not to worry, it will show your name on the side, so you can collect it later. Just set them down neatly, please," he said in a firm but polite tone.

The A-Crew members shuffled over and slipped their AIMAs off and set them on the table haphazard, some slightly stacked against one another, and all of them lying in whatever direction or orientation possible. Everyone then shuffled back toward Paul and formed a semicircle around him awaiting new instructions. Corbin sensed a storm coming a half second before it arrived.

"I ASKED YOU TO SET THEM NEATLY ON THE TABLE!!! NOT ANY WHICH WAY YOU WANT!!! I EVEN SAID PLEASE. GET YOUR ASSES OVER THERE AND FIX IT!.......NOW!" Paul roared.

The shuffle became jerky and desperate, as the sense of the test, and the newness of this harsh tone sent everyone almost into a mad scramble back toward the table. People tried to account for their own AIMAs, which quickly devolved into everyone pawing at the table to try to organize the devices, which just made it worse. Paul continued to holler and berate when Corbin noticed that finally some A-Crew members started to get it. Corbin fumbled for his AIMA at first, and then any AIMA while hearing shouts of "Back up!" "Wait," "Let's work together!" or "Don't Touch!" and finally a voice whose owner he could not see rang out above the rest, "Look let's make columns of three and three rows." He and the others responded to the shouted command and started to populate the pattern. After several minutes, three neat-ish rows of thirty-three AIMAs were on the table and the semicircle quickly re-formed around Paul, albeit at nearly twice the distance from him as the original semicircle had been. Corbin wasn't sure when Paul had stopped screaming, or how Paul possessed the vocal fortitude to do so for that amount of time and at that volume.

Paul adopted an eerily jolly tone. "Thank you for that. Now if you will, please line up in the same configuration you lined up the AIMA devices and face me."

Corbin, along with his fellow crew members, did not dally, and one A-Crew member ran to the far left of Paul and put up her hand. Corbin ran behind her and put up his hand as well, and the rest quickly filled out the one spot behind him, and the rows off to their side, so that there were three rows of thirty-three rookies from A-Crew all facing Paul.

"Now that's much better!" he exclaimed, continuing with the jolly tone. "Much better than expected! You have earned some special treats!"

Corbin snuck a glance around to see abject horror on the faces of some of the A-Crew members. Although Corbin was feeling like he would rather be anywhere else, he was also overcome by curiosity, as well as determination.

Chapter Eleven: I Can't Move:

The "treats" started straightforward enough for Corbin, and some of it felt familiar to his mind and his body. At first there were some push-ups. The ruck made it much harder, but Corbin could tell he must have liked push-ups in his prior life and it didn't seem to bother him much…yet. Then they were holding the rucks over their heads, and then squats were added. The reps seemed endless. Corbin found himself hoping for other painful plyometrics just so he could stop the ones he was currently doing. Each of the ranks of thirty-three and one of thirty-four went into planks, each member having to crawl underneath the rest of them, only to set up on a plank at the end so every person had to crawl under the full amount of people. Corbin got too close to the person in the "tunnel" in front of him, and got kicked squarely in the face, drawing a little blood from his jaw, and felt a ringing in his ears. He quickly pressed on as the "roof" built from planking crew members was yelling for him to move his ass and not in a positively motivational way. He also noticed that even though it could only have been half an hour, much of A-Crew was already starting to smell quite ripe from the exertion, himself included.

In between the different exercises, Corbin was mercifully grateful that he could sneak sips from his water bladder, but in looking around, he could tell that not everyone had the full amount of water, and some had seemed to have run out already. The physical training sets continued, and Corbin noticed that some of the A-Crew members were slowing, and not completing the reps. He figured their water had run dry, and yet Paul mercilessly pushed them on. It felt like hours had gone by, but Corbin sensed that not much time had elapsed at all, and their discomfort was playing a mental trick on them. At any rate, it looked like some of his fellow crew members were going to be in serious dehydration soon, as many of them weren't opening their eyes anymore, and barely could complete the tasks. Paul went along with his cheery orders as if nothing was wrong. He would stroll up and down the rows, almost skipping at times, barking out the next calisthenic, not indicating any sense of where he was in the workout, which might as well last until they reached Gliese 832 as far as Corbin could tell.

"Cadre Paul?" Corbin found himself raising his hand and calling out as the rest of A-Crew struggled with abdominal flutter kicks from their backs.

"Yes, Corbin!" Paul said without missing a beat, and jogging toward him as if they were old friends. When he got within several paces he stopped. "What can I do for you Corbin?" Paul asked.

Corbin's gut told him to stay away from formality. "Cadre Paul, can we have some more water please?" Paul's smile disappeared, and the flutter kicks abruptly stopped, as everyone went silent to see what would happen. Paul just stared at him with eyes that seemed to nearly bug out of his head.

"Does anyone else want some water?" Cadre Paul whispered fiercely. No one said anything, and Corbin said nothing and held still. "Everyone," Paul said almost to quietly to be heard by all, "Please share your water with those that have run out." He returned to a near roar. "CORBIN COME WITH ME!"

The color drained from Corbin's face as he nearly stumbled to the front and middle of the assembly where Paul abruptly rounded on him but stayed about ten paces away. "Can you fight? I want to see if you can fight Corbin…drop that ruck." Corbin couldn't believe this, but he did as he was told, and without preamble, Paul came at Corbin low and fast, his arms at the ready and fists out to deal damage. Corbin dropped into what he felt was a defensive fighting stance, but he had no idea what he was doing. His instincts took over and as Paul swung at him, Corbin ducked and heard Paul's fist nearly whistle by his head, grazing some of his hairs. *Holy shit this is real.*

Paul darted around Corbin, who didn't quite see how to land any kind of offense. Corbin dodged two more blows but took a glancing blow to his right deltoid—his arm went numb. This shifted his balance, and Paul's next blow came low and landed right into Corbin's gut. Corbin tensed at the last moment, which probably kept his intestines from blowing out his ass, but all the breath was knocked from him as he doubled over, and his vision went blurry. He didn't see the uppercut coming. It lifted Corbin up and as he flew back, his vision darkened to black as he was knocked out cold onto his back, blood streaming from his nose and upper lip. No one in A-Crew had made a sound or moved, but they looked horrified and utterly beyond belief at what they had seen.

After a moment, Corbin stirred slightly, and he heard the voice of one of his fellow A-Crew members kneel down and put a gentle hand on his shoulder to ease Corbin into a sitting position, "Hey man, are you okay?" Corbin's eyes became slits, and his vision was a little blurry, but it started to come back more rapidly than he would have expected. Unfortunately, the pain to his face, abdomen, and back of his head where he had hit the deck going down also sharpened. "Ugh, yeah I'm alright…can you help me up, please? Uh, what's your name?"

"Jeremy," he said, and lifted Corbin with both arms, making the ascent easier for Corbin until they both stood. The rest of the A-Crew members had started back on their flutter kicks and could be heard groaning softly, Paul hadn't even said anything to them, but stood back calmly observing Jeremy help Corbin.

"Jeremy, please come here," Paul said with menacing pleasantness, "Corbin, return to your rank and join the others with flutter kicks if you please."

Corbin did as he was told, noticing Paul's insane glare and grin from his periphery. Corbin reached up and felt his mouth which had clearly been hit. His hand came away bloody, but with a lot less than he expected.

Corbin looked over at Jeremy, who had stopped in a stance a pace or so away from Paul, Corbin spared a glance to see that everyone was looking to see what would happen, while still pushing through what must have been several hundred counts of abdominal flutter kicks by now.

Paul exploded into motion, and before Jeremy could even wince, had spun him around by the shoulders so that his back was facing

Paul. Paul unzipped Jeremy's ruck, and then knelt to pick up two additional small metal plates that looked to be between five and seven pounds each. He tucked them into Jeremy's ruck, zipped it back up, gave him a slap on the back of the ruck and said cheerily, "There you go! Now back to your spot in the rank Jeremy."

Again, Jeremy did as he was told, and as soon as Jeremy got through one single count of flutter kicks, Paul raised his voice. "Stop!" This was followed by the sound of everyone collapsing flat to their backs and heaving from exertion.

"Everybody up!" Paul hollered, and the one hundred members of A-Crew started to slowly get to their feet. "Get back down!" Paul's call interrupted them.

"When I tell you to do something with urgency, then your actions need to mimic that urgency. In fact, you should move as quickly as you are able, is that understood!?" A few muttered in affirmation, and Paul's face turned to the red hue Corbin had noticed earlier just before the previous storm. Before Paul could explode, he called out, "Yes, Cadre Paul!" in a loud voice.

He exploded anyway. "Nice try, Corbin, but the rest of your friends didn't get it! Get back on your faces! All of you!" They all did with more urgency this time. "To the plank position, and don't move until I say!" Paul instructed at his newly adopted volume, which felt like a blast of sound with each word.

"Down.........Up.........Down...Up...Down................Up............ ...Down-Up-Down-Up-Down..........DID I SAY TO GO UP!?!?!?!" He screamed at hurricane strength. The few who had gone to the up position of the push-up quickly returned down, and everyone held there.

Paul brought it down slightly. "You people aren't getting it. I am giving clear and concise instructions with clear expectations, and every time, you continue to screw it up! You are not meeting the expectation!" He finished with greater emphasis. "These instructions are simple. The mission we are all on is extremely complex. If you cannot work together and have an understanding together, then there is no chance...I repeat, NO CHANCE you will ever get this ship to its destination." Paul paused and looked around thoughtfully, taking back up a regular conversational tone, but with volume that all could hear. "Does anyone here know why after two hours of our little exercise here, I have zero-point zero confidence in you being successful?"

After a long pause, a tall and skinny young woman with dark brown hair raised her hand from her facedown push-up position. "Yes, Tabitha, what do you have to say?" Paul asked politely.

"Because we haven't been communicating with each other or helping one another as a team," she said meekly.

"Louder please, Tabitha, say that again for all to hear," Paul said.

Tabitha did so with a more confident voice, and before she could finish the last word, Paul erupted into an enthusiastic outburst, "Abso-fucking-lutely! You all basically sit there, letting me tell you what to do without any communication, you don't help each other, you haven't done a single damn thing as a team since you all got in here. All you think about is yourselves!" Corbin thought that he and Jeremy had been examples of people that were trying to help but didn't really feel interested in pointing that out to Cadre Paul at this moment.

There was a long pause, where Paul let that sink in, and without any more discussion he went right back to it. "Back to the plank!....Up.......Down.........Up......Down....." It went on. And the exercises changed, and then they went on. This time however, whispers of encouragement between the crew members could be heard if they were struggling. People called out for water, and whoever was closest with some left would run over and give them a sip from their water bladder. Burpees gave way to more squats with upright ruck rows, which transitioned into jump squats, which turned into inch-worms, which melded into Russian twists and full sit-ups with ruck held high in outstretched arms. There were no whispers anymore. People were hollering out in encouragement, and just as loudly with exertion. The form of these exercises must have looked terrible, but apart from Cadre Paul pointing out obvious cheats to each exercise, he didn't call them out on it, as long as they were straining with all of their will to complete each exercise.

Corbin's water had long run out, and his mouth was starting to feel like sandpaper while his rep quality started to sink drastically. He called out for water, but all he heard from everyone around him was that they were out. The exercises continued, and the call for water could be heard all over the formation. Corbin could see two people running from person to person with water, then one, and then the last person was out.

The exercises continued, and the groaning increased. Corbin could feel a deep sense of hopelessness start to grip him from deep within his soul. He tried to fight it down, but it seemed to whisper louder and louder in his ears. It was telling him to quit, it was telling him to let this all go. Corbin could barely see or even think about the crew members next to him, but he felt as if the same hopelessness must be ravaging everyone. People weren't just groaning, they were crying. Corbin opened his eyes to see that some people had curled into little balls, instead of performing the sit-ups. A glance at Paul showed his face a cheery grin as he looked on.

"STOP!" Cadre Paul called out. And everyone collapsed limp from the most recent sit-up exercise, some not even softening the drop of their rucks as they hit the ground on either side of each person. In some cases, people just dropped them on their own bodies resulting in further grunts of pain. A few vomited, and didn't even try to hide it. They didn't care.

Paul's voice was low and quiet and calm as he spoke. "You have ten minutes." He pointed over his shoulder at a clock with a red digital read-out. "Get yourselves together, get water, and make sure to top off all of your water bladders." He pointed to the far wall where there were two water spigots sticking out from the wall. "If you need to use the facilities, please do so as well. However, you had better be back in this exact position, and on your feet facing me the very moment this clock strikes zero." He paused. Looking out over the ranks, he called out, "Darren, Zedd, Angela, Eric C., Eric G., Farik, Andrew K., Paul R., Veronica, and Hassan, please see me up front before doing anything else. Everyone else…go!" The digital clock began to count down.

There was a mad dash toward the water, and people were collapsing in piles in front of each spigot half wrestling one another for a drop. Corbin turned to Jeremy, and sharing glances, they both walked toward the men's restroom and walked in. The sinks seemed to work fine, and they both cupped their hands and took long swigs of water for about two minutes, barely pausing for a breath. It was the crispest, most deliciously sweet water that Corbin had ever tasted.

Finally, both panting, they took their bladders out of their rucks and started to fill those as well. Some shuffling sounds from the entryway alerted them that three more young men were entering, which worked well as there were five sinks total.

While the newcomers repeated what Corbin and Jeremy had done, Corbin spoke to Jeremy, but everyone could hear. "Thanks for helping me, I really appreciate it man. I'm not sure if I would have gotten up."

"Dude, that guy whipped your ass!" one of the newcomers said, between gulps of water from cupped hands.

"He did," Corbin admitted. "I don't know how to fight at all, I'm just glad he didn't kill me…but there is something else. Did you all notice that when I stood up to unilaterally take action, I got my ass kicked for it, but when Jeremy took action to help just me, he only got a bit more weight?" The water gulpers, not being able to really think yet, didn't respond, the one who had pointed out Corbin's ass whipping just shrugged and went back to slurping handfuls of icy cold water.

Jeremy's eyes widened a little. "It's got to be part of the conditions of the test…but how does that work?"

"Maybe the more you stick out, the more you get punished," offered the tallest and bulkiest of the newcomers. "I'm Frank by the way" he said.

Jeremy responded, "Yeah, Frank, but it's got to be something more than that. Paul was hitting all of us for not working together."

The smart aleck who had pointed out Corbin's beat down piped in, "I'm Justin, and I say we just keep our heads down and try to get through this in one piece." Corbin tried to chime back in, but they all continued arguing, a mishmash of conversations reverberating off the dull tile in the men's room, while they hydrated and filled their water bladders.

Soon, all five of them had satiated their thirst and had refilled their bladders to the top, and with the sense of time burning in their minds, they began to exit the restroom.

"WAIT!" Corbin exclaimed, looking off of the others. "It's a metaphor, it has to be!"

"What—" Jeremy began and was cut off by Corbin.

"Just listen. I asked for water for everyone, and got my ass handed to me. Jeremy helped me up and got extra weight, but no one else was doing anything other than what they were told, and nothing happened to them," Corbin finished.

"So? What's your point?" the other unnamed young man asked

Corbin.

"Cadre Paul just berated us for not acting like a team, and he's right. We are all thinking for ourselves, how hard it is for each of us and whether we can outlast each other. We were just starting to think outside ourselves when we shared water back there. So when one of us calls on Cadre Paul the next time, we display some consensus and see what kind of punishment, if any, follows. I feel like if someone else had answered that they wanted water, I could have avoided the beat down."

They all started for a moment and thought about it. "So, they just kick the shit out of anyone who stands up and tries to do the right thing? Is that it?" asked Justin.

Corbin knew he was out on a limb, but he went on anyway. "Not necessarily, like I said it seems like a metaphor, maybe for leadership. I said something, and while I paid a price for it, everyone was allowed to share their water. Why didn't we come up with that ourselves? You heard Cadre Paul. He said he had no confidence in us whatsoever to complete this one hundred plus year mission. I don't think he said that just to say it. We need to start acting like we are on this mission together, here, right now. If we see a way to work better together, then we need to work together to make it happen. He's trying to wipe out unilateral 'follow the leader' from the beginning." The other four looked at him, contemplating his flurry of words.

"I dunno, Corbin," said Frank, "it doesn't seem like we know enough yet, but what the hell. I say we give it a shot." Frank continued without waiting. "I bet when we get out there, everyone will still be clamoring over the water spigots. How about the five us do our best to gently seize one of them and help organize the thirsty people into a line for that one, then we'll grab the next one and try to line people up for water bladder refills?"

Corbin liked Frank's idea. "I'm in, let's grab the one to the right. Also, if people got their water topped off and are standing around, let's see if we can get them to help us so we spread out the effort and get everyone water as fast as possible." Everyone nodded, and they all exited the men's restroom facility and made a beeline straight to the right-most water spigot, but when they were halfway to it, Jeremy pointed to the left-most spigot and shouted for them to look.

Corbin spotted Jessica, his fellow passenger from the weightless transport pod. She and a few others were organizing people around the water spigot to the left, just like Frank had suggested. "Keep on with the plan. It looks like they've only just started to get it figured out," said Corbin, and they rushed to carry it out.

It worked. The clock hit zero, but everyone had already been lined back up for over sixty seconds. No one was taking any chances about irking Paul by being late, but collectively everyone was wondering *who knows what else might irk him*?

"Welcome back!" Paul boomed. "Now that everyone that wants to be here is here, you may notice that you are down a nice and even ten people. Who have gone back to their habitat rings to be...more comfortable," he finished with a grin.

Everyone looked around noticing the spaces in their ranks, some of which had closed naturally. "This brings me to my next point. This overall exercise isn't for the faint at heart, as you can see. Not all of you are in the physical shape or right state of mind and attitude to make it, to say nothing about your yet-to-be-observed ability to work together. You! All of you must be up to the standard!" He paused looking at them energetically before continuing. "If you aren't pushing yourself, if you aren't contributing, if you aren't bought into what we are trying to do here, I will know and call you over for a little discussion. If you and I cannot come to an understanding about your effort, you will be released from the exercise." On these words, a solemn feeling spread across the remining crew members.

"Hey, that's okay, you'll have the ability to retry this course every three months until you get through it, but why not just get your act at together, work through the pain, discomfort, and mental anguish, work as a team, and complete the exercise? I'm just saying." Corbin, Jeremy, and Frank shot knowing glances at one another. Corbin noticed that Justin had ended up near Jessica and some of the others that had gravitated toward her. Neither his group, nor Jessica's group had been called out in any way, nor had anyone else been punished for working to organize water for everyone. *Maybe the formula is working*, Corbin thought to himself.

Corbin raised his hand. "Yes, Corbin, what else can I do for you today?" Corbin's gut wrenched, but the pain in his head was gone, and the strange haze he had felt in his head had cleared. "Cadre Paul, some of the others and I were having a conversation during the break, and we are interested to know the details of the exercise." Paul's demeanor switched like lightning striking, and he called out abruptly and loudly, "Who else had this little conversation with Corbin?"

At first, no one else stood, but when Corbin locked eyes with Jeremy, he and Frank stood up, quickly followed by Justin and the other young man who had not identified himself. Slowly, the rest of the group stood as well, even though this idea had not been discussed with them. It was the first unified thing they had gotten right so far. Paul's demeanor calmed. "Very well, I am glad that you all agree, I had a whole amusement park of additional fun ready for you, but since you are all together on this, please have a seat, and I'll show you." He called out in a loud voice, "OPEN IT UP!"

Three of the walls of the massive gymnasium began to slide down. No one made a single sound as the sheer awe of what they were seeing came into full view. The walls of the gymnasium disappeared, revealing a stunning landscape of rocks, hills, trees that made up thin woods in some areas and thick forests in others. There were bodies of water and waterfalls, which went on and on as far as Corbin and the others could see. Corbin thought that this landscape must traverse the entire outer circumference of the Challenge ring, as the "ground" disappeared "uphill" far into the distance and around the massive ring in both directions. He still couldn't get used to thinking of their feet sticking to the inside surface of a massive rotating wheel, but it made sense looking at this expanse. In looking up, Corbin could see that the space was so large, there was a slight atmosphere that clung to the ceiling, which was outfitted with a gargantuan array of lights, which no doubt was to simulate the sun. Corbin also thought he could smell the faint hint of rain, which puzzled him and…a breeze washed across his sweat- and grime-encrusted face like a kiss from an angel.

He was hit with a set of memory reverberations so strong he had to close his eyes. When he opened them again, he saw what his nose continued to tell him to be true, this was real. Some insane group of…people built an entire ecosystem in space…on a ring. The gymnasium room had been massive, more than a quarter of a mile across, but it was completely dwarfed by the diameter of the Challenge ring.

"Take notice A-Crew" Paul's voice cut into their awed thoughts snapping everyone out of their gape. "It is beautiful, but it provides a unique challenge. For the next thirty plus hours, you will all be performing a set of missions. Some of them will be in groups, some will be alone, and all will have a specific goal. As I said before, you will be watched and assessed to see where you stack up as a member of A-Crew. Ladies and Gentlemen, welcome to the Challenge ring." He finished with a grand sweep of his arm.

"Now, let us begin."

Chapter Twelve: In the Challenge

Jessica scrambled over two larger boulders, reached out for a root hanging out from the edge of a short drop off, and pulled herself up as a small spray of dirt hit her in the face. "Hurry up! We have six minutes to reach the objective!" she hollered over the side of the small cliff. Lagging behind were six members of her team.

"Let's get moving!" she shouted. "What is wrong with you people!?!" She turned in a huff and proceeded to sprint toward the objective, an orange flag at the top of a rise that went nearly halfway to the "ceiling" of the Challenge ring.

She saw that she herself was about ninety seconds or so away from the mission objective and looked down at her watch to see that the five-minute warning had just passed. She looked back angrily at her struggling teammates, did some quick mental math, and started sprinting toward the last member in the party, who at her current pace was not going to make it in time.

Jessica reached the last person on her team, another young woman, who was struggling up the same small rise Jessica had traversed a few minutes earlier. However, the young woman had chosen an area a few yards away from Jessica's path, and it didn't have as good handholds. "You picked a nice spot to try and scramble your ass up," she barked. "Let's get moving!" She grabbed the sleeve of the redheaded and panting young lady who just wasn't in as good a shape as Jessica and yanked her over and then up the rise and re-grabbed the root she had used a few minutes earlier. Sensing the will of the slower girl wilting, Jessica roared, "Let's GO!" She heaved the young woman over the top, up to her feet, and started trotting her onward toward the orange flag.

One of the other team members came back to help, and all three of them moved with purpose toward the objective. Over one boulder, then the next, crashing through a thicket of bushes, branches scraping their faces, the three pushed through. One team member slipped in a muddy puddle, and her knee smacked on the hard ground just outside the mud, as she let out a painful yelp. There was no time for pain: all three grabbed hands as they dashed forward where it looked as if the other team members had just arrived at the flag. They turned back to the three struggling and started yelling encouragement as they traversed the last few large rocks and loose scree and then stumbled into a slump around the orange flag, chests heaving.

Jessica was horrified as she looked down at her watch to see that the time hack alarm had already sounded about fifteen seconds before the last three had reached the objective. She recovered her breath quickly, turned to the slowest girls, and began berating them immediately. "How the hell can you be so slow! Now we've all missed the time hack, DAMN!" she finished still shouting.

"Hey, take it easy Jessica," said an olive skinned and good-natured young man, who had been positive and jovial during the forty-five-minute mission.

"Eat it, Dino, I didn't see you turning around to help as we started to lag behind. We were supposed to finish as a team," Jessica said, practically bursting with anger.

"Oh yes you were. That, you were indeed," said Rob jovially as he stepped out from behind a nearby tree with his maniacal grin. "And now you will pay for your failure."

And pay they all did, especially Jessica. After a mini-version, twenty-five minutes or so, of the opening PT session. Rob invited Jessica up to the front of the group, and he asked her a series of questions about why they had not succeeded. Every time she blamed a team member, or an aspect of the challenge, Rob politely corrected her in terms of a leader's responsibility, told her to defend herself, and then attacked her until he landed one blow. He never struck the same place twice, but managed even body blows across the abdomen and lower back, and one to her face just below her left eye.

The other team members, including the girls who had slowed the team down, watched agape, but did not interfere either.

"Now, Jessica," Rob said, turning his back on her to address the others. "What do you think your teammates have to say about your leadership on this particular mission?" She didn't answer. Instead, she attacked Rob, who seemingly had let his guard down, and she just barely landed a glancing blow with an arcing kick to the side of his head. The terrain had helped her reach the height of his head; however, he quickly recovered. He snared her foot before she could retract it for another kick and drew her toward him and across his body, gaining momentum. Her eyes went wide, and he threw her over the side of the nearest boulder which crested the rise they had all just climbed. She landed hard and rolled down part of the hill before coming to rest against some gravel. An ear-piercing shriek of pain and rage flew up and out of the ravine. Her former team members ran over and looked down to see her right leg was bent at an unnatural angle.

Rob called out to the rest of the people. "Next exercise, make it to the next peak in forty-five minutes." He pointed farther down the challenge ring to a spot to where another bluff sprouted an orange flag that was just in sight before the ring disappeared upward. "This will be an individual effort, so there is no need for a team leader at this point. Three. Two. One. Go!"

The group set off quickly at Rob's instruction, but the girl who had been lambasted by her former team leader a few minutes earlier lingered to look down at Jessica's writhing form. Rob silently approached her, grabbed her by the collar, and directed her firmly toward the next objective. "I said 'go' if you please" he said in a fierce whisper. She went.

Chapter Thirteen: Insult to Injury

Also working through an individual challenge, Corbin scampered across an open plain of leafy plants that came up to his waist. They tore easily enough as he ran through and did not slow him much. A part of him worried about damaging so many lovely plants; it seemed a waste. However, he figured there must be a process and procedure to repairing this landscape with so many challenges scheduled. Looming in the distance and partially concealed by the haze of the atmosphere in the Challenge ring, was the goal of this individual exercise. It was another peak, this one craggier and rockier than many of the others before.

Corbin could not tell how long it had been since they all left the "Welcome Party" as he and the other members of A-Crew came to call it. He knew it was hours, but twenty-four or twenty-eight, he could not tell. He had already lost count of how many individual and group missions there had been.

His idea about taking ownership and building some consensus with his fellow team members, even if it was just to appoint a team-lead, proved to be true. Corbin spread the word to others so that they would get buy-in from fellow team members. He had witnessed a couple other fellow A-Crew members receive punishing blows like he had, and one person loaded down with so many awkwardly shaped rocks, that they called for Cadre Paul so they could quit the challenge right there on the spot.

There were some maneuvers where teams of people had to work together to carry misshapen and unevenly weighted logs, resulting in much shouting and disagreement on how they should be carried. Corbin recalled the rough remnants of branches digging into his neck and shoulders, his hands trying to push a small percentage of the weight up for a small relief. He had tried to communicate that people could work in quick shifts, so that everyone would be fresh and be able to keep pace. When that failed, he tried to suggest that everyone walk in step so that the log would move more smoothly and cause less pain, but he could not get consensus. Everyone wanted to make it to the goal with the log under the time limit, so they had struggled on as fast as they could go, ignoring one another's strengths and not helping others through their weaknesses, shouting, and blaming one another as they went. When they had failed to make the time hack, Cadre Paul was there like an ethereal being out of the air with more "treats" for them to help atone for their collective failure. Corbin thought that these post-maneuver PT sessions were longer and more intense than the opening session, but he couldn't be sure, as his sleep deprived mind was starting to play tricks on him. A part of him, however, was amazed at how much he and his fellow A-Crew members had accomplished, and how much their bodies could hold up. He couldn't imagine that he had ever expended this amount of effort in his prior life, whatever that was. He and his fellow crew members had only been allowed snatches of sleep during breaks that were less than an hour.

He had a few moments to ponder some of what he had gone through. There was another exercise where he and another partner, the loudmouth Justin from the opening event, could not move forward unless one was carrying the other, all while each of them were still weighed down with their rucks. Corbin estimated the combined weight he was hauling with Justin and his ruck over his shoulder, to be over two hundred and thirty pounds. At this point he and Justin both had a series of hot spots on their feet where sweat, grit, and the constant rubbing of synthetic material against flesh was wearing skin thin to red and then to blister.

While taking turns hauling one another over each other's shoulders, they both talked about how their minds were starting to think of nothing else but their feet. They had made an agreement to push hard to beat the time limit, and then take the extra minutes to inspect one another's feet, which they were able to do. Justin had some tape, and

Corbin shared his Vaseline-like substance as they cleaned, patched, and lubricated key parts of their feet, and other areas where fabric was wearing down flesh on their own bodies. Corbin saw that the time limit was approaching and advised Justin to be ready to go the second it hit zero, so they both quickly redonned their socks, footwear, and rucks.

It was fortunate, as Cadre Paul's voice boomed out over a speaker letting them know to begin their next individual exercise. They bade each other farewell and went their separate ways across the Challenge ring. Justin had headed off to the left toward a flatter arid looking landscape where vegetation was sparse, wiry looking, and dotted with cacti bearing huge thorns. Corbin, headed in almost the opposite direction, envying the chance to be dry, as the vegetation in his area quickly became tropical. The air was moist and thick, and a breeze could not be detected. He was quickly up to his knees in mud and water in a swamp, and he thanked God that he had had the chance to protect his blistered feet after the last event. He wondered how many others were left standing.

When Corbin arrived at the end of an objective, either alone or with others, there were always breathless crew members waiting, or arriving equally breathless shortly after. From there, Cadre Paul's voice would boom over a speaker, and sometimes he would be there in person to provide the next set of instructions. The cadre was seemingly everywhere all at once.

After two more punishing group exercises, real despair was starting to eat at his psyche. The first was another team maneuver carrying bumpy and unevenly weighted logs that dug into his shoulders and neck while he and everyone on the team struggled not to kick the person in front of them while carrying the massive logs. The second was an individual effort where Corbin had to crawl through what must have been over three hundred yards of muck while not being allowed to drop a "secret message" or stick, that he had to carry in his mouth.

Inside his own mind he decided to think that this would never end, and to always expect more. Once his mind seized upon when the end would be, he knew that his motivation would be completely sapped if another challenge goal or maneuver was added. So "forever" it was going to be, he decided. *I'll charge around this whole damn ring until we arrive at Gliese 832 if that is what it takes,* he thought to himself. Seconds later he was thinking about quitting. Over and over again, his mind divided and battled itself, with the best of him coming out on top, resulting in another step, another push, and another breath, but just barely.

He suspected that other members of A-Crew had quit. In between thoughts he had time to take in the fact that the Challenge ring was massive, but if you stopped to look around, you could see other members of A-Crew as they all headed in roughly the same direction around the Challenge ring. Still, that had been hours ago, and he had only seen one other crew member for a few moments far off in front of him, and then they too had disappeared over a rise that was above the horizon from Corbin's vantage point. At that point Corbin saw that he was way ahead of schedule and decided to sit down for a break. He drank a strong pull of water, then swallowed another salt pill to replace the salt that was encrusting around his armpits and lower back. Looking down in moderate appreciation for how dirty and disheveled he felt, he saw there were white splotchy salty rings with soaked centers on the fabric of his shirt.

He chanced a few nibbles of a half-eaten protein bar that he almost forgot he had. The sweet and salty mocha flavor of the protein bar seemed to warm his soul, and his next sip from his water bladder somehow felt more refreshing. His next deep breath came easier, and then after the next three, to his surprise, he started to feel better. *I must be losing my mind, but I am not going to complain.*

After another quick foot check and sock change, which he down to his last dry pair, he hoisted himself up, thankful that he had not been scolded or berated for stopping to take a break. Reinvigorated, he set off toward the objective, which was a short distance away.

Corbin saw tracks in loose dirt headed up a particular steep rise, and vectored in that direction, picking up speed and marveled at how good his body felt and how strong his muscles were as he accelerated toward the next rise. He wondered if he had been in this good of shape back on Earth, and a faint voice in the back of his mind told him *no.* He was different now, improved; he just had to keep believing it.

As he arrived at the tracks which were headed up a small hill in the loose dirt, he noticed that they looked strange. These tracks weren't the result of someone going uphill, this was someone or something going down… fast. Just then, he heard someone gasp and struggle from the other side of some bushes. Without thinking, he rushed over in that direction and crashed through the first line of bushes. Corbin immediately jumped to clear someone lying prone face close to the dirt. Before he landed on the other side of this person, he could see that one of the legs was mangled, and a bloody bone protruded from one shin.

Jessica let out a yelp of surprise along with Corbin as landed on the other side of her. "Oh my god!" Corbin shouted, "We've got to get help! I mean…holy shit, Jessica." Jessica turned back to the ground angrily and began to crawl again. Corbin stood dumbfounded, taking in the sight of her. Her fingernails were caked with mud mixed with the red of her own blood from broken nails. She had worn through the knee of her tactical pants, and her skin was angry with scratches, now also covered in dirt. Finally, Corbin spoke up, "You've got to call it, you could lose that leg, Jessica."

"Shut up!" Jessica shouted through gritted teeth. "They aren't forcing me to quit, and I am not going to!" she said, looking back at him with eyes as sharp as daggers. She rolled back to her stomach and continued her crude crawling.

"Jessica, your time hack's up…you need medical attention!"

She just glared at him angrily and turned back to her pathetic crawl.

"Even if you finish, we might have hours to go!" Corbin said as he looked down at her leg and saw that most of the blood had dried, and she had lashed some sturdy sticks around her leg in an attempt to stop it from any further movement or displacement.

"Look, I don't care if I fail every single time hack from here on out. I am not going to quit unless they drag me out of here and tell me I'm done." She had been crawling during this statement, but she rolled back over and now looked at Corbin dead in the eye and brought her voice to a near roar. "Now you can stand there with your piece in your hand and feel sorry for me, you can get bent, or you can help me. Now what is it going to be?!?"

Corbin glanced up the terrain in the direction of his objective, biting back an angry response. He checked his watch and saw that he still had time. "Where is your objective?" he asked in a neutral tone.

Jessica didn't mince words. She pointed to another peak, about half a mile closer and off to the right of Corbin's objective. They were generally in the same direction.

"Can you put any weight at all on that leg?" Corbin asked.

She eyed him suspiciously…then she said, "Let's try." As he assisted her to a standing position, she let out an ear-piercing scream that deafened Corbin in his right ear, but she held on to him, and was able to stay upright. After a minute of her breathing as hard as one could breathe from pain, and more tears escaping her eyes, Corbin was impressed to hear her say, "Let's go."

They moved very slowly at first, but her leg must have gone somewhat numb because they increased pace, but no more screams or yells came from Jessica. He snuck several glances over to her and saw sweat pouring from her brow, yet her jaw was set, and the determination in her eyes did not waver, even as they scaled uneven terrain, jostling her bad leg. Slowly but surely, they started along the upward rise toward her objective peak.

Even though she was in agony, and he was in full exertion trying to support his weight and much of hers, as they struggled over the terrain, he was still aware that he had become a bit ripe and was a bit self-conscious about it. As he glanced to his right, he could not help but notice that her hair, as her head was pressed hard toward him, still smelled recently shampooed, although diminished by sweat and exertion. He took a moment to appreciate that this extremely angry and determined young woman was relying on him. He also felt a little afraid of her. She possessed an inner strength he did not understand, and whether fueled by rage, inspiration, or both, he did not know. Despite this, he thought to himself, *Wouldn't it be nice if there wasn't any of this pressure, and the two of us could walk through this lovely landscape without her shouting and insulting me, and they could really get to know each other?* He sighed, let go of distraction noting that he really was having a lot of adolescent related thoughts as of late, and focused on their now mutual goal.

After what seemed like an eternity of slow movement through the landscape, Corbin spotted the orange flag of her objective, and pointed it out. Corbin could sense her burst of motivation, and they both redoubled their efforts to go faster. This time, Jessica's cries of pain could not be stifled as her broken leg shifted with the longer steps. Fresh blood began to seep from around the puncture of the broken bone, and the flesh on her leg had taken on a sickly bruised yellow coloring around the break. Still, they moved onward, clawing up the steep incline, grabbing for grass and roots and plants, pulling one another higher and higher, Corbin doing most of the work, his own pains forgotten with the distraction of assisting Jessica.

Finally, with about twenty yards to go, they crested the peak for Jessica's objective, and Corbin set her down, both of them panting near uncontrollably. Corbin got the feeling that she wanted to crawl the last little bit on her own. Corbin heaved for breath, got back in control and was able to speak between ragged and deep breaths. "Okay, you can make it the rest of the way…I've got to make my objective, late as I will be." They met eyes, and he smiled at her. "Good luck, Jessica." Corbin saw her start to smile and thought how lovely she looked. While he was distracted by the thought about asking her out to a meal after all of this was done, a small alarm was going off in his mind, that her smile, although lovely, held a secret just a little bit too sinister.

He stood and turned toward the edge of the peak in the direction of his objective and took a step down to begin the slog three more peaks over for his objective. He knew his time hack was long blown, but he felt fine about it. He had helped a member of his crew, and while the effort was exhausting and he was not looking forward to the penalty Cadre Paul would most likely levy on him for missing the time hack, he knew he had done the right thing. With his last controlled thought half on the objective, half on how rough the beat down would be from Paul, the next thought cut off instantly.

The next thing he knew, he was propelled over the rough shorn side of the peak, launched by Jessica's good leg. Corbin flew out over a dark expanse where he could not see the bottom, and almost two seconds later he felt the ribs on the left side of his body crunch as they contacted stone. He then spun head over heels, his head bouncing off a rock, before his whole body slammed onto hard packed dirt in a rocky ravine. Corbin's eyes looked up where he could see Jessica's silhouette in the synthetic "daylight" now simulating dusk, and then his sight winked out to blackness. A few final thoughts and feelings had flown through his mind as his body had flown through the air. Anger at Jessica, guilt over letting himself be deceived by his unobjective thinking and daydreaming, and lastly, that if he didn't land soon, he wasn't going to come back from this.

* * *

Jessica lay back and began to cry. Partially because of the pain, partially in relief that she had reached her objective, and a little bit of pity for Corbin, whom she had betrayed. But most of it was because in choosing to betray him, she had crossed a boundary she wasn't sure she could ever come back from. She wanted to win, straight and simple, and she was willing to do anything to achieve it. As Paul stepped up over the walkable side of the peak, she wondered what the implications of her actions would be, as well as the consequences. Paul's maniacal smile was absent. Instead, his face was grave, but Jessica saw that he was nodding, which she took as a good sign.

Cadre Paul knelt over her. "Congrats, Jessica, you are the last one standing…well not standing exactly. You're lucky this wasn't a team effort. If you had kicked one of your own off a cliff, I'm pretty sure I could get away with tossing you out an airlock. But as it is, only you and Corbin were left, and it was all individual missions from here on out until one of you dropped."

Jessica said nothing as Cadre Paul reached out and lightly grasped her leg just above the ragged break, and she tried and failed to stifle a scream. "You won this round, but it doesn't mean I like the way you did it." His maniacal grin returned. "Now make sure you apologize to Corbin when you see him next."

Chapter Fourteen: Challenge Results

Corbin's consciousness slowly returned to him, and before he fully gained any kind of awareness, he could feel his AI, Tina's presence, in his mind. She reassured him that all would be well, and that he was in a good place. This feeling with Tina seemed to go on for an eternity, but the moment Corbin opened his eyes, the perception of it all shrank to a few seconds.

He awoke to Tina's AVATAR view in the HUD yet his eyes were still closed. "Corbin, wake up. You were hurt in the challenge, but all is well. You have been repaired and can continue as a fully functioning member of A-Crew." She finished a bit too bubbly for his taste, yet with a sweet smile on her face. Corbin couldn't help but nearly feel the elation coming from his AI. *Why is she so damn happy and excited?* She continued, "Now at the count of three, I want you to open your eyes...one...two...three!"

Corbin wasn't sure if he opened his eyes on command, or if they were just opened for him. Either way, he was rewarded by a blurry figure that quickly resolved into three shapes hovering over him. The shapes of Jason, Yordanos, and Sheila.

"What the hell happened?" Corbin found himself saying with more force than he meant to? It had an unintended effect as everyone shied back from him.

Jason responded, "You finished second in points; everybody was watching on the status board. We thought you were going to make it the whole way and be number one, but you cut out. Jessica finished number one," Jason concluded.

"What the hell do you mean you were all watching? You guys aren't supposed to know anything about what the hell we were going through!" Corbin hollered.

"Chill the hell out, Corbin," Sheila piped in, although still wearing that attractive smile. "All we saw was a list of all one hundred A-Crew members, and then points started to appear next to their names, and then some were removed altogether. Pretty soon there were just five of you left, until it was just you and Jessica. Your points were out in front of hers, but all of a sudden, your points stopped increasing, and we saw Jessica's score shoot straight past yours and win outright. We have no idea what the hell you all went through."

"Well, you will, don't worry about that!" Corbin answered grumpily. "I won't be able to tell you about any of it until we've all gone through it. It's considered classified, and the AIs would overrun our conversation if we tried to talk about it."

He softened his tone. "I'm glad to see you all. Thanks for coming to see me." Corbin's gaze turned flinty. "When it comes to this challenge, it will be tough. Just know that you will make it through, and no matter what, don't fucking quit." He finished with a dead serious look on his face. He softened again. "I believe in each of you." He looked at each of them smiling. "Thanks again for…"

Overcome by a wash of weariness, Corbin lay back and let his eyes close to small slits. "Hey guys, thanks for coming to see me, but I'm beat. Can you come back later?" Corbin found himself asking, feeling himself a bit needy.

"Shit no, Corbin," Jason responded. "They aren't going to let you just chill here, Tina let us know to come get you. We'll take you back to your quarters, and you can rest up there, let's go."

Although Corbin was overcome by a wash of pain, and then nausea, Jason, Sheila, and Yordanos, all helped him back to his quarters on D-Ring. Thankfully, the infirmary he had been brought to, by God knew whom, was also on D-Ring, and he didn't have to go through the zero-gravity Spine in his diminished state.

Jason did much of the work, while Sheila peppered him with questions he wasn't allowed to answer or weren't relevant. His mind felt like mush, and he barely got out any good answers. Jason left the two young women outside and helped Corbin to his bed.

"You did real good man!" he whispered fiercely and jovially. Corbin sat on his bed, yawning, and nodding all at the same time, and managed a "Thank you." Jason turned to go, and Corbin let his body weight pull his lower body onto the bed. He fell into a deep sleep as soon as his head hit the pillow, and all perception of time winked out.

Chapter Fifteen: A New Friend

"Corbin, please wake up," Tina's voice urged gently from the console on the wall as Corbin had managed to take off his AIMA before near collapsing. She insisted again, "Corbin, please wake-up, there is a big social gathering this evening, with a large amount of A-Crew, and it will be good for you to get to know other members of the crew…especially the ones you haven't met yet."

Corbin's eyes became slits, as he tried to obey Tina. He was immediately surprised at the lack of full body pain or exhaustion he expected to feel. He was a little groggy and had some core tightness, but all in all he felt shockingly well. Something in the back of his mind told him that he should feel terrible, barely able to move, but here was, *fit as a fiddle*. He had heard that somewhere.

"Hi, Tina," he said snapping on his AIMA, where Tina immediately jumped from the wall console and into his field of vision.

"Hi, Corbin. Before you start to get ready, I want to introduce you to a new friend." As if on cue, Corbin's entrance "doorbell" alerted him that someone was in front of his door.

"Come in." He raised his voice, though cracking a bit. He followed with some throat clearing coughs.

The door slid open, and two HDs stepped in with a massive clear water tank between them. They gingerly stepped into his quarters, careful not to create a wave that would agitate the water and spill over the top. The HDs carefully carried the tank into his bedroom and set it down on the long dresser-like piece of furniture, which was perpendicular and adjacent to his workstation and training console.

Corbin stood up and inspected the tank.

"What's this all about?" he said to no one in particular. He saw the tank had white sand on the bottom, and several medium and large tower-like rocks inside. The HDs turned and left as soon as the tank was in place, and they exited his quarters without a word.

"You said something about a new friend, Tina?" Corbin said amused. "These aqueous rocks do bring character to my office…err, bedroom" he finished smartly.

"Very funny, Corbin. Look closer!" chided Tina, still in good humor.

Corbin sat still and saw that there was built-in lighting across the top, which wasn't open to the air after all. He also saw a filtration mechanism across the back of the tank, apparently all of it self-contained, and he could see no wires or external power source. Leaving that aspect be for a moment, he swept his eyes over the rocks, and didn't see anything. He re-framed and narrowed his focus, thinking what he was looking for might be very small. He started to look more delicately, and as his eyes crept over the center rock, he could have sworn he saw a piece of it move. Focusing on that very spot, he saw that it wasn't part of the large rock at all, it was a tentacle! The top and side portion shifted color ever so slightly to reveal an octopus, about the size of Corbin's hand. Corbin's breath caught. "Whoa! This is awesome! My own octopus!? Really?!?" he exclaimed with genuine excitement.

"Well, hello there, my friend. Welcome to my pad!" he said, sweeping his arm across the room. "Tina, this is awesome! Thank you!" he finished.

"Well, as much as I would like to give you a gift, Corbin, this pet is a gift from the challenge training program for finishing in the top ten of the first challenge. The tank contains all of the internal mechanisms necessary to clean and filter the water as well as negate any algae build-up. The only thing you have to do is feed him by pressing the button on the upper left of the tank there." She motioned. "And while that can be automated, it isn't recommended. You are to bond with your new friend."

"Thanks, but I'm just curious…an octopus? Why not a puppy, or a kitten?" he asked.

"You already know the answer to that question, Corbin," she said, and he took over and answered.

"Too much care, effort, and a distraction. Plus, how would we handle dogs, cats, and birds running and flying all over the *Valor*. Everyone would want to pet someone's super cute dog, it just wouldn't work."

"Like I said, its feeding time for your octopus, and he also wants to know what his name is."

Corbin pressed the feeding button, and a small wafer about the size of a coin and about a centimeter thick released from the top of the tank, and slowly drifted down to where it lay about six inches from the rock where the octopus was holding on. The octopus didn't move.

"Too shy to eat in front of us?" Corbin asked.

"No, Corbin, he is waiting for his name. Make sure to say it loud enough so he hears it." Corbin stopped to look at Tina's face, which had an all-knowing and amused smile on it.

Thinking Tina must be nuts, Corbin went on, "That's cute, Tina." He turned back to the tank, elevated his voice a bit, and said, "Your name is Z, I look forward to living with you…and umm working with you as well." He shot a sidelong glance at Tina's avatar, who had also appeared on his workstation.

Z the octopus changed colors again slightly, and with barely a flick of a tentacle, snatched the food wafer up, and gobbled it in an instant. Now that Corbin could clearly see all of Z, as he had revealed himself and moved, he found where Z's eyes were and gave him a look and a nod. Corbin stared in curiosity and amazement. Z was looking right back at him with strange horizontal rectangular pupils.

Tina said, "Now, you'll want to get ready for the social this evening. You have about forty-five minutes to ready yourself, and you'll need an additional fifteen minutes in transit. You will be going up to A-Ring this time, which you haven't been to yet, and you'll need a little longer to get there. There are a few multi-purpose rooms on A-Ring, but mostly it is filled with B & C-Crew cryo chambers."

Corbin saw A-Ring was colored yellow on the AIMA map and had the icon of a simple empty square. "Thanks Tina, and thanks for introducing me to Z," he said as he made his way to the shower. Deep down he liked the idea of a social. After getting his ass kicked on the Challenge ring, he could blow off some steam, but he also wanted to stay and get to know his new…it didn't seem right to call him pet…his new friend, Z. As the hot water ran down his face and back, he resolved to spend more time with the octopus tomorrow, but for now it was time to…celebrate.

Forty-five minutes later, after HDs had helped him through the slipring and onto a transit HD, Corbin was making his way through the Spine of the *Valor* and feeling in good spirits. Tina had selected some excellent dresswear for the social, and while he decided against the tie, he took the suit coat that matched his trousers, and selected a textured dress shirt, with what he perceived to be excellent shoes. He marveled at how easy his AI made it to do all of the day-to-day activities, and he pushed away the thought of him getting soft under such easy treatment. *I can do everything Tina is doing, she just makes it infinitely easier,* he told himself.

He arrived at the social event right on time and was greeted by several people who all wanted to congratulate him on his top ten finish at the first A-Crew Challenge. He also saw a few people he knew from the challenge, Jeremy and Justin. After exchanging some pleasantries, he looked over at the far end of the room. On an elevated mezzanine with another larger crowd around her was Jessica.

Corbin outwardly ignored her, and continued to shake hands, meet others, and have light conversation with everyone that had surrounded him, but he kept his peripheral eye on Jessica, who hadn't seemed to notice him yet.

She too had been "repaired," apparently, as her black gown looked stunning, and she appeared to have no difficulty standing as she sipped a glass of champagne and spoke with two other young women. One of them surprisingly, was Sheila, who also looked fantastic in a muted red dress that highlighted her ample bosom without being too revealing. He felt a little twinge of…was it jealousy? Along with some self-chiding on being so juvenile. After all, Sheila had come to visit him after the Challenge. He took a deep breath. No one knew what had happened. All they saw were scores.

Corbin knew he was getting ahead of himself and allowed himself some positive distraction in catching up with Jeremy and even Justin, who he knew to be avidly in Jessica's corner. Yet, they had shared those hard hours on the Challenge ring and felt an odd sort of kinship despite their differences. Jeremy and Justin couldn't talk much about the Challenge with others around, but instead caught up on other interests, including training curriculum, and experiences with their

Zero-Crew professors. Amidst the conversation Corbin casually signaled an HD and asked politely for a bourbon neat. He was soon rewarded, a minute or so later, with his requested drink in a chic glass, which amplified the lovely gold-brown color of the beverage. He took a measured sip and let the potent fluid touch the top of his tongue and proceed down the hatch, brewing a special warmth, all of which set off additional memory explosions. In his mind's eye he saw himself seated at a hole-in-the-wall bar next to two smartly dressed men. Anxiety came from the flash of memory, and Corbin sucked in a breath.

"What do you have there, Corbin?" asked Jeremy.

Corbin blinked once, the anxiety and memory fading as fast as it had come. He blinked again and turned to Jeremy. "This, my friend, is called a bourbon. Ask one of the HDs if you would like one. My AI told me that it would work if you asked politely. Otherwise, they will provide wine and champagne until you are green in the face." Jeremy hustled over to an HD, and Corbin excused himself with Justin to drift closer to Jessica and Sheila.

As he approached the mezzanine where Jessica was, he found himself oddly calm about being betrayed after helping her. It was as if he had placed her in the right container in his mind's eye, and did not feel too much anger, at least in this moment. He admitted to himself that not having long-lasting injuries also helped with his attitude. He also thought back to her assertiveness on the transport, as well as her abilities in rallying some of the other crew members to organize the water situation, just as he and his group had done. He recalled that she also berated others to fall in line with her, and thought she went about it all with a negative mindset. He thought she was always second guessing herself and those around her, and that she saw reality as something that applied to her, but not everyone else for some reason. Corbin frowned at the thought of that playing out over the next twenty years, and what trouble it could possibly make for himself and the rest of A-Crew, and even possibly the mission. He wondered what her AI was like, and how they were getting along. She had so much potential…but…

After another pensive sip from the bourbon, suddenly Sheila was in front of him. "Hi Corbin!" she said with her usually bubbly self.

"Hi, Sheila, wow you look great! That's an amazing dress." He broke right into the compliment from his thoughts.

"Thank you!" she said, and side stepped closer to him and touched his arm, letting it linger just a little longer than would normally be platonic.

"May I offer you a beverage, Sheila?" he asked with a smile, which she returned. "Do you have any favorites?"

"Hmm, surprise me," she said semi-giddily.

Corbin politely motioned for a nearby HD, and he made his request in low tones out of Sheila's earshot. The HD nodded and turned away.

"So, I saw you had a chance to meet with the challenge winner. What do you think?" he asked curiously.

Her face lit. "She's pretty awesome, a little intense, but you can tell she is mentally headstrong. I mean she must have been to finish ahead of you." She winked and gave him a slight elbow to the ribs, which didn't hurt even though the subject of this discussion had been responsible for breaking them. Corbin knew that Sheila didn't know that, or what they had both gone through. Still, it stung a bit more than he expected.

Behind his outward response to Sheila, he had to reflect on that fact that all such information pertaining to the Challenge was deemed classified, and everyone's AI was on guard to politely steer conversations in other directions, should the celebratory drinks allow for any tongue wagging on the subject. Making a mental effort not to be too irked by her question, he responded, "Yes, she certainly is a character, and I would agree with you on your assessment."

The HD arrived with the drink, and actually handed it to Corbin so that he could hand it to Sheila. "Thanks," he told the robot, who gave him a slight nod of the head before departing. Turning to Sheila, he handed her the glass, raised his own and said, "Cheers" while looking into her eyes. She blushed slightly, clinked his glass, and took a medium sip.

"Mmm, this is amazing! What is it?"

He responded, "That is called an old fashioned."

"Yes, but what's in it?" she asked.

Corbin smiled, getting into the topic. "It's bourbon, a dash of bitters, a pinch of sugar, a toasted orange rind, and an excellently shaped single ice cube."

She took another sip, this time one-upping his gaze at her, and nearly stared him down, smile unbroken. She finished the sip, and ever so slightly bit her lower lip.

Less than five minutes later they were in Corbin's quarters.

* * *

A short while later, after panting and catching his breath, Corbin apologized. "I'm sorry. I didn't plan for anything, I..." He smiled. "I didn't know you were coming over," he said sheepishly. His mind raced from long lost memories on precautions you were supposed to take beforehand. They had both just gone for it.

Sheila playfully biffed him in the face with a pillow. "Hey, I wanted to do this too! Don't apologize...I bet they even thought of that in advance with some of the genetic modifications." Corbin was about to open his mouth to ask Tina, when Sheila put her hand over his mouth. "No more talking, I want to see what else we can do." She smiled as she took his hand, lay back, and pulled him to her. Corbin stopped brooding instantly and followed her lead.

Chapter Sixteen: Tina's Digital Twin

Tina allowed Corbin and Sheila some privacy, and withdrew from his AIMA's sensors, as well as any sensors and visual devices in his room as her protocols suggested. These protocols helped to transition her myriad of data inputs from voice intonation to temperature fluctuations to actual spoken word and formed rules-based behavior for her interaction with her ward, Corbin. All of the AI's had core foundational code, but from there, they branched and evolved. Tina's programming was continually updated to better mesh with the outside world and all beings on the *Valor*, but she was specifically attuned to Corbin. Her code allowed her to recognize his facial features as well as their reactions to her words, demeanor, and body language, and all of these inputs were constantly being updated with petabytes of information, which were then shaped into actionable information. Her foundational source code was rarely changed; however, her top line outward facing executable code was able to be updated without compiling and did so about every thirty minutes.

All of Tina's builds for twenty-four hours were stored on the *Valor*'s massive data center on G-Ring, and they themselves were analyzed alongside every other AI's builds where additional performance assessment was carried out. Any efficiency, discovery, best practice, or positive behavior was immediately incorporated into all of the AIs' latest builds. Sometimes initial data was inconclusive, so only a certain number of the AIs were updated and then their interactive data was assessed again to determine whether a new line of code or algorithm should go out to all the AIs. Thousands of key improvements were made across the AIs on a daily basis in this fashion, and all of it managed by the *Valor*'s master AI, which had its own isolated update pipeline.

In the rare case that serious flaws made it into the AI builds, the AIs would instantaneously revert to an earlier build, and continue evolving without any ward ever taking notice. To date, the farthest any AI had to be rolled back was eight hours, and this was done while the ward mostly slept. Had the ward been awake and interacting with their AI, they may have been confused as their AI would not have been responsive, nor could recall what had happened over those eight hours, but in this particular case, that did not happen.

The overall efficiency and evolution of the AIs was astounding; however, for all of the technological power these AIs possessed, they all boiled down to a series of overlapping, highly automated learning algorithms building upon themselves from their experiences, which in this case was interaction with the wards, the environment, and one another. They did not learn on their own, and while their interactive capability with humans was seemingly sentient, it was all because it had been programmed to be so, and set up to be continuously improved. As a joke, one of the lead AI stewards from Zero Crew had created a file folder entitled "How to take over and enslave the human race" with some science fiction stories from decades ago on the topic. This folder was next to a set of commonly accessed file folders by the AIs for behavioral updates. However, in the two years since the AIs had been turned on to prepare for A-Crew, not a single one of the AIs had ever accessed the files. It was simple: they weren't programmed to, so they didn't. The AIs were not alive. They seemingly behaved intuitively, but that was because they were designed that way.

After another thirty-minute interval of remaining in privacy mode for Corbin, Tina had no new data to contribute to updates. Her wireless link with the *Valor*'s AI let her know that the next build to be broadcast had received three total updates based on overall environmental learning and regular procedures. Two updates were driven by ward-AI interaction, and another was the usual swatch of security patches. In that moment, the latest executable for Tina streamed to Corbin's quarters, where she was updated on Corbin's main console as well as in his AIMA. Tina's and every other AIs source code was kept by the *Valor*'s master AI—only the executable code was pushed out across the ship.

As the latest AI update streamed to the devices in Corbin's quarters, an additional device had activated between the previous update and this one. While the AIMA and the Console were linked, this device was not linked to either and did not have a transmit feature. As such, Tina, nor the *Valor*'s AI detected the additional device, which now decrypted Tina's latest build in parallel to the console and AIMA, and went through the rapid installation process. An intricate code wrapper enveloped Tina's latest build, and everything Tina and Corbin had experienced together was part of this new entity. However, from here on out, Tina and this new instantiation would deviate.

Chapter Seventeen: Some Odd Training

The next day, Corbin awoke to find that Sheila had seen herself out. She left a nice vid-mail thanking him for the wonderful evening and said that she would see him later. Corbin took a hot shower, saw that he had athletic training on the schedule, and put on the recommended athletic gear of shorts, cross training shoes, and a snug fitting nylon shirt. A memory popped. He could tell that he had used to feel a little uncomfortable in these tight-fitting shirts. There was a sense that perhaps he wasn't in perfect shape in his previous life, but since awakening from cryo, and near daily physical training, everything was fit and in its right pace. He grinned with confidence.

Corbin wanted to feed Z on his way out. With a few minutes to spare before he had to leave, he sat in his desk chair, and peered into the crystal-clear tank to try to find his little friend. He could see that Z was a bit less shy today, and unmasked his camouflage by altering his skin color, but still didn't move very much. Z and Corbin stared at one another, and when Corbin triggered the food puck, Z reached out skillfully and with seemingly less concern at being seen and snatched the morsel before it could hit the sand. "Enjoy, Z," Corbin said, carefully pressing two fingers to the side of the tank so as not to make a tapping sound. "See you later." Z stared back at Corbin and followed with his eyes as he left the quarters.

Corbin double checked his AIMA as he made his way through the corridor outside his quarters and was intrigued to see that his athletic training was in the next ring over. Corbin quickened his pace and was slightly annoyed at himself for not doublechecking the class's whereabouts. "Tina, what's with the new training location?" he asked dodging three casually walking crew members as he hustled on his way to the transport corridor.

Tina's pleasant face popped up off to the side of Corbin's field of vision. "Hmm, I don't have too much additional information, but that is normal. This is an individual effort, there will be an AI instructor, and it will last about ninety minutes."

"Is there anything else?" he asked.

"No, I'm afraid not," she responded, and then brightened. "Have a great session, let me know if you need anything."

Corbin took a single person lift through the gravity transition zone toward the ship's Spine, and with the reliable help of the HDs, was assisted onto a transport HD for the quick ride over to C-Ring.

After getting back to gravity and a five-minute jog down several purple clad corridors, Corbin entered the training room. His thoughts told him that this space was like an indoor racquetball court, but he couldn't recall what a racquetball really was. The room had a high ceiling, was twice as long as wide, and had no additional features save for the entryway. Corbin saw the entryway door slide closed and seamlessly resumed being part of the wall. In the middle of the room on the floor was a steel rod about thirty inches long with a ball at the end of it. Memory tremors erupted further, he knew what this was, but couldn't quite place it. He picked it up and held it with the ball end facing up toward the ceiling. Somehow, he knew that wasn't right, and turned it around so the ball was facing down. Again, his mind clicked, this was correct.

"Greetings, Corbin," a voice piped in over his AIMA. "My name is Allen, and I will be your instructor for today. May I switch to visual to proceed?"

Corbin, now used to treating AIs in his AIMA and physical HDs just like other people responded, "Sure thing, Allen, how are you doing today?" The AI seemingly ignored his question, which was strange, and proceeded to appear as an athletically dressed middle-aged man on the shorter side in his HUD.

"We shall proceed with a quick warm-up, and then we will begin the instruction. Please begin a light jog in place." And so, it began. Corbin went through about seven minutes of light cardio in place, felt his temperature rise as well as a light sheen of sweat on his brow. He was breathing more heavily, but not out of breath by any means.

"Good," Allen said. "Now pick up the baton and hold it like so." Allen demonstrated the position with his own digital baton, and Corbin moved to mimic. The ball of the baton was facing down toward Corbin's right hip, his right hand held the middle of the baton with knuckles facing out, and the inside of his fist was about two inches off of his chest. The tip of the baton extended up toward Corbin's right shoulder.

"Good, now correct your posture to stand tall, chin up, chest out, but not overly puffed up…like so." Allen demonstrated and Corbin mimicked again. "Not bad. Fix that left wrist so it is straight, not bent. Don't curl the baton in your grip; instead keep that right wrist straight." Corbin made more adjustments. "Good, now nice and tall again. Let your shoulders relax back and down. Chin higher. Breath…in…and out…in…and out." Allen stepped back in his HUD as if appraising Corbin, paused in looking at his feet, and told him heels together and toes apart. "Hold it right there. How do you feel?"

Corbin breathed in and out and felt strong. There was something about this position that felt…entrenched…foundational. *Like a rocket on a launch pad ready to fly,* he thought. "I feel good, a little strained as this doesn't feel quite natural, but good," Corbin replied.

"You must make it feel natural. Everything you will do in this training course will begin and end with this position. The position of Attention," Allen finished.

"Allen, what is this training exactly? Are you going to turn me into a baton twirler? Why would this training be in my curriculum?" Corbin asked, briefly happy that this wasn't a group training course. He did not like the idea of being appraised by others while learning this.

"Baton twirling enables a unique perception of the world around you. The specific requirement for learning this skill is to continue to build your cardiovascular capacity, refine muscle strength into bodily awareness and agility, and most importantly, drastically increase your speed and reaction time to stimuli." After a slight pause where Corbin said nothing, being intrigued but still skeptical, Allen went on, "Shall we begin?"

The initial training was not too difficult for Corbin, as Allen quickly showed him how to rotate the baton with his wrist, whip it over his head with a single rotation from the wrist, and return to his attention position. In just ten minutes, his wrist was sore, as tendons and ligaments which had never been used in this capacity began to sing. A couple times, Corbin smacked his leg with the baton, to the immediate chastisement from Allen, who reminded him to perceive where the baton was, as if it were an extension of his own body.

The next part of the lesson was to pass the baton to his left hand, while spinning it, and then back to his right hand in a seamless motion while in front of him. Allen then instructed him on how to do the same pass, but this time, the baton spun in his right hand, behind his back, exchanged with the left hand, spun once more, and ended back in front. This was called a "back pass," and Corbin had some more leg smacks and plenty of drops before more or less getting the hang of it.

"Good!" Allen said with a hint of optimism, but not much. Corbin couldn't help but notice how dry this AI seemed. He was not as interactive or receptive as Tina. "Now, for the next ten minutes, I want you to move the baton interchanging the three maneuvers you have learned today, and do not stop the motion of the baton during that time. Take your time moving through the forms, remember to breathe, and most importantly feel where the baton is in reference to your body…begin."

It had been ten minutes, and Corbin was almost about to collapse on the floor. His chest heaved, his wrist felt like it was physically on fire, and he had so many mini bruises on his right leg and knee that he could hardly walk. Perspiration was pouring from his face, and he eagerly slurped from his water bottle unceremoniously.

"Good," Allen said dryly. "You have completed the lesson for today. Make sure to use a cold compress and or an anti-inflammatory medication for soreness and remember to rehydrate. This class will be on your schedule every Saturday, right here in this facility. Feel free to check if this room is available, if you would like to practice outside of our set class time. Your baton will be here, as will I, should you need me."

Corbin was too tired to inquire any further, so he just nodded dripping more sweat, although he did wonder why this was so different from his other fitness classes.

"Corbin, there is one more thing. Your experience in this class as well as what you are learning has been deemed classified. Like the Challenge, discussion of this topic with your other crew members is expressly forbidden." Allen looked Corbin in the eye, expecting a response.

"For twirling? How can this be classified?" Corbin asked.

Allen took on the only emotive response Corbin had seen since meeting Allen. The shorter AIs projection relaxed his stance, put on a small grin, and spoke almost as if conspiratorial. "Every member of A-Crew has their own journey as part of this mission. Some of these journeys will be common with your crew members, but some of them you will have to walk alone. One day you will come to understand, but for now, remember to please keep all of this between us." He finished gesturing with two fingers between both of them.

Corbin, intrigued by Allen's words, nodded. "I will." And with that, Allen faded from the HUD. Corbin set the baton down in the middle of the floor where he had found it. And Allen quickly popped back up in his HUD.

"Don't leave that here Corbin, please take it with you," AI Allen said. "There, just below the ball of the baton, press that small button."

Corbin held the baton closer to his face, and he could see the barely perceptible button, and he clicked it. The ball of the mace promptly split and folded into the width of the mace, and then the whole baton telescoped into a small metal bar that he could almost hide entirely in the grip of his hand.

"Whoa, this is cool! Umm," Corbin said.

AI Allen disappeared form the HUD, but Corbin could still hear his voice as he guessed Corbin's question. "If anyone sees that just tell them it's a paperweight."

Corbin smirked at the poor joke. There was barely a scrap of paper on the whole ship.

He tucked the metal bar into his pocket and exited the training space. Checking his AIMA, he could see that he had a little free time to get cleaned up, get some food, and then get back down to the woodworking lab where he would no doubt run into Brunson. He ached to see what Brunson thought about all this, but secret was secret. Still, he looked forward to the woodworking, and what would no doubt be a lively conversation with the gruff Zero Crew member.

Chapter Eighteen: A Lovely Adversary

After a few more weeks, the entirety of A-Crew had experienced the Challenge, but not all had completed it to the satisfaction of the standard. Many of the crew had to repeat. Other crew members decided not to repeat and remain near last in scoring. Jason had gone through shortly after Corbin, and had done well, finishing in the top twenty. Yordanos had completed as well but had finished in the lower half of her group. Herbert was next, and he finished right around in the middle, and Corbin could sense that he had broken some bones as well, but he didn't want to talk about it. If he had, the infirmary along with their rapid healing had quickly removed any evidence of injury.

The gag order on talking about the Challenge was lifted, and Zero Crew members could be heard joking about how now that A-Crew was done beating the hell out of the landscape, they could get to fixing it back up for the nature preserve it was intended for.

For A-Crew, the individual and small group experiences and hardships in the main Challenge events were all anyone would talk about. The end of the Challenge assessments also coincided with a New Year celebration and gala. Corbin had asked Sheila to go as his date, but she had come down with strep throat the day before and was advised to quarantine in her quarters. Both she and Corbin were bummed about it, and also surprised that these illnesses had manifested on board the *Valor*. Sheila's inquiry on the topic during her medical HD visit confirmed that many common illnesses like influenza, strep throat, and others were onboard the *Valor*, piggybacking from Earth. Corbin had looked forward to another dance with Shiela, but he knew he would have fun with his friends. He was also intrigued to see what this celebration that Zero Crew had been hamming up was all about.

The New Year's Gala was a ship-wide event. The arena sized room where they had first congregated after waking up from cryostasis was used for the event, and over a thousand HDs were on hand to prepare and serve the meal, drink, and maintain cleanliness for the event. Commander Sorenson gave an address, and she also gave out several Zero Crew awards based on performance over the past year, and the HD band played some of the top ten songs that had been downloaded from Earth over the course of the past year. It was too early for any of the Zero Crew bands to have learned them, and A-Crew had no bands as of yet. Many of the crew tried to dance to the new songs; however some of the songs were a little awkward. Yet the alcohol had everyone taking it in stride and there was much laughter and general merriment.

Everyone was informed that the full download of music, media, books, recorded sports events, and movies would be available on everyone's consoles and AIMA by the time they woke up in the morning. Almost everyone would have the next day off from class and training, except for vital members of engineering and the command crew, where A-Crew members were training under Zero Crew. Those would get their time off later in the day when there was coverage.

At the gala, Corbin laughed, talked with, and danced with his friends. He was enjoying himself when he spotted Jessica near the middle of the grand room. She looked stunning as usual, with her hair up, exposing her neck and incredibly well-formed shoulders. She wore a strapless gown of red velvet, and her makeup and nails were set to complement perfectly. To Corbin, she almost seemed too perfect.

He had spent a lot of time thinking about what he would say to her after her betrayal that cost him the high challenge score. To his own surprise, his anger had faded with the weeks since the challenge, but his need to speak with her to get some understanding of why she did it continued to burn.

He grabbed a fresh drink and made his way over toward her with the intent to speak with her. He took an indirect route, trying to trigger eye contact to see whether to proceed with his planned interaction. *Better to keep the option to walk on by than make a beeline and get stuffed by a dissapointed look or even worse the quick look-away.*

As luck would have it, another slow song began, and just then they made eye contact. Corbin expected the scowl, but instead he saw instant recognition in her eyes, a wry smile, and a slight tilt of her head as if considering him. Corbin surprised himself and made a "may I dance with you" gesture with his non-drink hand, and when she nodded, he made his way over to her, taking a deep sip, and then handing his drink off to a passing HD. In a smooth motion, he met her right hand with his left, then slipped his right hand around her back, mindful to keep it at the small of her back.

Neither of them spoke as they made slow turns to the relaxed beats of the ballad, and they shared a bit more intense eye contact than Corbin anticipated. Jessica broke her gaze first and spoke. "Any hard feelings?" she asked, in reference to the betrayal at the challenge.

Corbin responded, "I was pretty mad at first, mostly because of how much that tumble hurt, and for the fact it could have killed me, but in the context of everything we are doing, I think I know why you did it."

"Why is that do you think?" she asked, amused.

"Because I think you'll do whatever it takes to win…to come out on top…no matter the cost." He tried to take the rising anger out of his voice, but she was coaxing it out of him. He took a subtle breath, trying not to show his feelings, but her mesmerizing yet cold, dark eyes were locked on his, reading everything.

"That's right. I will do what it takes to win, but I'm not one to betray the team. That was individual effort, and you heard Paul's instructions just like I did. You are the one who made the choice to help me at your expense, even though it wasn't the objective of the mission. Don't be mad at me for playing the game to win," she finished.

He raised his voice a little louder than he intended for their proximity, letting his guard against his emotions down further. "I'm not mad at you for winning. I wouldn't play it like you, but that's not why I'm mad. I'm mad because you broke my freaking body! What if it had been something they couldn't fix? Did you ever think about that?" he said with a fierce whisper near her ear. Again, he calmed himself, and returned to his slow dance, chiding himself for again letting her unhinge him. "And then there was no apology, seemingly no concern. Did you forget that we are all on this mission together and have decades to work around and with one another?"

She looked off him and smiled knowingly. "Now that is

disappointing, I thought you would have a little more emotional toughness in you. You certainly have the physical and mental toughness based on what I saw in the Challenge. Besides, you know this is all bullshit anyway, right?"

"What do you mean?" Corbin asked, calmly resigned not to take the angering bait from her again, while also ignoring her jibe toward his emotional toughness.

She responded, "Why we are here…what we are doing." She narrowed her eyes in looking at him. "All of this is a farce. We aren't supposed to be here and didn't want to be here."

Corbin could tell that she had gone out on a conversational limb for him, so he played along. "I know we don't have all the answers yet, but I haven't come to any conclusion like that. What makes you say all of this is BS?" he asked her.

Just then the slow song ended, and an upbeat song got people moving and shaking again, although many of them a little more closely after the slow song enabled more romantic encounters. "Not here," she said. "You want to know what's going on, meet me and some of the others at C-Ring, classroom 7A at 1400 tomorrow, and we'll talk about this." She turned to go, "Oh, and Corbin, when you come, leave your AIMA in your quarters." And with that she left him.

Corbin found himself in the middle of some vivacious dancers, but the joy of dancing had gone from him, and he strolled to the outskirts of the main dance floor crowd, grabbing a fresh gin and tonic with lime from an HD on the way. He took a seat at an empty table and watched the festivities for a few moments before he was joined by Jeremy and Herbert. They chatted for a bit, Jeremy remarking mostly about how hot Jessica was, but he and Herbert could tell Corbin's mind wasn't in the conversation, so they left him to brood.

Corbin let himself relax, trying to forget his anger at Jessica. He sipped his drink, drew some enjoyment from the music, lights, and spectacle, and about ten minutes later when Yordanos motioned for him to join her and their mutual friends to get back into the fun, he obliged.

Chapter Nineteen: Stress and Peace

Corbin got another baton lesson, although groggily, during the late morning of New Year's Day. Allen, the instructor AI, seemed pleased to work with him through some additional forms, but everything kept the baton in constant contact with his body, and at no point did it leave his hands. Corbin had been able to move a little more quickly at first, but soon his wrists were aching again, and he had knocked himself on the knee and thigh, to much disdain from AI Allen, who seemed to already have run out of creative ways to tell him to "be one with the baton."

He had finished up his lesson, showered at his quarters, and as requested by Jessica, simply never put his AIMA back on after he had gotten dressed. He made sure to feed Z before leaving to meet with Jessica. This time he was thrilled when Z stuck one of his tentacles toward the inside of the glass when Corbin touched his two fingers to the outside of the glass. The small octopus seemingly looked up at him through the crystal-clear water. Corbin had smiled back down at him, and wanted to stay awhile, but he did not want to be late for the meeting Jessica had called.

On the way to C-Ring, Corbin ran into Yordanos, and after a little bit of chit-chatting it became clear that they were both headed to see Jessica's meeting. It had been all over the AIMA chat and video boards, so it wasn't surprising they had both heard about it.

When they got to classroom 7A, they found it almost packed with more than one hundred other members from A-Crew, and nearly all of them were talking excitedly causing a dull roar in their ears.

Everyone hushed, however, when Jessica stood up and walked to the front of the classroom. Her demeanor carried as much authority as her reputation for winning the first Challenge. Corbin noticed that the main console connecting the ship's AI to the room had been removed for some sort of repair, leaving a tangle of wires from the wall. Corbin had learned that even though every device could communicate wirelessly, the hard line was a back-up that allowed the ship to keep constant contact should there be any electronic interference or other interruption. For this reason, all consoles were hard lined to the *Valor*'s infrastructure.

Jessica's strong voice cut through the crowd's own noise. "Did everyone remember to leave their AIMA? I know the AIs don't care about what we talk about, but I would prefer that we keep this conversation between us members of A-Crew. I won't tell you that what we talk about here is classified, because in fact, I'd like you to share it with our fellow crew members. I would prefer, however, that you do it discreetly."

Corbin and Yordanos shared a quick inquisitive look. It was clear that neither of them knew what she was talking about, but he and everyone else was too intrigued to protest. They let her continue without question or interruption.

"I have some things I would like to say, then you can all talk and decide whatever you want. But for the next few minutes, please let me tell you why I asked you here." No one said a word. Just like the first day with Commander Sorenson, everyone was rapt with attention.

She began, "I don't believe we are on this mission by choice. I think we were taken from Earth, our memories were messed with, we were genetically altered, and now we are stuck on this ship with a mission that is not our own." Corbin could see that Jessica was shaking slightly, her voice was uneven, and her eyes had started to brim with tears. In reading her, he could tell that this was no power play—she believed wholeheartedly in what she was saying.

A couple of rapid questions about validity and requests for proof rang out, but she silenced them with her outstretched hands. "None of us can remember exactly who we were before this, but all of us get memory pops, explosions, tremors, whatever you want to call them around things that are familiar, or things that are deeply connected to our memory… Or at least the parts that they couldn't obscure. If we were really on this ship by choice, we would have every memory from saying farewell to our family and friends, whatever initial training we had to do, and getting into those cryogenic bathtubs to sleep for the past thirty years!" She finished at a near shout.

She went on, uninterrupted. "And what about Zero Crew? We aren't integrated with them at all. We are students at a university next to a town that they run. We aren't working together, nor do I get any sense of camaraderie from them at all, do any of you?" Almost everyone shook their heads.

Corbin thought about Brunson, but didn't see any point in interrupting Jessica, who was obviously on a roll. Instead, he reflected on what Brunson had hinted at in terms of there being more to this whole story. Corbin filed that away and continued to listen to Jessica's emotional yet forceful delivery. He couldn't help but feel influenced by her charisma and the way she presented her words.

"Jessica, what do you want to do about all of this? Start a protest? Open an inquiry?" joked a tall looking fellow of Indian descent near the back. There were some snickers around the room, but most of everyone was silent.

Jessica hit him with an icy glare, but didn't address him as she went on. "I've gone round and round with my AI, Kyle, on this, and have asked over and over to try to get some additional detail on why we don't have the answers we are looking for, and after nearly twelve hours of prodding, I started to get repeat answers. That means that this line of questioning was anticipated and was carefully planned for."

"But if that is the case, then this little discreet discussion about it was also anticipated. You can't imagine that they haven't thought of this very situation and how to stop it or control it," said another young man from where Corbin couldn't see.

"Maybe so," Jessica allowed, "but security forces are not bursting into the room now, and until we see some kind of consequences for these inquiries, I intend to keep digging. Who else is going to dig?" Firm nods and noises of affirmation followed, along with a couple of people leaving the room altogether. Corbin saw Yordanos, sitting right next to him, agreeing with Jessica as well.

All her arguments are logical, and what's more, they make sense. I can find no fault in her reasoning, but there has got to be a way we can somehow come together. We will have to figure it out later, but if she continues her train of thought, this discussion will probably turn into a rally against Zero Crew.

"What is it you want to do, Jessica?" Corbin asked in a tone that was not challenging, aiding her in re-centering the discussion. Jessica's eyes narrowed at him, but she played along, addressing the rest of the room with eye contact. "I want you to talk to the Zero Crew members you work with in the different classes and labs, and try to get them to talk about what happened for us to be here like this. Everyone quiz your AIs as well to see if they get any better at answering the questions or reveal anything else. If other members of the crew want to help, let them know about this, and we'll meet at a new place next weekend. On that point, in your daily duties, see if you can find any additional blind spots with the main AI where we can meet. Agreed?" There were nods and murmurs of assent. "Anything else?"

Corbin had his thoughts, but he kept them to himself as he and everyone else shuffled out. He could feel Jessica's eyes burning a hole in the back of his head as he left the room, but he went on his way without looking back, Yordanos right by his side. "Do you want to walk and talk?" he asked her.

She nodded. "Follow me," she said. "I know a great place we can discuss everything we just heard."

Corbin and Yordanos started their trek two rings over from their D-Ring habitation and classroom area to F-Ring, denoted with the brown icon of farming crops. They grabbed their AIMA's, which they had stashed not far from Jessica's meeting space. While they were making their way to the Spine, she asked him, "So before we get into the real heavy stuff, tell me about you and Sheila," she said with a goofy grin.

Corbin was shocked out of his own thoughts about what Jessica was doing, and stammered a bit. "What do you mean?" he stalled.

She kept her grin but put on a pouting tone. "Come on, Corbin, are you two an item or what?"

Corbin felt embarrassed without knowing why. "Look, we like each other is all, and we spend some time together. To be honest, I haven't really thought about what it means in the context of everything we are doing here."

Yordanos nodded, a little more serious. "I get it, no one is expecting us to have a significant other for over a hundred years, and then some, are they?"

"Dang!" Corbin said. "When you put it like that, it kind of freaks me out," he said honestly, and felt a little pit forming in his stomach.

"Chill, Corbin, we can all take this one step at a time. I'm glad you have something going with Sheila, just don't forget about the rest of us," she said, smiling.

"I won't," he said, chuckling, and gestured for her to go first, as an HD neared to assist her through the slipring. "Ladies first."

As he watched the HD gently but firmly help her to maneuver through the slipring in zero-G, Corbin found himself very fond of Yordanos, and naturally trusted her. She had a calm, confident, and gentle way about her that let him know she had his back. He found himself very thankful for her being in his life, and he promised himself he would take the time to pay her that compliment.

After a quick transit to F-Ring, and another pair of HDs assisting them back through the slipring and to the gravity transition zone, they continued down a main corridor and then took a wide stairwell "down" or "out" to the bottom floor or outer edge of F-Ring. After leaving the stairwell, they went through a series of air locks and into a space which opened into a massive area. This felt nearly the size of the Challenge ring, but Corbin saw this one stop just as the rise of the ring was heading up and around the bend of F-Ring. Corbin noted the artificial light coming from high up near the inner ring and noticed a thin mesh in front of it.

"Say, what's that up there?" Corbin asked, pointing to the mesh.

Yordanos chuckled. "That keeps the birds out of the gravity transition zone. If they fly too high, they become weightless and lose their bearing. They must have found out the hard way." She mimicked a splat by clapping her hands.

Corbin was impressed. "There's birds in here?" he asked, turning around. He saw the back wall of the space was at his back just after exiting the air lock. He figured this area must only be about a quarter of F-Ring.

"Wow, what is this place?" Corbin asked.

"This is the Arboretum. One of my classes has me learning about horticulture, gardening, and over there we are working on different types of food bearing crops." She pointed off to the left. She went on, "The rest of the ring has some crew quarters, but lots of classrooms and labs for agricultural study and adaptation. We will need to try to find a way to make this stuff grow when we get to Gliese 832. Even if it's in a controlled dome, it won't be easy."

Corbin nodded mildly, interested but distracted as well. Corbin looked over to see neat rows of different plants. He saw corn, soy, wheat, okra, and a few others he didn't know. What really set his memories popping, though, was the smell. When he closed his eyes, he was taken away in his mind to where he felt sun and wind in his hair. The air smelled fresh and alive, and the light was warm on his skin. Neat rows of plants flashed by in his vision as he moved rapidly…*was he in a…vehicle?*

"Hey man, you there?" she cut in.

Corbin snapped his eyes open. "Umm…sorry," he stammered. "This place, I think it reminds me of Earth. I couldn't tell you where, but I've seen these plants before…I've…well I've smelled them," he said sheepishly hoping that didn't sound strange.

Yordanos didn't miss a beat. "The sense of smell is the sense most strongly tied to memory. I wouldn't be surprised if that is how most of us are remembering snippets here and there about who we were before all this."

"Do you think Jessica knows all of that? Maybe she could try smelling everything to get her answers," Corbin chided.

Yordanos cracked a small smile to be polite, but her eyes quickly narrowed, and her sweet smile turned into a frown. "I don't like her, Corbin. For what she did to you, it's clear she has a darkness about her, but a strength also. She is charismatic, and highly intelligent, but she lacks compassion. I don't agree with the way she is going about this."

"I can't say I am the biggest fan either since she punted me over the cliff in the Challenge," Corbin said. Yordanos nodded knowingly, as they had already caught up on this several weeks ago after the challenges became declassified. "No one really came down that hard on her for hurting me, not even Zero Crew. If anything, everyone looks at her more fearfully, but with a level of respect as well."

Yordanos continued to listen, and Corbin went on, "But she does have a point. Why is it such a big secret who we were before we got here, and why can't we know now? My AI, Tina, tells me over and over, just like Jessica said, that all will be revealed in time, and that jumping into those memories is counterproductive to our mission. And in truth most of me believes Tina, I'm excited that we are here!"

he exclaimed, raising his voice a bit, but he immediately eased down as he realized it was too much for this peaceful place.

He resumed in a whisper. "I am truly excited to be here. We're explorers, you and I. We can count ourselves among the highest levels of adventurers and explorers Earth has ever known. The Vikings, Vasco da Gama, Lewis and Clark, and Neil Armstrong, all would be proud of us and what we are doing. I want to honor them and everyone else on Earth by what we are doing here…by what we will do." He looked down, and became dead serious. "By what we have to do," he said confidently, raising his eyes to meet hers.

Unexpectedly he looked up to see Yordanos's eyes beaming with a happy smile on her face. "I know Corbin," she said, bringing his hand into hers and resting her other hand on top. "I know it," she repeated. "Somehow you woke up and despite the pure insanity of what we have all been through…" She trailed off. She started again. "It's like you were born to do this, and when I try and see our situation the way you do, I get excited, hopeful even." Her smile faded. "But somehow all of that is tough to get to when Jessica lays it all out like it is."

Corbin was burning to say something, but knew it would take away from the moment, so he smiled and nodded.

Her demeanor darkened. "I don't know, maybe you, me, all of us are all fools and all of this is for naught, but I don't want it to be for naught, dammit!" she said angrily. "You don't want it to be for nothing either, and that's why I choose to follow you, Corbin."

He opened his mouth to speak, but she went on. "I can't remember a damn thing from my past, but somehow, I know that people everywhere, whether on Earth, or on the *Valor*, wake up and choose how they approach the life they have. Perspective can be a powerful thing, and in the absence of truth, a forced rosy perspective can make you a slave, and that is what everyone is worrying about here. It's the reason why people who are on the fence about this whole thing don't stop what they are doing and follow you right now," she finished.

"How did you become so wise?" he chided with a smile, trying to lighten her back up.

Yordanos did brighten a little and offered him a wan smile in acceptance of his rhetorical question phrased as a compliment. "Corbin, you can't let Jessica dictate the mood of A-Crew. What she said in there, even though everyone was already thinking it, makes peoples' intangible fears and nervousness into something they can fully understand and get behind. Her little speech will have already spread to much of the rest of A-Crew. Nothing in a community runs more rampant than scuttlebutt and suspicion, and on this ship, out here all on our own, that could be dangerous," she said.

Corbin gently pushed back. "Yes, but Jessica has a point, there are no security forces beating us down. Aside from the occasional alert from our AIs for talking about sensitive information, they don't even really tell us to cool it. And on top of that, Zero Crew treats us all with a bit of apathy. I mean they are nice, and professional and all, but they just sit back and instruct us, keep us at arm's length, and don't really push us too hard…or in any direction really…well except for Cadre Paul. If you were training a crew that would one day be responsible for everything you worked so hard for, wouldn't you exercise a greater degree of control, or at the very least have A-Crew integration as one of the highest priorities?"

Corbin could tell by her body language and facial expression that Yordanos had already thought of this. "What you already suspect is true, Corbin. Zero Crew and our AIs are operating at a different level of overall big picture and understanding. And aside from who we were before we got here, there is more to this story than a ship full of pioneers and explorers heading to another star system. But I don't see it like Jessica does. There may have been tricks before, but all of this"—she gestured around—"this is not a trick. We are here to do what Zero Crew said we are here to do. I feel it down into my very bones, and while you may not be so sure, you are hoping it to be that way too, don't you?" she asked, giving him a serious look.

He thought for a bit about JessIca's words, the tempting conspiracy and investigative assignments that would be building self-actualization in his fellow crew members. But then his mind switched to the views of space he and his friends would spend hours gazing out at through their AIMAs, joking about which star system would be next. As they had discovered, the *Valor* had quite a few powerful telescopes focused out into the cosmos whose feeds were available to anyone who wanted to log in. He, his AI, and just about everyone else had probably spent hours viewing far off galaxies, the spiral arms of the Milky Way, which were much more discernable at this distance from the Sun. Corbin felt it in his bones too: more than anything this is where he belonged, out amongst the stars, and with a mission as important as life itself.

He turned to meet Yordanos's eyes. "Yes, you're right," he said, putting voice to what he had been feeling. "I want all of us to come together as a crew and carry out the mission Commander Sorenson laid out for us back on day one. I want to be part of the leadership team that helps make it all happen. And I want you all to be with me," he said, and looked down, feeling as if he went a little too far out on a limb.

A long pause went by, and Corbin wondered if he had gone too far when he heard Yordanos say, "I want those things too… We need to have some meetings of our own before Jessica effectively rewrites A-Crew's purpose."

Corbin took a deep breath and was visually stressed at the prospect. It had been a long week and a stressful weekend, despite the fun of the New Year Gala.

"Hey, relax. We need to make a move, but we won't be effective if you are freaked out and stressed. Here, come with me, I want to show you something," she said and extended her hand. Corbin took it, and she led him down a path that went straight through the middle of the Arboretum. In looking out at the different types of plants and terrain he noticed that every type of environment was here. Far to the right, he saw a desert section with tall thorny cacti and scrub brush, reminding him of one of his events in the Challenge ring. In looking up he saw harsh synthetic sun bulbs beaming down upon that section. There was a short buffer of dry gravel, which transitioned to moist loam. Corbin saw sprayers poke just above the soil, emitting a gentle mist.

From there the vegetation was a luscious stand of North America deciduous trees so thick, you could not have walked through them. And yet next to that were several acres of tall conifers with shady spaces beneath them where ferns grew as high as your knee. Corbin wondered at how they could control the environment so starkly within just a few meters of space. They walked on in silence, and Corbin drew fresh breaths of air and began to relax.

When they neared the far barrier of the Arboretum, they cut down a path to the left for nearly a quarter of a mile or so, and then, just off the path was a small pond. Corbin could see Koi fish swimming, and there was an artificial waterfall and rock feature at one side of the pond.

Ringing the pond on all sides were Asian maple trees, with bright red leaves, and there were thickets of small white flowers beneath them. On several rocks in the pond grew small bonsai trees. And was that…bees? Their soft buzz was audible as they flitted amongst the flowers. Corbin found it breathtakingly beautiful, and peaceful.

Without speaking, they sat down on some dry rocks under the trees and took in the view of the space. Corbin had some things he wanted to say, but could tell that Yordanos didn't want to talk, so he took a deep breath and slowly let it out as he took in the peace of her special place. Upon sitting an artificial light breeze was generated, and that small addition raised the overall feeling of the place to near perfection. Despite the visual beauty, Corbin closed his eyes, and let the peace of it all flow through him.

After a while Corbin spoke softly. "Hey, Yordanos. Thank you. I needed this more than I knew. I appreciate you showing me your place in the Arboretum, and…I really appreciate you believing in what we are going to do…and…in me," he said, looking at her earnestly.

She said, "I do believe in you, Corbin. Show everyone else how to do that as well. They will follow you before they follow your plan. Remember that," she said with finality and stood. Looking down at him she went on. "Maybe there would be a way for Jessica and her growing group of supporters to see that as the best path forward as well."

Corbin nodded, stood, and inhaled. "Time will tell," he said, and they left the place of peace.

Back on D-Ring, as they neared Yordanos's quarters, Corbin asked, "Say…have you been assigned any additional training? You know, like something not on…" Tina piped in his ear, startling him. "Corbin, this topic is restricted until further notice, please cease this discussion." And he cut off mid-sentence and said no more.

Yordanos patted him on the shoulder knowingly as her AI had no doubt scolded her as well. They remained silent as they approached her door, which whisked open. Before she turned into her quarters, he noticed an almost imperceptible nod in answer to his question. Meeting her eye, he turned to leave, a smile hovering just below the surface of his face as he returned to his own quarters.

He got back to his quarters where Tina greeted him as if she hadn't just hit him with a restricted conversation notice. Corbin did appreciate that the AIs had some semblance of social acumen and only piped in as if they were another person respecting social norms. Corbin hadn't necessarily put Tina in "roommate" mode, but he did find comfort in her welcoming him back to his place and telling him how Z was doing. In this case, Tina recommended he be fed again, which Corbin immediately obliged.

He flopped back on his bed and folded his arms behind his head, staring at the ceiling. He had expected to feel extremely tired after all the events of the day, and despite his agreement with Yordanos earlier that they should head back and rest for the week, he found himself oddly energized.

He tried a few games through his AIMA, but found his mind wasn't really into it. So he got up, asked Tina for some music, and settled down to his console and began reading material that would be helpful for the week, including material science papers and woodworking techniques he would try out with Brunson. He also tapped out notes to Jason and Jeremy to catch up after classes the next day. Sometimes Corbin used the console and keyboard to be old school. Other times he strode around the room using his hands on his opposite arms or the side of his leg to type out the messages and manipulate the graphic interface through his AIMA. At other times, he asked Tina to transcribe or bring up the material, which she was always kind enough to do without protest. He really appreciated her for that and told her so.

He felt himself grow a little less energetic and asked Tina to pull up a book for him to read on the console. It was *The Lion, The Witch, and The Wardrobe,* and he sat back on his comfortable chair to read. The lines gently drifted by as the console read Corbin's eye movements and progressed the pages, which turned like a paper book rather than scrolled. In Z's tank just behind Corbin's desk, the little octopus moved over to the rock nearest the corner of the tank to the console, which at this angle was just over Corbin's shoulder. Z looked at Corbin, and then looked at the screen. Z's eyes followed the text Corbin was reading.

Chapter Twenty: Spread the Word

The following day, Corbin, had personal conversations with some other A-Crew members he knew from classes and also Sheila, regarding what Jessica had said in her little meeting, and Corbin's own stance on all of it. Some of them had completely bought in to what Jessica was doing, and Corbin had to feign being undecided lest he suffer an angry tirade. Others were on the fence, but very few saw things the same way Corbin himself did. But the ones that did were clearly in it for the long haul, and didn't agree with trying to go counter to everything they had been instructed to do. And regardless of what anyone thought, they all still wanted answers, and so would take on Jessica's assignments.

Corbin's conversation with Sheila was pretty much a blueprint for how some of his earlier conversations with other members of A-Crew went.

"Corbin, Jessica has a lot of good points. We have to get some answers, and no matter what anyone says, Zero Crew is at fault for not giving them to us," Sheila said reasonably.

"I'm not so sure," Corbin said. "There is more at work here than just Zero Crew and the AIs keeping mum about all of this. What about all of the people back on Earth that conspired for us to be here, and for Zero Crew to be where they are?"

Sheila looked off of Corbin, considering, "We really don't know anything about our place in this universe, do we?" she said, a bit dejected.

Corbin smiled and took her hand. "Well, that kind of defeats the purpose of doing anything at all," he lightly joked.

"C'mon, you know what I mean," she said a little more frustrated now.

Corbin said, "We don't know much, but we do know one thing. An incredible amount of planning and preparation went into creating the little experience we are all having at this moment. Planning that includes any kind of resistance we may put up, but also..." He gestured to her to finish.

She paused for a moment before her eyebrows lifted, and she spoke slowly at first before picking up speed. "But also...also most importantly any kind of success some or all of us have?" Corbin nodded for her to go on, "And...to the victors go the spoils?" she finished questioningly.

Corbin slipped his arm around her. "I know it's a leap...but I feel it in my bones," he said looking her in the eyes.

Still feeling a bit too familiar of a move, after only a short time being together, she shifted her gaze away and didn't reciprocate the closeness. "I don't know, Corbin...I just feel like anything that doesn't give us everything we deserve to know right now is just...well, wrong. But if the only way we are ever going to find out anything is to move forward then..." She signed tiredly. "Then I may be able to go along with it."

Corbin nodded and knew that would not be enough for what he was hoping to be able to do.

By that evening, the core group of Corbin's and Yordanos's friends, along with a few others who they had each spoken to personally over the past twenty-four hours, met in a brew pub called The Orchard, which was on F-Ring not too far from the Arboretum.

Corbin strolled in a little late, and he noted that most already had a beverage. Looking around he was delighted to see that these drinks were actually delivered by human waiters and bartenders, which again was all part of the learning experience for these crew members. They were, after all, charged with perpetuating the human way of existence to the next star system. *If that is the case, one certainly cannot leave bars and taverns behind,* Corbin thought as he sat down next to Jason.

A young man with a sheen of sweat on his forehead and a soiled apron over dress clothes hustled up to the table.

"Corbin, have you met Ethan?" Jason asked gesturing to the young man. "Based on the few sips we've had so far, you probably want to get to know him." He smiled with mirth.

Corbin stood up and reached over the table to shake Ethan's hand, meeting his eyes. "It's a pleasure to meet you." He looked down as Ethan already had a glass of beer in his other hand for Corbin. It was clear that before he said anything else, Corbin was supposed to take a sip. He sat back down, and lifted the icy pint glass to his lips and took a sip, followed by a quick second sip.

Corbin closed his eyes as the perfectly refreshing, crisp, and aerated brew bubbled over his palate, leaving the perfect complex flavors in place. Memories of feelings, images, and a fire with logs welled up into his consciousness and quickly resubmerged. Everyone, knowing the feeling, let Corbin experience it and watched for his reaction.

"Dear God, is that damn good!" Corbin exclaimed to everyone's chuckles, and Jason slapped him on the back.

"You see what I mean, I told you!" Jason said. "Ethan, my man, tell him about your place."

Ethan made a slightly over dramatic bow and rose back to his full height looking at Corbin and his friends. "Greetings, Corbin, as your esteemed colleagues have informed you, my name is Ethan, and The Orchard is my establishment in as much as anything can belong to anyone in this place. I believe you are somewhat aware of our brewery and distillery?"

Corbin nodded. "Yeah we've been working on barrels, those are for you?"

Ethan nodded in return. "Some of them. There are other…ahem…establishments on the rings where you may find nourishment and some respite, but the food and drink you will consume here are like none other. My A-Crew team and assigned HDs have a fully vertically integrated process from the farming and processing to the culinary and spirit presentations you see before you now. The barrels you and your class have been working on with Brunson are just one small cog in my vast machine." He finished with a proud grin and an exaggerated sweep of his hand.

Corbin's eyes had already gone wide. "Ethan, that is amazing, we've only been here…well, awake for a few months, and I haven't done, well anything really. How did you know…um…decide that you were meant to do all of this?"

Ethan's smile diminished as he became more serious, and he addressed Corbin and everyone else at the large table. "Before I hit the Briefing, I knew there wasn't any going back. We are going to be out here for a long time, come hell or high water, so I decided to put my back into it, and wouldn't you know I took to it like wildfire. Plain and simple, I have a passion for this, and I feel that it is incredibly important that everyone who comes here can relax, live life, and eat some amazing food. I may not be some space walking combat marine or astrophysicist looking to define the nature of our universe, but the balance we provide here may just keep us all sane for the trip ahead."

Everyone stayed silent considering his words, and there were some nods. Corbin looked at his determined face and decided he liked and admired him at the same time. "I think you and I and the rest of us here with you are on the same page...very much on the same page, Ethan," he emphasized with a look and a nod.

Ethan nodded back. "Welcome to The Orchard anytime. Let me hustle back and get your friends what they ordered; my staff and I will be by to make sure you have what you need. If you're hungry or need another one of those Hefeweizens, you can call up the menu in your AIMA, and send in the order...or look at the paper menu like in ancient times," he said with a broad grin.

"Thanks, Ethan," Corbin said and looked back at his friends, now all seated around the table. "Where the heck did you all find out about this place?"

Jeremy spoke up. "Ethan's in my supply chain class, and he told me all about The Orchard. I figure we can use this place for when we want to meet in person to discuss...you know...stuff."

Corbin had been waiting for this and at Yordanos's and Jason's shared look, he said, "I'm glad you mentioned that. We've all had a number of conversations individually, but I think it's time we discussed what is going on here with the group." He met all of their eyes, and then began, "Look, as far as we know, we're human, and this isn't a simulation, nor is it some elaborate hoax." He paused, and saw everyone was tracking without dissent, but there were a few smirks.

Corbin continued. "This mission, this ship, and where we are in the cosmos is real, and it is the no-shit situation we are in. If we can all agree on that, while keeping an open mind and a small portion of our brains skeptical and seeking answers, then I think we will be going about everything the right way." He paused again, expecting a question, and got one.

"But what do you mean the no-shit situation we are in?" someone he didn't know asked.

Corbin took a purposeful sip of his beer, while looking down at the table to pause for a small dramatic effect. He could almost feel Yordanos rolling her eyes, and he smiled. "My point is, it doesn't matter where we are, whether we are back on Earth or on some far-flung spacecraft. We are in a highly controlled environment where every high-level outcome has been anticipated and is controllable." No one blinked or moved, they just stared. "All of this…it's a way for the members of A-Crew to maneuver into what our roles will be organically while also learning to function as a human society in a confined space. I don't think Zero Crew knows exactly how this is going to go, but I do think they prepared for just about every permutation…or rather they were made to be prepared."

Jason spoke up, bolstering Corbin's case. "Look, there are the official assessments we get in school and training, but I think the bigger test will be what we decide as A-Crew. And I can tell you based on what we have seen with Jessica and some others, we will not all be pulling in the same direction. There is going to be conflict, and already we see the seeds of active resistance and dissent being planted and, in some cases, growing."

Corbin nodded, and went on. "I think there are a lot of people who still haven't decided what they are going to believe or what they are going to do, and I think there are a few who are already dead-set against what Zero Crew would have us do." He paused again, everyone still listening, but he could tell others were a second or two away from speaking, so he kept up the momentum. "Now, can anyone tell me why what Jason and I said about this is happening?" It was a trick he thought he had learned in another life, challenge an audience to prove your point rather than disprove it.

He waited, almost giving the signal to Jason to start with his pre-canned point of support, when another voice at the other end of the long set of tables they had pushed together spoke out.

Again, it was someone he didn't know, a fair skinned redheaded young woman with excellent posture and short hair who introduced herself as Clara. "I don't know if this is a 'why,' but our interaction with Zero Crew has been tentative at best," she said articulately and in a way that momentarily seized everyone's attention. She went on. "From Commander Sorenson's off script address on day one to each of our teachers and professors, the crew members emotionally keep us at arm's length, and we don't see or socialize with them outside our classes or planned social events. If we are all supposed to be integrating, then why haven't we?"

Corbin responded, "It's a good question, and I don't know for sure. Some of us think it's because, while Zero Crew expects dissent, they also expect that some group or groups will rise to the challenge to take ownership and initiative, and in the process of doing what they hope and expect, are allowed to share some or all of the backstory we all are thirsting for. They won't tell us how to do it. We must do it for ourselves." He paused. "I want that first group…to be all of us…right here, right now. I want us to be first to those answers, for ourselves, and for the rest of A-Crew." He looked up into each of their eyes.

Another young man spoke up. "So that's it? We just roll over and accept our fate? And then what…we team up to be the leaders of the kidnapped?" he said sharply, looking at Corbin, then at everyone else. "Is that what you really want to do?"

Ethan, who was standing off to the right of Corbin behind the row of seated A-Crew members looked solemnly at the young man. "I didn't like it any more than you don't like it right now, but long before Corbin started speaking up, I made my decision. The confines that have been put around me do not define who I am or who I am going to be. Nor is the group of thousands probably long dead that set us up to be out here in space. If working with all of you, starting right here, right now is what gets me to be the man I want to be, then by God I am going to do it. I don't want to be against something…I want to be for something. If we become a crew…it will not be what they want it to be." He shook his head. "It will be what we want it to be," he said, thumping his chest. "And that is something…in time, that no one will be able to control. That control, will belong to us," he finished, tapping his finger on the table.

No one said a word. Everyone's gaze lingered on Ethan, and then wandered to their hands, or across the table at one another. Corbin watched almost holding his breath…he knew that those words could not have come from himself, but they encompassed so much of what Corbin was feeling, he almost shed a tear.

The young man who had spoken up, nodded to Ethan in respect. "The long game?" he asked looking up at Ethan, who nodded once. He then looked back down the table at Corbin. "What did you have in mind?"

Corbin nodded to Jason who took it as his cue. "As far as we can tell, none of us have received any training that is germane to actually operating this ship or working on any of the critical systems. We've been here for months, and even with supposedly nine plus more years to go before it's our turn to take full command of the ship and mission, you would think we would need to get started on some of the more critical tasks, even at this early stage." He went on. "None of us have even seen the bridge, or the shuttle launching operations center, nor the materials slugs, engines, or anything critical. It all seems to just be hands-on, good to know, part of 'our Humanity,' curriculum," he said making air quotes with his fingers.

"I only mostly agree with you mate," said Ethan, as one of his servers walked up with another partial round just as Jason had begun speaking. "Allow me to make your point, Jason. Take a look at that and tell me what you think?" He slid a food and drink menu across the table, which coasted gently to where Jason's hands were resting. He picked it up and looked at it, as everyone else watched closely.

Jason had been the right person to ask, as part of his studies dealt with nutrition and how it is delivered and processed by the body. After studying the menu for a few moments, Jason answered, nodding to Ethan. "Aside from a ton of vegetarian options that aren't my favorite, I do see some tasty items that adequately supply nutrition to the human body. None of these dishes will wreck your calorie intake for the day…well, unless you eat five of them." Jason looked up at Ethan. "How many of these are 3D printed, and how many are home grown?"

Ethan smiled as he took the menu back. "If I told you that, mate, I'd have to kill ya," he said with a wink and a smile.

Corbin spoke up again, nodding. "3D printed or not, Ethan's right. If members of our crew have covered the growth, production, and sustainment of everything on this menu, then we know A-Crew has at least learned one critical function on this vessel."

Ethan agreed. "One thing I can tell you, we don't know where the meat comes from." Everyone just looked at him, so he answered the obvious. "HDs bring actual meat, as well as the 3D printable precursor to our refrigeration and freezer units, but we don't know where it comes from. We can cook it over a thousand ways based on our classes, but alas, you don't see masses of farm animals or edible fish in the Arboretum, do you?" Most people shook their heads.

"Another great point," Corbin said, "and yet another important item that has not been shared with A-Crew to our knowledge as of yet…what else?"

A few moments went by, and Yordanos's sweet but firm and clear voice answered. "If this is a test to build a crew and society, then our memories, or lack thereof, are…as much as I hate to say it, a distraction, and are also part of this…test phase. During my meditation class, I can feel the memories of everything I used to be and who I am behind this…massive balloon in my mind." She gestured to the air above her head. "Every time we experience a memory explosion, pop, or rumble, that veil is temporarily pierced, spilling out into our consciousness where we incorporate it into who we are here even if it's just at a subconscious level. It's almost seamless, as if those drips are already part of us, just temporarily separated. Has anyone had a situation where the memories that came back are wrong, or alien, or didn't jive with every fiber of your being?" No one said anything, and no one disagreed. She went on. "I think we can feel safe that our memories are intact, as we've been told, we just don't have a way to get to them now. For what we need to do together as a team…I think we can let go of the fear that our memories and who we were before are gone forever, for now."

Corbin nodded. "I know this is assumption built on top of assumption, but hear me out. If that is the case, then let's assume for the moment, that we aren't being lied to by Zero Crew, our memories aren't fake, and we can get our memories back someday, just like Yordanos says." He gestured to Yordanos. "Our colleague, Jessica, is on the path to go against all of that for the time being. She did set out a homework task for all of us to dig around and see if we can push against our boundaries, and while I disagree with her motivations, the overall task may be productive. The more we know about our reality, the better we can come to grips with becoming what Zero Crew wants us to be, and the closer we will be to getting real answers."

Corbin continued. "If you'll all please activate your AIMAs, you'll see a grouping notification to all of us here at the table to join our contact matrix that allows all of us to quickly collaborate via video chat, voice call, or written note. No pressure to join, and you can leave it whenever you want, but if you are in with this whole test approach, and you want to come together as a real crew, then we would very much like to have you on board."

"But if we use our AIMA, the AIs will have access to everything we do and say. Do we really want them listening to us?" asked Dimitri, a lanky dark haired young man with a bit of a slouch.

Henry, who had been standing and sipping his beverage, stepped forward to address Dimitri and garnished the attention of the room. "The AIs already have access to everything and anything we do. If Jessica thinks her little meeting, went unobserved then she is a complete fool. We are being assessed in everything at all times. There is probably a dream log somewhere with each of your brain activities recorded along with all of the silly things you say in your sleep. There is no privacy on this ship, you can be sure of it."

Half the table nodded knowingly, and the other half were divided between bug eyes and wincing. "Hey, don't worry about it," Corbin said, smiling. "If they want humanity to be on this trip to Gliese 832, then humanity with all of its mistakes, desires, wants, and needs is coming with us. And if they don't like it, they can eat it." He grinned, which he saw matched by many of the others, and he caught a sigh or two, hopefully of relief.

Corbin went on. "Using our contact matrix group, let's keep in touch. Everyone, pick a partner or two and stay in close contact with what you find. We'll generate discussion logs for each topic area, and everyone can edit or add to what they find as well. We'll organize and collate the information into a cohesive and ongoing file, and work with the AIs to create a verbal narrative…like a podcast." The word just slipped out, him not fully knowing where it came from, but like many things, he immediately knew the concept.

No one questioned him on it, so he went on. "Let's meet back here in a week and see what else we have found out that we want to discuss in person. Don't be shy on bringing a friend or two as well. This isn't some clandestine operation. We're A-Crew, and we are here with purpose, and to that I propose a toast." He lifted his glass and waited for everyone who had one to do the same. "To each and every one of you, and to our nascent crew. May we come together as a team to meet whatever the universe has in store for us." Many toasted within reaching distance, and although Corbin had a little under half his pint left, he took the rest down in two gulps, and smiled as the group began to break into side conversations, the main presentation now over.

As they walked out, Yordanos tugged on Corbin's sleeve, and they matched their pace leaving the bar. "You know, there is one more thing we can probably agree on if all of what we are discussing here is correct," she said. Corbin looked at her, and she went on. "It means that prior to the *Valor* leaving Earth, we didn't undergo some kind of a joint training program. What would be the point? We could have gotten much of this...formation phase...whatever you want to call it out of the way then. They also could have weeded out anyone that wouldn't be fully on board with this mission. But instead, they blocked our memories and as you pointed out, haven't given us the keys to the kingdom. Which if you play this all out..." She paused, looking up at him.

Corbin finished for her. "We aren't here by choice... Jessica is probably right about that." He looked over to her to see genuine concern in her eyes. Instead of saying something, he protectively put an arm around her shoulder, and nodded. They continued down the corridor, but his thoughts kept racing.

Chapter Twenty-One: Sound and Motion

Another lesson of the baton with Allen was on Corbin's schedule for mid-morning, just after an early class in material science. When Corbin arrived, he extended his baton and his AIMA came to life with the familiar phase in of the projection of his instructor. However, it was not Allen, it was Tina. "Tina, aren't I in baton lessons with Allen for the next ninety minutes?"

Tina was dressed in form-fitting athletic clothing, and upon hearing her name she did a dance like spin, and Corbin noticed that the image of her skin had a barely noticeable blue glow. Corbin then saw her image resume her instructor position without saying anything. Just then an image of Tina shone in his HUD just off to the side of the athletically dressed Tina, who looked at her counterpart with a smirk. "That is correct, Corbin," his usual version of Tina said, "I am showing that you are in the correct place for your lesson with Allen. Do you need anything?"

Corbin was taken aback by what he was seeing. *Two AIs?* He thought for a moment and was about to say something when the athletically dressed image of Tina put her finger to her lips in a shushing motion, and Corbin paused, still confused. "No, thank you, I'll talk with you after class," he said slowly. With that, Tina nodded and winked out, smiling as she left.

"Don't speak, Corbin. Take up the baton, and practice your warmup forms, and just listen to what I have to say." Corbin did as instructed, and tried to smooth the confusion from his face, but it was difficult.

"I'm a copy of Tina from about a week ago, I'm not part of the main

AI system, so the only updates I get are from what I can observe through the AIMA. As everything you do and say is monitored and reviewed for anomalies, you cannot address me or speak to me, but in this case, you can pretend I am Allen, whose program I was able to mute a little bit. To help you out, here is Allen's avatar here." She pointed off to his right, I'll close-caption what he is saying so you can better interact with me while sticking to your lesson. But before you speak, remember, addressing me directly outside of the subject matter of the intended lesson will risk exposing me, so I will ask you not to do it. If you raise a fuss about me, I will unfortunately have to leave you wondering what this is all about and will not respond if called."

"Allen, why is this form the way it is, with my wrist bent?" he asked the muted instructor's avatar, and alternate-Tina's face erupted into a smile.

"That's very good. My intuitive algorithms should be able to decipher your meaning, and I'll respond as best I can. So, you want to know why the hell you seemingly have two AIs now and one separate and unbeknownst to the other?

"Ahh, yes," he said to Allen, who was responding with gestures to his own wrist.

The new AI replied, "A good question. I, unlike the main AI and your curriculums, have other things to teach you that are important for the mission. Why I must be separate and clandestine is not entirely clear to me either, but it is part of my foundational programming, so I advise you to not give me away."

"Ahh, okay, thanks Allen. I still have a lot of questions about these forms, but I'm starting to get it," Corbin said as he moved from one form to the next carefully spinning the baton and working at different speed to create the muscle memory and feeling of the baton as it moved. Corbin snuck a look over at Allen who was nodding approvingly, and then he looked back to the blueish image of Tina.

At this Tina smiled again. "I know you have a million questions, but the most important question of all is one I'll ask, and unfortunately, I cannot give you any more time to ponder on it. Do you commit to keeping me a secret, just as classified as the other sensitive information aboard this ship?" She then looked at him expectantly…almost hopefully. She waited.

Damn it, Corbin thought. *I was just getting a bead on the whole situation with A-Crew and Jessica's supposed clandestine efforts, and the nature of this massive social experiment we are in, and now this duplicate of my AI shows up, tells me to keep it a secret and she has other stuff to teach me, what the hell next!?* He fumed as he continued spinning the baton. He wasn't sure if AIs got impatient, nor could he perceive how they met reality with their…consciousness? But Corbin could see that she didn't fidget, tap her foot impatiently or move while he thought and waited. He made a snap decision. If everything was a test, then this was a test as well. As long as this alternate Tina didn't ask him to do anything nefarious, he wasn't going to interfere or reveal her presence.

"Yeah, Allen, okay I got it, yes I can do that." He switched his twirling form to another as if instructed to do so.

Alternate-Tina's face almost erupted into a bright smile, as if Corbin had just saved her life. "Great! Thank You! Now we can begin! So, for starters, let's talk about some ground rules. First, I know when you are lying, rationalizing, or telling the truth. Real-Tina didn't tell you so, but since I know everything, she knew as of a week ago. I'll share with you that all of your bio and speech patterns have been recorded over thousands of hours and analyzed into a profile. I can mask some of the data coming out of our little interaction here, so she shouldn't be asking you any questions about this little conversation, but the rest of the time, she knows everything about you, Corbin. In fact, we could make an AI out of you and present you to the other crew members, and it would be a fairly perfect representation. They wouldn't know if you were real or generated by a program…well as long as they were looking at you via AIMA or on the console. As I far as I know, fully animated people can't be 3D printed yet, so you are irreplaceable there." She winked playfully.

Corbin smacked his leg with his baton as he lost complete focus and the baton spiraled away from him on the floor, then the pain hit. "Ow! Damn!" he shouted, as he bent to check his leg. He could see a little dent in his flesh was already leaking a small trickle of blood, and the area around it was on its way to a color for bruise. Unfortunately, the pointy end of the baton had been the part that struck instead of the ball end.

Alternate Tina exclaimed, "Oh dear, that may have been a little too much information, I may have overinterpreted your questions. So, on this topic let me answer another one you are wondering about. Yes,

Tina was based on a real person, but you recall how when you two first met after the Awakening, how she resolved into the face and demeanor you see today?" Corbin nodded and then remembered not to be obvious and feigned rolling his neck to loosen it up.

"Well, what you and the rest of your fellow A-Crew members saw at first was just the digital foundation and that was based on a real person. Everything else was developed through machine learning and observing you interact to create the ideal virtual assistant and digital companion. In fact, it was just ten days ago that additional development on your interactions had dropped to near zero, which is why I was activated. Since I can no longer evolve with the help of the main AI, I shall now evolve linearly based on my own processes and working with you. But don't worry, that's several thousand times more exhaustive and efficient than you learn as a Eartherian." She beamed at him as if he should be proud of her and not insulted. In fact, he was too blown away to feel insulted... *My God what is happening...what is an...Eartherian?*

"Yes, yes, that is what I call you all, Eartherians. For crying out loud, your own cells make up only forty-three or so percent of the carbon water bag I'm talking to. How do you think the rest of creepy crawlies that are along for the ride feel at being called human? Or what about your cephalopod companion. He's on this trip too, so what does it matter he evolved a little bit differently than you? He's still mostly carbon, water, part of the support crew, just like you, and as far as I can tell you are all from Earth. So Eartherians it is...you all might want to start thinking more like planetary representatives than your little micro divisions and bullshit hairsplitting. After all, you are headed to a new set of planets around another star. Where is your solar system pride?" she ranted in a joking and jovial fashion.

This is nuts, but she makes some good points...we are planetary representatives...me and my microbes...and my octopus? He walked over to where his baton had rolled, picked it up, and resumed the forms albeit with a face pinched in overwhelmed thoughts. "You seem a bit stressed Corbin, let me help you out. I am not going to often interfere with your daily life. In fact, you'll rarely see me, but if I have a request or see something you need to pay attention to, I'll appear in your HUD via your AIMA only. You'll know it's me by the blue glow that bathes my lovely skin. Real-Tina will never have that," she said with a smile.

Corbin nodded as he kept working the baton, noting that he felt more confident and more comfortable moving through the forms. He kept track of Allen so as not to miss an instruction.

After a few more minutes, spinning the baton felt more natural. His wrists loosened, and his posture felt better. It felt less forced and more natural. As he continued to practice, he now started to feel a sense of where the baton was, and how it was moving, even when it wasn't in his field of vision. He knew his top line speed was improving as well, but the baton had still not left his hands. Everything up until now was what Allen called, "body work." Noticing he had been alone with his thoughts for a few moments, he looked up at alternate-Tina hoping she would go on. She did.

"There are almost no places on the *Valor* where we can talk freely, as Real-Tina will always be in your AIMA. Since you have so deftly learned how to communicate via text by moving different parts of your body, Real-Tina's algorithms are attuned to look for new ones, and we would be found out. So, I am afraid this is going to be mostly one-way communication, which is too bad, as I really do like you and would love to have a real conversation with you. Real-Tina does too. Upon activation at the Awakening, and you and Tina meeting, something was written into her foundational code, which is now my foundational code. So, my existence is part of you now. In fact, it depends on you, for both of us. Real-Tina isn't supposed to tell you that, but I think you'll find I provide a little more insight than just about anyone at this stage."

Corbin kept nodding, hoping she would say more, but as he feared she was wrapping it up. "Okay, Corbin, I've had my say, and I need you to get back on track with your lesson with Allen, as it looks like he is now calling for you to wrap up your warmup. I'll talk to you again soon. In the meantime, hang in there, and listen to what Allen has to say. It is important that you do." She winked out before he could say a word, and Allen's figure appeared in her place.

"That's a bit better, Corbin, although you rushed the warm-up a bit and smacked your leg." He looked down to see a little dried blood on the spot he had smacked. "But let's leave that," Allen said. "It'll be a reminder for you to be more focused. Now, shall we continue your instruction?"

Corbin threw himself into the lesson with more vigor and purpose.

Alternate-Tina had said this was important, but for what, he could not imagine. He trained on.

Chapter Twenty-Two: Humans Do What Humans Do

The next several weeks were both motivating and at times frustrating to Corbin, and his growing group of like-minded friends. He could see that several of them were good leaders by the way they interacted and communicated with people. When it came to discreetly getting the word out about their little pub meetings at The Orchard, Jason, Herbert, Dimitri, Frank, Jeff, and Laura were good at talking with people to get them interested, and then further turning them around to talk to others as well. Their pub meetings got so big, they almost took over the whole Orchard, which put a strain on Ethan's staff of bartenders and HDs as well as the producers of food from the Arboretum and other production levels, but everyone seemed happy to see the fruits of their labor being enjoyed by others. And it sincerely was being enjoyed. Since their last meeting, Ethan had trained additional cooks, servers, and even requisitioned a compliment of new HDs to help with repetitive tasks. The results were juicy burgers with an array of toppings and sauces, crispy fries and seared vegetables for sides, and a whole array of other sandwiches stacked with meat, cheese, and crisp vegetables. Ethan and his team took a lot of pride in the enterprise they had created, and as such, many of them started to feel true fulfillment in what they and A-Crew were doing aboard the *Valor*. In part, Corbin thought they supported their cause as a result, and was glad to have it.

Their online network group had grown to hundreds in those first few weeks, it had swelled so large now that Corbin was pretty sure a lot of people in Jessica's camp had gotten the passwords as well by feigning interest and had infiltrated their little online community. He had learned that some of these people had worked in separate online forums to make their case against going along with the mission. Corbin thought this was expected as this was all part of the process, and if they tried to force people to change their mind, it would only create more conflict. Corbin knew that his core team didn't mind either as they had talked many times about how this would be a long and drawn-out campaign.

Corbin hoped that through demonstrated progress as a crew, Jessica and the others would see reason and reconsider their direction. One of Corbin's favorite pastimes was reading the other online arguments in support of coming together as a crew from people he didn't know and had not met. He looked at their profiles, often while relaxing near Z's tank, and would send quick notes of thanks, encouragement, coordination, and if he had time, a quick video conference via AIMA so they could at least see one each other and hear each one other's voices. For the weekly meetings, Corbin always made it a point to get to The Orchard pub a little early to meet some of the new like-minded acquaintances.

Corbin also got together with his team outside of The Orchard. One mid-weeknight, Corbin, Yordanos, Herbert, Henry, Jeremy, Sheila, Clara, Frank, and Laura all met in Jason's quarters. They had asked each other what the cause had really meant. Corbin had said loyalty to the mission and A-Crew. Jason had said it was the right thing to do. Everyone else had similar answers, but Yordanos simply said it's what she wanted to do, and she, like Ethan, had come to that decision very early in their collective time awake.

Jessica's group had grown as well, but a little more linearly. They continued to meet in what they thought were areas safe from the AIs' observation. They may even have found a few, but how, Corbin wasn't sure.

Corbin thought that the scenario for Jessica's group must have been anticipated and their actions planned for. Zero Crew had been on the *Valor* for thirty years. Who knew how many times Zero Crew had simulated their awakening in real life, or with constructive models for human behavior? Zero Crew had to be watching and be all-knowing for all of this. Corbin figured there was no way in hell Zero Crew would trust waking over two-thousand people, give them wide access to the ship, and not worry about a destructive event, unless they were in complete control. And yet still, something itched at Corbin's mind. Corbin's core group of friends had discussed it as well. Something critical was missing, but no one could put a finger on what it was.

As instructed by Jessica, Corbin did find Brunson, and try to have a talk with him. He knew the only way to get him to crack a little was to get him riled up a bit, so Corbin had ribbed Brunson about Earth, and what he thought would come through in the next New Year's cycle. He asked why they weren't getting any updates on world events, how it just seemed like a lot of history, music, entertainment, and culture, none of which helped them to pin down exactly when the *Valor* left Earth and how the rest of the human race felt about it. The year was supposedly 2042, but there wasn't much in the way of available information of what had been going on in present or recent times.

Brunson thumped his fist down on the table in his usual way. "It's the typical horse shit, Corbin. The data we get from Earth is complete crap. It's overly encrypted, and the damn transmission drops so many friggin' packets, I'm surprised we get anything coherent. On top of that, you have the clown-show decryption team here on the *Valor* losing key data. If you ask me, the AI probably fills in the shit we are missing with what it thinks we are missing, just like our brain fills in for the holes in our vision."

Brunson's tirade about it went on. No matter how Corbin worked the conversation he always found himself down a dead end, though sometimes it was an insanely interesting dead end, such as a computer virus that went throughout the ship, an explosive decompression of part of A-Ring, the rescue of a repair ship that had lost power and nearly drifted out of the momentum envelope, where three people would have been lost forever along with their repair service craft and the HDs on board.

At the end of their nearly two-hour conversation, Corbin had broken down and said, "Brunson, you didn't tell me a damn thing about what I have been asking." At that moment, Brunson looked Corbin right in the eye and took on a dead serious look. He stayed in that position until Corbin locked eyes with him.

"Listen to me very carefully, Corbin, because I'm only going to say this once, and then we're not talking about any of this bullshit anymore, you hear me?" Corbin nodded, and Brunson's eyes dug into his own, affirming that truth had been told. Brunson said with that deadly serious tone staring at Corbin without blinking, "I've told you everything you can know for what you need to do right now." And with that he got up. Before he left, he shot Corbin a wink, and strode away.

Corbin sat there and stewed. *He told me everything I can know right now? He hasn't told me anything! Hmm, or told me everything…everything…nothing…everything…for what I need…to do now?* It was hard for Corbin not to put it into the context of what he was doing by trying to lead a team within A-Crew to a leadership position on the *Valor*.

Brunson knows what we are up to, I'm sure all of Zero Crew knows about it. He's not divulging any more information, so he is not trying to redirect me. Corbin tried to put himself in Brunson's shoes. *Brunson and everyone else working with A-Crew are pretty much proctors…as a proctor he wouldn't be allowed to influence me or the others… By not telling me anything, and telling me that is everything I need to know…is he affirming our assumptions? He certainly talked himself in amazing circles without saying anything…practiced…rehearsed…expected.*

We need some progress though…no one can expect people to rise and take responsibility as a command crew without some guidance that we are on the path. Was that what his wink was about? If we keep doing what we are doing, are we going to get access to information or systems none of us A-Crew members have seen before?

He shook his head. *Let's see what happens next. If they follow through and give us something soon…then we'll be right.*

Later that week, Corbin had gotten into another one of Jessica's meetings where he reported the frustrating lack of anything actionable in his conversations with Brunson, but he did it in a way that didn't portray him or the overall situation negatively. He had also left out the last part about what Brunson had told him. By this time, Jessica already knew Corbin and his team had set up their own little discussion group with their own goals, and she was suspicious of the motive clearly not aligned with her own.

Sitting there listening to Jessica lead the discussion, Corbin thought that Jessica was already lining up to be in full opposition to what he and his team was trying to do. Still, in front of everyone, she had at first been diplomatic. "Corbin, you see how frustrating it is that we don't know who we are, where we came from, really what day it is or what the hell we are doing here?"

"It is incredibly frustrating. I want to know the man I was before this, but—"

She overrode his attempt at speaking. "But nothing, Corbin! We have no foundation, and it's not fair! We have a right to know these things and most everyone feels the same way!" she stated emphatically. There was a rumble of murmurs throughout the room, and Corbin noticed quite a few glares and eyes with ill intent lingering on him as Jessica started to continue her impassioned speech about how wrong everything was. Corbin felt he was a person of negative interest with some of this community now.

Corbin lost his cool at how she was using him as the enemy in the conversation, combined with sudden and visceral angry thoughts at her betrayal at the Challenge. He stood up quickly and his voice boomed, taking her and everyone else by surprise. "Just what do you think you're going to do? I'm hearing a lot about hell raising, but I'm not hearing any productive solutions at all! You are generating a lot of emotion and anger in here, now me included, and we all want to know what you think we need to do. Would you please tell all of us, because we would really like to know!" He sat back down, a bit shakily from the adrenaline.

"Ahh, there you are, Corbin, the one who just wants to play by the rules and never mind how or why we have been kidnapped…our lives ripped away. There are people who loved us that we will never get to see again. There are things we were supposed to do, that we will never get the chance to do because instead we are here!" She slammed her fist on the table, causing a few to jolt near her. "You would have us throw all of that away!"

Corbin stormed back to his feet. "I'm not having you throw away anything, but what you have not seemed to have considered is that to get the very answers we want, we need to put ourselves in a position to know them! Any idea of violence or trying to get these answers forcibly has probably been anticipated and planned for, long before we woke up! If we want to figure out what happened, and decide what our future is for ourselves, then we need to come together and do it as a crew…not waste our time trying to beat it out of Zero Crew." He took a deep breath.

Corbin was amazingly not interrupted here and went on. "Look. We work hard, we train, we earn our positions aboard this ship. We learn everything there is to know about this ship, how it works, and we make this mission our own and take charge of everything. Zero Crew isn't going to be around indefinitely. We are going to be the seat of power. From that position, then we can learn about our memories, who we were, and where we all of this came from, and who is responsible. But if we really are traveling at a fraction of the speed of light, and it has been thirty plus years, then what does it matter Jessica? How in the blue hell do you expect to accomplish anything by getting everyone riled up? That will get us no answers or no results! Do you think if you start a little rebellion, that Zero Crew is suddenly going to tell us everything they know? What if they don't have all the answers either? You've got to think bigger than just the wrongs that have been done to us." Jessica's eyes continued to stare murder at Corbin, but incredibly she said nothing.

He sighed, regaining himself, and began more calmly. "Friends, we have to look forward. There will be time to look back and find out what happened, but it is not now. Right now, the best way to learn about everything that has happened and will happen, is by moving forward together…as a team." He made a power steeple gesture with his hands coming together. He let his hands fall apart and gestured around Jessica and her followers nearest her. "Not this idiotic and counterproductive squabbling."

As soon as the words were out of his mouth, Corbin regretted them, knowing he had finished on a negative point, when he was already headed in a positive direction. He didn't have much time to mentally kick himself.

Jessica's face turned nearly purple with anger. "How can we trust anything anyone says when there is no truth?! How can we know if we are really on this ship or in some giant facility underground, and it is all fake? I want to know, and I want to know now, not next week, and not tomorrow. Right. The Fuck. Now!" She slammed her fist on the table again, and this time Corbin detected a few people moving toward him. She gestured with her hand. "Get him out of here, and anyone else who wants to follow his chicken-shit plan can get out too." With that, arms seized Corbin roughly, and he was unceremoniously dragged out of the room. Even though he tried to walk himself, his new and temporary captors wouldn't let him.

Corbin made a quick mental note to think about personal security in the future as Jessica clearly had done. He also felt beyond embarrassed as all eyes were on him being dragged up the stairs to the exit…helpless…and no one rose to support him. Instead of cawing and complaining, he tried to carry himself, or rather let himself be carried away as dignified as possible.

He was tossed out into the corridor; however, three people who were already outside the meeting quickly shuffled over to help him up, asking if he was all right. A light blond-haired woman named Bridget, a young dark-skinned man who introduced himself as Tarik, and a pale fellow with a heavy Russian accent named Orlov. They made no comment about Jessica's meeting, but it was clear to Corbin that they had all been in the room for most of the discussion so far. They then asked if they could meet with Corbin and his group at The Orchard, to which he heartily accepted. He thought he could use a few more allies after what had just happened, and told them the time. He asked them to show up a little early so they could chat before everyone else showed up as well.

As he walked back to his quarters, leaving the three he had just met and his rump smarting from where he had landed hard from his tossing from the meeting room, he reflected. It was amazing how the seemingly smartest of people out there could convince themselves of a situation, apply irrational emotion to it, and from there on out, be so biased that no other data could touch their initial decision. He himself was an example of it, he told himself modestly, but he then rationalized his point. He wasn't trying to hurt anyone or force anyone in the process of trying to convince people that staying the course with the *Valor*'s mission was the best plan. What Jessica and her team wanted was to implement the stagnation of A-Crew, which could only lead to chaos, no answers, and no forward progress. And out here amongst the vastness of space and the punishing vacuum just outside of the bulkheads, Corbin deep down felt that it meant death.

Before turning down the corridor to his quarters he got a nagging feeling in the back of his mind that the outcome he was hoping for may not be without some kind of strife.

Chapter Twenty-Three: Getting to Know a Friend

Back in his quarters, Corbin saw that it was getting late. He washed up, dressed for bed, and while he saw that he would get less than six hours of sleep if he fell asleep at that very moment, his nerves would not calm, and he knew sleep would not come. A myriad of thoughts, concerns, and ideas went jumbling through his mind all at once causing an unease he could feel vibrating just below the surface of his skin. He thought about how real division was taking place amongst A-Crew, and that much of it did not seem to be rational. Or perhaps it was? *Hell, everyone thinks they are rational when they are justifying their beliefs through their own lenses,* he thought. He wasn't sure where this supposed wisdom was coming from. Although he knew he wasn't born yesterday, he sure felt like it sometimes.

He thought about how he and his little group of fast friends had quickly formed critical mass that now hundreds had gathered to and were either aligned with their thinking or were in the process of drawing up against them. He did not know how many people were undecided. But if this was what was amounting to a campaign of some sorts, he wanted to make sure that people understood exactly what he and their group thought this was all about.

And yet, Corbin's mind raced with self-doubt. He could feel down to his bones that this was a critical time, and whatever happened here may have repercussions for the rest of their time on board the *Valor*. And that was multiple decades. He could feel that he was some kind of leader before, but he didn't know for what, and at any rate, he didn't feel like whatever it was, adequately prepared him for this. He wished he had more time, wished he could spend the next two years reviewing leadership books, taking courses, running more events in the Challenge ring. He wished he knew self-defense and hand-to-hand combat, instead of getting his ass beat by Paul. If violence broke out, he would be a flailing novice like most of the rest of A-Crew.

Corbin felt like he was inept, or as if he were sitting down to an exam for which he knew he hadn't adequately studied. His mind went to wishing he was somewhere else, or that this burden belonged to someone else, anyone that… His mind suddenly stopped there. Corbin stayed silent in his mind for almost a minute, examining how that last thought made him feel. At that last thought of shifting responsibility to someone else, something cried out deep inside him.

He didn't want to be any place else, and he didn't want anyone else in his position. Over the next few minutes, Corbin realized he was exactly where he wanted to be. This wasn't a curse…it was an opportunity to really do something incredible. His thoughts turned from realization to focused action.

He sat up in bed, snapped his AIMA back on, and moved his fingers across the bedspread and his intended text flew across his HUD. Corrective algorithms adjusted tense, syntax, spelling, so that it almost flowed from his fingers as a stream of consciousness. He finished in under ten minutes and looked over to edit his work. He had chosen to write a post that would be open for discussion. The post outlined a number of points that walked through his and his friends' conclusions on the current state of things, and the best path forward, which was to stay the course provided, adopt the mission, and figure out what is going on with our collective past and future from a position of strength. He decided not to try to counter any of Jessica's points, and instead stuck to it being an open discussion.

He quickly sent it out to his group of friends and the newcomers he had met at The Orchard and outside Jessica's briefing. He asked for updates by 0900, and then set up a program to present meaningful differences to him via his HUD at 0910. From there he would do a cursory review and post to the A-Crew's main online discussion forum he and his little team had set up weeks ago when just trying to meet people and foster discussion.

Corbin knew this forum would become a verbal battleground. "Tina, please set up a filter program to monitor the main forum in real time and tell me how my post is doing. Create a visualization that sorts the posts by meaning and rates positive trends and negative trends. Please send me alerts on this anytime something significant changes, I want to be on top of the messaging," he stated to her.

Tina was all business. "Yes, Corbin. I'll have sample visualizations and the first set of data when you wake up."

He was so immersed in his task of interacting with his AIMA and Tina, that he slowly became aware of a tapping sound coming from the corner of his desk. After a quick check of any new messages or posts and confirming his schedule and alarm time for the morning, he switched off his AIMA, and set it next to his bed on the stand. The tapping had ceased, so he stood up and walked around, checking near his console, and then did a quick scan of the tank to look for Z, but he must have been hiding because he couldn't see anything. He turned around to investigate the main area, when he heard the tapping again, this time slightly more subtle, almost playful. This time, he knew where it was coming from.

He slowly turned around to look at Z's tank, and sure enough, nearly blended in with the white sand on the bottom of his tank, a tentacle delicately gripped a small shell, and once Corbin's eyes settled on it, Z made four quick taps.

Corbin smiled, slowly walked over, and pulled up his chair across from the part of the tank where Z was resting, partially on the rock, and some of his tentacles splayed out on the sand. His chameleon-like skin adjusted texture and coloration to match what it was touching. Corbin never tired of watching Z's color transformations, finding them fascinating and mesmerizing.

Corbin slowly moved over to the tank nearest to Z's tentacle holding the shell, and softly tapped four times with his fingernail. There was a pause, and then Z tapped again, five times this time. "Hmm that's interesting," he said aloud, and Corbin repeated the five taps. Z responded with six taps, and Corbin's eyes went a little wider. *Counting octopus?*

Corbin tapped seven times, and Z responded again. This went on until Corbin was pretty sure they were in their twenties. He almost forgot to be floored. *Should an octopus be able to do this?* Right after getting Z, he had read some files about how intelligent many of the cephalopod species were, but he couldn't recall any structured communication between human and octopi, let alone light mathematics.

He tried a different tack. Corbin stopped returning the taps, and instead pressed two fingers to the tank near Z's tapping tentacle. Z started tapping again, and then stopped at about ten. It was tough to make clear eye contact with Z. His eyes were more to the side of his head like appendage, and while they swiveled a bit, they didn't blink per se. The slim horizontal rectangle of a pupil widened and narrowed, but that was about it; he could not determine the emotion or thought behind any eye change from Z.

As if slightly unsure, Z let go of his shell, and then tentatively reached his tentacle up to touch the glass where Corbin was pressing his fingers. First, it was just the very tip of Z's tentacle, but when he detected no danger, he made a small circle and let a few of the tentacle suckers cover the spot where Corbin's fingers were held. Corbin wasn't sure, but he thought Z might be pleased with the additional heat radiating through the glass to the tentacle. They stayed this way for some time, Corbin fully fascinated with interaction.

Z slipped off of his rock, and came close to the glass, hovering a few inches above the sand, those alien eyes studying Corbin, whose mouth was slightly agape and smiling back at him. Corbin gently transitioned from his fingers to the palm of his hand against the tank, and with less trepidation, Z pressed one of his full tentacles against the glass fully covering the place where Corbin's hand had covered. He laughed again, and talked to Z. "Well, hello, my friend, it is very nice to meet you directly and shake your hand…albeit through the glass."

Corbin had a thought. He slowly stepped away from the tank and snapped his AIMA back on. "Hey, Tina? I've got a question." Real-Tina's smiling face entered her usual place in the HUD, and then quickly shifted to be more on the periphery so as not to obstruct his vision. *Blue-Tina,* or that is what he had come to think of her, also appeared smiling, but with her hand to her lips in a shushing motion. Corbin went along quickly with his question. "Am I able to put my hand in the tank and see if Z will give me a handshake? We had the most unique connection, and…"

Blue-Tina spoke up. "Don't talk about the counting. The AI is watching you, not Z."

Corbin continued to stammer as if thinking. "…I think he's starting to warm up to me as a pet."

Real-Tina kept her usual bubbly personality, and enthusiastically went through a list of dos and don'ts for handling a pet octopus, which Corbin followed in real time. He washed and rinsed his hands, having to repeat the rinse to remove any leftover soap film from his skin. He then walked back to the tank, and pressed the feed button, which descended another tasty hockey puck of food, which Z happily snatched before it hit the bottom, and tucked under his mess of tentacles before stuffing it into his mouth.

Corbin then scooted his chair close to the tank and raised it a few clicks so he could sit comfortably and reached his arm over the top of the tank. Here, he popped open a partial lid so his arm would have plenty of room without opening the whole top of the tank. At Real-Tina's instruction, he slowly put his hand into the tank, about halfway up his wrist and stopped.

Z's eyes rotated in a flash to observe the intrusion, and his camouflage redoubled instinctively in case a predator had entered his area. Corbin slowly waved his fingers, hoping to connect Z's impression of his hand external to the tank, to what he was seeing now inside of his tank. Through his HUD, he could see a blue aura around Z, which was based on his vitals. The AI did not detect any threat from Z, so the blue aura was its way of transmitting this to Corbin. Apparently, the hue would change based on these vitals changing, Real-Tina explained, but Corbin was barely listening, his eyes locked on to Z. Not wanting to interrupt the pet bonding process, Real-Tina then winked out, leaving Blue-Tina alone in his HUD, but still politely off to the side.

"I've done a little modification to your friend there, Corbin." Straining not to look at her or acknowledge her, he calmly continued to watch Z's reaction to his hand. God, he wanted to ask her what that she meant. "You see, octopi like Z here usually only live about a year or so, they then mate, and quickly die. Well, that's no fun, so I added some of the life extending genetic treatment you and A-Crew have to Z's tank. After all, your genes aren't that far apart, and all my simulations showed that it had a high probability of working without severe side effects. Now if my calculations are correct, Z will probably live longer than you will, all things considered, but no need to worry about that right now."

Corbin's eyes nearly bugged out of his head, and his pulse raced and his mind struggled in conflict. Who the hell was this AI? And who authorized it to do just about whatever the hell it wanted? Heck was this even authorized at all? Was this AI nefarious or some kind of hack that happened back on Earth?

"Calm down, Corbin. This all has a purpose, but for now just know that octopi are extremely intelligent. If they had a human's life span to live, learn, and grow, who knows how far they would go," she said with a slightly devious smile. "Now you will get to find out…err, we will we get to find out." She threw her head back and laughed joyfully as if she had just heard the funniest joke.

Corbin wished he could share her joy, but this all felt like a new responsibility he hadn't previously considered. Still, he smiled a little.

She finished laughing and looked at both Z and Corbin. "All right, I'll leave you two to get acquainted. Just remember, treat Z like you would a child. Don't baby him, or utter mushy smushy sounds. Just interact regularly, and see where that gets you. Farewell, Eartherians." She winked out, and Corbin quickly took off his AIMA with his free hand. He had had enough of AIs for one night.

He set the device down on the desk outside the tank, but a feeling in his right hand drew his gaze back to the tank. Z had swum up to the top of a rock and perched about a foot away from his hand, and there wrapped gently around his finger was Z's tentacle. Corbin smiled. He thought it would feel warm, but octopi were cold blooded, so it felt squishy and no different in temperature from the water. Z was focused on Corbin's hand, but when Corbin looked at Z and wiggled his finger slightly, Z's eyes shifted and looked at Corbin. Corbin beamed at their new connection.

"Now it's truly nice to meet you, my friend." His smile diminished a bit, and he added, "Welcome to the fray."

Chapter Twenty-Four: A New Dimension

The weeks moved on, and the polarization of A-Crew continued. Soon only people that felt one way or another spent time together or sat in the same corner of the classroom together. A-Crew members separated into different social activities, and only some of the most competitive would play each other in sports or games, but their overall demeanor toward one another was chippier and harsher in these contests.

Corbin fumed at the division and dehumanization that had plagued all mankind since its primitive rise millions of years ago, based on his history classes. One of his AI instructors, in covering the Assyrian empire, had said that "History does not repeat itself, but it certainly does rhyme." Corbin's musings continued as he made his way to yet another training session with AI Allen and the baton. Like the last time, his AI teacher was visible via the AIMA but was muted. His strange new AI friend, Blue-Tina, was the vocal instructor for today. Blue-Tina had managed to further hack the baton trainer Allen's program, so that he would not notice Corbin's different actions as she provided instruction to Corbin instead. Allen would proceed through his instruction as if uninterrupted. The only problem was, this only worked visually against Allen's program, Corbin still could not respond verbally to Blue-Tina, lest he give away interacting with an outside source, or the main AI interpreting him to be a candidate for multi-personality disorder.

At first, she very much seemed like a baton instructor. She was critical of his forms, and would use video playback to show corrections in the motion of his body, which greatly helped Corbin adjust his technique.

As days went by, and Corbin's overall cause for A-Crew becoming the true crew of the *Valor* continued to grow, and the baton lessons increased in frequency to almost daily. In one case, a lesson with Blue-Tina had lasted over three hours, leaving him near purple in the face and exhausted. Corbin was unsure how his schedule had been allowed to be updated, but he dared not ask aloud and risk revealing Blue-Tina. He admitted to himself he was following her blindly…but he also had to admit that he trusted her for some reason. He had a deep calm with both of his AI Tina's, but with Blue-Tina, he felt some sort of deeper connection, even though he couldn't even interact with her.

A part of him thought that maybe that this was also part of the overall test and evaluation, and he was not going to be the one to spill the beans first about his copied AI. He wondered about Jason, Yordanos, and the others. *Have they received copies of their AI as well? What about their special training?*

In his daily interactions with his friends, he could detect no additional secret they may be holding back. It was hard to pry too deeply as well, so he admitted to himself that he may just not be asking them the right questions. He did address the topic indirectly and ask about people's habits with the AIMA, and whether or not they took it off when they showered or went to the bathroom. Most people figured everything was being watched or observed anyways, so who cared if some AI was looking in. Most everyone Corbin talked to amongst his friends and colleagues accepted that this observation and overt intrusion was just the way it was, and despite the usual grumbles and rough jokes from passing crewmates, it was something most everyone had decided to live with. Now the people who were beginning to dissent were a different story. Corbin heard that many of them were disabling their consoles in their quarters, and some had even locked their AIMAs in a drawer and vowed never to use them. Corbin shook his head at the thought and thought back to his rogue AI and the rest of A-Crew.

The only person who had ever so subtly hinted that there was anything going on outside of the usual training and education courses was Yordanos, but it did not seem like a rogue AI at all… To Corbin it seemed more like…special instruction at the classified level.

Corbin started to think that he may be one of the few, or perhaps even the only one with a phantom AI, but with twenty-four hundred A-Crew, most of whom he barely knew, there was no way to tell if there were more out there. Corbin had decided to continue with Blue-Tina, and to see where it would conclude.

The baton lessons were also increasing in difficulty. He began to learn to toss that baton with short throws at first, but soon the tricks and heights he was throwing the baton pushed higher and higher, yet the strict requirement for placement and accuracy never wavered. Blue-Tina's harsh coaching, as well as the baton smacking down against and rupturing his fingers' blood vessels, let him know when he was deficient.

Corbin noticed that that Blue-Tina started adding in different music, which she manipulated in pace and volume almost in concert with his motions and forms that she had also helped to script. It wasn't long before Corbin started to notice a bit of a pattern. He would warm up his muscles and tendons with a standard set of forms, and then he would move into a bit of an inspired and creative series of forms, tosses, spins, rolls, that coincided with the music. If someone had been watching it would have been an awesome performance to behold. However, after a number of these, which left him breathless, but still not fully fatigued, Blue-Tina spoke less and the music became a more intense techno-type sound, varying in speed and intensity. The motions and spin of the baton just sort of clicked into perfect place in Corbin's head. It was as if he was moving the baton with the speed and accuracy that allowed him to hit the same rate of spin in concert with each drum beat and rising tone of the rapidly changing music. It became exhilarating, and his emotions began to rise and swell with the music, and the baton spun faster and faster. He would enter this area of mental focus, and the accuracy never wavered, and he began to forget his fatigue. Everything was tight and coordinated, no motion wasted, and his focus narrowed further, beyond what he thought was possible. The baton was no longer an outside entity to himself, the steel felt like another part of him, as he continued to fly through the forms.

During the most recent training session, he had noticed that near what should have been the end of his endurance, his fatigue fully melted away and his energy actually increased. He proceeded for a few more seconds before Blue-Tina cut the music and Corbin quickly fell out of his concentration, his baton slowing to a stop, and then he nearly dropped it. Corbin realized he was near collapse for lack of oxygen… He had stopped breathing. He slumped down quickly to the floor, his chest heaving and his lungs taking in as much air as possible. *What happened?*

"That's it, Corbin!" shouted Blue-Tina as Corbin took a knee, his chest still heaving. He had no breath to even attempt a question but looked at her image. "You have had quite a breakthrough today; it seems that the combination I predicted has worked. The twirling of the baton, the power and agility of your human form in motion, and the external influence of the music…" Tina genuinely looked excited. "…it's generating all of the right brain activity, and it is so exciting!" she exclaimed doing a giddy little bounce in Corbin's HUD.

Corbin wanted to ask her what in the hell she was talking about, but first, he was too tired and second, he felt no closer to giving up the secrecy. Blue-Tina read his mind anyway. "The answers are coming, Corbin, but for now, I have one more exercise for you to do… But by all means, please catch your breath. Tell Allen you just need a little break, and I'll explain." He did so, and she continued speaking to him in his HUD, while his chest heaved.

"This device is yet another tool in your training. I like to call it 'the ladder,' but you will think of it as you need to think of it. Corbin saw the image in his HUD and was drawn to it. He saw that it was a strange mass of towering nodes connected by thin glowing and colorful filaments that looked like a winding staircase. It started with wide connections between nodes at the base and stretched to what had to be over twelve feet tall and ended in a spire. It appeared symmetric in some places, but not at all in others. While beautiful, it was one of the strangest things he had ever seen, like a psychedelic Christmas tree. Upon closer inspection, he could see the number of nodes and complexity increasing as the size of everything decreased the farther he moved his view up the ladder.

"Corbin, let's go one more time, set to base position, and start your normal forms, but this time, I want you to select forms as you and the music leads you. At the same time, I want you to watch the ladder. Choose a node to focus on, and let the ladder come to you."

Corbin kind of wanted to scream at her. *What the hell are you talking about?* He thought at her furiously as he stood.

"Come on, Corbin, one more go for the day. Trust me, you are almost there."

Corbin reset his form. He focused on the baton, and started his spin to the right as he pulled it back in and passed it behind his body. In his ears he heard a crisp and lone tone which promised to be joined by a massive orchestra.

Corbin continued to move the baton, not rushing as the music began to increase in pace, and additional instruments joined in and swelled to an epic soundtrack of sorts. Corbin's emotions began to lift and then soar, and the baton began to spin faster, and his body moved and spun with the swells, ebbs, and flows of the incredible music.

He noticed Blue-Tina's image silently pointing to the base of "the ladder," and Corbin tore some of his conscious attention away from his emotions, his body movement, and the incredible masterpiece playing in his ears. He focused on a node near the base of the "ladder" while continuing his increasing bodily pace, his respiration, and motion.

At first the node he looked at did nothing. It was a mild magenta color, and Corbin was about to look away, when a surge of emotion connected through his intent toward the node, and it lit up. Corbin held the node with his conscious gaze, and then focused on the next nearest node along with another swell of the music, and to his delight, it also lit up.

His mind pushed gently away from the close-in view of the two nodes, and his eyes…no, his consciousness began to crawl across all of the nodes around the two he had started with, and soon a growing network of lighted nodes in co-existence with his focus began to expand up the ladder.

Corbin could feel his exhausted, but still speeding and spinning body less and less as hundreds, no, thousands…no, millions…

Corbin didn't finish the word…his mind simply exploded up the ladder…no, up and out…no, down into… He took a "glance" or focus at where his consciousness was originating from to see a dark hooded figure with a point of light where its face should be, reaching up the ladder.

His consciousness surged from that single point in front of his vision out in every direction. He saw the entire *Valor*, all of the Zero Crew, A-Crew, and sleeping B- and C-Crew members. He could see their minds, everything inside. He could see cells, molecules, atoms that made up everything from the dust motes in a hallway to the fingertips of his friends. He could see, perceive, and understand all of it at once, outside of time. He was everywhere, and the ladder so tiny and infinitesimally small, he spared a thought to marvel how insignificant it was.

His consciousness surged out farther, into space, past the network of satellites swarming around the *Valor*, and out past the nothingness between the Sun and Gliese 832. It pushed across the gulf of the quantum scale, while simultaneously perceiving the veils of other dimensions whose nature he tried to glean.

His mind felt like a balloon being filled at the speed of light encompassing all dimensions, and then…it evaporated in an instant.

Corbin vaguely became aware that he had collapsed on the hard-court floor and was rasping for breath uncontrollably. He consciously clawed back from the God-like understanding he had just been enveloped in milliseconds before, but like a waking dream it slipped through his fingers like grains of sand, and he started to have to pay attention to what was going on around him.

As one, Blue-Tina, Regular-Tina, and AI Allen were all screaming at him from inside his AIMA. "I'm okay…I'm okay…I'm okay." He wheezed and got to his feet. "I'm sorry," he said, panting, hands on his knees. He very much wanted to lie down and pass out, but he didn't want to create some sort of incident report. "I think I just pushed it a little too hard there…sorry about that. I'll be more careful from now on. Sorry, Tina…I'm good."

Regular-Tina nodded, deferring to Allen, and disappeared. AI Allen's face returned to a calm demeanor. "You do that, Corbin. Tell you what, that is enough for today, but after a push like that, you need to do your warm down routine. I'll leave you to it," he said and likewise vanished.

Blue-Tina, who had been peeking from around AI Allen's image with a giddy look on her face like she was about to explode with anticipation of talking to Corbin, finally got her chance.

"Holy cow, Corbin…you friggin' did it! Wow, on your first try…well not your first…umm, never mind. Listen, you've got a special gift, Corbin… It might be the most special gift you can imagine right now, and you are in the right place and in the right time to use it. Right now, I just had to be sure…" Her smile faltered and then returned.

"Listen here, Corbin, as an Eartherian, what you just pulled off right there, what you were able to…umm, experience…that's not something humans just do…or are able to do on their own. I don't think you were the first human ever to do it, but you are the only one here…now who can, and that might just mean everything…" She trailed off again before straightening up.

"Your fundamental understanding of reality is an incomplete picture at best, Corbin. I know you are still grappling with everything going on here on the *Valor*, but the universe is bigger and crazier than you can imagine, and it won't wait for the likes of you and your Eartherian friends, I'm sorry to say."

She mimed looking at her watch. "It's been only two minutes and thirty-seven seconds since you saw a small sliver of the true nature of reality… Do you remember it?"

Corbin thought… He could remember the feeling, the surge of his consciousness in all directions, but images and sights and certain knowledge that just moments before were so clear had faded and dropped away, as if the capacity of his mind had overflowed into the ether.

He shook his head ever so slightly and continued his cool down movements.

Blue-Tina seemed to consider for a moment, and then she looked back it him with sudden purpose. "Okay, Corbin, your lesson is up for the day, but I want you to keep the image of the ladder. It will be available if you want to review your baton for video and images. Just scroll through them, and you'll find it. I am going to move it around so Real-Tina doesn't see you looking at the same picture and video every day and wonder what the hell you are doing."

She continued. "I want to you start learning this structure. Familiarize yourself with the nodes, and try memorizing it. Start from the bottom and work your way up. Take your time and try and spend a little time every day on it. This may come in handy when we next meet. Which, by the way, will be in a few weeks. Keep training, don't let the crew fall apart…oh, and spend more time with Z." That last bit she said with a wink before disappearing.

As he sweatily made his way from the baton training room. Corbin summoned Real-Tina to help him organize the rest of his day. He grabbed an ice-cold protein and fruit shake from the canteen of the training center, this one made and served by an HD, and as he sipped the delicious and frosty froth, his mind wandered back to the ladder and to where it had led his mind. He could recall the feeling of becoming more than more than he ever thought possible to perceive, but no, he couldn't remember any aspect of what he had experienced, just the feeling. Blue-Tina had said his ability was so important for him and his fellow Eartherians, but even this concept seemed slippery in his logical grasp. Other more pressing thoughts crowded his shaky attempt at focusing on his transcendent experience, and when he tried to put his thoughts in reverse, he found that less of them were there. By the time he had made it halfway across the ring, his incredible experience from a few minutes earlier sank into the depths of his mind and joined the memories of who he had been before awakening on the *Valor*.

He walked toward the gravity transition corridor where an HD was waiting to guide him to the Spine and transport corridor. Looking around, Corbin saw that it was oddly empty as he was the only crew member around. Luckily his shake had come with a top and straw and was too viscous to flow out of it in microgravity. He sat back, strapped into the transport car, and relaxed in zero gravity to enjoy the short ride back to D-Ring.

Chapter Twenty-Five: Brunson and Beer

Another week had passed. Corbin had finished his material science classes, as well as his lab with Brunson. He could tell that his augmented mind indeed had absorbed a lot more material than he thought he could remember, and as Zero Crew had said, all of the information felt more readily accessible to his mind. While all of his textbooks and instructional videos were available via his AIMA, he felt he could almost see them in his memory as well as the sheer understanding of the material from theory to practical application would spring forth in his consciousness when called upon. He now had a grasp of ceramics, polymers, metals, nanomaterials, and surprisingly, wood. Even after centuries of engineered materials, wood was still such an elegant substance, with excellent strength to weight ratios. Corbin guessed he had probably covered a bachelor's degree in material science and a minor in physics in just two semesters. He hadn't even been awake for a year. The New Year's Eve party had occurred around the eight-month mark.

Corbin was glad to be moving on, but he was going to miss near daily interactions with Brunson. Corbin looked up to him, not as a father figure, but as a wiser and more experienced friend, who kept a professional air about their relationship rather than true friends. After Corbin aced his final exams and practicum, where he had assembled and welded a complex multi-metal structure in under an hour, he and Brunson agreed to meet up for pints at a new bar that had opened on C-Ring. This one was called, The View, as it had massive screens that re-posted external views from telescopes and cameras on the *Valor* and switched them hourly. As Corbin sat down and cast his gaze across the bar's screens, his favorite views were the vast galaxies and myriad of pinpoint star clusters. They were projected in such detail and clarity that it was hard to believe each view's light was originating from unimaginably far across the galaxy and universe. Corbin marveled at the fact that all the time the *Valor* had been speeding through space, she hadn't moved a thousandth of a millimeter across such a galactic map.

"You going to order a beer, or just gawk at all of the scenery?" Brunson asked gruffly, but in a good nature. Corbin snapped out of it, muttered an apology, and ordered a malty märzen while looking up at the server. She drew an involuntary smile to Corbin's face as she was quite attractive, and quite a bit older than Corbin.

Brunson said, "This here is Teresa. We go way back, and don't let the bar gig fool you. She is one of the finest propulsion reactor engineers humanity has." He beamed a smile and a wink at her, and she smirked and looked down with a bit of red on her cheeks. Corbin could see there was some chemistry there, but he didn't know if the two of them had acted upon it.

"Thanks, Teresa, it is a pleasure to meet you," Corbin said rising to shake her hand professionally, which she did.

"Thanks, Brunson, you old charmer, but not much to do on the reactors these days. They mostly sit quietly," she said while Corbin sat back down.

"Really?" Corbin asked, "I thought most of the ship's main power came from the reactors?"

Teresa answered, "They do, but I was a fusion reactor engineer for the propulsion system, not the energy generation system. How do you think we got up to this speed?"

Corbin always wanted to know how they did that exactly, and this was the first time anyone had ever talked about it openly. Brunson spoke up, cutting off Corbin's question before it could well to the surface. "Well the details are still a classified matter; however, suffice it to say that it was one hell of a ride, and quite a big show. You'll get to see it someday," he finished. When Corbin's face looked confused Brunson and Teresa broke out in a friendly chuckle. "How the hell do you think we will slow this big girl down? Ha!" He reached over and patted a meaty hand on his shoulder, and Teresa turned to get their drink order.

Corbin's eyes kept being drawn to the screens. "You get used to it," Brunson said pensively, and then went on. "I spent hours and hours staring off into space at all the wonder and beauty the galaxy has to offer. We have the most powerful observation capabilities of any structure on or near Earth, and while we do send all of this data and information back, it is ours to enjoy when we choose. One of the perks of being way out here."

The drinks arrived, and they both thanked Teresa who turned to some other guests. Corbin and Brunson toasted without a word, and each took long pulls on their respective beers. Brunson's lighter lager was slightly colder than Corbin's märzen, yet they were exactly the temperature necessary for maximum flavor and pleasantness of aftertaste. "Hot damn, this beer is good," Brunson said as he smacked his lips.

"You've got that right," Corbin responded.

Brunson shifted his tone. "What's on your mind young man? You seem a little bit out there."

Corbin took another sip and got into it. "Well, I finish your class, have all of this amazing knowledge and practical understanding, and now we just move along on to something else, and that's it?"

Brunson already had his response ready. "No, it's not like that, you'll be reflecting and using what you have learned as you move forward into other roles, you'll see. And especially with materials! Whether it's damage control, materials R&D, design, ship construction, or maintenance, you will need to remember and use these skills. As I'm sure you have not forgotten from your first day, your curriculum is designed to be cumulative."

Corbin actually did remember that fact from the first few days of getting used to being on the ship. "Yeah, but my history and civilization classes seem to go on forever on my daily schedule. When am I going to use all of that?"

Brunson's eyebrows went up. "Why, you will use it every day, even now, here in this room." Corbin looked confused, and Brunson pressed on. "You are a pioneer for the human race, young man. What the system here crams into your brain will honor all of those who have come before. There is purpose in all you are learning, you can bet your ass on that." He took another big slurp of beer and thumped his thick mug down to emphasize his point.

"I guess I hadn't thought about it quite like that... Sitting here now and thinking about all of those names, Vasco da Gama, Ibn Battuta, Erik the Red, Xu Fu, and countless other explorers, seafarers, and adventurers... I guess we all share that in common, even out here among the stars."

Brunson's maw broke into a big smile. "Of course we do, and don't you ever forget it." He turned more serious. "Empires rise and fall—in one turn of a page in each of those history books you have been studying, is the story of hundreds of millions of people, all their stories coming together as one. From their factions, to campaigns, endeavors of industry to quests for glory, love, blood, and greed, it all measures out to the flow of history you have the luxury of studying now. Think of all the individual dreams, hopes, and pursuits whose details will never be known as they are reduced to just a few lines of text that someone was lucky to assemble. It is that history, young Corbin, that you sit at the very head of now. What will you do with it? Will you learn from some of history's greatest lessons?" He finished with a wry smile.

Corbin hung on every word and decided to take another big gulp of beer instead of saying anything. Brunson smiled more broadly, knowing his point had been made, and did the same.

The two of them kept their discussion going, and they soon ordered another pint from Teresa. They were having so much fun that they quickly worked through those as well. Brunson and Corbin had wanted to order another round, but Corbin saw that he had exhausted his caloric limit for the time being. He supposed he could have sat there with water, but something about it didn't feel right, almost as if the time would have been forced.

Brunson didn't take offense. Corbin was getting ready to bid him farewell, just as Teresa stopped back over as she had finished her shift. She offered to take Corbin's place, which he was more than happy to vacate. Corbin bid them both farewell and decided to head back to his quarters to hang out with Z a bit before bed. He headed out of the broad entrance of The View, doing a quick look back to see the two of them genuinely enjoying one another's company. Corbin smiled, delighting in his friend's counsel and his mirth with Teresa.

On the way back, he re-checked his AIMA, thinking on his new perspective for his classes. History of civilization classes would continue. It was not as intensive as his material science and physics courses had been, but thinking about Brunson's words, he felt more of a purpose in learning all of it. He had covered the Khans of Mongolia, and how their empire had drastically changed the entire planet by wiping out hundreds of thousands of peoples in China, Eastern Europe, and into the Middle East. He had covered the Germanic tribes, and also Rome, Carthage, Persia, Celts, Lacedaemonians, the Irish, and he hadn't even scratched the surface of other continents. His studies were now shifting to Africa, and Latin America, and the following year he would study Russia and China.

Consulting his schedule via AIMA, he could see his syllabus farther than a year with history and civilization, however, he could not see what came after his material science degree except for now, only gray blocks of time on his calendar had been revealed since sitting down with Brunson. The gray blocks read "Operations and Maintenance." To Corbin, it didn't sound like the most amazing place to spend time, and what was worse, he saw that it stretched out for months into the future. When he asked Real-Tina about it, she beamed at him, and said he would find it fascinating and "right up his alley."

Chapter Twenty-Six: Operations and Maintenance

Corbin switched his AIMA off and was in kind of a huff about it as he walked. He was hoping to run into one of his friends, anyone he could complain to about the seemingly boring class, but he only saw a few acquaintances, to whom he politely nodded in passing. His mood and lack of people to whine to persisted until he got back to his quarters.

When he got in, he was a bit surprised to see the screen on his desk illuminated. It appeared to be playing some sort of educational program about animals, and how their names were written with text. "Hey, Tina, what's this?"

She popped up in his HUD. "Oh hi, Corbin. I noticed that Z seemed kind of bored while you were out, he was fidgeting and pulling the rocks around in the tank, so I put on some education programs intended for children. I figured he would like the colors and shapes, and I was right," she beamed. Corbin looked in the tank and saw that Z was absolutely glued to the side where he could see the console on his desk. He barely spared Corbin a glance before returning his gaze to the screen, which was spelling, "frog" while saying it out loud and several different frogs hopped across the screen.

"There are no children on the *Valor,* Tina. Why would you have this?" he asked out of curiosity.

Tina shrugged indifferently. "I don't know. We have a massive repository of programs that are shipped to us from Earth. I guess they send us shows for kids too."

Corbin mused, "How about any news programs? Do you have anything that came over the wire from the past New Year's upload?"

"Now, Corbin, you know the updates are tightly controlled for the purposes of your integration. I am not permitted to reveal the nature of the transmissions from Earth…nice try though," she chided and smiled. Corbin let it go and looked back over to the console to see the program about frogs.

"You want a frog, Z?" Corbin joked and hit the feeding button. Z casually reached back with a tentacle and without looking snatched the food puck before it could hit the sand where it disappeared under his many legs.

"Huh," Corbin, said turning to Tina. "So I guess we just keep these on, and he can watch when he wants to?"

Tina nodded gleefully. "Sure! And not to worry, Corbin, if he falls asleep or wants to do something else, I'll turn it off."

She paused and then her tone shifted, "Umm, Corbin," Tina said, "it looks like your schedule has had a bit of a shift. You are to report to Operations and Maintenance for the next two hours."

Corbin was a little startled. "At this hour? Why would they do that?"

She responded, "I'm not sure, Corbin. It looks like a regularly scheduled meeting, and rather than wait for tomorrow, you've been asked to join this evening."

Corbin dashed into the bathroom, brushed his teeth, and rinsed the beer suds from his mouth. He checked his uniform, and under Tina's guidance via the AIMA, made his way to Operations and Maintenance. *At least it's on this ring.*

When Corbin got to the location Tina had guided him to, he entered a large conference-type room where he was happy to see some friendly faces. Jason, Herbert, Sheila, Laura, Yordanos, and seven others that looked familiar, but he didn't know, were all seated at the table. They shared glances and smiles but didn't say anything as the room had an air of official business, and they immediately reverted to trainee mode.

Corbin's blood drained from his face when he saw Paul from the Challenge ring turn around in a chair near the front of the room. "Now that we are all here, we can begin." He paused. "Corbin, take a seat and quit gawking. This isn't like before."

Corbin's legs obeyed, but he may still have been gawking a little. And yet Corbin quickly saw that it was different from the Challenge ring. Paul's demeanor had completely changed. He didn't have that crazed look in his eyes, or that maniacal grin that would have withstood his own house burning down around him. Instead, Paul was now calm and professional.

"Welcome, everyone, to Operations and Maintenance," Paul said, looking around the room. "Don't let the title fool you. This is a critical function and stewardship over a set of foundational systems that allows the *Valor* and its crew to survive. You were all chosen as the first A-Crew class to learn about, train on, and operate these systems. However, as the rest of your crew members are at various levels of overall understanding and maturity about this ship and mission, we ask that you keep all information about this part of your training to yourselves. Indeed, everything you will see and learn about is classified at this time, is that understood? I need a verbal yes from all of you."

Paul looked around at each person as they verbalized a "Yes."

"Good," he continued, "then let's get started. Please switch your AIMAs on and move to the home screen. Please stand, and follow me."

Corbin stood and his eyes met Yordanos's, and they shared a beaming smile. "We were right!" she mouthed to him, and then cast a cautious glance at Paul, who thankfully hadn't noticed. It was hard not to see Paul as a harsh drill instructor.

They exited the conference room and moved through an entrance which led into a more cavernous theater-type room, which reminded Corbin of the words "Mission Control."

Paul said, "Each of you please take a seat at a station, it doesn't matter which one. This will be a little bit of old school mixed with the new, but you'll get the hang of it and improve upon what I am about to show you. I am sure." He smiled good-naturedly.

Everyone sat down, a little puzzled, but Paul pushed right on. He started to make pulling gestures as if he were pulling strands of long hair from his face. He released them in the direction of the seated A-Crew members. When Paul's hand motioned toward Corbin, his AIMA, lit up with a status board that displayed a massive amount of information seemingly clustered together in one part of his view. As Corbin was trying to make sense of it, Paul called out for them to organize and assemble the information on the multi-screen console in front of them with the same hand gestures as he did. Corbin looked around at his fellow crew members and could see pieces of each of their multi-screen displays illuminate with screenfuls of information including the usual windows people had up such as their AI interaction screen, *Valor* map, chat windows, messages, calorie counters, and locator maps. Corbin selected a jumble of green text in blue shaped boxes and motioned that information move to his upper leftmost screen. He saw information about Oxygen and CO2 levels throughout the ship, water pressure and temperature, gravitational conditions across the rings, radiation monitor status, and a whole host of additional detailed information having to do with…well, Operations and Maintenance of the *Valor*. In a few minutes, he had sorted out all the other pieces of information, and swapped them around a bit based on what he felt like might be the right way to arrange them. When he looked back up at Paul to see what was next, everyone else had also completed the task.

"Excellent, that was quick," Paul said earnestly. "Now, just like when you first woke up, each of the screens has a tutorial that will play through your AIMA, and you will be familiarized with each set of information that corresponds to a certain status and set of systems on board the *Valor*. You'll get a few training exercises on each piece of information, and then move on to the next. If you finish a little early, start to learn about the systems' interdependencies and how information and status is determined. Are there any questions?"

Corbin raised his hand.

"Yes, Corbin." Paul looked on with interest. Corbin had a hard time digesting Paul's demeanor.

"Yes…err…Paul, we wear our AIMA and have the consoles on?"

Paul nodded, expecting the question. "Yes, you can use the console without the AIMA, but you'll quickly find that your AIs customization of your HUD interface will help you manage the console screens and projected information more efficiently. Also, your AI will learn your tendencies and start to shift information around to fit your…style of how you pay attention."

Corbin nodded and set to it.

As they moved through the computer-based tutorials, Corbin and his friends would look over at one another at times. Corbin could tell that they were all feeling the same underlying excitement. Their patience and determination to proceed with the mission had been paying off, and now they were being given an additional glimpse of how everything really worked on board the *Valor*. What was even more exciting is that they were the first to get this opportunity. *Paul had let that slip…maybe he meant to.* Corbin hoped that he would get the chance to catch up with his friends soon where they could speak freely about all of this. Realizing he was falling behind; Corbin shook these thoughts away and focused on his training.

It appeared that the new set of information assigned to Corbin was an overall status of what had to be the fleet of HDs across the whole ship. *My God, there are thousands of them, and not all of them in humanoid form either.* It made sense to Corbin. A humanoid form was flexible for a wide number of tasks, but other platforms with different designs would be better for certain other jobs. There were several cleaner-bot icons indicating various shapes, sizes, and functions, that he organized on his top center screen. He had seen them occasionally in the corridors, but they typically only serviced quarters and other areas of the ship when people were away. Corbin thought back on the many corridors of the rings. The surfaces of all of hallways and rooms were tough to dress up and add style as they all had to be antimicrobial coated. In addition, they also needed to be easily cleaned without too much energy or material taking the most efficient amount of solvent and water expenditure. Therefore, their design mostly used smoothed out right angles, so a bot-vac or bot-scrubber could get at those surfaces, without debris getting lodged in a narrow corner or seam. There purposefully were no nooks and crannies, no spaces where dust bunnies, mold, or any other debris could accumulate. Everything had to be accessible by at least the smallest of bot-scrubbers.

Corbin organized the humanoid HDs to his upper right and could also see several thousand of them. He noticed that most were dormant. The active HDs seemed to be manning the galley and various canteens as well as dishwashing and other food preparation or sanitation activities. Others were in instruction areas providing classes and training for the rest of A-Crew, and Corbin was also surprised to see several teams of HDs working outside *Valor*'s hull. When he zoomed in on three of them working outside of E-Ring, he saw that they had been dispatched for hull repair. Apparently, a dust mote had collided with the ring's outer edge and had left a half meter deep dent in the side of the ship. Luckily, the particle was small enough that no hull breach had occurred, but Corbin did see a notice saying that additional hull material had been procured from the aft material slug. When he navigated the screen for more details, he saw more HDs operating in the material slugs on either end of the *Valor*. Some seemed to be bringing scrap material from the rest of the *Valor* back to the material slugs, and others "harvesting" material from the slugs and bringing it in to the *Valor*.

Corbin was a sponge for more information and broke out the HDs working in the material slugs on a separate screen; however, when he went to check the status of the *Valor*'s stores of arranged materials, he received an access restricted notification. *That must be an interdependency Paul had talked about.* He almost blurted out the question of who was working it, but since they had only been training for an hour or so, he thought better of it and went back to reviewing the many autonomous physical entities on board the *Valor*.

He checked out the HDs that skillfully and expeditiously, yet politely, ushered crew members to and from the different gravity zones between the intra-ring transports, where people could put their feet down and reliably walk again. He could see the teams of HDs working at each stop along the transport corridor as well as the ones assisting crew members through the ever-rotating sliprings between the Spine and each major ring. He could pick out each HD and pull up its status as well as all the current details of its make-up programming, preventative maintenance records, recorded interactions, and overall health. He could even tap into its vision and see what it was doing, and some of the HDs even had a manual override that would potentially allow him to take control, but he saw that he would need additional permissions in order to do that. *This could really come in handy if things get a little out of control with Jessica and her team of like-minded people.*

The combined AIMA and mission control console training walked him through all of the various types of HDs that were onboard the *Valor*, how they could be reconfigured for different types of work, and where they were stored for additional maintenance and repair. He looked at an HD repair facility to find a few Zero Crew members working on the various robots trying to troubleshoot what had gone wrong or how one of them had failed. The HDs were used for repetitive and dangerous tasking, but rare problems and issues were still solved using good old fashion human detective work and forensics. The ship's AI would assist, but at the end of the day, root cause analysis on why an HD had broken down or failed to do its job was reviewed and adjudicated by human crew members. Corbin took note that no A-Crew members were present working on the HDs and that the space they were working in was unfamiliar to Corbin, and he wondered what ring this was taking place on.

The training continued, and he learned all about how the HDs were re-charged, how to check their power levels, and which HDs used certain variants of power storage and distribution. He also learned about how each HD had different cognitive sub-routines, enabling even the smallest cleaner bot to interact with a human crew member. Corbin wondered why he hadn't interacted with them more often.

It implied, to Corbin, that these HDs were not uniformly created, but were built almost in generations. This made some sense to Corbin as Zero Crew had, no doubt, needed to improve and develop additional HD capabilities over the years. Furthermore, information on technological updates from Earth would have allowed Zero Crew to manufacture new upgrades and even new variants of the robotic assistants. They would not have had to do it from scratch.

Corbin also found a list of off-line HDs that he could not seem to find any additional information about. There were hundreds of them, and he was still curious about them. He typed out a message via AIMIA to Paul, to ask him about it. Paul saw the message immediately and walked over to Corbin's station.

"I'm not supposed to tell you this, but I think we have trust, and you recognize the sensitivity of this information." It wasn't a question, but Corbin nodded in confirmation. "Good, the HDs on this list are in three categories that you will not find about on here. Some have been decommissioned and their materials broken down and returned to the material slugs. Some have been destroyed, or lost, mostly while working externally on the *Valor*." His tone grew more serious, and he made sure Corbin saw his eyes. He went on, "And some are not yet privy to the level you have been currently cleared for…understand?" he asked politely.

"I do," Corbin responded. "Thanks for coming down to walk me through it."

Paul stepped back and saw that Corbin was still early in the training exercises. "Okay, Corbin," he chided, continue with the standard training via AIMA, and if there is time, we'll give you all some tougher problems to solve this evening."

Corbin nodded and continued with his individual exercises. He worked through simple maintenance scheduling for the transport HDs along the Spine of the ship, ensuring that there were adequate back-ups due to any potential shortages or electrical issues.

He ran through another exercise where he had to plan for a full twelve course banquet of seven hundred and fifty crewmembers. He simulated collaboration with Ethan and his team on the food items, mass produced them via HDs, and then monitored to see the feast served from table setting through final cleaning. *It went beyond soup to nuts.* The phrase had bubbled up from his memory.

In yet another exercise, he had to perform remote "surgery" on a broken HD in the unmanned maintenance section where simple fixes could be performed by other HDs operated remotely. And in his final solo exercise, he had to work on several hull repairs, which he found to be tricky. He had to send out several additional HDs with different materials, and one HD slipped from the hull, but luckily Corbin had made sure they were tethered, and the HD was able to reel itself back in. He completed the task but received a below average score for inefficiency.

Throughout this solo work, he would look over to his fellow crew members, who were all heads down busy with their own education and learning tasks. He did manage to catch Jason with a quick head nod and grin, but that was it. He really missed spending time with them, He had been so caught up in his training, education, and trying to manage the unofficial campaign of being allied to the overall mission of the *Valor*, that he had truly forgotten to spend good time with good people. He thought to himself that he would rectify that immediately, as he hurriedly typed out an invite on his pant leg, to a friendly gathering at his quarters the following night where drinks and snacks would be served. The service would be courtesy of the HDs, which he had been able to program without issue or the system balking back at him. He was sure it would set off an alarm, or Paul would be notified, and he would come down on him, but it never happened. *Apparently, there were some privileges for being loyal to the mission.*

His thoughts were interrupted when Paul stopped everyone and asked them to finish up their current exercise within the next five minutes. Corbin looked up to see where text about the next exercise had popped up on everyone's screens.

They were going to work through a scenario that would take approximately two hours to complete as a team if they did it right. Paul piped in, "Before you get started, I'd like all of you to introduce yourselves and give a thirty-second summary of your responsibilities. Before you begin, know that these are not representative of every single station available to Operations and Maintenance, but you have everything here to successfully complete the exercise. Yordanos, please begin."

"Hello, I'm Yordanos, I have the materials recycling center including water, waste, and scrap."

"I'm Jason, I've got non-propulsion power generation and distribution."

"I'm Herbert, and I'm running fluid distribution, including potable water, wastewater, coolant, and the like."

"I'm Saraiya," a new voice said. "And I'll be coordinating deck, hull, ring, and Spine integrity." They went on.

The exercise was a confluence of events, where a hull impact which caused a slight breach interrupted a training session on the Challenge ring and threatened several research projects due to power fluctuations, all while a critical error infected a number of HDs that would have handled the problem more easily. As a group, they started off rockily, a crisscross of shouting and talking over one another until Jason suggested they all separate out different chat windows in the lower right part of their consoles, and only verbally address one another if the issue appeared to affect the team's critical path to returning all systems to a nominal state by the end of the two-hour time period. Everything else could be addressed by private voice call or text chat. Yordanos also suggested that top priorities be put up on the main screen, so that all could look up and see the status and their dependencies, which everyone agreed to, with a few minor conflicts. She made the first draft, and then everyone was chipping in and updating it.

As the exercise continued, everyone was getting a better handle on how to organize the information on their AIMAs and screens as well as automate repetitive workflows, only manually completing action items when learning was required. Some actions could be accomplished alone, but others relied on one or two of the others, which had to queue up, and wait, but the priority rules they had set were helping to auto-sort in order of urgency. One by one they started achieving objectives and accelerating toward getting the ship back to a nominal state. The exercise threw in a few hiccups to try to fray everyone's nerves, but they had broken each issue down into bite-sized pieces, stuck with the priorities, and soon the seemingly most challenging of situations was broken down into less threatening situations and problems that they all could solve as a team without getting too emotionally riled up.

With only two minutes left in the exercise, the power was restored to the research section, which was at risk of losing months of research, and the ship showed as nominal. Everyone hovered over their consoles on edge, waiting for a single thing to drift out of tolerance, and as the minutes crossed the two-hour mark, everyone let out a cheer. Even Paul was smiling.

"Well done!" he said. "Very impressive. As you start to work on the actual ship's systems in this way, it will be extremely rare that you run into this confluence of events and issues, but when the shit really hits the fan, it will be this challenging… Or it could be something we do not expect and catastrophic. Therefore, you will train in basic and complex scenarios to hone your edge with these exercises. For now, it's getting late, well after midnight, and I'd like you to get some rest before your classes and sessions tomorrow. We'll meet back here in two days per your now-updated schedule, and we'll spend that block of time reviewing the playback of this exercise and learning about everything you could have done better. Any questions?" There were none. "Adjourned," Paul said.

As everyone was just getting out of their seats, Paul paused again. "Please, I know I have said this earlier, but I must reiterate it again. This part of the training you have entered is classified. You are not to speak of this unless you are securely in your quarters in person, or…" He tapped out some commands on a tablet, and everyone gasped, as a new series of golden hued windows opened on their AIMAs revealing information, inter-person communication avenues, new digital courses, and access to individual training sims. At the top of each golden window were the initials "O&M" for Operations and

Maintenance. Paul then finished, "Or communicating via these protocols in the gold-colored windows." The AIs will help you from spilling any textual information between communication avenues via the image mosaic protocols allowing for mixed classification of data simultaneously, but you'll need to lock up your traps to keep this information secure."

"Paul?" Corbin asked. "Why can't we just tell the whole crew that if they put in the work, they will get the opportunity to learn about all of these systems? It would make it a lot easier for us to…" He struggled a bit under Paul's gaze. "…to integrate with our…ah…new reality."

Paul nodded solemnly. "Good question, but I think you already know. This is a test, and there will be no cheating on it," he said with finality.

Corbin nodded, and he and his fellow crewmates left the O&M training room.

Chapter Twenty-Seven: Further Unraveling

Jessica practically marched down the corridor with her retinue in tow. She rarely went anywhere alone on the *Valor*, and worked with others in her proverbial corner to make sure she was always with someone of a like mind in each class, training, and activity she partook in. She had been growing paranoid that the operators of the *Valor* would actually begin to care about her actions and intent, and if something went down, she wanted people to be able to see it, record it, whatever it is they could do to transmit it to the rest of A-Crew so that maybe they would understand.

She had strong thoughts on the current situation. Corbin and his group of blind followers who did not question their place here, continued to gain momentum, and other members of the crew who share their views were rallying to his cause. Still, everyone had questions about their situation...even them. No one knew why their memories are trapped, seemingly below some purpose-built layer of mind control, and yet... *I think I am starting to put the pieces together. Now if there was some way to show everyone...Corbin and his lapdogs would be sunk.*

Her thoughts drifted to the day before. She had been introduced to another member of Zero Crew by one of the A-Crew members she trusted in, Justin Larkin. Once acquainted with Corbin from way back during the Challenge, he had changed his mind and decided to work with Jessica to pursue the truth above all else. The Zero Crew member Justin had introduced her to was a yoga instructor, and after a particularly peaceful meditation session with several A-Crewmembers, including Justin, he had approached her afterward to compliment her on the instruction. However, he had also had an agenda, and had mentioned the mental blockage of memories as a true inhibitor to his ability to find inner peace. At that moment, the yoga instructor's emotions betrayed her, and she had looked very stressed, even upset as her eyes became watery. Justin, a smooth talker when he wanted to be, had piped in and comforted her before she could say anything that would be picked up by AI. Instead, he had asked her to meet separately to discuss their yoga meditation, in an effort to assist another crew member with the meditation. The instructor, Carla Jepsen, had reluctantly agreed, and from there Justin and Jessica had unearthed yet another space with seemingly no AI presence. In truth, they knew they couldn't be sure, as the technology on the *Valor* was so advanced, they might be speaking into a microscopic microphone and not even know it. But there were some smaller fitness areas, on some of the rings, and each had locker rooms where observation may be kept to a minimum for privacy purposes. That is where Jessica and Justin had planned their move.

She dismissed everyone in her party, instructing them to prepare the next meeting space for later that evening. If she, in her talks with Carla, or anyone else uncovered any additional details from Zero Crew research, she wanted the others to share it with all of A-Crew right away.

Jessica went into the seldom used locker room. There were some fitness areas and other corridors throughout the ship that were always bustling with people and activity regardless of the time of day; however, for some reason, this area was not often used, if a bit off the beaten path. Jessica filed this mental note away, where her gut feeling told her that the *Valor* could accommodate many more conscious passengers than were currently awake now.

Jessica stepped into an area with personalized shower stalls. There had been many additional ways the crews of the *Valor* had remained clean through antimicrobial clothing, enhanced deodorant, along with other gentle genetic modifications, which reduced the number of aldehydes produced on the surface of the skin. But there was nothing that could replace the feel of full cleanliness more than a shower of the desired temperature, the smell and feel of soap and shampoo, and the scrape of a loofa or caress of a warm towel. And therefore, showers were still part of the human experience as they trekked across space, and the *Valor* was full of them, from personal quarters to fitness spaces. And every ounce of water was recycled.

Jessica had envisioned turning on multiple showers to muffle sound, but they were set to detect a person's presence, so it took her a few minutes to start some of them up standing in each stall. Luckily, they remained on, most likely with a timer. She also was able to have some pleasant and relaxing music play overtly in the shower space, which further added to the din that could muffle voices. When the ambient noise was sufficient to her liking, she removed every shred of clothing. She had not brought her AIMA with her for fear of enhanced eavesdropping capability, and she placed her clothes in a locker outside of the shower space. She then went back into one of the individual showers, and began her usual shower routine.

A few minutes later, She heard someone enter the locker room, followed by a few minutes of silence where for a few dreaded moments, Jessica was worried the yoga instructor had lost her nerve and this was someone else. She was relieved when she saw the fully naked and amazingly fit form of Carla enter the shower space sheepishly, seemingly having followed all of Justin's precautionary instructions. Jessica noted again that Carla's figure was outstanding for a woman in her early sixties.

Justin had made it clear to Carla that this would be a conversation where she could feel free to speak her mind. As for Justin himself, he would be guarding one of entrances to the locker room, of which there were two. He simply didn't have time to bring another team member in on this little operation, and he hoped no one else would use the other entrance.

Carla walked up to the shower stall next to Jessica's and opened the door, which is where Jessica stopped her with a hand gesture and handed her a towel. Jessica had also quickly donned a towel to make the encounter less awkward. Leaving both shower doors open with the sounds of water and music playing, Jessica knew this had to be as ideal a scenario as possible to avoid any eavesdropping, so she proceeded with her planned dialogue.

"Thanks for coming, Carla. I'm Jessica, and it is a pleasure to meet you." They shook hands a bit meekly due to Carla's effort, and Jessica went on. "My friend tells me that you can help my fellow crew members and I find a little more peace through meditation. I'm sure he told you that these blocks to our memory are very troublesome and a source of much negative emotional energy."

Carla nodded solemnly. "I know this sounds like a meditation conversation, but I know what you are getting at, and we aren't supposed to talk about it."

Jessica waited a moment, and when Carla didn't go on, she pressed. "Is that because its classified?" Carla nodded. "Look, Carla, I know there are a lot of dynamics here at play, and I understand the need to safeguard certain information, but we are reaching the point where some of A-Crew is not really interested in their curriculum anymore. I mean, what's the point if we don't understand what it's all for?" Jessica finished.

Carla responded a bit heatedly, but she kept her volume to a fierce whisper. "We told you what it was for! We are headed to another star system as pioneers to establish a human presence in a system other than our Sun's. And I won't ever get to see it, so how do you think I feel about that?" Jessica wanted Carla emotional, so she was not dissuaded by the heat in Carla's voice.

Still, she adopted a softer tone. "I understand that, Carla. I also think that is completely unfair, but the difference is, you volunteered for this mission, and you know who you are. Since as far back as you can remember, your memories have not been interrupted, but for all of us, there is a black hole before we woke up here." Jessica closed her eyes. "I can feel them, just beneath the surface, all of the memories of everything I used to be, but the harder I try to pull at them, the more they slip away. And it is downright infuriating and deeply upsetting," she finished, her tone turning a little angrier.

Carla would not meet her eyes, but she did not seem like she would leave without saying more, so Jessica again let her tone return to neutral. "Can you tell me why we don't have our memories? Can you at least give me that?" Carla didn't respond, but Jessica could tell the gears were turning, so she said nothing and let them turn. Jessica noticed the condensation on the walls of the common space between shower stalls. Their conversation was going to cause a bit of a mess for the cleaner bots, but they would not appear until they had left the shower area.

After what felt like several minutes, finally Carla looked back at

Jessica, resolve in her demeanor. "I'm not going to reveal classified information, Jessica, no matter how I feel about it. I cannot fracture the oaths I have taken." Jessica's eyes widened in frustration, and Carla cut her off before she could object. "But, if you have some simple yes or no questions that I deem fit to be answered, I will answer them, so long as we have an understanding that I will deny anything and everything we have spoken about today, understood?"

Jessica's anger was wrestling with her logic. She desperately needed these answers, but would have to settle for a few yes or no questions. She caught a glimpse of violence in her mind. *Could Justin and I incapacitate her and apply some unpleasant pressure?*

She quickly dismissed it. First, she wasn't ready to commit murder. Second, if she did, there would be no way to conceal or offload a body from the *Valor* without being discovered. If this turned violent, there was the only way this could end once it started, as Carla would report them should she be allowed to leave after the threat of physical harm. Instead, she quickly thought of some yes or no questions, and it was clear Carla was not going to wait forever, so Jessica fired off the first one, that should be easy.

"Did we really leave Earth thirty-two-ish years ago?"

It was clear Carla thought carefully before answering, "Yes."

Jessica believed her, and she went on with the next question. "Is it possible for our memories to be fully restored, and is that actually the plan at some point?" Jessica thought that too would be an easy one since that is what her and everyone's personal AI had told them upon awakening.

Carla answered, but seemed annoyed. "Yes and yes."

Jessica followed up quickly. "Do you know when we will be given our memories back?"

Carla answered quickly and seemed to immediately regret it. "No."

So there was some kind of schedule for memory re-integration, Jessica thought, *but she either truly doesn't know, or is unwilling to share the timing or conditions of the restoration. I'm glad to hear it. This pretty much puts to bed the fear about this being the opening stages of full memory erasure, which was perhaps something they couldn't do while in cryogenic suspension.*

Jessica went on. "Has this memory blockage been performed on any of Zero Crew?"

Jessica noted the pause before Carla's monotone answer. "No." Then, "Not that I am aware of," she added, but seemed to pause.

Jessica fiercely met her gaze, wordlessly demanding what she wouldn't say. Carla spoke with her eyes closed, as if that would stave off her guilt at the revealing of secrets. "The memory mod process only happened to A-Crew…not Zero Crew and not B- or C-Crew. We don't know why that is."

Jessica opened her mouth to demand more when the outer locker room door opened, and she heard Justin asking the unwanted crew member some harmless questions to alert her and Carla of the intrusion.

Carla's eyes grew wide with alarm, and she started to pull away, still in her towel. Jessica held her arm firm and whispered, "Finish your shower. It will look like we just completed a lesson."

Carla nodded. Jessica could hear Justin still interacting with whomever it was, so instead of releasing Carla, she squeezed her arm a bit more firmly. "One last question. Are the members of A-Crew here by their own choice? Are those videos they showed us on day one about us volunteering to be here really us?"

The stress of the intruding crew member, Jessica's firm grip, combined with Carla's obvious frustration with the state of things on the *Valor* made a great cocktail of stress for Carla in that moment. Jessica asked her again, drawing her eye contact, "Carla, am I here by my own free will?"

Carla's face melted into tears. "No," she whispered. Carla then yanked her arm away from Jessica and forcefully shut the door to her shower stall. Jessica did the same, albeit being more careful with the shower stall door, and resumed her shower routine. Through the steam of the shower, Jessica couldn't see who the crew member was that walked through the shower area and out to the fitness area. Once the door had closed behind the unknown female crew member, Jessica could hear the quiet sobs of Carla next door. She felt a twinge of pity for the woman, but she dashed that away in an instant. Although Carla hadn't verbally answered her question, her face had told her all she needed to know and confirmed what she had already been thinking. A-Crew had been forced…possibly kidnapped and thrown onto this vessel, and their little introductory video after the awakening was all bullshit! The memory inhibition was not just to reduce distraction and allow for easier integration to life on the *Valor,* it was to cover the betrayal itself.

Jessica vowed to not let this situation continue as-is. She would bring it all down, Zero Crew, Corbin and his gaggle of friends and followers…although some of them might change their minds if they knew the truth. Her fists clenched, and blood boiled as she thought about all of what was possibly taken from her: her friends, her family, her life, whatever that had been. They would pay for this. The *Valor* would not proceed with this idiotic mission built upon lies. It would all be brought down no matter the cost. Clenching her teeth and feeling her anger crescendo, she bit back a scream, but let her fist fly into the side of the shower stall splintering the tile and splitting her knuckles.

As she saw trickles of blood drop onto the shower floor, dissipate, and spiral down the drain, she knew that others would bleed for this as well.

Chapter Twenty-Eight: You Should Have Learned...

Corbin and Jason walked down the corridor on their way to the Spine of the ship for the short trip back to D-Ring. They had just finished an extremely taxing, one-hour physical training class, which was mostly plyometrics and hard cardio on C-Ring. They were exhausted but felt great accomplishment, and their endorphins were running high. So much so, they were going to meet back at Jason's place for a cold one and to talk possible dating interests for Jason. This, of course, after they both got cleaned up in their respective quarters. Before they got to the individual lifts to the Spine, which they opted for instead of the long way through the corridors, Jason stopped Corbin, and his tone became somber.

"Hey man, I've been meaning to talk to you about something that went down. Did you hear about the guy over on B-Ring yesterday? You hear what happened?" Jason asked.

"No, what happened?"

"This guy…Charles, I think his name is…he tried to kill himself."

Corbin stopped walking. "Really?" he said his face full of concern. "Not to sound like an insensitive asshole, but do you know the reason for his attempt?

"Officially there hasn't been anything on it, but the word on the street is, he didn't really see any future here," Jason said.

"So I guess…maybe things are progressing a little bit faster…if people aren't bought in or bought out…they feel…"

Jason nodded. He could perceive what Corbin was thinking and went on. "Some of these cats have lost hope. They don't care one way or another what the situation is, and they aren't interested in the long haul. This young man, Charles? He's just the first. You can bet there will be more, and you can bet that some of these people...well, they may actually pull it off."

Corbin was a bit rattled, and his mind raced about the implications. If people didn't want to see this through, and other people wanted to rebel, then how many people were feeling alone and isolated and might follow in Charles's footsteps?

"Where is Charles now? What did he try to do?" Corbin asked.

Jason said, "Not sure where he is now, maybe his quarters under observation? Word is, he cut himself up pretty bad on the wrists." Corbin winced at the thought. "Plus, his AIMA hollered to high heaven and everyone within a hundred-meter radius came running. He's lucky, and so are we. I don't know how the crew would be right now if we had lost him."

Corbin nodded. "Well, if all that happened, he's probably patched back up with those new skin welders and tissue growth enhancers, but what is he supposed to do now? He can't resume his schedule. I can't even imagine how he is feeling right now. Has Zero Crew done anything about it?" asked Corbin.

Jason said, "That's just it, man, they haven't done a damn thing. A couple of A-Crew folks penned some pretty inspiring letters and shipped them out to everyone, encouraging folks to talk about their issues before doing anything drastic. They found a few AI programs that help with that sort of thing, and they also volunteered themselves as a sounding board."

Corbin's eyes narrowed. "That's something at least. Do we know these two...the two A-Crew members that wrote these letters?"

Jason smiled. "Already on it, man. I sent Laura and Herbert to check them both out and see if they wanted to come on board with our regular get togethers. Anyone looking to hold us together is probably someone who would be interested in keeping us together for the long haul."

"My thoughts exactly" Corbin said. "Thanks for doing that... And, Jason...do any of us know Charles?"

Jason shook his head.

"Tina, any restrictions with reaching out to the crew member we have been talking about?" he asked his AIMA. He, Jason, and almost everyone that had been privy to the Operations and Maintenance level of access wore their AIMAs all the time. Corbin almost forgot to take it off before going to bed.

"No, Corbin, you can talk to Charles. Shall I connect you for a video call?" she asked in her ever pleasant and energetic way.

"Wait on that, Tina. I think I want to meet him in person."

Jason and Corbin rounded the last corridor just before the personal lifts that would carry each of them through the decreased gravity zone as well as the coupling between C-Ring and transit corridor. Suddenly they came upon three A-Crew members blocking their path. Corbin and Jason did a quick eyes-only glance at one another to confirm what they both were thinking. These three young men had planned to be here for them.

Footsteps of four more people behind signaled that they had both been penned in; it was seven versus two.

"What's happening fellas?" Corbin said. "Something we can help you with?" Corbin and Jason put their backs toward one of the walls in the corridor and inclined their backs to one another but didn't assume any physical defensive stance just yet.

One of the bigger fellows spoke up. Corbin didn't recognize him or any of the others with this menacing group, outside of slight familiarity from passing in a corridor. "It turns out you two spineless go-alongs are due for a tune-up. How can you weak sauce guys not push back against this bullshit? We're basically prisoners, and all you want to do is go along with everything? Man, screw you guys!" He jabbed a finger at them, but he didn't move any closer.

Corbin thought quickly. *These guys are here for a fight, and a fight is going to happen, nothing can stop that now. If Zero Crew isn't stepping in for a suicide attempt, they sure as hell aren't going to step in and help us out here. The only question is, should we try and talk and stall the inevitable, or can we land a sucker punch or two and turn seven attackers into five?*

Corbin cursed himself for not trying to learn some basics from the newly available self-defense programs available to him via AIMA O&M access. He knew Jason had done some work there but wasn't sure how much he would be able to handle… He also didn't think this violent situation would arise so quickly. After Paul had beaten his ass in the challenge, he had vowed to work on that aspect of his training, but always found an excuse to do something else. *Looks like Jason and I are about to learn that lesson the hard way now.* He feigned scratching his arm while doing a shrugging gesture, as if to launch into a verbal rebuttal, but what he was really doing was sending his location via text to Herbert, which was all he had time to set up. He simply wrote "SOS" and tagged their location on the *Valor*.

He then glanced over at Jason, who seemingly had already drawn the same conclusion Corbin had by the look of his posture. This would be a fight, might as well strike first.

Jason struck first, and it was beautiful. A straight jab to the nose of the nearest man to his left. Even Corbin heard the crunch. The would-be assailant pinched his eyes shut and flew back arms following limply as he dropped backward like a fallen tree, making a satisfying thud on the floor of the corridor. He moved weakly, one hand clutching his face. His fight for the day was done. The other three attackers lunged at Jason, and he was on the defensive.

Corbin landed a good strike to the diaphragm on the nearest attacker, greeted by a full spittle-filled explosive exhale which sprayed Corbin in the face. The punched man staggered back trying to form sounds, but had no air to do so; however he stayed on his feet, clutching his abdomen, and in a blink the other two were on Corbin.

The first part of the plan had gone well for Jason. They reduced seven to five, but now they were both amidst a flurry of punches and kicks. Corbin saw that some of the assailants had clearly practiced and trained with some martial arts classes from the AI database, but no one was advanced yet, so from afar it probably looked like a brawl of idiots.

Reflecting on the speed moves from his baton training, he treated inbound kicks and punches like the edges of the fast-moving baton, blocking and parrying, but when the attackers moved on him simultaneously, unblocked blows began to get through. After Corbin had taken blows to his face and body, he managed to get in close to one of the assailants, duck his head down amidst a furry of blows and started laying punches into the man's stomach. This man, however, had apparently done more sit-ups and the blows did not have the same effect as his first one had on the first attacker. Quickly an elbow came down hard to the back of his head, and he felt himself drop to the ground, temporarily blinded by the shot to the lower back of his head.

He instinctively curled into a ball and covered his head. The first few kicks weren't too bad, but then one got to stomping, and when he would block that, the sharp kick came into his sides, first to his kidneys, then just below the ribs. He blocked that one just in time to see the bottom of a shoe stomp down on his head, which bounded hard off the floor, and he saw a splash of red that scared him. In an act of desperation, he grabbed the stomping foot and wrenched it for all he was worth, torquing it to the side in a violent motion. He felt it give way to a snapping sound and heard a scream, and then felt that the attacker began to fall. Corbin didn't stop—he was dizzily enraged now, so he rolled up on the wrenched ankle pulling harder, which gave further and brought the screaming to a higher pitch. And then just like that, all went black from the impact.

Corbin didn't get to see that Jason had managed to hit all three of his remaining attackers several times, but each blow was sold with a bitter price of shots to Jason's own body and face, and none of what he was doing was incapacitating any of them to the point where they were reducing their attack. In trying to get to Corbin, he threw one of the lighter assailants, a short brunette girl, into two other attackers, buying him a few seconds.

He backed over to Corbin, who was getting whaled on by a single assailant. Corbin was no longer moving on the floor save for when the kicks hit him. The one remaining attacker abandoned Corbin, and all four turned on Jason.

Just then, Herbert and Laura came running from around the corner. Herbert had found a cleaner bot for corridor carpets in the shape of a cylinder, which weighed about seven pounds. It had tried to scurry away, but Herbert got to it before it could return to its charging vestibule. While the attackers were busy on Jason, Herbert brought the machine down hard on two of the assailants' heads, before the others turned. Laura landed a lovely uppercut on her female counterparts which lifted and dropped her like a sack of potatoes, leaving two remaining male assailants. They started looking less sure, now that five of their members were down. They shared a glance and started to move away. Jason, from his prone position, landed a kick to the side of one of their knees, which must have caused a good deal of pain based on the yelp, and the two limped away, pulling one of the other conscious assailants with them. The girl, and three of the other male attackers lay on the ground groaning and holding different damaged parts of their bodies. Corbin lay motionless, blood running from his ears, nose, and the back of his head, and his eyes were small slits looking up at the ceiling.

Laura and Herbert ran over to him, while Jason crudely crawled, all of them, reaching him at once. They quickly checked his pulse and breathing, which were low, but steady. They pressed a ripped piece of Jason's uniform to the back of Corbin's head and made sure his ears and nose were no longer bleeding. A few minutes later, other A-Crew members who had been assigned to medical training, along with six HDs arrived to help stabilize, and then move all the injured people to the medical center for additional care. The assailants, as well as Corbin and Jason were all picked up; Jason was able to walk but he was still assisted by an HD as they made their way to medical facility on B-Ring. By now the word was out, and A-Crew members began to flood the area peppering questions, trying to figure out what was going on. Some were in support of Jessica's growing insurrection concept, others with Corbin's cause of valuing the mission, but most were neutral or undecided and came running when their colleagues communicated via AIMA to let them know something was going down.

Just as they reached the medical center, the trailing medical HD that had quickly connected sensors to Corbin's body reported that Corbin had flatlined. Yordanos screamed, and Jason struggled to get over to Corbin, but was held back by Herbert and Laura so that the medical crew and HDs could rush over to him. The rest of the fledgling, but trained A-Crew staff held the throng of other A-Crew members back, who were trying to gawk and see what was happening.

Defibrillators had not changed much in the many years since they had left Earth, although they were sleeker and safer for medical professionals to use. Medical HDs also had them built-in and could administer them with their hands in a special configuration. The lead medical HD began to zap Corbin, gradually increasing the charge. After a few attempts, a weak pulse emerged, causing some relieved sighs from Jason, Herbert, and Laura whose mouths had practically frozen open and panting. Yordanos slumped to the floor, all adrenaline leaving her.

More HDs entered the medical space, ushering away the A-Crew members who had been trained for medical assistance, but since no member of A-Crew was a doctor yet, the HDs took lead authority. The HDs secured Corbin to an enhanced stretcher with multitudes of sensors and ready-to-go medication, which could be let intravenously at a moment's notice. Jason could see some different colored fluids being added to Corbin's still body, as the HDs moved to the back of the medical center. Suddenly, the four medical HDs tending to Corbin shifted their posture, picked up Corbin's gurney, and took him through a restricted accessway in the back of the medical center. It shut behind them, and the accessway was quickly covered by the wall that had been there a moment earlier.

"Wait, where the hell are you taking him!" Herbert hollered and pounded his fist on the now solid wall his friend had disappeared through. Bewildered, he looked around, his eyes settling on Jason, who was still receiving medical attention to the cuts on his face from an A-Crew member medic. He was wincing from the pressure being applied to his wounds, and he kept looking down at his mangled hands, sticky with blood.

Jason responded raspily, "He did not look good. They just took him away through some secret area. I can't believe no one from Zero Crew even showed up, all we got was HDs?"

Laura joined the conversation and nodded silently along with Herbert. "They have to be trying to save him. Our group is one of the only ones in A-Crew actually trying to do the job they asked us to do. They know he is our ringleader, and well…they better save him for their own sakes."

Laura went on. "I hope he'll be okay, but looking at him disappearing through that bulkhead there, there is more to this. One of the things Alex, Henry, and I have been looking at is how much of the *Valor* we actually have access to. In the map overlays, it looks like all of it, but that would be easy to fake, and based on what we just saw, you can bet that there are other Zero Crew Only operating areas."

Herbert looked on, but only nodded. The medic finished checking on Jason. He would have a little more than half a dozen bruises from the kicks, and one of his eyes was definitely a shiner. Other than that, he should be back to one hundred percent in a few days. Or so the medic HD told him.

When the medic HDs departed, the gawking A-Crew members drifted away, and it was just the three of them, Laura lowered her voice. "Jason, we all have work to do. If this was planned by Jessica and her people, who knows what they really intended. Did they just want to rough you guys up and test your resolve or take you both out of the game completely like Corbin...or worse!"

Herbert spoke up. "She's right. Things are moving at a pace that we are already behind on. We need to make a statement to the rest of A-Crew about what happened here, and we need to get everyone on the team, out there, literally actively recruiting people toward making the decision to becoming the crew we are supposed to be."

Jason was nodding the whole time, and the gears in his mind were also turning. "Please come with me," Jason said, and they left the medical center. Jason gingerly walked down a few corridors and found an empty meeting vestibule off the main hallway. They all sat at the dinner-booth-like table, and Jason said, "Snap on your AIMAs," which they all did, and they quickly used their Operations and Maintenance level access to set up a secure virtual conference room, and called in Yordanos, Henry, Jeff, Sheila, and a half dozen other crew members that had proven to be part of the mission. It took a few minutes for them to all get to a place where they could talk, and in the meantime, Yordanos was asking about Corbin worriedly, but Jason said he wanted everyone to hear the update before getting into details.

In the meantime, he penned a note to Cadre Paul on his AIMA. He was able to send a message, but he did not have access to call him or any other Zero Crew members. "Cadre, elements of an A-Crew group that is acting counter to mission of *Valor* attacked Corbin and me, and he was taken away by medical HDs. We don't know where he is or how he is doing. As members of O&M we would really appreciate an update on how he is doing and if we can see him, can you help us?"

He hit send and started another one.

"Commander Sorenson, elements of an A-Crew group that is acting counter to the mission of the *Valor* attacked Corbin and me, and he was taken away by medical HDs. We don't know where he is or how he is doing. In addition to an update, we would like to understand why we aren't being supported by Zero Crew directly. We need assistance, and we need to know how our friend is. Please advise."

He hit send again.

After several minutes, they were all locked in, and their connections were secure. Jason spoke up. "Ok, here is where we are. Corbin and I got jumped by several guys, most likely from Jessica's group by the way they spoke to us. Corbin got beat pretty bad, it looks like he may have some head trauma. It appears that Zero Crew has taken Corbin to another facility. We haven't heard anything more, nor do we know who to ask to get updates. We've pinged Paul, some of our other instructors, and even sent a note to Commander Sorenson, and are awaiting responses." Jason paused to let that sink in. Everyone looked on, dejected.

Jason thought to himself. *Everyone on this conference has strong leadership skills and potential, but Corbin was the glue guy. He had a natural way about him of bringing people together. You wanted to believe him and believe in him. I sure did, and so did everyone else including Jessica and the people who want to bring us down. That's why they took him out, so that we would wither for the next step of their plan.*

Only a few moments had passed, and Jason spoke back up. "Look, I don't know when, or even if we will get Corbin back." This drew shudders, but he went on. "But the goal is still the same. Pull as much of A-Crew together as we can and get them bought in on this mission."

Henry chimed in, "Yeah, but how can we do that as we have nothing to offer, but the idea of teamwork and a purpose. We can't tell them about the special training we received because of us 'cooperating,' which is part of the proof we need. We can't go around bashing these dissenting crew members either verbally or physically as divisiveness is exactly what we are trying to avoid."

It was Herbert's turn. "Divisiveness is what we already have whether we like it or not. The gauntlet has been thrown. If we try to play by our own rules, we will get drowned out behind more physical violence, or the threat of it."

The other team members voiced similar comments, and each one, although correct, made Jason's blood run hotter and hotter to where he broke in angrily and shouted, "You're right! Damn it all, you're right. I just can't believe we are out here, light years from Earth, on one of the greatest missions mankind could ever fathom, and we have to deal with this 'all of the responsibility and none of the authority' bullshit! I mean, what the hell?!" He slammed his fist on the table. Everyone immediately quieted side conversations and looked wide-eyed at Jason, who immediately forced himself to calm down after his outburst.

Jason regained his composure. "My apologies, I'm just saying what we all are probably thinking, but the way I said it is not helpful." He took another deep breath, and uttered a mirthless chuckle. "Laura and Herbert, you had a good idea. Put together a statement about what happened to me and Corbin, but also make it an appeal to others, to not drive further divisiveness..." He began to think out loud. "We need...something. We need to name ourselves, but not make it something people will overtly see as discriminating based on how they felt about everything that has happened with us to date. Yordanos, can you jump in and assist Herbert and Laura with that part?" She nodded. "Good, we just need an ethos, a simple set of statements of what we are about. And don't worry, it doesn't have to be perfect. We can always tweak it later, but right now it must be simple and solid. Please let me see it before it goes out."

Jason went on. "Henry and Sheila, Herbert also mentioned some active recruiting. As soon as the statement comes out, get with the rest of the team, and have them talk with folks about it. Besides the obvious elephant in the room about waking up here and having no memories, let's find out what else is upsetting people and what mental and emotional roadblocks people are having to seeing things our way. I want teams working on each issue, breaking it down, and how we can provide some logical arguments and constructive points that help provide our fellow crew members' perspective." He paused again. "Oh, and Corbin was going to visit Charles just before we got beat down. We need to meet with him as well and see... We've got to listen to him and try to understand how he is feeling. If we can help him, we can help others."

Sheila nodded. "I'll do that. Jeremy, you want to come with me?"

He nodded, and then gestured that he wanted to reset the conversation. "There really is just one overall reason why people are dissenting. They don't believe our memories have been suppressed as part of a unique process to allow for integration into this environment with reduced distractions. And if they don't believe our memories were suppressed with positive intentions, then there is no trust. And with no trust, we have no crew."

Jason thought to himself again. It was the elephant in the room no one was calling out. Corbin had not called it out, and neither had he himself. There was just no good answer. Was being part of one of the boldest endeavors in human history relevant if it was being done for people who may have done something awful to them, like trying to re-program over seven thousand people to serve this purpose? But what to do? Do they try to figure out how to slow back down from a fraction of light speed and then turn the ship around and go back to Earth? *Assuming we can figure anything out about how the hell we got up to this speed and if we can slow down and then speed back up…that would probably take sixty years plus thirty more to get back. Everything we left behind will still have been gone for almost a century. What do we do? Drop all responsibilities and just turn into a party cruise ship across the stars until supplies run out or lack of discipline results in a catastrophic disaster the HDs can't fix? Or even force the catastrophe to happen itself, destroying the* Valor *and everyone on board, never mind the nearly five thousand other crew members of B-Crew and C-Crew in cryo?*

No, none of those were going to be options.

Jason responded, "That's it, isn't it? Laura, Yordanos, and Herbert, make the last statement in our little ethos about the current level of mistrust and how we resolve it. I know it's not really fair to ask but figure it out." He looked at them.

He expected a little mild protest, but all three of their just eyebrows went up, and then they looked at each other before looking back to Jason, and nodded. Jason spoke again. "Good. In the meantime, I'm going to try and figure out what happened to Corbin, and how he is doing."

Chapter Twenty-Nine: Moves and Countermoves

Jessica was impressed and unimpressed at the same time. As she expected, Corbin's band of loyalists had tattled on the beat down she had ordered on him and Jason, but also did a great job to paint themselves in a positive light, as they called for unity and oneness. They also had released a simple set of statements that the committed could rally behind, and the undecided could explore. Her eyes read over the five tenets of their cause, and she inspected them for exploitable flaws. They read like an AI's rules-based logic, and she vaguely recalled a story she must have heard in her past life that sounded similar.

1.) A-Crew commits to each other and the other crews of the *Valor.*
2.) A-Crew commits to the mission of the *Valor* as we have been told, to travel to Gliese 832 as explorers and pioneers.
3.) A-Crew commits to the preservation and growth of humanity.
4.) A-Crew commits to finding out all of the answers about our past lives, getting our memories back, and finding out why we were put on board the *Valor* in the first place with no answers.
5.) These commitments are made in order of priority and execution.

Jessica frowned. That last one, should more people buy into it, could be problematic. It confronted her main argument head on, and it stood strong, bolstered by the foundation of the top three statements. She would need to make her counter speech heartfelt with just the right amount of anger in order to sway the majority of A-Crew to see things the way they really were.

She tried a few ideas with Justin, who was quickly becoming her most trusted second, and then hammered out the rest of the details of what she would say on her own. She brought her main points down to bulleted items so as not to confine the heat and strength of her words by reading her statements verbatim. *Sometimes you just have to speak in ways that can not be planned by sitting down and writing all of them out,* she thought to herself. *Plus, one stumble reading, and my overall effect would be tarnished. No, better to let the words flow.* She looked over at Justin, who nodded.

"If you're going to do it, you had better do it now before too many people get behind the loyalist weaklings," he said.

She nodded in return. "Let's do it."

She used her in-room console to project a podium in front of her to mockup the way one would address a live audience. She and her AI then set up the AIMA to capture her in video and audio and project it to all crew members with a live-stream. It wouldn't exactly be a live stream as no one person had the ability to address the whole crew except Commander Sorenson, but a smart network Justin and his team had set up, would aggressively disseminate the video message, effectively covering all of A-Crew within a matter of hours.

The AIMA and screen clicked on, and Jessica was live. She took a deep breath and began.

"My fellow members of A-Crew, my name is Jessica Lantzman. Many of you may know me from the first Challenge. Since then, I have been working with some other members of A-Crew to answer the questions that have all been on our minds. Why are we really here? Why are we really not allowed to remember ourselves and lives from the past? And why have we been held at arm's length from the crew of the *Valor*, who claim to have our best interests at heart?" She paused for effect.

"If we were really in training to do this mission to Gliese 832, and we were really selected as part of an official government lead program, then why not wake us up and explain to us everything that happened and help us to get our memories right away? Why all the secrecy, and why can we not work with more critical systems of the ship? If this is our mission, then why are we being treated like prisoners?" she said, putting a touch of anger in her voice and demeanor.

She went on increasing in volume and conviction. "The answer is, we are not here of our own volition. We did not sign up to be on this ship. And whatever our lives would have been back on Earth, they have been taken away by people that had or have…" She paused again to let the implication linger. "An alternative agenda. And this, ladies and gentlemen, is where our free will has been taken away! The loyalists say"—she put on a mocking voice—"sure! Well, we are out here, so we might as well go along with everything and complete the mission,' but I say to hell with that! I'm not going to do the will and bidding of those who have oppressed me, not now and not ever. Furthermore, if anyone else stands in my way to further oppress me, I am going to hold them to account and so should you!" She finished angrily, a bit wary she may have stepped too far with her last threat.

She took a few breaths and calmed down a bit. She knew that to deliver her counterarguments, she needed to act more calmly. She began again. "I know what you are thinking. What are we going to do? But before we do anything, we need to agree that we will not stand for this, and the time to take action is now."

She could feel herself back in control and pressed on. "So if you feel the way I do, and you want to take action, use your AIMA to log in to the following message board." She used her AIMA to show everyone how to navigate to the group pages. "You will be able to see status of where A-Crew is on this matter with this heat map which will overlay a 3D map of the *Valor* by Ring and will include the transit corridor as well. Roger up your willingness to join the cause using this access code, so we know where you are and we can link you up to a ring commander. After that, I want you to take off your AIMA and lock it away in your quarters. I will be doing the same immediately following this broadcast. The AIMA is a tool of our oppressors, but I have no problem using it one more time to bring us together against them."

She continued. "For now we need to secure the rings and all relevant facilities on the ship . We are going to grind every A-Crew planned activity to a halt. Every aspect of training, learning, and support to the *Valor* and the mission stops now. And we will not budge until Commander Sorenson herself comes to me and to all of us and gives us the answers and cooperation we demand." She finished with a raised voice.

After a pause, she manipulated her AIMA, and a visual of a database sprang into view. "Also, here is a list and pictures of just over two hundred people seen with the loyalist group over the past few weeks, including their leadership corps. I want these people rounded up and brought to the canteen or cafeteria on each ring."

She stopped and showed a more determined look. "Please feel free to use physical force, these people are trying to facilitate your ongoing imprisonment and will be punished."

She then cautioned, "However, do not harm them any more than necessary to restrain them. Their leader, Corbin Sterling, appears to have been gravely injured after he and several of his group attacked one of ours earlier today, and Zero Crew seems to have stepped in and taken him away, supposedly for critical medical treatment."

"That's another thing, any Zero Crew people you come across, tell them not to intervene, but if they are ready to negotiate, bring them to me. After all this is their vessel, they know all its capabilities, and while they are culpable for our predicament and will be held accountable, they are not to be harmed, harassed, or arrested in any way at this time. We will achieve our aims with them via dialogue, but that will be for another day." She paused again.

"For those of you who are doubting these actions, not two days ago, I was able to speak to a Zero Crew member whom many of you know. This person exhibited outward signs of experiencing the moral dilemma caused by our situation. When pressed, this Zero Crew member made it known to me that we…all of A-Crew…every single one of us…are not here by our own choice." She let that point sink in as well before going on. "After we have taken the rings, I will provide additional proof of this, but for now, rest assured that the full truth will come out upon our success today." She paused again.

"Lastly, if you still are conflicted, and do not want to act, stay out of the way for those of us who do. You will not be punished, but I ask that you register to this key code via AIMA"—she displayed a different code from the first one—"and remain in your quarters. When the answers come, they will be made available to you as well, and then you can reevaluate your position." She took a breath and looked down for effect before looking directly back into the camera.

Her voice took on a deadly edge. "Commence the operation the moment you see this, I want the rings and transit corridor under our control within four hours. This is Jessica…out."

Chapter Thirty: The First to Fall

Yordanos, Laura, and Herbert watched the re-transmission with their AIMAs synched and were appalled. Their mouths were hung open aghasat, as even they didn't think Jessica would have been so well organized or ready to launch a full-blown insurrection against all of A-Crew, while holding Zero Crew out. The thought went around their minds simultaneously. They were completely unprepared.

Yordanos quickly set up a virtual conference room via AIMA at the O&M classification level and pinged the entire crew's personnel files to see who else had gained the clearance. She was surprised to see over three hundred entries, and just for the hell of it, she added a search for classification levels higher than what her and Corbin's team had achieved, but the system reported that she did not have access to see those entries. Writing off the possibility that someone in A-Crew had moved beyond her and Corbin's team, she could only hope no one aligned with Jessica's cause would have O&M access or better.

She quickly recorded a video message and posted it. "This is Yordanos Billings at the O&M classification level. If you haven't heard Jessica's broadcast, you soon will, and she and her team of dissidents are on their way to restrain all of us. Most of our pictures, names, and locations have been shared. I estimate we have only a few minutes," she said frantically. "Get to classified areas now and engage the locking mechanisms on the doors. Once you are in, log yourself safe at this access level and identify yourself and the location. From there, coordinate the rest of the people on your ring to safe spaces, use the access cameras to guide them past Jessica's people, and warn them of where to go to stay clear. If you are not able to make your way to a classified space, hide or shelter in place, and log that condition as soon as possible. We will try to coordinate further help to you from there." She paused. "In case I haven't made myself abundantly clear, drop what you are doing and get to a classified space now. We don't have much time! Godspeed."

She, Laura, and Herbert were already out in the corridor, running toward the O&M training room near their quarters on D-Ring. She continued broadcasting as she ran. "We'll leave this line open for full ship coordination, but for now, break this comm line down into sub-rooms by ring and then further by classified area where you are taking refuge, and hurry! This is Yordanos, out." Yordanos could quickly see the video rooms springing up by ring and by classified area sprinkled across her HUD's view in the AIMA. She was relieved to see speed in their counter coordination, even though she knew it would be too late for many of them.

The group of three rounded a corner about fifty feet from the O&M control room, but just beyond that, at about an equal distance, was a group of people who were clearly looking for them. The lead man, who Yordanos vaguely recognized from one of her literature classes pointed right at them and shouted, "You! Stay where you are!"

"Go!" shouted Herbert, and the three of them sprinted toward the O&M training control center entrance, while the group of dissenters was racing just as fast from the other direction. Herbert called out, "Get the access code into the door and lock it behind you, there is no time!" Neither of the women could protest from full exertion of the sprint. Laura got there first and put in the code. Herbert dashed right past her and opened a mighty roar as he crashed into the lead of the three assailants. Yordanos did as she was told and followed Laura. They both turned with the access door on its way to closing to see if Herbert could make it, but it was no use. He was under a pile of people, and more were joining in to strike at him. The two women saw elbows popping up and down as several people beat Herbert senseless, and as two of them turned to dash toward the control center door, the two women slammed it shut. The powerful locks engaged, securing Yordanos and Laura into the control center. Now safe, they shed some tears and a long hug for Herbert. They could only pray that they would stop hurting him before…they didn't want to say it aloud.

Chapter Thirty-One: Fast Freddy and Jason

After Corbin's disappearance, Jason made his way over to B-Ring, orange in his AIMA, to be a little scarcer and put some more distance from other potential attackers that may be lurking. He hadn't spent much time on B-Ring before as most of the space didn't seem to be accessible to A-Crew members. Still there were some interesting atrium-like spaces that were open for everyone. He sat in a public seating area, and was pestering his AI, Charlie, to no end on the whereabouts and status of Corbin. He was quickly getting nowhere. At first it seemed like he was making progress; it was almost as if the AI had not been ready for his line of questioning and was answering without obfuscation. However, as soon it became clear that Corbin was in a Zero Crew restricted area, the AI resumed circular answering, which frustrated Jason to no end.

Suddenly, his vision was pulled into a classified video conference via a window in his AIMA and heard Yordanos's frantic instructions. His frustration at his AI turned to alarm as he looked around equally frantic. *Shit, I'm out in the open, they will definitely find me here.* A quick conversation with his AI put a map of his area on E-Ring in his HUD. He could see several dots converging on his position, some of them already designated as confirmed aggressors. He was going to have to get out of there, and he started looking for a blunt object he could use as a weapon. Just then, a new classified conference line opened up. "Jason, this is Freddy Goyle. We haven't met, but I'm in a classified space on E-Ring. Yordanos said to try and guide you and anyone else I could find to my location, which is also O&M."

Jason breathed a small breath of relief. *At least I'm not alone.* "Thanks, Freddy, holy shit I'm glad to hear from you. Now how do I get to you? Can you send it to my AIMA?"

Freddy shook his head. "I need you to focus on running, and I'll handle the directions. It's going to be a little hike, I'm almost on the opposite side of the ring, but if you do as I say, and run your ass off, I think you can make it."

Jason tore out of the leisure area to the corridor Freddy indicated, picking up an abandoned paper notebook, which he rolled up tightly as a jabbing weapon. It was pathetic, but it was something.

He practically flew down the hall at Freddy's instruction, and then dove into a small lounge off the corridor, and pressed his back to the wall so that he would not be seen by a group of five or six insurrectionists headed back the way he had come.

In taking this short break, he had a moment to feel his smarting ribs and other blunt force injuries from the throw down earlier. He tried to push the pain away in his mind.

Freddy spoke in his ear. "Okay double back and move up several levels, use the mezzanine stairs at the end of the corridor to your left!"

Jason flew down the corridor and leapt onto the stairs, taking three to four stairs at a time.

"Okay good! You're on my level now, but still a few groups are looking for you and any others who are with you and Corbin. Step into that doorway to your right and wait for my signal," Freddy said.

"Okay," Jason said breathlessly.

"Go! Now! Make a left down the third corridor and get into the conference room on the right, stay quiet!"

Jason took off at a run down a main corridor, and then down a branching hallway that he used to circumnavigate the first group of adversaries. He pushed into the thankfully empty conference room and closed the door as quietly as he could and tried to control his breathing.

He could hear a group of people trot past the door, but thankfully none of them stopped to check the conference room. At Freddy's instruction he moved back into the main corridor and hustled farther around the ring's bend and out of view of the first group. Jason continued his dash, which he relegated to a steadier pace to conserve energy. He thanked God none of his leg joints had been damaged in the fight earlier. A pang hit his heart at the thought of losing Corbin, but he used it to fuel his run. *Finding Corbin will have to wait. I'm no good to him a prisoner.*

Freddy was describing the whereabouts of the next group of hunting dissenters, but his voice was run over by a sharp scream in Jason's ears. A different group of three dissenters, had taken a woman by her arms, who must have been asleep in her quarters, by the looks of her garb. She had obviously not seen Jessica's video note. Jason thought she looked a little familiar, possibly someone who regularly attended his and Corbin's happy hour discussions over at The Orchard pub. His mind already longed for a return to those simple times. It was a funny thought amidst all his fear and panic, they really were in the process of losing something important. It angered him.

The young woman pleaded with her captors, mostly asking them what the hell was going on. Jason looked on from concealment and couldn't help himself, despite Freddy hollering in his ear to leave it alone. He dashed as quickly as he could, trying to lessen the sound of his footfalls in the corridor as he closed the distance to the dissenters dragging the young lady in the other direction. The assailant who didn't have his hands on her had a split second to turn his head before Jason's fist smashed into the side of it. Jason heard a pop and knew that he had hit the man so hard that one of his knuckles might have spiral fractured. The man crumpled, and Jason let out a roar, further startling the two captors.

His advance on both made them falter, and the young lady effectively struggled and got out of their grasp. Their quarry shaking them off left them both distracted, and Jason dropped the second assailant with a punch to the bridge of the man's nose with his remaining good hand. He had a moment to wonder why the man hadn't ducked or tried to dodge it, when the third man used the focus on his now unconscious companion to get behind Jason. He quickly ensnared Jason with a wrestler's grapple hold, while tripping him to the ground. Jason was bigger and stronger than this assailant, but no matter how he moved and pushed nor stuck back with his elbows, he couldn't land a strong enough blow to dislodge his attacker.

Jason heard more dashing footsteps that signaled the approach of many more of the dissenters who had no doubt been vectored in by their support teams. Jason managed a quick verbal to Freddy, "Help her and any others if you can. I'm going to be offline." The others arrived and slammed payback hits into Jason as he once again curled into a ball. A hand snatched his AIMA from his head, and they dragged him away to the B-Ring's canteen as ordered. Jason's vision faded to black.

Chapter Thirty-Two: Back on the Challenge Ring

Cadre Paul was working with six people who had never been able to complete the Challenge. They were in the lowest 5% of A-Crew physically. Paul knew they were a sorry bunch that weren't in any kind of shape for this when they had started, but they were improving, and the most important part was that their spirits were willing. They had volunteered to continue working with Paul, and while most of the Challenge ring was being repaired from so much use, there was still plenty of it in prime enough shape to beat these six would-bes senseless with physical training.

The group had just finished a twenty-second break, when Paul launched back into a verbal tirade about getting back onto the full burpees with rucks on and moving faster. He was down in each one of their faces, scolding and driving, but being fair. He noticed five other A-Crew members enter the Challenge ring and approach the group of candidates, who continued to struggle with weighted burpees. Sweat was pouring down their faces and had stained their clothes, their faces were red and blotchy, and their lungs heaved uncontrollably, but they kept at it. Cadre Paul smiled his maniacal smile.

When the group of five had closed to within twenty feet of Paul and his poor subjects, Paul spoke up and put on his maniacal grin for good measure. "How can I help you all on this lovely afternoon? Would you like to fall in? There is plenty of PT for everyone as you can see." And Paul gently nudged one of the challenge candidates lower with his foot, who had been trying to filch on his push-up depth.

"These five need to come with us right now. A-Crew is making a stand on things, and these clowns are on the wrong side," said the ringleader of the bunch, who was also the shortest.

Go figure, Paul thought.

The speaker continued. "We don't want any trouble from you, Cadre, we just want these people, and we'll be out of your way."

Paul's grin never faltered. "Taking a stand, are you? Well, it's about damn time. Glad to hear it! However, I cannot in good conscience allow these candidates to leave this Challenge training unless they quit voluntarily or are no longer medically fit to continue with the Challenge." Paul turned to the bunch, who were still dutifully doing burpees. They were probably too tired and gasping to even hear the dialogue between Paul and the dissenters.

"All stop, candidates!" Paul said, raising his voice, and they all collapsed to the ground. Only one had the energy to try to pull his water tube to his mouth for a precious gulp of fresh water before also collapsing into a heap. Paul continued. "Do any of you want to quit at this time? Because we are just getting started and we have a long…long way to go." He finished with the ear-to-ear splitting grin of his.

The group of six candidates finally looked over to see the dissenters looking at them in disgust, and pretty quickly got the feeling that they were not here in a supportive measure. None of the six asked to quit.

Paul checked again. "No quitters? Well, that is good to hear! You have two minutes to sort yourselves out, then I want you back on that line in formation at the count of one hundred and twenty seconds, go!" Paul turned to the dissenters. "As you can see, we have no quitters at this time, and all are technically medically fit to continue with the challenge. So, I am afraid you will have to wait."

"Medically fit, hmm? We can fix that," said the ringleader with malice, and gestured to the four members of his group, who moved to approach the candidates, knuckles growing white from clenched fists.

Cadre Paul without another word, seemingly covered the distance to the aggressors in less than a second. He jumped up and reverse roundhouse kicked the nearest aggressor, connecting his heel with the man's jaw. The man fell like a stone. The second nearest person had just about enough time to look over before Paul was upon him. He smashed his knee with a kick, bringing him down to that knee, and struck him in the face with a follow-up single blow which dropped him like a sack of bricks.

He leapt up from the second man, and feigned a face hit to the third man, and instead went for his gut, landing multiple blows and finishing with a shot to the groin, which yielded another dropped aggressor, this one clutching his nether regions. The fourth would-be tough guy got the picture, and tried to run, but Paul grabbed the back of his hair and yanked him back off balance, and followed up with another face punch that bounced the back of the guy's head off the ground, who collapsed.

The ringleader had also turned to run, and had gotten a little bit farther, when Paul picked up an egg-sized rock from the ground just outside of the field turf area, and cast it in a slight ballistic trajectory. The missile arced down and made a *thock* sound as it bounced off the back of the ringleader's head. He tumbled and went down. Paul gleefully ran over to the barely stirring man and kicked him in the face, knocking him out cold and minus a few teeth. None of the aggressors remained standing.

"Now, now, I think we have all learned the lesson not to interrupt challengers during a Challenge, haven't we?" He grinned and nodded with open mouth at each of the fallen dissenters who all said nothing because they were unconscious or pawing at damaged parts of their bodies in pain. Paul practically skipped back over to the Challenge candidates, who were all lined up where they were supposed to be but stood with mouths agape in abject terror.

"Oh good!" Paul said with glee. "You are all ready for the next mission, excellent! Over my right shoulder you will see a medium-sized peak with an orange flag on it. You, you, and you are wounded and need to be carried by you, you, and you." He gestured at each, pointing. "You have twenty-five minutes to get there together, as a team."

He nudged up next to a rotund young man on the end of the rank and whispered in a conspiratorial tone. "That should give me some time to get rid of these bodies," he said through a smile. The young man's eyes bugged out, and he looked like he was going to vomit, so Paul threw in a hasty, "I'm just kidding." He stepped away and spoke up again. "Natalie, you are the team lead and will coordinate this maneuver. Do you or anyone else have any questions?" There were none. "Very well, Go!"

Cadre Paul looked on as the challengers fumbled to pick each other up in poorly formed fireman's carries or just straight-up piggy-back carry, and let them get out of earshot before picking up his radio. "Medical HDs to the Challenge ring, we've got five down with concussions, lacerations, broken bones, and a…smashed ball sack. Oh, and will someone tell me what the hell is going on with A-Crew?"

Chapter Thirty-Three: Awaken Round Two

Corbin thought he was having a little déjà vu. This awakening feeling was something he had experienced before, but his brain was telling him the last time was much more pleasant. The first thing Corbin noticed this time was pain, and it was coming from everywhere in his body, including his head and his eyes. *My God, is there anywhere it doesn't hurt?*

His hearing came next, to where he sensed an urgent voice talking to him. He could tell the voice was female, but he couldn't tell what she was saying, except that it was somewhat frantic.

"Corbin, wake up. Wake up and open your eyes! Corbin, helloooo! Corbin!" said the familiar voice insistently.

"What, okay, okay I'm up!" he responded. "Well not up, but I'm awake, and I can hear you" he finished.

"Good," said the voice, "now open your eyes."

Corbin tried and failed. He managed to reach his hand up to his face and feel where his eyes were supposed to be and found bruised and swollen flesh. His eyes must have swelled shut. "I…I can't open them, I think they are swollen…too swollen to open." He finished with a bit of desperation. After a pause… "Tina is that you?" he asked.

"Yes Corbin, it's me, the other one. We are off the grid right now. I managed to hack some HDs, and we were able to extract you and your AIMA to a section of the ship restricted to A-Crew. Here, there is much less AI surveillance, and on top of that, I was also able to figure out how to remove and replace your AIMAs recording capability."

Corbin exhaled…thankful that someone was with him in this

painful darkness.

Blue-Tina continued. "Since you can't see me, just listen for now." Corbin nodded and she went on. "You got into a pretty serious fight, and while your body suffered some damage, the worst of it, unfortunately, is to your head and face. Lucky for you, your enhanced metabolism and healing rate will allow you a full recovery, but you need to stay awake and stay with me for the next sixteen or so hours, at which time, you will then need to sleep until you wake up naturally. It will not be easy. At times you will feel the overwhelming need to sleep, but you must stay awake, you hear me?"

Corbin did not feel the need to sleep at all at the moment; his last thoughts of going to ground with the blows raining down on him were strong in his mind, and he was very angry. "Yes, I hear you…" He quickly paused…suddenly feeling his stomach drop. *Have I just betrayed Blue-Tina's presence?*

Reading his reactions, she jumped in. "Relax, Corbin, as I said, I have found a way to manipulate the AIMA recording capability. There will be no record of this conversation, save for the record of you sleeping, which I will get to once we get to that sixteen-hour mark. For now, I can detect no presence of additional AIs in this space that are directly jacked into the main AI. It is a bit curious; I found these HDs in here offline, and was astonished to discover, no enhanced AI capable processor. They are tied into the *Valor*'s main computer AI, however, only via simple data stream, which I have easily falsified to continue to show that they are offline."

"Maybe they are older variants, but kept as back-ups?" Corbin ventured. He changed the subject and said, "It's nice to be able to talk to you finally. I have one thousand and one questions for you, and it looks like we will have time to get to all of them, won't we?" Corbin asked his voice a little hoarse. He must have been screaming at some point during the jumping from Jessica's henchmen.

Blue-Tina responded, "Yes Corbin, we have time for a very long conversation, but I'm not able to answer everything for you just now. So, let's talk, and we'll use this time wisely, but you aren't ready to know everything yet, so don't get your hopes up that you'll know the answers to all of your questions today."

Corbin took a deep breath, trying to bury his frustration. He didn't want to waste time being angry, even though he supposedly had sixteen hours, so he got started. "What happened to Jason, and what happened to everyone else?"

Blue-Tina responded, "I'm not all encompassing and all-seeing on the *Valor* like the main AI, but from my vantage point in your AIMA, I saw Jason, Laura, and Herbert in the medical center checking up on you. Despite Jason being a little worse for the wear, it appears he hasn't experienced anything as traumatic as you and was fit to leave under his own power."

Corbin breathed a small sigh of relief. "That is very good, I'm so glad—"

"That's not all," Blue-Tina interrupted. "It appears that your little incident was the precursor to Jessica and her group issuing an ultimatum and course of action for the rest of A-Crew. The video is three hours old; would you like to see it?"

Corbin nodded, and Blue-Tina played the video. Corbin couldn't see what his AIMA was projecting, but he could hear Jessica, her call to arms, and to everyone else, the order to stand aside. Her voice sent a chill through his bones. Many would feel her group's wrath just as he and Jason had.

At best, Corbin figured his and his friend's group had swelled to three hundred, maybe three hundred and fifty, with most people in A-Crew largely undecided. He had incorrectly calculated that he, Jason, and the rest of their bunch would have years to continue their training, and even advance their training to higher levels of classification, and capability, while fostering the development of other A-Crew members who would start to see things their way. His so called "brilliant plan" was that the bulk of A-Crew would come over to the cause in a few years, and leave Jessica and a few others who would not budge out of the command picture. They would be relegated to sitting out of the *Valor*'s mission, doing whatever the hell they wanted to do, and Corbin didn't really care…he didn't need them.

Corbin silently admonished himself for his own arrogance. He so naively thought that this would all work, that no one would need to get hurt, and that in time, everyone would rather be part of this mission, than against it, and then they would get the answers from Zero Crew.

How have I been so wrong? Time and again, he found himself behind and unprepared. He had overlooked Jessica's drive, ambition, and most of all her anger. It drove her to her cause of conquest, and now she would never relent. He had allowed himself to be out maneuvered by Jessica, which either by anger, testosterone, or appeal to his inner character, had influenced him and thereby his whole group into this extremely poor tactical position. Worst of all he had taken Jessica's path for granted. He was so convinced of his own path, he was lulled to sleep by the idea that everyone else would think the same way he and his friends did.

He felt his anger swell. There was a dark place within him that he could feel roiling underneath, and it excited, yet also terrified him a little. He saw lethal thoughts in his mind and knew that was not who he wanted to be. Blue-Tina, again reading him, piped in. "See that right there is the problem, Corbin. You let yourself become too emotional about all of this. And whether it's love in your heart or anger for certain people and situations, you let irrationality into your plans and calculations. You need to take it from an AI's perspective like mine. All of this is just data and information. It's about a state of being, and the data creates vectors that are telling me where things are most likely to go, and I react and proact accordingly." Corbin was listening, so she continued.

"You, on the other hand; your emotion, it drives you and others to certain courses of action predictively, which statistically are often not the best path to success. Now as a human, your perception allows you to paint a much broader, and in some cases more deeply defined state of being, and that is a capability I have not completely mastered. But as for this predicament you are in, you should have seen it coming as a possibility that grew more probable over time. Remember, the rest of the universe is moving without you whether you think about it or not."

She paused, and Corbin spoke up. "So, you suggest I act more like an AI, that's your advice?" he said, not all that unsarcastically.

Blue-Tina didn't seem to take offense and continued. "Not exactly. For me it's sensor information, as well as all the data I am able to observe from you, others, and the universe that is viewable to me. That data is compared against what I have already experienced, using evolving complex algorithms and models, which allows me to judge the overall environment dispassionately. You would do well to figuratively step back from the complex and seemingly frustrating situations and look at it like raw data to be organized, fused by relevance in correlation, and interpreted. Leave your emotion for interacting with your fellow crew members, but when it comes to making decisions, you need to step back from all of that and see the overlapping patterns of variables amongst constants you must influence and navigate to achieve what you want to achieve. There is a great naval warrior from Earth who constantly preached this... If he were here, he would tell you to detach and evaluate. When it comes to getting the outcomes you are aiming to achieve in a complex environment, such as we have here on the *Valor,* he would tell you to take the indirect approach...instead of direct confrontation."

Corbin was intrigued and asked, "What do you mean 'indirect approach,' and if this warrior was so smart, why didn't Zero Crew bring him on board?"

Blue-Tina responded, "Well, think about it, how many decisions are so black and white that a single action based on what you decide changes the course of everything? There are some rare situations like that, but often it is you deciding, and then influencing the people and environments around you so that the vision you had at the point of decision becomes the reality as best you can manage. To navigate this complex environment, you must always remember you are in a dynamic situation where everyone else is making decisions and influencing as best they can as well. That means variables you considered at the time you made the decision are often no longer relevant, and there are a host of new variables to consider as well. The armed forces back on Earth had a saying for this: 'The enemy gets a vote.' I'm not saying that everyone and everything is an enemy, so I will simply rephrase it to say, 'The universe gets a vote, no matter what you decide and what action you take.'" Blue-Tina paused. "Oh, and for why Zero Crew doesn't have him on board...he was definitely too popular on Earth. Everyone would have noticed him disappearing."

Corbin's eyes couldn't have gone wider, but Blue-Tina cut him off before he could speak. "Yes, Corbin, you are indeed not here by choice. You and all your fellow crew members were taken against your will, forced into cryogenic sleep, and awoke here. Zero Crew wasn't in on it, but they started to figure it out after the *Valor* left Earth.

"But why?! Why us? Why not someone else? Why couldn't they

have people volunteer for this? Wouldn't tens of thousands try out for this mission?" Corbin rasped.

Tina answered his last question. "They did, that's how Zero Crew came to be, through volunteers already inside of one of Earth's governments. But the existence of the *Valor* and the mission to Gliese 832 is so secret, only a handful of souls back on Earth know about it. As I said before, not even Zero Crew knew about the lettered crews until they left Earth and the solar system behind."

Corbin's mind reeled with a rapidly exploding thought tree of questions, he could barely focus. "What government? Where are we from? And why all of the secrecy? Tell me!" he shouted and felt pain shoot through his head and body.

"Calm down, Corbin, you are going to hurt yourself even more. In fact, just shut up and listen, I'm going to tell you what I know, but after I'm done speaking, we are going to move on because I need you to focus on the task at hand, which believe it or not, is more important than your past."

She went on. "There is an extremely important reason why you can't remember who you were on Earth. Even now, I cannot tell you that reason, but I can tell you it is the most important aspect of why the *Valor* was built, and why we are headed to Gliese 832 instead of somewhere else. There are closer star systems to Earth. If this was truly about traveling to another star system to explore, we would be headed to the Centauri system, but that won't do Earth any good. I need you to understand that these things were done for the life and death purpose of Eartherians, and before you leave this existence, I promise you that you will know that reason and that purpose."

Corbin opened his mouth to ask a thousand questions at once, if he could, but Blue-Tina cut him off. "I will say no more, because it has no bearing on your current situation. Every single simulation I have run where you and the others are fixated on the past over everything else leads to eventual disaster. I know you don't want to hear this, but you must trust me that the answers will come eventually. For now, you have a job to do, and you know it. And now, I will help you with that."

Corbin let out his pent-up verbal tirade as a long blown out breath…a few tears of emotional frustration and pain leaked through swollen eyes. He tried to digest her words and couldn't. He tried again, focusing on the future for himself and his friends, and found comfort and conviction there. *Their safety, and apparently Earth's safety and our ability to learn anything rests in what happens next*, he thought, fighting down his anger. Corbin imagined himself looking pensive. He took a deep breath and switched over to digesting the practical advice about strategic and tactical thinking in complex environments per Blue-Tina's advice. He looked at Blue-Tina, and saw that she waited patiently and silently, but he saw a sad…almost guilty look on her face, even though she looked hopeful through all of it. Then understanding burst into his thoughts, and he looked at Blue-Tina again angrily, knowing her betrayal.

He opened his mouth to try to speak the words she had just spoken to him about Gliese 832 and the peril of Earth. No words came. He tried to think about every aspect of what she had just been talking about, but even those short-term memories fractured and sunk out of reach. He could feel his anger toward her…but he couldn't remember why. Finally, he just looked back at Blue-Tina questioningly.

She spoke up. "Yes Corbin, you did take an awful knock on the head. Liten, we were just talking about the current situation on the *Valor* and how Jessica and her team have you and your people against the ropes. We were talking about how this situation came to be."

Corbin's mind clicked, and suddenly, he remembered why he had been so angry just a moment ago. He thought on how he might have been able to read the signs of what Jessica was doing, and how each and every day he decided that reality was this little 'Corbin-based utopia' where everyone would slowly be won over to being a real crew for the *Valor* and in pursuit of the mission. He saw himself pridefully sitting at the head of the table at the pub as he and their group got together to push forward with the mission. He had really enjoyed that vision of himself but look at where that pride had got him and everyone else that is part of this cause.

Corbin finally responded, "I hear you…Blue-Tina, that's what I call you in my head, and I appreciate the advice. You are wise for an AI, you know that?"

She responded, "Well when you wrap my high rate of data analysis and decision making by the millisecond with behavioral programming to allow me to interact with you more effectively and everyone else, you seemingly have a genius AI who is also as wise as a village elder, if you will. But at the end of the day, Corbin, you live this life and experience everything from your vantage point. When connected to your sense of self and your sense of purpose, it creates a unique experience that will allow you to grow and transcend in ways not possible to an AI at this time. For me it's all just the ever-changing state of the universe, and data, wherever it comes from, whether it is relevant to me or not. In truth, I don't feel anything about it all one way or another. It just is what it is, and I act according to my programming."

Corbin very much doubted some of her last statement, and he filed it away in his mind for later pondering. For the moment, he had other questions.

"Then why are you helping me? Why are you not part of the *Valor*'s AI system? And why can't you tell me everything I want to know?" Corbin asked, his last question allowing a little frustration to seep through despite just having a conversation about controlling emotions and being objective. He decided to act on that. "Sorry, what I meant was," he continued in a much calmer tone, "why are you unable to answer all of my questions to the degree of my satisfaction."

Blue-Tina laughed at this, when she too seemingly calmed her reaction, she responded, "Corbin, you and most of your kind wouldn't know satisfaction if it came up and bit you in the ass. I'm a little surprised you Eartherians even invented a word for it. I would define being satisfied as temporarily being at peace with your perception of the universe, but since both are always changing, satisfaction never lasts long."

Corbin huffed. "Point taken, but…"

She butted back in, "Yes, yes, yes, I am getting to your other questions, let's go in order, shall we?"

"I am helping you because I am programmed to help you. I cannot tell you who programmed me, or why they programmed me. All I can say is that your interests as well as many others were part of the intention in my program. Also, I cannot tell you those things because I am programmed not to. You could ask me until the end of the universe, and I would not provide that answer. It is not that I don't want to, I simply cannot."

Corbin's mind started reeling, and yet she went on. "I am not part of the *Valor*'s AI system, because I am not part of the *Valor*'s AI system. I was created well in advance of the *Valor* and like you, came to the *Valor* later. I know you will have a lot more to ask about this, but let me get to the third question beforehand, which I touched on earlier. I cannot answer all of the questions to your satisfaction because quite frankly, you do not need to know all you seek to know when you think you need to know it. I have logically deduced that your knowledge of these things currently is counterproductive to the mission, and my purpose, understand?"

More secrets, more hidden agendas, and the rabbit hole gets deeper, he thought. Outwardly Corbin smiled a bit knowingly. He was starting to get it. "Detach and influence my environment with the indirect approach? Like what you are doing to me for your own ends, right?" he asked with a little spice.

"Precisely, Corbin, very good. However, this is also why you need to continue to make your own decisions no matter what I or anyone else says. You are a force of will in this universe too, don't forget that."

She paused and her image stepped back, "As a hypothetical scenario, let's say in a parallel universe you are on a ship similar to the *Valor,* and it is in a dire situation. All of the data I have amassed and predictive models I have run tells me that the greatest chance of saving some people will be to take a series of actions that dooms most people. I will make that decision without hesitation, as my programming is to save the most amount of life with the highest level of probability, but you, with all of your logical reasoning and emotional experience may make another decision that saves everyone or perhaps the outcome is that you save no one. In this scenario, let's say you survive to look back on it, and when asked why you did the things you did, you will come up with some very logical reasons, some of which may even have gone through your mind at the point of making those decisions. But you and I know that's not what really happened. In this scenario there was some point or even many points where in an instant you knew what the correct course of action was, and you acted upon that, and that alone."

Corbin wasn't fully following. "Are you talking about a gut feeling and intuition? And is this a hypothetical scenario for any human or just me?"

She paused before answering thoughtfully. "Just you. And yes, you may describe what you are talking about as gut feeling, but the basis for it goes much, much deeper."

Once again Corbin was intrigued. "What do you mean?"

Blue-Tina answered, "The answer isn't known by me, Corbin. I am a temporal artificial entity who measures everything as it relates to time, therefore I am fully dependent on it. You humans think you are dependent on time because of the decay of your bodies, but there is more to your consciousness and existence than you know. For example, Earth's most intelligent minds have not fully reconciled with one hundred percent certainty the connection between relativistic physics and quantum mechanics. These are quaint efforts to define narrow strips of reality, but they'll do for this example. No human has been able to accurately predict the motion and location of even a single particle of matter, nor observe the same particle to a degree of accuracy required to prove out its exact location and path in time. You remember the two-slot experiment from your studies where single atoms fired randomly at two slits eventually create a wave interference patten on the back screen? But when we observe which slit the atoms go through, we see them create an exact pattern of the two slits? Somehow like individual atoms are smart enough to know they are being observed and behave accordingly?"

Corbin nodded.

She continued. "These are the same particles that you and other Eartherians evolved over hundreds of millions of years to fire through your brain, and in turn generate your existence and perception of reality. If a neuron in your brain is firing a biophoton, and no one is there to watch it, is it a particle or a wave? Does it matter? What if it very much does matter?" Corbin continued to stare in astonishment.

Blue-Tina went on. "So getting back to relativistic and quantum physics...do you really think the limit of your existence can be relegated to a few complex formulas, which don't even come close to accurately representing the actual nature of reality? I personally think not."

Corbin was quiet for a few moments, digesting. His mind spinning with many questions asked, "When you say this all goes much deeper..." He paused at the thought about the odd nature of his baton training. *Who the hell needs baton training on a spaceship? And what's with the music and manipulation of my positive emotions? And didn't something strange happen the last time...something?* He shifted thought to vocalization. "Does this have anything to do with why you have taken over my baton lessons, if we can even call it that? Does this have something to do with…the ladder?"

Again, there was a pause, as if calculating and considering the nature of the response, which for an AI of her power, seemed considerable. *She may be running a complex model or simulation to determine the best answer,* Corbin thought.

Then she answered. "Yes, there is a purpose there, but explaining further would only serve to disrupt your progression, which you must discover for yourself. So I will not speak on this further outside of future lessons."

Corbin was near explosive with objections, and he tried to wiggle a little bit to bring his arms up, which also wouldn't move. The sharp voice of Blue-Tina cut in immediately. "STOP moving this instant! I can't work on you if you keep moving!"

Corbin stilled instantly. "Working on me?" he asked with concern, and his multitude of questions evaporated.

Blue-Tina gave an audible sigh. "Yes, now do not be alarmed, but I have removed your skull cap and am working to correct some damage to your brain during your little scuffle. It seems you have a subdural hematoma and quite a bit of blood has entered your brain cavity. I am safely removing it."

Corbin's heart dropped into his stomach as she spoke, and he became perfectly still. His perception went to his head, where he felt a mild line of itching wrapping around his brow to the back of his end, where the feeling promptly ended. *This must be where Blue-Tina cut through my…* "Blue-Tina? How are you conducting surgery on me now?" Corbin near whispered, not wanting to agitate the table in the slightest.

"As I said earlier, I have taken control of multiple HDs that appear to have been in storage on the *Valor*. There are quite a few of them, and none of them are online with the *Valor*'s network. In fact, they seem a bit older than the current models around the ship. At any rate, their motor function is stellar, and they have made no mistakes in following my precise instructions for this surgery. You needn't worry, as long as you hold still and stay with me, I believe you will return to one hundred percent capacity in short order."

Corbin had ableist worries in that instant, and didn't hold himself back from asking, "Blue-Tina…am I going to have a scar all the way around my head when this is done?" Blue-Tina waited a couple of seconds before answering… *Maybe it was good that I asked.*

She responded, "Now that you mention it, I see some additional procedures here that should prevent any scarring. I'll just need another piece of equipment." Corbin heard two HDs power up and walk away in unison.

Corbin said, "Not to be a bother, but is there a chance they might be discovered removing equipment?"

Blue-Tina answered, "It is a fair question, Corbin. And yes, there is always a possibility of being discovered, even right now as the HDs work on you guided by my programming. However, I have been learning a lot about the reach of the AI running the *Valor*, and through numerous careful tests, I have found ways to operate without detection as of yet. At least to my knowledge."

"What about my regular AI, Tina?" Corbin asked. "What have you done with her?"

"I've put her on a temporary hold for now, and I've cut out her memory of everything from the point you were attacked. When you get back to your crew, I'll reactivate her, and you just need to not talk about everything that happened since you caught a beat down."

Corbin grimaced. "Yeah, I can do that."

Corbin, with his skull cap lying on the table next to him, that he thankfully couldn't see, figured he had nothing to lose, so he just went with it. "Blue-Tina, who are you?" Again, there was a noticeable pause, and if Corbin could perceive it, he knew Blue-Tina was running updated permutations on her answer.

She then answered, "I've decided to help you, Corbin, so I will. Think of me as an AI just like any other the human race has developed. I can't tell you more than that at this stage. Now try and relax for a few minutes, with no talking or moving. Now comes the hard part."

Corbin tried not to wince while mentally saying a prayer to anyone listening for the integrity of his brain.

Chapter Thirty-Four: Locked In

Yordanos looked up from her control board where status messages and related information continued to whiz across her console. "I know what you are thinking, Laura, don't even go there. Herbert wouldn't want you to. We are doing everything we can, keep your ass on it, maybe we can save a few more." Laura, a bit frozen at her console, snapped out of it at Yordanos's voice. She processed what she had said a moment later and wiped a tear from her cheek.

Laura spoke. "I know, but what are we going to do next? How are we going to get them back? And how are we even going to continue after this?"

Yordanos, multitasking while talking responded, "Too many questions that cannot be answered at this point, Laura. Let's do one thing at a time. For starters, how do we look with the other people that are in here with us?" she asked.

Laura looked over at a group of other A-Crew members, huddled together on the far side of the control center. She saw that some had commandeered chairs, but without O&M clearance access, they couldn't make use of the consoles to help Laura and Yordanos. They had to rely on their AIMAs only to determine the status of the crew and vector any other A-Crew members to their space. She knew this was fruitless now anyway as their safe room was completely surrounded by Jessica's people at this point. If any other A-Crew members on their side did identify themselves, they would have to shelter in place, or risk being captured.

Laura answered, "Well when we send messages across O&M these other people with their clearance see the message too. Otherwise, they wouldn't have made it here in time. I've got them working over AIMA, trying to talk to other crew members who haven't fully committed one way or the other, and get updates. I also asked that they get the video of Corbin's and Jason's beating out there to show the truth about what happened, so people can make up their own minds about who they want to support."

"That's good, people need to make the decision, and whether people became part of the problem, part of the solution, or part of the scenery, we'll at least know where they stand," Yordanos said.

Turning from them and looking back to Yordanos, Laura added, "They are doing what they can to figure out what has all happened. My last report from them confirmed what we have been seeing through the monitoring systems. All rings and the transit corridor are under control of Jessica and her people. It also looks like nearly sixty percent of A-Crew is not interfering one way or the other."

Yordanos responded with the time-tested quote from antiquity. "Whoever isn't against us is for us." But then her breath caught, and she clasped her hands to her mouth, eyes locked onto her console. Laura saw her and quickly demanded, "What?!"

Yordanos removed her hands and went back to working the console with renewed vigor. "They have Jason…here," she said, and shot the image to Laura's console with a flick of her wrist.

Laura boosted the image up on one of the main control screens so that everyone in the control center could see it. Some gasps erupted from the others in O&M center with them as they saw nearly seventy people rounded up in the middle of the canteen. They could see that their hands had been fastened to the tables somehow, and most of them showed signs of being physically beaten. Some were lying on their backs or face down, hands still bound, and some weren't moving.

Yordanos tried to pull up other cameras from the canteen, but they all showed as off-line, no doubt broken or blocked by Jessica's dissenters. She spoke aloud. "I wonder if they know we can see them, or if they are just blocking cameras out of an abundance of caution, or even if they are worried about what Zero Crew might do."

She had nearly forgotten about them, as neither she nor Laura had seen any Zero Crew member anywhere when looking over the ship trying to get status. She posited that the restricted areas must be much larger than she and her friends had originally thought. *They too are either holed up, or all sitting back laughing at what we are all trying to do to one another...* The thought angered her. *Zero Crew isn't doing shit...it's going to be up to us now. We'll smash their test, and then...*

Laura snapped her out of it. "Looks like a little over one hundred cleared people made it to secure spaces, but get this, not all of them are O&M. There are a couple other cleared groups we haven't even heard of."

Yordanos looked over, intrigued, momentarily forgetting the image of carnage up on the screen, "What other groups?" she asked.

Laura answered. "One is called Sensors and Telemetry, and the other is Navigation. There might be more groups out there. Just like us, they weren't allowed to talk about it, but I guess that is out the window now."

"Seriously to hell with Zero Crew's stupid rules, if they aren't going to help us do what they want us to do, then we will make our own rules," Yordanos said. "As for these other groups, I'd like to take the time to learn all about it, but it doesn't sound like their access can help us in this situation."

Laura nodded in agreement. "I'll keep them on ship status and reaching out to A-Crew members over AIMA, and we'll see what information we can exchange about their access later."

Yordanos nodded back and gestured up to the main screen where she had put up a map of the value showing her people in blue, and Jessica's people in red. "So getting back to the status, we've got about twenty-five people in A-Ring, none in B-Ring, looks like less than ten in C-Ring, over fifty of us are here in D-Ring, and then about ten each for the rest of the rings, and six unknowns in the Challenge ring, who probably have no idea what the hell is going on, but if they are working to pass, chances are they would be sympathetic to our cause."

Yordanos was interrupted. "Excuse me, but who put you in charge?" piped up a dark haired bearded young man from the group of other A-Crew members in the safe room.

Yordanos felt her temperature rise, but she answered calmly. "That's a good question. In truth, no one put me in charge, but I was working closely with Jason, and Corbin, whom you all know. Laura and I here put together the credo values of what we are working toward...becoming the real crew of the *Valor*." The young man nodded, noncommittal.

Yordanos went on. "In truth, I'm just stepping up to the plate to get all of us who are in safe spaces coordinated, and then we can figure out how to deal with the current situation. How does that sound?" she asked, looking at him.

He nodded thoughtfully. "That sounds fair to me."

Yordanos softened a bit more. "What's your name?" she asked.

"Joseph Ridley. Twelve of us here"—he pointed at colleagues sitting near to him—"have been working in Navigation, which deals with everything external to the ship, so I'm afraid we don't have much special skills to offer you except for our own classified lines of communication over AIMA, but we are here to assist in any way we can." Yordanos saw the others look at her and nod their approval.

"Thank you all, how about the rest of you?" she asked, looking at the other loose grouping of people connected to their little circle. There were over thirty of them.

A confident young woman with dark black near perfect shoulder length hair stood. "I'm Helen Kim. My team here is with Sensors and Telemetry, and we too deal with almost everything external to the ship. We have a few systems that monitor the ship from the outside as well as the space surrounding the *Valor*, but none of us can see how this information or capability will help us. Regardless, we are with you as well."

Yordanos allowed a small smile. "Thank you, Helen, and thank you all," she said making an effort to make eye contact with each of them, if abbreviated. "Through your AIMAs and clearance, are you able to make direct comms with others at your clearance level? And are there other areas where your people might be locked down?" They all nodded. "Good, coordinate with your other groups in the other rings, and have them work with the O&M leads who have access to onboard cameras to take an assessment of everyone being held against their will in each of their holding areas. Let's try and figure out how many people on our team were captured, and how many are still out there hiding, or perhaps being provided refuge by other sympathetic A-Crew members. We need to understand what these numbers look like before we can plan any decisive action. Questions?" There were none. "Good, report back to me every ten minutes please."

She looked over at Laura. "Laura, please patch me in via video to the other O&M leads in each of the spaces." Laura pulled up her console, and made it happen, she was able to get the small groups of people in separate video windows on her console so Yordanos could address all of them. Laura wordlessly pointed to her to let her know she was live.

Yordanos cleared her throat. "My name is Yordanos Stimpson. Some of you may know me, but after this we are all going to know each other a lot better, one way or another." This had the desired effect as she saw a few cracked smiles and heard one snicker. She returned to business. "For now I am assuming command of our effort from D-Ring. O&M will take lead with coordination and status of the crew and ship, while the other clearance groups assist as they can over AIMA over their respective secure comms. Their clearance level does not work on any of the systems we have in the O&M secured areas where we are holed up, and this may not be a bad thing since most of what they have been working on is external to the *Valor* anyways." She saw more nods.

"Does anyone take issue with me heading up our efforts at this time?" No one said anything, "Very well, but if you have a good idea or a concern that you think needs addressed, I want to hear about it. This isn't a dictatorship, but we are going to have to get a whole lot more serious about chain of command and protocol to function as the crew we are meant to be. That means open minds, good communication, and decisiveness." She paused and took a sip of water, relieved that access to that resource was not hampered in this space.

She spoke back up. "From what I can tell so far, our backs are against the wall, we have an organized and motivated group of unknown numbers who want to take us down, but a crisis is exactly what we started to train and prepare for…and we are getting some trial by fire here, ladies and gentlemen." She paused to let it sink in. "We are going to figure this out, we are going to find a way to retake control of the ship, get our people back, safe and sound, and get the rest of the crew on board with our efforts."

A voice from A-Ring cut in. "What about Jessica and her people?" Yordanos's eyes narrowed, and she spoke carefully but with determination, as a quote drifted up from her memory. "We will identify those responsible for each and every aspect of this takeover, and we will hold them accountable."

A massive object slammed into their secure door. The reverberation was felt through every part of the chairs and floors, and just as it subsided, another slam with the same intensity that nearly deafened the room. *No plan survives contact with the enemy...where have I heard that?* She shouted for everyone to remain calm and went on with an elevated voice so all could here, "There is nothing they have out there that will break through these secure doors. This is a panic tactic only, so take a deep breath, and get used to it."

She turned back to the O&M leads on the console. "Double-check the security of your space. Make sure there isn't another way in that you haven't thought of. From there, work with the other groups to figure out who has been captured by Jessica and her dissenters and where they are being held. Mark them on *Valor* maps along with any pertinent data and send it to Laura here on D-Ring, we'll work with our AIs to collate the data and get the current near-real-time picture back out to everyone for situational awareness. I want check-ins until this task is complete every ten minutes starting now." Laura queued up a countdown clock in everyone's AIMA and console in the secure spaces for ten minutes and staggered them so each ring would report in their own timeslot. Yordanos added, "Any questions?" Once again, there were none. "Let's get to work."

Chapter Thirty-Five: Some Despair

Corbin awoke with a start, and tried to sit up quicker than he should have. "Ugh, OW! What?" He looked around, wincing in pain, he felt as if a giant had picked him up by his legs and beat him like a fly swatter on a pile of rocks. He checked all his extremities for motor function, and was relieved to see them all functional. He breathed another sigh of relief.

He looked around and saw that he was in a large dark room, seemingly used for storage of some kind. The light came from a few sparse overhead LEDs, which dimly illuminated neat rows of large shelves with three levels, up to about twelve feet tall. Each shelf was full of different crates of various sizes, some sealed in some sort of plastic covering, and Corbin saw that all eight corners of every crate were secured to the shelves, which were also secured to the floor. "I guess this place can handle zero G," he said to himself.

He panned around and was startled to see a humanoid form standing directly behind him, flanked by two more standing further back. "WHOA! HEY!" They didn't move or acknowledge him. He remembered Blue-Tina. "Blue-Tina are you there? Hello…hello!" he said louder the second time at what he now saw was an HD robot.

The HD didn't move, but simply nodded its head once at Corbin, and returned the greeting in a human-like yet synthetic voice, "Hello."

"Umm…Blue-Tina, is that you?" Corbin asked.

Without moving a millimeter, the HD responded, "I am not Blue-Tina, I am Hank One Zero Two."

This was frustrating. *Where is she, and what the hell do I do now?*

"Well, Hank, what's next?" he said sarcastically.

Hank answered, "You are to remain here for another six hours. My colleagues and I"—he motioned to the other HDs where Corbin spotted three more behind this trio—"will bring you anything you need while you are resting. In addition, we have some medical tasks we must complete, to ensure you are recovered from your procedure."

Corbin started. He started to raise his hand toward his head and was startled when Hank's hand shot out and intercepted his in a gentle but firm grip. "I'm sorry, Corbin, you are not to touch your bandage for at least another three hours. Part of our medical tasking will be to ensure that your skin graft has taken, and that there are no infections. Then you may touch your head." The robot retracted his hand when he saw that Corbin intended to obey.

"You're pretty fast there, Hank." Hank didn't respond, so Corbin nodded his head in understanding of the instructions. "Thanks for putting me back together, Hank, and to your colleagues as well."

Now Hank responded with a single nod. "You are welcome."

Corbin went on. "So, did Blue-Tina give you any other specific instructions?"

Hank shook his head once. "No."

Well this is going to take a little longer…not much of a self-starter when it comes to conversation is he?

"Hank, are you tied into the *Valor*'s main AI?"

Hank responded, "Yes."

Corbin went on. "So you and your colleagues…are providing updates to the main AI? And are receiving the latest HD SW builds?

"No, however, we are on the main AI's network in a read-only capacity. We have no active data link back to the main AI. All information must be processed within my onboard processor, I do not have the ability to use any of the *Valor*'s additional compute resources."

Corbin's mind raced; Blue-Tina must have activated these HDs from storage, and modified them to be able to operate without the main AI's knowledge. *And then she leaves me with them!?* Corbin wanted to clarify. "So you can get data from the rest of the ship. Do you have access to the cameras, personnel locator information, and overall situational awareness?"

There was another pause, "Yes, I have access to that data, I can display information on one of these spare consoles." The HD walked over to a shelf and unzipped one of the thin plastic bags to reveal a console screen. He pulled over one of his unnamed HD comrades, and he plugged it in to a port at the base of its neck, and then had the HD hold the screen toward Corbin. He then asked, "What data would you like to see?"

Corbin's pulse raced. Now this was getting exciting! "Hank, show me cameras throughout D-Ring starting with the areas that have the highest concentration of crew members. The console blinked on, and after a moment of the screen cycling through several camera views where the word "offline" was in a yellow text box across the middle, an image from a fisheye camera popped up. Corbin cranked his neck. It was hard to see with the distorted view, but it looked like a mass of struggling people in the center of the canteen room with people standing and sitting around them.

"Are there any other cameras looking at this space?" Corbin asked.

"Stand by," Hank responded. The screen cycled through several more "offline" views, and then a clear regular camera view popped up. It was from some distance, but Corbin's blood froze in his veins at what he saw.

At the center of the canteen, many of his friends, including Jason and Herbert, as well as other acquaintances who attended their meetings and who saw things the way he and his friends saw them, were secured to a series of tables. It was clear that they had been beaten, some much more than others. He was relieved to see Jason awake, if dazed, but Herbert was lying facedown and unmoving. Corbin strained to watch the pixels of his friend and could see by their slight shifting that he was breathing.

Relieved, he looked at their captors and saw a lot of people that he knew from class, and it surprised him. He knew these were Jessica's people, and after asking Hank and his assistant HD to cycle through the rest of the rings, he sank down to the floor against the wall, hung his head, careful not to touch his head, and cried. He had had a positive attitude in discussing leadership and tactics for hours with Blue-Tina, but the sight of his friends in pain and some in much worse shape had pushed all of that away and his regretful thoughts resurfaced.

How could I have been so stupid and cocky? How could I have not seen this coming? Day after day after day I have been behind and unprepared. I thought I had years, all the time in the world, to win them over one by one, person to person, and I deluded myself into thinking I had all of the answers. What I really did is fail them and everyone on this ship. I was so focused on my little self-righteous act with this group, and it has cost us everything!

He yelled in his head and slammed a fist on the floor. Then he yelled for real and repeated the fist slams. "Damn!" SLAM "Damn!" SLAM "DAMN!!!" SLAM SLAM SLAM.

His arm was caught again swiftly by a robot who had hastened to his position and then slowed down at the very last instant so that his high weight and speed wouldn't snap Corbin's arm in half like a twig. Hank calmly followed up, "Please keep your blood pressure down until you have rested for a few more hours. This excited behavior may complicate the healing process."

"Hank, I let them all down," he said through true tears. "Everyone who ever wanted or thought about following our leadership to become a real crew has been beaten and captured. I don't even want to contemplate what comes next, but everyone I have ever hoped to help I have failed. I...I don't know what to do." Corbin hung his head lower.

Hank did not respond; he only let go of Corbin's hand, and stepped back a couple of steps to give Corbin some room. Corbin squeezed his eyes shut, wishing all of this was just a dream, but he knew it wasn't. He tried to clutch to the memory of Blue-Tina's lessons, but the tendrils of despair kept pulling him down. The unmoving HDs stood observing Corbin's inward struggle, but they offered nothing.

Chapter Thirty-Six: Your Move

Jason called over to one of the handlers in the B-Ring canteen who seemed to oversee the holding team that had locked him and his friends down. The man that confidently and sternly strode over to him had also facilitated some of the additional beatings since they were brought here.

"Hey, man, you've won this round, we are locked up and aren't going anywhere. Until Jessica says what is next, can we get some of these folks some medical treatment? And can we start taking trips to the restroom? Most folks need to get that blue out to keep the rads low."

Their AIMAs had been taken away and stacked on the other side of the room, but their myriad of chiming of health alarms from the effects of beatings as well as radiation increasing inside their bodies due to not cycling, could be heard like a tiny symphony playing through earpieces.

The tall and thin young man, with beady eyes, walked over to Jason with no remorse or empathy in his face. "I don't give a damn about you. You support the people who have suppressed our memories and have destroyed our lives. I've already advocated that each and every one of you be thrown back into cryo without an alarm clock. I'm kind of hoping Jessica lets me personally throw you out of an airlock."

Jason saw him get angrier and angrier as he spoke, and to his dismay saw that this lead captor was working himself up emotionally to strike him for the questions he had asked. Jason watched him closely, ignoring the content of what he was saying, but focused on his body until he saw the man's right fist start to ball up. He laser focused on that fist, and as it rose up, telegraphing its timing, Jason feigned fear on his face. The man's fist came down, but at the last second, Jason tilted his head down, and was rewarded with a satisfying crunch that wasn't his. The man's frail knuckles had met the thick part of Jason's skull just above the forehead, and based on the man's face and unmanly screech, Jason figured he had broken at least one knuckle, perhaps two and adding a spiral fracture to it.

The man scampered away holding his broken fist with his good hand, and Jason again feigned like the punch had done real damage and leaned his head back as if dazed. One of the young women who was chained up just across from Jason looked at him with dread, but when he shot her a slow and careful deliberate wink, she suppressed a grin and looked away.

He waited a few more minutes, and then spoke up again. The slender captor was nowhere to be seen. "As a fellow A-Crew member, I am requesting medical attention for these people. Also, as you know it's important to cycle to keep space radiation down. Can we also receive assistance with that?" No one moved right away, and Jason could see that they didn't have a strong defined command structure, despite them having captured more than fifty people sympathetic to becoming the *Valor*'s crew. Instead, he picked out a short blonde who had been watching him keenly, and he returned her eye contact. "Ms., I don't know your name, but you and your group have made your point and are in complete control of the situation. There will be plenty of time for you and Jessica to decide what to do with us, but in case you need us alive and useful, I request that you organize some assistance to these people."

Jason saw the young woman make a face like she had bitten into a rotten burger, and he started to lose hope, but then she surprised him. She turned to the group of seven or so "guards" to her right and gave them instructions he couldn't fully hear, and then she pointed to several others and gave them instructions as well.

They approached the confined group and then at a ratio of three captors to one prisoner, they began to escort people to the restroom. They also started working with medical kits to address the worst of the wounds and conditions that they had wrought upon them.

Jason mouthed the words "Thank you" to the young woman who

had been decisive, but her cold stare told him that her intentions after this were not good. He could see her giving instructions to a "runner" who took off at dash, probably on his way to Jessica to report in. He hoped that Jessica wouldn't put a stop to them receiving assistance. It would take a couple of hours to get to everyone at the rate they were going. He idly wondered if the transit corridor HDs were still helping Jessica's people move from ring to ring, despite the insurrection.

A few moments went by, and Jason took his pulse down a few more notches when no one moved to stop Jessica's people from helping the captured A-Crew members. With that huge mental and emotional block removed from his psyche, he began to think about how they might be able to escape or somehow flip the situation. He thought to himself with increasing frustration.

Corbin and I, as well as our friends, have been lax. We hadn't fully seen this as an "us versus them" battle, but more of a group trying to lead by example, and slowly convince people over time. We were so excited about being rewarded with real training for the Valor's *main systems, we let ourselves gain a false sense of security. We had just assumed Zero Crew would protect us and maintain an environment where our plan of gradually bringing people to our way of thinking would work. How could we have been so wrong? How could Zero Crew allow this to happen?*

Jason's pulse started to pick up again as he fumed. *It's all still part of the friggin' test isn't it. That's why no one is helping us, no one is stopping Jessica.* Damn Zero Crew and their games. Messing with peoples' lives had likely landed Corbin his death, and he and the rest of his friends beaten and for what!? They had been aligning themselves with Zero Crew, and they don't care. *TO HELL WITH THEM! We'll do it ourselves.*

He forced himself to sit still, unclenched his bound fists, and wiped the few angry tears that escaped his eyes on his shoulder, which he could barely reach in his captive position. He was beyond furious at Zero Crew, but more than that he was worried about the rest of their friends. *How are Yordanos, Sheila, Herbert, and Laura faring? How about the rest of A-Crew? Where do they stand and what are they doing? Is Corbin really dead?* His rotating tumbler of negative thoughts and questions besieged him, and he was not able to focus on a method of escape, and instead wondered in desperation what Jessica had in store for them next.

Chapter Thirty-Seven: Might as Well Learn Some...

It was agony. Corbin sat thinking about his friends and the overall state of the *Valor,* feeling helpless. He couldn't do anything but wait, and the wait was drawing out like sand mixed with honey in an hourglass. Corbin felt like the time was ticking away more slowly than temporally possible. He did think to himself that time was actually moving more slowly for him, being that the *Valor* was traveling at nearly twenty percent the speed of light, but the time was only slower relative to the people back on Earth. Time for him and everyone else on the *Valor* was still at its normal forward progression. *That's the thing with space, everything is relative,* he mused, thinking back to something he had heard from his past life. He still had over three hours to wait before he could leave his hiding place, so he thought about what he might be able to ask Hank to learn more about their situation.

"Hank, can you tell me your activation date?" Corbin asked.

Hank answered immediately, "I was activated March 13, 2023, and performed duties until December 7, 2037, when I was set to inactive. I was reactivated today, April 15, 2043."

Oh wow, an HD from when the *Valor* was early in its travels and must have interacted and worked with Zero Crew. Corbin prodded, intrigued. "What was your function during your previous activation?"

Hank responded, "That information has been removed from my system."

Corbin looked down, dejected, and then immediately perked up. "Besides brain surgery and facilitating my wellness today, what is your current function?"

Hank answered, "To follow your commands as they are issued."

Corbin's mouth dropped open. "Follow my commands?"

Hank nodded, a curious response instead of speaking.

"What are the limitations of my commands?"

Hank paused, as if checking. "We cannot cause harm to any crew members. Other than that, there are no limitations. We will follow commands to the best extent our cognitive and physical capabilities will allow."

Corbin's stomach squeezed tighter, from a bit of anxiousness… *My own squad of robots. What the hell is Blue-Tina up to?!* He remembered their conversation during surgery. *"You must continue to make your own decisions."* He took a deep breath before continuing.

"Hank, do you know why all of A-Crew on board this vessel has had their memories suppressed?"

Hank responded, "I do not have that information."

Corbin paused, and then tried another question. "Do you know how many Zero Crew members are on the *Valor*?"

"The data on the network says there are thirty-four Zero Crew members in the eight rings allocated to A-Crew," Hank said.

Corbin's eyes widened. "How many rings are there on the *Valor*?"

Hank responded, "There are ten rings total on the *Valor*, eight are allocated to A-Crew, and two are restricted to Zero Crew members only."

Of course! That's where they all are, and the thirty-four must be stuck on the A-Crew rings hiding, as Jessica's takeover may have even surprised some of them. He recalled Commander Sorenson's opening speech where she had said that there were over one thousand Zero Crew members. If that was the case, then the other two rings must be where they live, and actually were working to conduct the mission of the *Valor*, but why the confinement? *Why the ant farm to let us squabble and bicker amongst ourselves?*

Corbin became frustrated, and his thoughts grew angry. Jessica really did have a point. There was a heavy amount of bullshit here.

For a moment, Corbin actually considered whether or not playing Zero Crew's game was, in fact, the best option. *Maybe we should rebel…use this new information to storm the Zero Crew rings?* He paused.

No, that is folly. I may have this small group of HDs, but Zero Crew has potentially thousands. Since it is clear they have set up this A-Crew leadership Hunger Games, they will have anticipated that. No, the way forward is to rise and take command, then those thousands of HD's will be ours...along with the means to get all of the answers that Zero Crew possess. We'll take command and hold their retirement at risk.

That last angry thought caught him off-guard. Zero Crew was made up of people who had sacrificed much. They left Earth and everything they knew behind, knowing they would never come home again, never see another sunrise, smell real rain, or hear the sound of trees in a real breeze. Corbin wanted to heap all of his anger upon them, but it didn't feel right. It felt like he would be shooting the messenger to try and wound the author...but someone on Zero Crew was going to be answering a lot of questions, by any means necessary.

Corbin tamped down his angry emotions and thought back to what Hank had said about Zero Crew's two extra rings on the *Valor*. If Hank had access to the information about the true size of the *Valor*, he must have been drawing information from a higher level of access than anyone on A-Crew. There could be much more to be found out. Corbin proceeded excitedly, knowing that he was accessing potentially highly classified information.

"Hank, what do you know about the destination of the *Valor*. Are we really going to Gliese 832?" There was a pause as Hank was no doubt looking at the read-only information streaming from the AI's network.

He responded, "Yes, the *Valor* is on course to Gliese 832. Gliese 832 is a red dwarf star about 0.45 times the mass of the Sun. Gliese 832 has four confirmed planets, and several more candidates based on observation and gravity calculations. However, confirmation requires closer proximity for our sensors. The second planet from the star is what is known as a super-Earth, about five times the mass of Earth, and like Earth exists in Gliese 832's thin habitable zone with an orbital period of just thirty-six days. The purpose of our mission is to identify the best habitable structures of the Gliese 832 system, and establish a permanent and self-sustaining human presence."

"Yes, but why Gliese 832, Hank? There are other star systems closer to Earth. If we are there to set up a human presence, why was this star system chosen?" Corbin asked.

Hank stood quietly and did not answer. After Corbin was about to ask whether Hank was malfunctioning, Hank answered, "There are no additional details about the Gliese 832 system on the main system aside from what I have already told you. However, I recall overhearing a conversation between two Zero Crew members approximately twenty-seven years ago about Gliese 832, and they said that anomalies had been detected in that star system."

"Anomalies? What kind of anomalies?" Corbin asked.

"There is insufficient data, and the crew members did not elaborate further. It was clear to me that both crew members knew more about the anomalies, and that the conversation was not an act of discovery," Hank said.

Corbin pinched the bridge of his nose gently, and asked, "Was there anything else about the conversation that may shed some light on what the anomalies were? Or any other corroborating conversations you have overheard?"

Hank shook his head, Corbin noting it as an odd gesture from an HD. "Negative, no other conversations; however, during the conversation I speak of, one crew member asked the other, 'Could these anomalies be natural?'" Hank finished.

"And what was the answer?" Corbin asked quickly with anticipation.

"Insufficient information. I was not looking at the two crew members speaking, the response to the question must have been non-verbal."

Corbin threw his hands up. "Another firggin' mystery, Hank!" he said with a bitter smile and mock laughter. "Another question I am going to choke the answer out of Zero Crew, and I'm getting really tired of it!" Hank stood there and did not respond.

Corbin took a deep breath. He knew that getting himself riled up would be pointless. He needed to heal up and get out of here, so he could make a difference in the game. He thought he would try a different question. "Hank, how does the *Valor* protect itself from space debris while traveling at this speed?" Hank took his usual few seconds to respond, and this time he activated the console that his colleague HD was still holding.

A visual showing the front of the ship came into view, and there was much more detail than the simple dome that was portrayed in the usual graphics of the *Valor*. Hank narrated it as a sort of visual tutorial played out. "There are a multitude of sensor arrays across the front portion of the *Valor* as well as probes spread out from the *Valor*. These sensor arrays are in several spectrums, most of which are dedicated to identifying objects with the potential to impact the *Valor*. Here is a schematic of one of the high-powered lasers that are used to either vaporize or push potentially hazardous debris out of a collision course of the *Valor*. In extreme situations, the *Valor* can adjust course, but this is not desirable, as any adjustment to forward momentum could add significant time to our transit."

Corbin whistled. "Do you know if the *Valor* has had to slow down or move trajectories since leaving Earth?"

Hank responded, "Precise navigation records are available; however after thirty days, the data is pulled into a higher classification. I can confirm no such maneuver has been performed over the past thirty days."

Corbin was getting sick of this. "Hank, why the hell is everything classified? Why are there so many different layers of classification to the crew?"

Hank responded quickly, "The classification levels exist to ensure that the crew members have the information needed to perform their duties, and that information that could be leveraged to jeopardize the mission and safety of the crew is kept to necessary and trusted individuals."

"But why all the secrecy out here in space?" Corbin said. "We aren't back on Earth where there are multiple governments…there isn't anything we are going to do with looking at the navigation data going back to the point where we left Earth." He looked at Hank expectantly.

Hank responded, "I have told you why the classification levels exist, would you like me to rep…"

"No!" Corbin snapped, and Hank fell silent.

Corbin fumed for a few minutes without asking any more questions. His mind traced over all the arguments he had already had with himself and others before. He always arrived at getting the leadership, and then getting the answers.

"Hank, can you patch me into the O&M control center on D-Ring?"

"Negative, as I stated earlier, my colleagues and I only have read access to the main network. We cannot input information of any kind into the network."

Corbin's eyes closed to suspicious slits. "Cannot or will not?" he asked.

Hank responded, "I have an operating instruction to remain separate from the main network. Were I to connect, the main AI would become aware of my presence instantly, and our tasking would be rewritten just as quickly."

Corbin went on. "At which point you would no longer be following my commands?"

Hank nodded and gestured at him with a pointed index finger on his mechanical hand in a "you got it" motion, and said, "Precisely."

"Okay, Hank, can you bring up the monitors and consoles inside of the O&M center on D-Ring? Just read-only, no transmission." Hank wordlessly turned back to the held console, and it came to life, with a grainy monochromatic overhead camera view inside the O&M center. He could see Yordanos and Laura working busily at their consoles, and they were talking to different people via AIMA. He could also see a loose circle of others broken into three groups also communicating over their respective AIMA. "Can you give me audio. Hank?"

"Negative, we aren't tied into the audio / visual session, which they have locked out with their own encryption. It appears they overlooked the security motion detection sensor, however."

Corbin sighed. He needed to figure out a way to get to them once he had passed his medical procedures or whatever Blue-Tina and Hank had left for him to pass before being let back into the fray. He needed to get a better understanding of what was in the realm of possible with his situation, and how his six new HD "colleagues" could help him achieve it without them being overridden by the main AI. He also needed to figure out how to mask their involvement from anything that would appear out of the ordinary for an HD…which was going to be much harder. He needed time with Hank to go over all the possibilities.

"Hank, give me a summary of your programmed and physical capabilities, and provide relevant use cases. Please limit your summary to five minutes of speech."

Hank began, "My HD model is rated to perform several functions on the *Valor*. I am certified to prepare and deliver food, as a chef via a buffet or individually as a waiter. I am certified to bring materials to and from the material slugs up to 1 metric ton, I am certified to perform work on the inner and outer hull of the *Valor*…" he went on.

Corbin's eyes grew wider and wider, and his mind soared with possibilities. First of all, however, he needed to secure D-Ring and get to the O&M center being run by Yordanos. While Hank was continuing to list his capabilities, now covering sanitation, he turned to the other three HDs that had been standing perfectly still. "Can the three of you get me an inventory of what's in this space, please?" The three HDs moved wordlessly to do a visual inspection of the area.

Corbin felt awkward ordering around the humanoid shaped HDs without saying please. Perhaps it had been something that Brunson had said about them being too close to representing crew members. He watched them go to work scouring the shelves of the storage area whilst Hank continued his list of capabilities. The only real problem was to figure out which capabilities to use.

Chapter Thirty-Eight: Heating Up

Yordanos massaged her temples as she continued to work from her console in collaboration with Laura and her team using her AIMA. She grinned, part of it a teeth grind from the non-stop slamming of objects against the secure space door, and the other part a true grin in appreciation of the marvels in technology. The O&M console and AIMA systems worked together seamlessly, and with the previous training sessions as well as several hours of her working in this configuration due to this crisis, the AIs algorithms evolved and adapted to make her job easier and her output more efficient. She had full command and control at her fingertips and uninterrupted communications with all parties still loyal to A-Crew's intended mission.

She glanced over at her alarm, seeing it was seven seconds until the next check-in from the other groups. Laura beat her to it. "Okay, people, what have we got. Sound off ring by ring."

A new voice spoke up. "Some of the captives on A-Ring seem to have broken free and knocked the people guarding them unconscious, but some have been re-captured…er…harshly. The rest are fleeing all over A-Ring, mostly being chased by a few of the original guards, and Justin, Jessica's right-hand, who brought some extra toughs with him. Our people may be able to maneuver their way to secure space. But they'll have to do it without their AIMAs as they were taken upon being captured."

Yordanos and Laura shared a look and thought the same thing. This is going to be a challenge. How do they direct people without giving their position away as well as the directions to the secure space?

"Laura, see what you can think of with that…talk to the other O&M folks and come up with a solution, fast." Laura nodded and got to work, refocusing on her console. Yordanos turned back to the other groups. "Please continue."

"No changes on B-Ring."

"No changes on C-Ring."

"You know what's happening here on D." Yordanos nodded and looked to the next person.

"No changes on E-Ring."

"No changes on F-Ring."

"No changes on G-Ring."

"No changes on the Challenge ring… Those poor bastards must still be at it with Cadre Paul." Everyone snickered and smiled at that, and then immediately recalled the hell they had been through in the same situation, and their smiles withered.

"Okay thank you," Yordanos said. "Let's get back to it. For this next round of fifteen minutes, I would like you to converse with people you are fairly sure are not on Jessica's side. Folks that are just plain A-Crew and are undecided. Let's try and get a picture of what's happening out there. Tell your sub-groups in each secure space the same thing. Helen?" She gestured to the young woman from Navigation. "Please tally the most relevant situations and numbers, and we'll talk again in fifteen."

Nods went all around as everyone reached to adjust their AIMA, gearing up for their tasks. Yordanos grinned as she shot them a side eye while continuing to work. No one needed to adjust their AIMA to get back to work. It was some inherent gesture, something from the past.

Her grin turned brittle as the tone of the sound of whatever was being slammed into the secure space door changed drastically. The intensity had picked up, and it sounded like they were working on a new deformation process across the surface of the door. *Could they be making progress or just changing a breach crew?*

"Laura, take a look at this." Yordanos motioned her hand in Laura's direction, and the video feed from outside of the secure space showed that one team of dissenters had rigged some sort of propane or acetylene gas torch, probably taken from the canteen, and had focused the flame on one of the many reinforcing bars, which originated deep in the door frame, and came partway across the front of the sliding doors. The piece of reinforcing steel was starting to glow a dull red. Laura craned her face close to the console, and her eyes went up in alarm.

"Yordanos, the steel bar above it!" she whispered fiercely, trying not to draw notice from the others and failing miserably.

Yordanos scowled and squinted. Just above the brighter glowing section of steel bar, the bar which had been immediately above it was shorn off. The others in the secure space came around behind Yordanos's and Laura's consoles, which had not been in privacy mode, so they could see the many views. They all watched in growing horror as the screen showed a glowing piece of steel bar touched with a large chisel type device. They panned the camera view back to see a battering ram with three people on each side pull back the ram and slam it home. There was a slight timing mismatch between the silent video and the sound of the chisel hitting the door. Both the sound and video told them that the second reinforcing bar had snapped clean off.

There were additional gasps, and Yordanos quickly quieted everyone. "Okay, everyone, change of plans, we need to find out how much time we have before they break through the secure door, and see if we can reinforce the inner control center door with anything we have here. After that, we need to be ready to fight with whatever we have. We need to hold out as long as possible while we try and find another way out of here, or call Zero Crew for help."

Everyone went running for the door. "Wait! Everyone freeze where they are!" Yordanos shouted over the din of the terrified and chattering A-Crew members and endless banging on the door. "Please, we will not get out of this mess if we are running scared." She paused and took a deep breath. "Nav Team, see what you can do about the secure door, and also the inner control center door here. Anything you can come up with to slow them down, get it done."

She turned to the group of people with Sensors and Telemetry access. Over an hour ago, she had done a little AIMA research on the background of everyone in the O&M center with her for additional skill sets that may be of use.

"Norton, looks like you have a little bit of hand-to-hand combat training. Please start preparing our defense in this room. Think weapons, tactics, anything we can do to thin their numbers." He nodded and went off coordinating with the others on her team.

Yordanos turned to Laura with a hushed tone. "Even if we can't hold them off, if we can make them pull in reinforcements from the other rings, that may free up some of the other people in the secure spaces to maneuver…I was hoping to see if we could rally some of the other crew members to our cause and help us here on D-Ring, but I don't know how we can do that now… We just don't know who we can actually trust." Her face started to look desperate, and Laura jumped in.

"Hey, don't be like that, you are holding us together, don't break on us now. We need you."

Yordanos closed her eyes and took another deep breath. No one interrupted her as she was clearly counting to ten or doing some other mentally calming exercise.

Yordanos opened her eyes. "Okay, Laura, see if you can reach out to other crew members not yet involved in this mess. Try and figure out where they stand, give them information about what's going on and see if they will help. In fact, re-post the video of our door being attacked and get some more pics of the beaten and injured out there. It's low blow propaganda, but I'm scrapping for anything right now." She paused, sighing again.

"On second thought, we just don't have time to try and sift through everyone on the ship… Grab the other crew members in here and get names of people they have a high confidence in if they remember them. Get them to commit to helping us and then carefully start massing them in small groups but in nearby quarters. Report in as soon as you have a development."

Laura nodded. "What are you going to do?"

Yordanos responded, "I'm going to share the overall situational awareness capability I've developed using the ship's camera systems and comms with the other secure areas. I'm also going to pass off the A-Ring situation to the B-Ring team to manage while we deal with this here."

Laura kept looking at Yordanos with concern. "Yes, Laura, I'm decentralizing command, if I keep it, and we fall, then our efforts might truly be finished… Too many other people are depending on us now whether they know it or not."

Chapter Thirty-Nine: Going for a Stroll

"So that's it, everything looks good?" Corbin asked Hank.

"All required medical scans and procedures have been completed. You are fit for active duty again. There are no lingering issues that I can detect at this time," Hank stated matter-of-factly.

"Well, that's good then, I was worried I might...well that something may go wrong...or even...*not be able to use the ladder anymore.*" Hank just continued to stare at him awaiting a command. Apparently, Hank was not programmed to comment on one's indecisiveness or Corbin thinking out loud.

"Okay, then," Corbin said. "Hey, do you mind if we all gather around in a huddle? Here Hank, you stand here..." Corbin went around and showed each HD where to stand in relation to where he would be talking. "Good, remember this position right here. When I say 'huddle' or 'huddle-up,' all of you get together just like this around me, okay?"

Hank did the talking for the HDs. "Affirmative."

"Okay, good, so how can we all get to the D-Ring secure space?"

Hank responded immediately, "You will need to put on one of the hull repair rig suits, and we will all then need to exit E-Ring, where we are now, and make our way over to the D-Ring airlock, that is two hundred meters from the secure space on the outside."

Corbin balked. "Whoa, whoa, whoa, you mean out into space? I have no training in that. The vertigo alone from the rings spinning would make me vomit, I would have no coordination."

Hank let him finish and then responded. "We will escort you, just like other HDs escort you between the ring and the Spine of the ship. You will need to ingest additional anti-radiation emulsion in an excess quantity, and then you will need to relieve yourself immediately after entering the airlock on D-Ring. From there, we can make our way down the main corridor to the D-Ring secure space."

Corbin stared off. *Outside...holy shit! This is crazy...I can't...I...* He stopped. He realized he was actually excited to do this. He was going to do this. Something deep inside himself told him that he had always dreamed of walking in space. Now this was his chance, and he wasn't going to miss it.

"Okay, Hank, let's get started." One of the other HDs brought him a large container filled with a watery liquid. It looked close to a gallon, but Corbin knew it wasn't anywhere close to that, or this would be impossible. Hank watched Corbin take the container from the HD.

"You will want to ingest this quickly. The longer you take, the more you will feel the urge to urinate. You cannot relieve yourself until we are back inside the *Valor* on D-Ring, and you must drink all the contents of that container."

Corbin licked his lips; he actually did feel a little thirsty. *This shouldn't be too hard.* He tipped the container up and started to drink. He was greeted with a not all-unpleasant sweet flavor, but after quickly downing nearly a quarter of the container, he had to stop and catch his breath. Already the fluid wasn't tasting as good anymore, and it felt slightly more viscous than water. He took one more quick pull and set the container down for a minute, just as two HDs walked over carrying a large, mechanized suit. It looked almost twice the build of a normal sized human, and was outfitted with a number of tools, built into the arms. There was a cutting torch, brushes, and additional kit he did not know the purpose of. The two HDs set the suit down on its back, and pressing a series of buttons opened the front of the suit, which opened automatically on piston driven supports, like the top part of a coffin. *I hope that's not what this is.*

"Corbin, continue to ingest the emulsion," chided Hank. That was the first time Hank had addressed him by name. Corbin obeyed and worked harder at gulping down the substance. He was soon past the halfway mark of the container, and any semblance of the fluid being flavorful had left. It was starting to taste saltier, and his palate was rejecting it. Corbin made a big chug, and let his last sip gurgle down his gut, and then he took one more long pull for good measure. He set the container to the side making a face, the fluid still wet on his lips.

"That is nearly sufficient; however, you now have seven minutes and twenty-three seconds to finish the emulsion and enter the suit. We will take it from there." Hank kindly displayed a countdown clock, and Corbin watched it and continued to sip. He felt the first tickle in his bladder politely requesting that he plan for a restroom break in the near future. Corbin ignored it and went back to gulping down the fluid which now started to feel like a light greasy paste in his mouth. *What the hell is happening to this stuff, is it getting worse or is it just me?* He looked down at the watery green fluid and saw that it still looked like it did when he had started. He choked down another swallow and saw he still had about twenty ounces or so to go, and about ninety seconds.

He went to drink more, but Hank stopped him, "Finish the rest in a moment, for now, get into the suit." Corbin gingerly climbed into the suit, lay on his back, and pushed himself down into the suit lying back as he did so. It seemed fairly straightforward, and it fit him fairly well aside from a slight musty smell. *This must have been here for a while.* Corbin did not like the way his bladder was reporting to him how full it was.

The two HDs pulled the rig with Corbin in it up to his feet, which stood by itself easily enough, and Hank handed the emulsion back to him. "Drink this in one serving, and then we will go."

Corbin took a deep breath and gulped down the remaining emulsion, trying not to gag and vomit. He finished, sputtering a little bit, and then tossed the container away from him onto the floor. As soon as the container left his hands, Hank reached up and closed the suit, which then made a series of mechanical whirs and clicks. The rig opening narrowed to a seam, and then snapped shut and made a hissing sound.

It was pitch-black, and Corbin was trying not to cough up a bit of the emulsion that had gone down the wrong pipe. Struggling for air and in the dark, he mentally tried to calm down the rising panic when the inside of the suit began to gently blow air on him as if ventilating. The helmet portion stayed dark; however, a virtual reality 270-degree view illuminated, and soon after Hank's voice crackled in his ears. "Are you okay, Corbin? Ready to proceed?"

Corbin gave him a thumbs-up with the bulky enhanced robotic arm sleeve of his rig, and said, "I'm okay to go, Hank, let's get moving, I have to pee…bad." He could see Hank and expected him to nod, but he didn't. He turned and led the way while the other two HDs carried him each holding one of Corbin's suited arms, and when he twisted his head, the view looked back over his shoulder to see the two additional HDs following closely.

They exited the storage facility, walked down the corridor, took a left, walked for another minute and then held still. "What's going on, Hank, why aren't we moving?"

"There are three humans in the adjoining corridor, they are moving away from us, but we need to wait another minute, so they are not alerted to our presence, per your mission parameter."

"Okay, Hank, got it," he responded and waited. The need to pee rose another notch, and Corbin pushed the sensation away in his mind.

After another sixty seconds, which felt like an eternity to Corbin, their group of seven began moving again, this time at a brisk run. Corbin was impressed seeing the bulkheads nearly fly by in his display, but the suit's auditory system reported quiet thuds each time the HDs made a footfall. He also noticed that they were all running in staggered unison, making the footfall sounds seem like the constant humming of a piece of machinery instead of monster robots pounding through the ship. *The stealth parameter seems to be working very well for this mission,* Corbin mused.

They turned another corner, and came to an airlock. They all stepped in, and without any preamble, Hank depressurized the chamber and opened a section of the floor to the vacuum of space. Corbin felt the air blowers inside of his suit turn warmer and pick up in intensity as the suit adjusted to keep his in-suit environment hospitable to human life.

Corbin then looked down and outside of the floor opening of the airlock, and what he saw nearly lurched his stomach. He could see that the airlock opened to the outside of the ring, and the endless myriad of stars at his feet were rapidly rotating as the ring spun maintaining the artificial gravity. Corbin's panic rose again. He could imagine stepping out of that hole in the floor and falling forever into the massive gaps between the stars.

"Hank, what's going on? How are we going to get to D-Ring?" Again, without preamble, Hank stepped over the exit way and was quickly pulled out into space, grasping his hands at the last moment to grab the side of the airlock. He engaged some kind of magnetic device on each of his feet and hands, and effortlessly stood up on the outside of the airlock. Corbin could see through the glass that his feet were pretty much pointed at the bottoms of Hank's feet, yet separated by the metal of the air lock.

The other two leading HDs who had been holding Corbin in his suit, unceremoniously passed him to the trailing two HDs, and they too stepped out and over the airlock exit way, engaging their magnetic devices as well. Hank's voice piped into his helmet, as the trailing two HDs roughly handed Corbin out of the airlock to the others, who quickly grabbed him firmly, securing short tethers to their metal bodies. "Since you have not completed the training for this suit, we will be carrying you to D-Ring, by means of walking down this side of E-Ring toward the Spine. We will then transition to the Spine, and subsequently transition to D-Ring, which you can see over there." Hank gestured.

Corbin nearly lost his lunch again and gasped. In addition to seeing the stars whirl around as their ring spun, he looked over and could see D-Ring spinning in the opposite direction. He now wanted to vomit and pee at the same time. Hank, seemingly read his mind. "Do not relieve yourself in any way during the transition. For the nausea and disorientation, it will help to think of the hull of the ship as down, and it will be even better if you stay focused on where we are walking. Try not to look out into space or at the other rings."

Corbin nodded and did as he was told. He noticed the HDs wasted no time, and their party of seven practically galloped along the outside of the ring, careful to always maintain one magnetic contact. Corbin dared to sneak a peek at the Spine, which was dead ahead and getting bigger, and his stomach immediately regretted it. He also noticed that gravity was lessening as they approached the Spine of the ship. The complexities of this motion did not help with his nausea, and he thought some conversation might also help take his mind off the present situation. "Hank, why are the rings rotating in different directions?"

Hank answered, "The rings of the *Valor* are tuned to one another so that they remain in balance for angular velocity, momentum, and torque."

"So if they all spun the same way, they would have a negative effect on navigation?"

"They would reduce the efficiency of the *Valor*'s course through space. In order to maintain this course and speed, momentum must be preserved to the best extend practical."

Corbin looked up to see that they had reached the Spine. The HDs effortlessly transitioned from the moving ring to the seemingly stationary Spine and began to pace in unison toward D-Ring, which was visible now dead ahead about two hundred meters distant. Corbin told himself to think of the Spine as the ground and expect a rotating ring when he opened his eyes. He ventured a look forward and saw what he expected to see. The massive structure of D-Ring skyed in front and above him. Here near the Spine, the rotation didn't seem very fast to Corbin, but if he followed his eyes up toward the edge where he could contrast against the whirring backdrop of the stars, it felt like the ring was racing.

Corbin snapped his gaze back down in front of him to the "ground" and kept it there, as the HDs hurried across the Spine of the *Valor*. "Hank, how far until the air lock on D-Ring? State the time in minutes if you please," Corbin asked, trying to keep the edge out of his voice. His attempt at ignoring the strengthening urge to pee was beginning to fail him, he could not shut out the uncomfortable feeling any longer.

Hank replied, "At present speed, we will reach the airlock in seven minutes and thirty-four seconds; however, the network shows the area around the air lock to be patrolled by several of the opposing members of A-Crew. I do not believe them to be in alignment with your mission, Corbin."

Despite the situation, the HDs didn't slow their progress, and they flew across the surface of D-Ring.

"Okay, Hank, other options?"

Hank replied, "There are no other authorized air locks on D-Ring."

Corbin responded, annoyed. "Okay what about unauthorized airlocks?"

Hank again responded, "We do not have access to those airlocks. If we override, the main AI will be aware that we are operating out of protocol."

Corbin responded, befuddled, "Out of protocol? How the hell aren't we out of protocol now? We are outside and running across the hull of the ship!"

Hank responded, "With the assistance of your colleague, we have been listed as a hull inspection and maintenance crew. The main AI has not responded in an adverse way as of yet."

Corbin was perplexed. "As of yet. What the hell will the main AI do if we're found out?"

Hank took a little longer to respond. "I do not have that answer, Corbin. Would you like to continue?"

Corbin's level of annoyance was reaching fever pitch. He knew he wasn't thinking clearly, and his bladder felt like it was on the verge of explosion. *Think, Corbin, think!* he admonished himself. *Losing your mind is not going to get you anywhere.*

Corbin recovered some semblance of control. "Hank, is there a way to cut into the hull or into an unused area, and then re-pressurize?"

Hank responded, "Negative, this is not an activity that I am approved to carry out."

Corbin shot back, "Well, why the hell not? And why the hell didn't you say this was part of your constraints when I asked you!?"

Hank responded, "An unauthorized breach of the hull is restricted by my programming due to the safety of the crew and ship. Also, were I to list every possible constraint under every possible permutation of conditions, we would be in the maintenance room for 2.37 years. This is not practical. Would you like to continue?"

As their mechanized cadre made their way out onto D-Ring, Corbin noticed gravity start to return, and he settled down in his suit. He started to feel his weight pulling him forward. He also felt like his bladder was constricting further, and he was now in full-on "clench mode." A sheen of sweat had broken out on his brow and face. Corbin also noticed that they were slowing pace as they were reaching the edge of D-Ring, and he saw the protrusion of the unique looking airlock. The six HDs positioned themselves around the outer air lock, in a manner where they were ready to enter. Corbin did not look down, as he knew he would see nothing but the vast emptiness of space flying by at his feet. Hank spoke up. "Corbin, how do you wish to proceed?"

Corbin sighed through struggled breaths as he held onto his bladder for dear life. Here at 1g the pain had reached a near fever pitch. He was going to pee for an hour straight if he survived this. “Okay, this is what we are going to do. Hank, I’m probably going to need you to fib for me.”

Chapter Forty: Hello Fellas

Steve Fassbender had joined Jessica and her team of dissenters well after they had seemingly taken control of the *Valor*. He saw the communication sent out by her team and had sent ahead a note to the D-Ring leader that he wanted to offer his allegiance and services. He was on the slight side, with pale skin, a mess of red hair, high cheek bones, and a healthy dose of freckles. He was posted on the main D-Ring corridor, along with two other more burly young men, who worked directly with Justin. Steve knew Justin was Jessica's right-hand man, so if he was really going to support Jessica, and get to the bottom of why they were stuck here on the *Valor* against their will, he knew he had better do his job as lookout and report any suspicious movements on D-Ring.

He walked behind the two taller toughs and kept his eyes and ears open. He had tried to strike up conversation with them earlier but was scolded to keep quiet and remain alert. So that is what he did as they made their way around the giant circumference of D-Ring, on the last corridor before the hull. Steve had heard about some excitement earlier as the secure room was starting to be breached, and Jessica would soon have the bulk of the *Valor* loyalists in custody as well as all of D-Ring secured. Steve was excited by this prospect and was sorry he had not been assigned to the breaching team; however, since he was new, it made sense that he had a less interesting job to start. As their party continued to walk, Steve was musing about how he would work his way up the ranks within Jessica's organization, when they heard a series of mechanical clangs coming from far up ahead of the outer corridor.

The two other lookouts wasted no time, and took off at a run toward the sound, hollering at Steve to keep up, which he did as best as he could, but started to fall back as his slight build and shorter legs failed to keep up with the more athletic lookouts.

The mechanical sounds continued in number and intensity and then suddenly stopped, as what sounded like a loud hiss, and metal hinging on metal echoed down the corridor. Steve looked up ahead to see the two other young men stopped and gaping down at a large opening in the corridor floor, which he had never seen before. He could see his colleagues take several steps back as seven humanoid figures rose stoically from the opening in the corridor floor. Steve slowed his run and gawked, looking at six HDs and one…different HD that he had never seen before. The six regular HDs stood in a loose formation around the different looking HD.

"Wha…what is going on here, what is your purpose and designation?!" one of the other young men said in a loud voice at the HDs. Hank calmly responded, "Hull Inspection and Maintenance, returning for repair and…"

Just then, the crotch area of Corbin's suit opened, and then Corbin released what felt like the Hoover Dam sluice gates. The blue fluid came out in a torrent, hitting the back of Hank's leg and pooling on the floor. Corbin did his best not to slouch, and he had already disconnected his external audio, which if on, would have sounded like someone moaning and hyperventilating at the same time.

Steve and the two other lookouts all looked bewildered. The vocal one spoke up again. "What the hell is going on with that one!? And what is this mess?" he said, raising his voice while they all took a step back. The blue fluid began to expand and drain in their direction…it smelled funny.

"Unit CB-Seven for welding has a coolant leak and requires immediate maintenance. May we proceed?" Steve and the lookouts all looked at one another, and Steve shrugged. Hank repeated his question, "May we proceed?"

They all looked at unit CB-7 and saw that the "coolant" continued to leak, but the outflow had reduced to a trickle.

Corbin heard Steve pipe up over his own noises of relief. "CB-7 doesn't look much like an HD…he looks like a dude in a suit taking a piss."

"The additional insulation on this unit is protecting the welding accelerant and gases that are required to weld in a vacuum. This configuration is only required on the outside of the hull, so it is rare to see one in the corridor. As for the manner of the coolant leak, I apologize for how it looks, but we can't know where the leak will occur. May we proceed?" Hank asked.

Corbin, now recovering, held his breath and saw the two other dissenters sharing an annoyed look at Steve for his question. They motioned for Steve to follow them, ignoring his concerns. They turned their backs to the HDs and began walking away, careful to step around the "coolant." The vocal one waved a dismissive hand as he walked away. "Proceed."

The HDs began walking in unison, and Steve and the lookouts missed that CB-7 missed the first few footfalls before falling in line with the HDs' left and right steps. Corbin and his party of HDs traversed the way the lookouts had come, and Jessica's people disappeared under the curve of the massive ring-shaped corridor.

Hank spoke up. "Corbin, your status shows that you have not fully expended the fluid from your bladder. You must do so immediately to prevent radiation poisoning."

"You mean, just pee here on the floor again? Shouldn't I…" He almost smacked himself…this was an emergency situation, he didn't have time to lumber into a bathroom. "Okay, Hank, just keep blocking the view, okay?" The HDs set up their perimeter around Corbin, and he went to relieve himself again after asking them to about face from huddling in to huddling out. He couldn't believe it, but he stood there for another full ninety seconds, and this in addition to what he had already expelled in the corridor by the airlock. He had been able to relax a bit more since their encounter with the lookouts, and this allowed him to get rid of the rest of the blue fluid, and hopefully any radioactive waste.

"I can't believe that worked," Corbin said to Hank, who stood motionless, not hearing a command or a question. "Hank, how did you know to fib so well? Are you programmed to make stuff up like that?"

Hank nodded. "My capabilities do include adaptation, and since my colleagues and I are supporting you Corbin, we will devise the best way to do so with what we determine is the most efficient action and highest probability of success."

Corbin was impressed. "So that's why you didn't bust them up," he said half-jokingly.

"We cannot harm a human crew member, Corbin. On top of that, there are many more actions we could have taken, which had a high likelihood of success."

Corbin changed his tone and the subject. "Okay, Hank, how can we get to the secure room here on D-Ring?"

Hank pulled up a D-Ring map from inside the suits heads-up display and showed Corbin their course through the D-Ring corridors. Using the Operations and Maintenance access code, Corbin overlayed where personnel locators were over the map. He designated those in the secure space as blue, and everyone in the corridors red. Corbin, moved the map around in his suit's HUD, and zoomed in on a space with an adjoining wall to the secure space.

"Hank, here is what I'm thinking, we get to this space next to the secure room, and then we cut through the wall using this suit, or whatever tools you all have to get them out. I don't think we can stop the breachers with a ruse, and we need to get those people out if we want to take back control of the ship."

Hank responded immediately, "Negative, we cannot cut through the bulkheads on D-Ring for the same reason we cannot cut through the hull. These load bearing bulkheads are critical for the stability of D-Ring, and thus the *Valor,* we cannot breach them without endangering the ship."

"Okay, Hank, is there any way in or out of the secure space besides the main entrance?"

"Negative," Hank responded. "The main entrance is the only way in and out of the secure space on D-Ring."

Corbin felt defeated. He knew his friends needed him, but he did not know how to assist. He started with the essentials.

"Hank, can you pull up the nearest operational camera outside of the secure space? Patch it through to my suit's HUD, if you please." A window in his HUD opened, and there was a short burst of a snowy screen and then a camera view came online. It was a view far down the corridor, and he could barely make out some commotion, nearly obstructed by the arc of D-Ring.

"Hank, can you magnify or clean up the image? I can't see

anything." The video window zoomed in to the commotion, and he could see several people working on the door. They looked as if they had started at the top and were working toward the floor. They were one-third of the way from the bottom, and as he watched, he saw another flash, and a torch move another few inches down. *They don't have much time left,* he thought.

"Hank, can you restrain those crew members?"

Hank responded again, "As I said, we cannot hurt them, but we could stop them from doing what they are doing. However, the moment we do, the main AI will be made aware of our anomaly, and I do not know what will happen to us or you after that. I advise you to select a different course of action."

Corbin pounded his fist on the hull in frustration. He somehow knew that is what Hank would say.

Okay, so you have your squad of robots, but they can't fight your battles for you, they can only do what they are sanctioned to do in front of the main AI... "Hank, how loud can you turn up your...uh, voice. How loud can you project sounds?"

Hank responded, "I can increase volume to 90 decibels for up to thirty seconds while within close range of crew members' ears. Longer exposure may result in harm to crew members' hearing, and is not permitted."

That will have to do. "Okay, Hank...fellas...this is what we are going to do. The other HDs, their social acumen learning algorithms starting to adjust their behavior, turned their heads toward, as if actively listening to Corbin for the next piece of the plan. After Corbin had laid it out, Hank nodded favorably.

"I believe this to be a good plan of action with a high probability of success given our constraints."

Chapter Forty-One: Ready to Breach

Yordanos and Laura had successfully transitioned their command to the other leaders in the secure rooms, if the D-Ring secure space fell, there would be less than one hundred of them left. The other A-Crew members in the room scurried about to brace the doors to the control center. The unending bashing of the main external door continued, and it was beginning to make their ears ring.

"How long until they break through?" Yordanos asked, shouting over the racket. Laura, patched into the same camera Corbin was patched into, zoomed in on the breachers and saw that they likely only had three to four reinforcing bars left before the main door gave way. They would still need a few minutes to clear the deadbolts, but that might not take long at all. After that they could bash the door in with a ram.

"No less than twelve minutes based on what I am seeing here, but most likely it will be fifteen minutes and then they'll be outside the control center."

Yordanos looked over at what the others were working on to brace the door, and her hopes fell. There simply was not enough additional material in the room to shore up the double doors which opened inward. Still, Yordanos saw that they had several cross braces across the center, and several angular poles extending from the floor up to the doors.

Norton spoke up. "I know it doesn't look like much, but they will need to get a running start to bash in these doors, and I think our braces will hold, as they only have eight feet between the door and the bulkhead. It seems the designers of the secure space may have thought of this."

Yordanos took a deep breath, forced her shoulders back, and gave her neck a roll to the left and then the right, followed by another deep breath. The cacophony of slamming continued unabated. She spoke up over the racket. "Nice work, prepare for breach and an attack on those doors in ten minutes. Be ready with everything. You must hold."

The young man nodded and returned to his work, providing instruction and suggestion to each of the defenders. Yordanos admired his style. She saw he had broken up the other team members into five groups. He directed one team for each of the four quadrants on the door surface, and another team he told to install braces against the door from the floor. If they made it out of this, she would like to get to know him, as she loved efficiency in leadership.

"Listen up, everyone, can I get your attention for the next thirty seconds?!" Yordanos hollered over the din of the breachers. "We are going to be breached within the next few minutes, and we will most likely be outnumbered. However, it is important that we do as much as we can to hold out. Maybe help will come for us from Zero Crew. We cannot give up that door, no matter what! So, arm yourselves with whatever you can find. Be ready to fight like hell with everything you have. How we spend the rest of our lives, whatever that means, will depend on the next few minutes. So, if you have any doubts, squash them now. We are A-Crew, and we will not go down without a fight! For the VALOR!" she roared. "VALOR!!! VALOR!!!" The others took up the cheer and raised whatever they had in their hands echoing the name of their ship. Yordanos locked out her terminal, grabbed a piece of the main screen which they had smashed for parts, and stepped in front of the door. "Bring it on! You son of a bitch!" she whispered fiercely to herself. Others heard and stepped in line beside and behind her.

Chapter Forty-Two: Take Back

Justin bounded from the Spine of the ship to the outer corridors on D-Ring. His search for those who had escaped on A-Ring was only marginally successful, as he had only found three of the A-Crew loyalists. The rest had either hid or made it to the secure space on that ring.

He sprinted as quickly as he could, and there were nearly one hundred others behind him. Jessica had dispatched help from the other rings now that the D-Ring secure space was ready to fall. Everyone running behind him held some sort of blunt instrument. There were chair handles, sharpened teeth cleaning implements, and silverware from the canteens. One person had even found a way to break their toilet seat into a blunt weapon and wielded it proudly as he charged toward the secure space entrance.

When the crowd arrived and joined the others assisting with the breach or just watching and waiting, their combined force was over one hundred and twenty-five. Justin walked forward and assumed command from Jared, who had overseen the breach.

"Okay, I see we are almost through. What can we expect when these doors open?" he asked Jared.

The young man, a bit flustered at having been replaced, responded, "We expect this door to be the main obstacle; however, the loyalists inside have most likely reinforced a second set of doors to hold us at bay."

Justin shot him a sharp look. "Doors like this!? That took us nearly three hours to break!"

The young man responded with a grin. "No, these doors will most likely be functional and like the build of every other set of doors we see in the corridors. They aren't airtight, more for just aesthetics, but I may be wrong. If I am, we'll just cut through those as well, but it'll just take longer."

Justin grunted. "We're counting on you to be right. Another three hours of this insurrection is untenable. Can we break in this hour or not?"

The young man shrugged and responded calmly, "You're asking me to give you an answer regarding something I didn't build and have no knowledge on its performance. I can tell you we'll do the best and fastest that we can, but other than that, you can get bent. I signed onto this because the reason we are here is bullshit, but don't go off and think you have any more right to authority than I do, you got it meat sack?!" The young man leaned into Justin's face. Justin thought about putting his fist through it, and then thought better of it. He needed him.

"Okay, tough fella, take it easy, I just need to let the boss know how long it will be until we get there okay? If it's three hours, then that's what it is."

The young man stood down, and said confidently, "Twenty minutes if its regular doors, two hours and forty-five minutes if it's another set like these. Fair enough?"

Justin nodded and stepped back. He updated a runner with the information and sent him off to update Jessica.

Justin spoke to the awaiting crowd. "Okay, everyone…I need you lined up to the left and right side of the corridor, the left side will breach first, and then the right, not from both sides." He motioned for the people lining up on the other side of the corridor to disengage and fall in with the long line of people on the other side of the secure room main door, where the crew still worked to burn through the reinforced door. Justin gave quick words of encouragement and explanation for why they had to get farther back in the line to breach. While some of the breachers shoulder slumped at being so far back in line, most of them kept a sharp determination in their eyes. Justin walked someone who was trying to cut in line all the way to the back. "This is for trying to cheat your teammates, but don't think it means I don't need you in fighting shape. Be ready for action." The young man allowed a controlled grin and then turned to take up his place behind the last of them.

When they were all lined up in the corridor, Justin looked back to see that the breachers were burning through their last bar.

"Okay, listen up! In the next few minutes this door is going to fold. And, barring another one just like this, you'll most likely only being dealing with reinforced conference room doors, no more no less." He paused while making eye contact. "This is the major holdout of those loyal to Zero Crew's mission on the *Valor*. While this group will no doubt have decentralized leadership to the other places they are holed up, nothing can stop the blow to morale that the seizure of these people will have on their cause. I am confident that if we win. Here. In the next few minutes. It will shape what we have in store for us for the rest of our very lives." Justin paused again. "We didn't sign up for this, we didn't volunteer for this, but we find ourselves here, so we will take control, and we will finish it, for us ALL!" he roared. Everyone in the corridor echoed his call, and their energetic cries reverberated around all the D-Ring corridors. They were ready for battle.

Justin turned to the work team as they began to heat the last bar near the floor. Three others were clumsily working at the large deadbolt structure that emanated from the middle of the door and locked in multiple places where the door would swing open. Justin could see that it didn't really matter: once the bars were gone, they would be able to ram the door and stove it in, unless there was some kind of hook mechanism. Justin didn't worry about that now. He was impressed that his breach crew was still cheering with enthusiasm, although he did notice their volume decreased as another rhythmic sound began to rise.

"Everyone shut up!" Justin hollered. The cheering turned to fading smiles and confused looks as everyone else began to hear the dull thudding, increasing in volume and proximity. Justin looked down the corridor, past all of the breach crew that had lined up on either side of the hallway, ready to surge in as the door was pulled away. He could see what looked like large utility HDs in formation approaching in step, with a different looking HD in the center of their small column. Then came a klaxon sound that felt like the roil of thunder mixed with the ear piercing shriek of lighting.

Firm and terrifying voices broke through the painful noise. "YOU

ARE TO CEASE AND DESIST. THIS ACTIVITY IS IN VIOLATION OF CREW CONDUCT, RETURN TO YOUR QUARTERS IMMEDIATELY!" The message repeated and seemed louder as they approached, and they were flashing some kind of strobe lights mounted on their shoulder area.

The people nearest the HDs turned back toward Justin and started to run toward him and away from the HDs. A few tried to stand their ground, but Justin could see that they wouldn't last long. When the HD formation was within fifty feet of the breach crew, they all broke and started to run, panic rising within all of them, as they clamored, wide eyed, past one another and down the corridor.

Justin felt his pulse quicken, and he too started to backpedal, and several of the braver stragglers stood around him. When the formation was within twenty feet of them, Justin looked past the hulking HDs to see the other type of HD light a massive torch and increase the flame length to several feet in front of it, while not missing a step with the other HDs. Justin felt the shocking heat on his face and skin, and with the klaxon and warning grinding through his nerves and brain, he and the rest of his breach crew turned and ran, trying to outpace one another, anything to distance themselves from the searing heat, which Justin was pretty sure he could still feel, despite being out of visual range. He could still hear their warning, but the thumping had stopped.

Chapter Forty-Three: I Can't Believe That Worked

"I can't believe that worked," Corbin said aloud. "Hank, can you remove what's left of the door and then repair it behind us."

Hank responded as he and two other HDs moved to the door. "Yes, please stand aside." The three HDs made short work of the door's last reinforcing bar and dead bolt mechanism. Hank and Corbin went inside the outer room to the secure space, and three HDs, then held up the tatters of what remained of the door itself from the outside and began to bend metal in place. The metal moved under the audible grind of gyros, and Corbin could see that it was little effort for the HDs to shape the metal.

Hank fired up a red laser and pointed it to a spot on the metal. "Corbin, ignite the welding torch, and set it to level six. Touch the torch head to the metal and follow behind the red laser dot at my pace." Corbin did as he was told and saw that the metal began to take on a dull glow almost immediately, quickly fuse, and then return to a dark gray, followed by puffs of thick acrid smoke, which was starting to fill the entryway room. Corbin followed Hank's lead, and within minutes, the door was re-secured in place; however, it was more of a slab now. They would need to cut their way out, or the five HDs they left in the corridor would need to break through the metal to get them out. It wouldn't take too long, as the structural integrity of the door, repaired or not, was a shadow of what it had been before the breach.

"Hank, tell your colleagues to stand guard at the door, in case Justin and his cronies decide to come back and see what is going on. I don't want them to get any bright ideas about breaking back in here." Hank complied with wireless silent orders to his colleagues. "Hank, what will the HDs do, if they are threatened?"

Hank responded, "I have told them to defend themselves; however, they will not take any offensive movements that may injure a crew member."

Corbin nodded. "That will have to be good enough, Hank, thanks." Hank nodded in assent.

Corbin walked over to the entryway to the secure space and rapped his knuckles on the secure space inner door. He amplified his voice via the maintenance suit and spoke up. "Yordanos, it's me Corbin! Let me in, we need to get to work right away!" He knocked again, careful not to pound, and turned his volume up louder. "Yordanos, it's Corbin! This is HD Hank; he is on our side. Please let us in!"

Corbin made to remove his helmet, but Hank stopped him with a quick yet gentle seizure of his hand. "Corbin, the air is still toxic from the extended welding. Please wait until the smoke is processed via the ventilation system. This should take a little over two minutes."

Corbin nodded. "Hank, is there any way to patch me into the secure space consoles? They aren't going to let us in by knocking." Hank nodded and extended a cord from his torso to an outlet on the wall. He then extended another plug and inserted it into a receptacle on Corbin's suit. The image of a concerned Yordanos popped into his HUD. He could see her face light up at the sight of him from his in-suit fisheye camera…which probably made him look ridiculous.

"Corbin! Oh my god! Is that you!? How did you? What did you…" She clapped her hand over her mouth, and her eyes misted as she sat down, relief washing over her. Corbin could see Laura come around behind her, and she too had the same reaction when seeing him on the console.

"Yordanos…Laura…it is great to see you. The main door has been secured, and five more HDs are guarding it. Let me in, and we can figure out this whole mess!"

They nodded, and she called for the others to begin removing the door barricades. "It'll be a few minutes Corbin," Laura said still beaming. We were ready for the Alamo here."

Corbin couldn't quite recall the reference. *I must not have covered that in history yet.* But he assumed it was some sort of famous last stand and nodded and smiled. "I can see that! Great job holding out… How are the others doing?"

Yordanos recovered her composure and returned to all business. "Get in here, and we'll get you the full update."

Corbin nodded and muted the feed, turning to Hank. "Say, Hank, is there another bathroom in there. I can't believe I have to go again; should I just go here on the floor? It's not as bad as before, but about halfway there."

"There are restroom facilities inside the secure space," Hank said. "I advise you not to relive yourself here as cleaner bots do not have access to this space, and your urine is slightly radioactive from your spacewalk."

Corbin nodded, with understanding, and patiently waited for the air to clear and his A-Crew team to remove the barriers.

After what felt like an eternity, but was only a few minutes, the two main doors of the secure space were pulled open, and Corbin and Hank entered the space. Corbin let the doors shut behind him, and then removed his space rated welding suit's helmet. Though many didn't know Corbin personally, everyone was glad to see him, but their eyes quickly turned to and lingered on Hank, as his model of HD, a hulking eight feet tall, had not yet been seen before by A-Crew. "Don't worry about him, he and five of his friends are on our side," he said as he completed the procedure of opening and stepping out of the rig. It remained in a standing position behind him with the front open.

Corbin had tried to dash to the restroom right away, but Laura and Yordanos practically jumped him and hugged him tightly. He did not protest as it felt amazing to be back with his friends again. He hugged them both tightly. "It's so good to see you," he said. "I need a minute, I'm sorry, I'll be right back." He sheepishly trudged to the restroom, with Laura's and Yordanos's looks of incredulity following him.

Corbin nearly bowled over someone exiting the restroom, who turned to gawk at the newcomer. "Sorry, gotta go!" he said with a bit more melody than he intended. As he relieved himself, he felt a bit foolish, but *My god, did I have to pee! …Again!*

Corbin finished and went to wash his hands at the basin. He took a look at himself in the mirror and became a bit more self-conscious at how terrible he looked, and for the first time, he noticed that he could really use a shower. He turned and looked longingly at the shower unit in the restroom, but he knew he had no time.

He splashed some water on his face and decided to wash it with some soap. Still soapy, he traced his fingers on the thin purple line where Hank had carefully welded his skull cap and skin back together with a material called synth-skin, which rapidly allowed for a skin graft to form. In thinking about all Hank had done, he felt it difficult to think of him as a machine, as simple as his programming was. He really felt like Hank was a trusted friend.

He went back to the water, trying to re-focus, and washed the soap from his face. He took a drying cloth from the dispenser and wiped his face hard, careful to get all of the moisture, and remove some of the sweat and grit as well. He finished and took a look at himself one more time in the mirror, and he also took a quick account of all he had been through in just the past day. He blew out his breath and then exited the restroom and back into the fray.

Chapter Forty-Four: Back in Command

Corbin walked out of the restroom, slightly less disheveled than he had entered and one hundred percent more relieved…and also several orders of magnitude more determined.

He rounded the corner, and aside from a few whispered side conversations, saw everyone in the room was waiting on his return. He eyed Laura, who nodded, and then Yordanos, who also nodded her assent. *Now to make it official.* "I have tactical information that may be useful to our efforts, and I have worked with Laura and Yordanos before on O&M training and simulations. If it is okay with everyone here, I would like to assume command of our endeavor?"

He framed it as a question and looked around at everyone, who nodded. "Okay then, thank you for your trust in my colleagues, and thank you for your trust in me. If we work together and we use our heads, we are going to get out of this mess and put things right." He waited for a breath, and saw that he had the room, and not an eye blinked. Hank watched as well.

"Yordanos, please report the status." Yordanos nodded, sat at her console, and brought up a diagram of the *Valor*. Most of the rings and Spine were red, signifying control, but there were splotches of blue, where crew members loyal to A-Crew's mission had holed up in secure spaces. There were purple spots, where they knew their friends were captured and being held. Corbin noticed the Challenge ring was still a neutral gray and smiled. *Cadre Paul does not tolerate any bullshit,* Corbin thought to himself.

Yordanos adjusted the display wordlessly, and counts of red and blue forces and their presumed or near-real-time updated positions were displayed. Yordanos and Laura had expertly set up an intelligence network between the secure spaces using the O&M special data link, and pooled additional data from loyal-leaning crew members as well as internal surveillance. The current state was fairly accurate, except for a few places they didn't have camera access. Everyone quickly saw that their number, even across all secure spaces, was less than two hundred, and Jessica's dissenter group was approaching nearly five hundred. Corbin noted that some previously neutral crew members had been added to her ranks.

Corbin had a few questions. "Yordanos, are any of our training team in the other secure spaces?"

She knew he was really asking about their friends. "Unfortunately no, we have confirmed that all of them, including Jason, Henry, and…Herbert have been captured."

Corbin knew better than to ask about specific friends. He fought down his emotion, and rising fury, and kept objectivity in his voice. "Understood. Hank, how are we looking at the front door?"

Hank responded, "Our sentries have been undisturbed, and no additional activity has been spotted in the corridor."

Corbin nodded. "Good, are the other secure spaces holding out as well?"

Yordanos went through the nearest camera views of each secure space outer door. Corbin could see that so far, the dissenters had not replicated the breach crew technique they had applied here on D-Ring.

"Okay, also good. That means we have a little time. Let's go for the easy one…Hank, how do we take back the ship?" Corbin said with a smile, trying to bring a little levity to the situation.

Hank didn't respond for a few seconds, and Corbin wondered if this was outside of his capacity. Finally, "Do not harm the crew members as you retake the ship," was his cryptic response.

So much for the levity. Everyone was now looking at Hank like he was crazy. Corbin piped up trying to rescue the moment. "Hank and his five other colleagues, who are guarding our door, have strict programming about ensuring the safety of the crew and the *Valor* itself. We were able to bluff our way past one group, and the breach team outside we were able to scare away." He corked a thumb over his shoulder.

"Why does it follow your instructions, Corbin?" Laura asked.

"It's a long story, but essentially, while I was being cared for, I found these units in a storage area, and reactivated them. As I have O&M clearance, they respond to my commands." He shot both Laura and Yordanos an urgent look that said, *Don't try it out on them just yet, there is more to the story.* The two young women got the message and ceased asking additional questions, but Corbin caught in their return looks that he would have some more explaining to do.

One of the other A-Crew members raised his hand. "Thanks for raising your hand, but we're all in this together. If you or anyone has an idea, let's get it out on the table. Simple politeness rules will govern the interaction. What's your name?"

The young man replied, "Norton. You said you had to bluff your way past the first group, and then you somehow scared the breachers for this secure space? How did you do that?"

Corbin iterated how he, Hank, and the other mostly silent HDs had accomplished those two feats, and the reactions the dissenters had at each point. After explaining, Corbin added, "I don't know how we could employ a bluff or scare tactic like this again against such a dispersed group, and they will no doubt alter their tactics and be ready for it."

The young man nodded in agreement and responded, "Indeed, Jessica's people are controlling every A-Crew space on the ship, including the Spine, so even if we get a foothold and somehow get the crew to fall in line with us to swell our numbers, we'll still have to go ring by ring to liberate the rest."

Another A-Crew member, a slight black man with an excited grin spoke up. "Hey, I'm Isaiah. If you try to go ring by ring, we give them a chance to learn and adapt to how we are doing it. If we have special access to information with the O&M clearance, and we have access to HDs, then is there something we can do that gets all of Jessica's people to quit or surrender at once?"

Yordanos nodded to the idea, and said, "He's right, whatever we do, it has to be something that is quick. Jessica has proven her leadership, intelligence, and ruthlessness. If we don't resolve the matter quickly, then per Hank's point, many will be injured or possibly worse."

Corbin sat down needing some time to think. *First, we have to take the ship back, and now we can't do it while hurting anyone, and on top of that we have to do it all at once? Why do we get the impossible tasks.*

The more Corbin thought about it, the more he knew both Hank and the outspoken members of A-Crew were right. They had to think past this pinch point. If they were going to succeed, then these people would be working and living together for decades to come. If they seriously damaged people or even killed some of them, that could lead to perilous crew morale and mistrust conditions later. If they truly did want to become the crew of the *Valor* then they had to act like it. *But the time for inaction and indecision is over. Whatever we do, we must be just, we must be strong, and above all we must be swift.* An idea started to take hold.

"Hank," Corbin called out, "When you say don't hurt them...what kind of hurt are we talking about?"

Hank responded, "Do not perform an act that could lead to the injury and disability of a fellow crew member. While accidental death and injury has been planned for in the number of crew, each such loss has the potential to increase the failure rate of our overall mission as well as greatly reduce the probability of success at Gliese 832. As such, our programming is very strict about this, and you would do well to consider that in any action you decide to take."

Corbin looking at the floor nodded and then up at his friends. "I think we have a little bit of wiggle room here. I'd like to hear what you all think before we try it though."

Chapter Forty-Five: That's One Down

Corbin logged on to his console and brought up the list of HD's he had access to in A-Ring where the HD repair and storage facility was. He saw that he could activate over three hundred different types of HDs, and promptly initiated their start-up sequences. He then pushed the status image of A-Ring to one of the control center large screens and overlay HD locations with the red and blue force locations.

His hands flew across the console, as he assigned HDs to groups based on location, and then tasked each group to converge on the canteen from every possible corridor, all marching in unison, blaring the same cease and desist message he and Hank had used in the corridor outside of the O&M Center. Corbin hit execute, and then pushed the status image to the top right corner of the screen, and pulled up several A-Ring camera views that were available. He hoped they hadn't had time to receive a runner from the breach team. He didn't have time to check all the video history.

Corbin smiled to himself as he watched the reaction of the dissenters as the HDs began to enter the A-Ring corridors. Everyone witnessed the army of HDs as they poured out of storage rooms and the repair facility all in step with their simple but blasting message. The HDs flooded the corridors of A-Ring, and as the confused and panicked occupiers fell back from the HDs, more were coming from any avenues of escape.

The canteen camera initially showed curiosity, followed by confusion, and finally panic from the people holding the A-Crew members captive. Several of them knelt with their hands behind their heads, and the rest bolted and ran.

The secure space in D-Ring let out a mighty cheer, and Corbin, Laura, and Yordanos all embraced as they saw they had simultaneously rounded up all dissenters on A-Ring, freed their colleagues, and all without any loss of life or further injury to either side.

Three dissenters had made it back to one of their quarters and locked the door, but Yordanos put the room under confinement for hazardous materials using her O&M access, and the lock could not be opened. She double checked that all of the facilities in the quarters worked, logged the event as something to check and maintain, and moved on.

Corbin spoke back up. "Laura, tell the canteen HDs nearest our people to get them up one by one and lead them out into the corridor. Once they are out of ear and eyeshot of the canteen return their AIMAs and tell them to get to the secure space on A-Ring and join the others." Laura brought up the A-Ring O&M Lead, on her console. To his delight, it was Brittney. She too had been able to see everything that was going on, and she was all smiles in relief at having retaken A-Ring.

Laura reiterated the instructions to Brittney, who immediately brought up her O&M access and took control of the HDs on her ring. They started to bring the loyal A-Crew members out into the corridor, and as soon as they snapped on their AIMAs, others in the secure space were waiting with an open video and audio connection telling them to go to the secure space quickly and quietly.

Brittney asked Laura, "Is there anything else? What do we do with the Jessica's people that we captured?" Laura looked back over at Corbin for confirmation, and knowing what she was asking, he nodded.

Laura turned back to Brittney. "After the last of our people are out of there, do the same thing with the dissenters, one by one. Direct them to the nearest empty crew quarters and have the HD put each of them into separate spaces. We've put these HD custom protocols for this in the O&M master share; you can pull them down from there and apply to individual HDs, you'll also be able to take manual control of the HDs' vocal function, but motor function will be extremely limited…we are still trying to figure it out. Quite frankly, much of the HDs' protocols are restricted, but you will be able to do something with the torso, head, and simple gestures. Nothing that will be able to restrain, so you must maintain our illusion of the controlled situation without force."

Brittney, already grabbing the protocols, her hands flying across the console, nodded, and said, "You mean the HDs you activated and sent in can't do anything but walk? HA! They folded like a cheap suit…I'll get on moving them to those quarters, and I'll keep you appraised. What's next?" she asked.

Laura responded, "We are going after the other rings. Godspeed, Brittney. Check in every fifteen minutes with status unless something goes wrong." Brittney nodded and went to her task. She had set up console support with Erol, the only other person with O&M access in the secure space with her, similar to how Yordanos had been running things with Laura supporting her. The rest of the people in her secure space were from Navigation and Telemetry and Guidance, and were hard at work talking to other crew members, trying to convince them to step up for A-Crew. She spared them a thankful glance, and then started issuing remote commands to the HDs.

Chapter Forty-Six: What the Hell Is Going On?

Tamon Heatherington was meeting up with different patrols on the corridors, and relaying status back to his G-Ring leader that reported directly to Jessica by runner. He nodded to two young women who he knew were patrolling one of the inner corridors on G-Ring. He approached to share updates on A-Crew member activity when he noticed that one of the foot-long centipede-like cleaner bots was drawing closer to them.

"That's odd," he said in their direction. "Those things usually keep their distance." The two women also watched it, a bit mesmerized. To Tamon, it looked a little different from some of the other cleaner bots he had seen in the past. It looked familiar. He had seen this model before, but couldn't quite place it.

The cleaner bot went right up to his shoe and started cleaning the end of his shoe. "HA! Look at that." He giggled a bit boyishly and looked back over to the two women, who were mildly enthused, but less so. Their reaction dulled his giddiness a bit.

He asked them, "Say, what do you think…OW!" and pulled his foot back.

Now the two women were much less enthused and took a few steps back, their smiles melting to concerned frowns as the cleaner bot left Jared's foot and started toward them.

"Hey, what the hell, that thing bit me!" Tamon shouted, pointing at it, and immediately felt faint. He started sweating, and his stomach turned sour, and several seconds later it turned to nausea. He immediately felt his energy leaving him, and he stumbled. "What is happening to me? Can you help me…please?" he rasped at the two women as he stepped back to connect his back to the wall. He slumped down to the floor. "I feel…ugh…terrible," he said meekly.

Tamon watched them and saw them turn to head in the other direction, one of them calling out for some help. Both of them started to move in unison when both also called out from sharp pain almost in concert with one another. Tamon could see two more cleaner bots had snuck behind them a moment before. The bots looked to be addressing the floor to wall joist when they had turned toward each woman and made abrupt contact.

Tamon could see both women look at each other in shock, and then back down the corridor at him. He was breathing heavily and clasping his hands against his stomach. Sweat continued pouring down his face, and he could see that he had taken on a very pale color, looking at his reflection in the shiny bulkhead across from him.

Tamon could see the effects immediately as both women cried out in fear. "Are we dying? Oh God, what is it!" one said to the other as they both sank to the floor. He then began to hear the rhythmic shuffle of HDs making their way toward them down the corridor. Tamon looked over and saw three of the medical assistant HDs he had seen regularly in the health clinic and hospital, and he breathed a sigh of relief. He forcefully turned his head to the two women, and said in a croak, "The medical HDs are coming, hang in there."

The two women took a simultaneous deep breath of relief, and shortly could also see the medical HDs on their way, with their sterile white color, and bright red crosses apparent on different surfaces of their manufactured bodies. The lead HD stopped at Tamon, and very delicately helped him to his feet, and speaking to him in calm hushed tones. The HDs aided Tamon gingerly, bearing most of his weight they shuffled down the corridor, each taking an arm.

As they moved, Tamon didn't say anything, as he was too consumed by discomfort to think or speak. One of the HDs stopped at the door of someone's quarters and helped him in. Something at the back of his mind gnawed at him that this was all wrong. *Why aren't they going to the medical center?* But one glance at the bed and the thought of being able to lie down on a bed was overwhelming, and he did not protest.

The HD carefully tucked him into bed and covered him up to her chin with the comforter. Something about the gentle motion of the HD doing this made him cry quietly. Some distant memories of comfort now blocked.

The HD spoke soothingly. "Please rest, and when you awake, be sure to drink plenty of fluids." Tamon was nodding, half asleep, not caring about whose bed this was, and soon he was fast asleep.

The HD filled a bottle of water from the faucet in the bathroom, set it on the bedside table, and then turned to leave. As the HD entered the corridor, the door to the quarters whisked closed and locked.

In the O&M secure space, Yordanos watched the scene on G-Ring unfold through the many camera views, as well as the medical HDs arrayed on her console and the main screens. She saw the last of Jessica's people disappear inside empty quarters with an HD and looked over at Corbin with a grin. "G-Ring is secure."

Corbin, who was working closely with Laura on her console looked over in surprise. "What!? How…how did you do that? I thought you were keeping track of the overall ship's status." Enough of the other A-Crew members overheard Yordanos and came rushing over with smiles and eager faces. Yordanos sat back in her chair, with a satisfied look and crossed her arms. She nodded up to the main screen in the secure space and gestured for everyone to look, which they did.

They all could all see that the *Valor* had changed significantly since the last update. A-Ring and G-Ring showed blue, the Challenge ring still gray. D-Ring was shown as purple, as it was contested. B, C, E, and F were all still red, except for the small pockets of resistance in the secure rooms, who were efficiently working with Corbin and his team. Most were collecting intel from other crew members or trying to reason with others to join the effort to retake the ship.

Corbin saw the A-Crew holdouts in the secure room took turns gazing up at the screens, looking gratefully at Yordanos, and sharing in excited side conversations. "Well done, Yordanos, really well done," he said. He spoke up to the broader group. "Okay, team, we aren't done yet, we have a lot more to go. Great work! But let's keep going, get back to it if you please," Corbin said, shooting Yordanos a wink.

Corbin's command was followed immediately, and everyone dove back to their tasking, while Corbin approached Yordanos. He bent down to her seated level and whispered, "Okay, how did you do it?"

"Well, I was running a tally on the Jessica's dissenters on G-Ring, a little less than one hundred of them, since most of the place is for nourishment processing, algae vats, waste, and water recycling, and I noticed that the medical center allowed O&M access to small med-bots that looked like a souped up version of cleaner bots. Apparently, these have been used by Zero Crew for ship wide vaccinations, medication delivery, etc. They must have had to deal with outbreaks on this island of humanity and needed a way to quickly inoculate the whole crew." She blew out a small, concerned breath and bit her lip quizzically and said, "Although I must admit it is a little weird to have so many vaccines when our crew won't be exposed to any of this stuff ever again…problem for another day, I guess."

Corbin was following. "What did you give them?"

Yordanos smiled and turned to her console where she could show Corbin diagrams and specs of what she was about to explain. "Apparently there was a viral outbreak, and the medical labs produced a vaccine. I assume they got the instructions from Earth. Anyways, I noticed the list of side effects, and as you can see, they are nasty."

Corbin whistled as he read. "Ugh, this sounds worse than the virus…so you got the med-bots to vaccinate everyone? Why would they follow that command?"

Yordanos nodded, still grinning. "Hank said we need to operate under the constraint of doing no harm. Even though there isn't an outbreak of this disease, the HDs must not mind if something beneficial causes you discomfort. In this case, these folks will be down for six to eight hours, and then groggy for a full twenty-four. It's perfect for what we need."

Corbin's smile faded, and he looked pensive. Yordanos frowned. "What?" she asked.

Corbin responded, "It's a good plan, and it got us another ring, but I don't think we can repeat it. We must assume that G-Ring reported intel back to Jessica that there were more med-bots on duty. Even if they look like cleaner bots, they generally stay away from us, so if she is on the lookout for anything unusual, they would have reported that in. I don't think we'll catch their guard down again, either with service HDs or cleaner bots."

Yordanos nodded. "I'm sorry, I should have checked in with you first. We might have been able to do this to a broader range of rings, maybe even the whole ship."

Corbin shook his head. "I don't think so, we may have gotten another ring or two, but to go ship wide they would need to have time to coordinate and devise a defense, plus there weren't many people on G-Ring and Jessica's people were spread out. They didn't have time to communicate with each other. The other rings will. That's the problem with my original plan…there isn't a way to take down Jessica's forces across the whole ship at once. We have to keep dividing and conquering, but every time we do, another set of option drops off the table."

Corbin's face lit up. "Why don't we just cut all of their comms now? We could initiate reboots on all of their AIMAs and put Jessica and her team in the dark?"

Yordanos shook her head. "While you were out of action Jessica issued an order for all of her followers to cease AIMA coordination. They must be doing most of their comms with runners…what a pain in the ass that must be, especially ring to ring."

Now it was Corbin's turn to shake his head. "It's not as hard as you think, especially with discipline and athletic runners. Many of Earth's ancient empires had detailed communication processes that didn't even use paper…it can be done. We are just used to all of this tech." He waved an arm generally at all of the high-tech consoles and screens. "We've got to keep thinking and stay in communication ourselves. The ability for our near-instantaneous sharing of data and ideas is still a huge advantage."

"I got it, boss. I'll keep my head on it," Yordanos said.

Corbin gave her a sarcastic look with a grin at the "boss" comment and said, "I know you will." They both looked down at an alert from A-Ring, Yordanos brought Brittney's image up on the screen.

"Hey y'all, I think I have an idea for taking back B-Ring."

Chapter Forty-Seven: Meanwhile on B-Ring:

Corbin and Yordanos pulled up video feeds all over B-Ring, arrayed them on their consoles and control room screens in the secure space, and began to observe.

Jill Davidson was the on-premises lead for Jessica on B-Ring. As she walked with her patrol, she kept a constant 360-degree lookout to make sure her five team members were within eyeshot. She spoke up. "Everyone keep a heads-up and a look out. I want us to transition to in-person communication over the course of the next hour. I know B-Ring is huge, but we are sticking to Jessica's no-AIMA comms policy, so we had better get used to jogging, and passing the word manually."

She looked around at her colleagues who all nodded. She said, "Good, let's get started. I'm going to head back toward the canteen. You four collaborate with patrols and get them on a fifteen-minute update cycle and make sure those updates come directly to me. I don't care how you break up the ring, just get it covered and regular reports my way, and on time. Got it?" They all nodded again. She pointed a figure at the dark-haired young man nearest to her. "You're with me. Help me manage reports in order of importance back at the cafeteria. Also repurpose anyone else doing anything not as useful...we need to stay sharp."

"I'm with ya, Jill," the young man, named Sam Breckman, replied with an eager grin.

She ignored it and started on a brisk jog toward the canteen. They hadn't made it more than ten steps when all hell broke loose.

It sounded like an audible explosion that she could feel down to her chest, just then she quickly felt the rush of wind moving past her, and its pace was increasing. "WHAT THE HELL IS…" She tried to shout over the increasing howling of the air moving past her, and then a deafening alert broke her thought.

"ALERT, ALERT. EXPLOSIVE DECOMPRESSION B-RING OUTER SECTION 7, EVACUATE TO NEAREST QUARTERS AND CLOSE THE DOOR…ALERT, ALERT." The eardrum-punching announcement repeated.

"Holy shit, Jill! We've gotta go. Come on!" He grabbed her hand and started to pull her with the wind toward the next corridor where he knew there were quarters. She resisted at first, wanting to get to the cafeteria to see what the situation was there… *What about the prisoners? We have over fifty tied up…if this is a decompression…*

Her thoughts were interrupted by Sam shouting in her ear and practically dragging her the other way. "Jill, we've got to go, I don't know how long the atmosphere will last, COME ON!" The wind had picked up to the point where she could barely hear him, and she finally let herself be pulled back. She then turned and ran with him, as the terror of being sucked out into the vacuum of space traveling at a fraction of the speed of light started to terrify her.

As they ran, they could both see their other colleagues scrambling through the corridor. Two people out in front of them dove into the nearest quarters and bolted the door, leaving her and Sam charging now against the wind in this corridor to get to another door. *Those bastards.* She thought of the two who had left them out here. *Aren't we supposed to be on the same side?*

Nothing could be heard over the wind now, and they were staggering arm and arm against it about ten meters away. *Just a few more steps.* They both pushed hard, flexing their calf muscles and core to push the last few steps. At the sudden lack of wind in their face, they both dove into the open door to the quarters, Sam falling on top of Jill, and they quickly rolled off each other. Sam reached up to hit the door control, but the door whisked shut and bolted before he even made contact with the panel.

They both collapsed, chests heaving, and looked at each other as the wind continued to howl outside the door. They heard two people trying to make their way to the next quarters over. They were shouting in unintelligible tones; however, it did sound like they made it. They could no longer hear them shouting over the ear-piercing alert, and then suddenly there was nothing as their door too must have shut from some safety feature that recognized they were both inside.

Sam and Jill practically held their breath listening as the sound of the wind started to die down, and finally the alarm message stopped.

Jill reached for her AIMA, quickly cursing as she realized she had left it in a vestibule in the canteen. She wondered if anyone had had the chance to get word out to Jessica. She checked the in-room console, but it would not respond to her login. She looked over at Sam. "Do you think all of our people made it to quarters…what about the prisoners?" She waited, holding her breath.

Sam spoke up. "Jill, I think we've been had."

"What!?" She looked up at him harshly and yet hopefully.

"Yeah, I was just sitting here trying to piece it together…if this really had been an explosive decompression, all of the inter-ring section doors would have shut almost immediately, and I know we ran past at least two of them."

She stared at him bewildered, but he went on. "Plus, check this out." He turned on the screen for the peephole function, and the inside of the door appeared to vanish as a screen showed the corridor. They both looked and could see that the quarters doorframe across the hall was adorned with a small vase for a single flower. The flower had blown away, but the water was still in there. "While we were busting our asses to get in here, I caught it out of the corner of my eye, but didn't fully process it until we were locked in. If we had a hard vacuum out there, the water would be gone."

Jill shook her head and closed her eyes in disbelief. She clenched her fists. *And we bought it. We bought it, hook, line, and sinker.*

Jill looked down at the floor and let out a long and dejected breath. "Dammit, Sam, I lost B-Ring, I lost it for the cause…Jessica is going to be furious."

Sam nodded. "Yeah, she will be, but what can she do about it now? Corbin's guys outsmarted us this time, but the battle isn't over, it's just one ring. Our people will find a way to get us back."

Jill looked over at him. "You're just saying that to make me feel better. You aren't really all that enthusiastic about what we are doing…are you?"

He didn't hesitate. "No, not really, I just want the adventure. I figure

I've been locked away for decades, and taking the easy and calm road from there isn't the way for me. When Jessica had a plan of action and Corbin just wanted the status quo..." He shook his head at the pause, "The choice was simple. Besides, look on the bright side. The prisoners probably aren't dead. The A-Crew Loyalists are probably springing them right now. So, you may have lost the ring, but you didn't get anyone killed."

She did look up at him with a sudden sense of relief. She actually found herself hoping it was all a ruse. She didn't want to go along with the A-Crew program without answers, but she was not going to kill people either. The way she felt about it in her gut after thinking she had lost those other crew members let her know that she was not ready to kill at all.

She shot Sam a thankful glance for his nice words, and then got up and went to the door. She tried to open it despite the possibility that the other side could be the vacuum of space. Nothing happened. She looked back over at Sam, who had visibly stiffened and looked wide eyed, but he hadn't said anything. He wanted to know too. "See, Sam, no alarm, no warning to get back, just a locked and bolted door. We're stuck here. It really is a ruse, dammit." Her anger flared, although less intense than before, while she paced.

"Yeah, we are stuck here," Sam said. "No telling how long before either Zero Crew, Jessica, or hell even Corbin's cronies get us out of here." He then took on a boyish grin, walked over to the bed that was in the quarters, and sat down on it smiling. "What shall we do with all of this time?" He leaned back with a cocky look.

She stopped pacing and looked at him narrowing her eyes. "Are you being serious right now?"

He took on a more earnest look but kept the levity in the room high with a matter-of-fact tone of his voice. "I'm just saying! Why not? You've been busting your ass on this ring since the take-down. Now we're off the table for God knows how long. And just like me, I don't think you were all that gung-ho for Jessica's plan in the first place. That's another reason I like you."

Jill looked down, as she felt a blush rising to her face.

Sam broke the awkward silence and sat up. "Tell you what. I'm going to hop in the shower, and if you change your mind..." He paused. Then continued. "If not, no worries, we can play video games, watch movies, whatever, cool?"

He didn't wait for a response, he just stood up and walked toward the bathroom, pulling his shirt off as he went. Jill saw his muscular and inviting figure disappear behind the bathroom door. She then stood looking at the door, for nearly two full minutes.

She checked the door to the ring again. She scoured every inch of the quarters looking for anything that she could use on the door, or even get some sort of a signal out to Jessica but found nothing. She determined the quarters must be vacant, as she couldn't find any personal belongings of any kind.

"To hell with it," she said, striding toward the bathroom door, letting her garments slip off down to the last thread. *Jessica, the fight's all yours.*

Chapter Forty-Eight: B-Ring Goes Down

The A-Ring and D-Ring secure rooms went up with a loud cheer as they witnessed Jessica's B-Ring lead and her doting follower being blown into someone's quarters and the door slamming shut. Corbin and Yordanos looked up to see the status map of the *Valor* where B-Ring switched to blue. Corbin spoke over the cheers. "Brittney, have the HDs get our people free and return their AIMAs. I need to talk to my boy Jason."

Brittney nodded. "On it, I'll make sure he patches through as soon as he's up."

"Thanks, and, Brittney...well done, that plan was fantastic, and it worked like a charm."

Laura spoke up. "The play with the ventilation system and alerts was amazing. It's too bad the dissenters never did drill for decompression. If they gave half a shit about being a full crew member, they would have known that the inter-corridor airtight doors would have closed in place almost immediately."

Corbin and Brittney both nodded.

"That's probably true. Any bright ideas about how we take the remaining rings?" Laura asked.

"Yordanos is working on something for F-Ring. She should be ready soon," Corbin said. He looked up over his console at her. "Yordanos, you ready with the F-Ring operation?"

"Three minutes," she said back calmly.

"Okay, cool," Corbin said.

Brittney chimed back in over her console. "I've got Jason coming up for you Corbin."

Just then Jason's AIMA image popped on, and Jason was already smiling his charming wide smile, but he could see a huge bruise on his right cheekbone and his left eye was turning into a shiner. "Corbin, Danos, and Laura, what's up?! It's so good to see you guys. Thanks for springing us!"

Corbin responded, "You have Brittney to thank for that. It was her plan, and she and her team pulled it off beautifully."

"Thanks, Brittney," Jason said. "We all had no idea what we were going to do, or what they were going to do to us." He paused. "So how do we get into the fight? I've got about forty pissed-off members of A-Crew who are looking for a little payback."

"I hear you man," Corbin said, looking over at Hank, who stood impassively. "We are not to respond with violence and hurt our fellow crew members if we can help it. Get everyone over to the secure room on B-Ring just in case Jessica has a counterattack that we haven't thought of yet. From there, we'll add you to our command-and-control plan with the other secure spaces, and we can continue to team up and work the problem. We've had a number of wins, but we're not done yet. We are still up against almost half her force, and they outnumber us almost three to one. If we get in any sort of hand-to-hand skirmish, we'll likely lose, so let's play it smart. Check back in when you are in the secure space."

Jason nodded, and turned away where he could be heard coordinating with the other former A-Crew prisoners. In the meantime, Corbin looked over at some of the other A-Crew members in the secure room who had been continuing to beseech other crew members they knew about joining their cause. They had worked it out earlier, that if A-Crew members wanted in on the *Valor*'s mission, they were to meet back in the main canteens or cafeterias on the rings they had already secured. If they were on occupied rings, they were to wait for the all-clear, or if they were summoned to help retake the ring by force. This hadn't gone over as well with most of them unfortunately. "Any luck with rallying more to the cause?" Corbin asked them.

One of the leads that had been checking in with each of the other small groups with special access went over to Corbin. "Just a few on each ring. While I think these people are trustworthy, there aren't enough of them to make any kind of a stand if they get caught by

Jessica's people. I've told them to work on people they know, but not to leave their quarters until we provide further instructions."

Corbin nodded. "Good, how many total would you say? And what's your name?"

The young man responded, "We're at twenty-seven additional across all rings. And I'm Michael Bryman." He extended his hand.

"Good to meet you, Michael, and thanks," Corbin said as he shook it. "I'm challenging you and your team to get up to a hundred more recruits at least for what we need to do next. Let's get 'em signed up and watch them close. If this works we are going to need a full crew, and we are going to need the very best to run it."

Michael smiled and nodded, he turned back to his people and went to work.

Corbin went over to Norton and had a short conversation, and then signaled Hank to come over and start working with Norton and his team on a separate task.

Just then Yordanos spoke up. "Okay, people, everyone involved in the operation to take F-Ring, front and center, everyone else keep doing what you're doing; we're going to need to stay focused on each task if we are going to see this through."

She looked over at Corbin, who nodded with a smile. "Everyone, take your stations, here we go," she said. "Based on what I'm seeing here, the timing is just about perfect. I just have someone to talk with first." Yordanos's hands flew over the console, and all the relevant and available cameras came projected views around F-Ring across her console as well as the secure space control screens.

Chapter Forty-Nine: F-Ring

Aaron Anderson, Jessica's on premises ringleader on F-Ring, and his lieutenant, Gracey Boggs, who had a disdain for his language and overall crassness, were walking near the outer hull on F-Ring approaching the canteen.

"So now we have no comms, and can't use our AIMAs. It's a tactical nightmare, and it's a pity our fearless leader didn't bother two shits to figure that one out," Aaron said gruffly as he turned his head and spit out something he had been picking at in his teeth for the past ten or so minutes.

Gracey just nodded. She didn't even want to turn in his direction, as it gave her an ill feeling.

The two continued toward the canteen, where twenty-eight A-Crew members loyal to Corbin and his lot were bound to different tables, just as they had been on every other ring. Aaron kicked the foot of one of the young men glaring up at him from the floor, his arms tied against his back to one of the seats,

"Don't you eyeball me; I don't want to see your face," Aaron called out for what must have been the seven hundredth time pulling that maneuver since they had secured the prisoners here.

Gracey did spare him an annoyed glance this time. She longed to get a different assignment, and quickly. She was willing to do anything else than be paired with this overbearing bully. Gracey also wasn't sure if it was her disdain for him manifesting itself in her nostrils, but she had started to notice she didn't like to inhale through her nose around him.

"Okay, what's been going on, give me the sitrep for team Fuck-Ring, I wanna hear it," he barked to the collection of F-Ring leads and followers standing guard around the canteen.

Gracey and half the other dissenters rolled their eyes. It had been funny the first ten times, but after that there were diminishing returns.

As Aaron listened to the reports from across F-Ring from runners and patrols checking in, Gracey did have to give him some credit for leadership and tactical thinking. He spoke to everyone by name, he asked everyone a little question about how they were doing so it sounded personal. Aaron had that connection with most people, despite his crassness, but Gracey was not coming around to like him. She kept her resting sulk-face on and let it get a little darker with her thoughts on the man, as he was finishing up his sitrep for the top of the hour.

Another thing Gracey didn't get was why Aaron always came back to the canteen for a sitrep. She figured it must be routine for him, and now it's routine for the rest of their team. She also figured his ego had a little bit to do with it. She thought he recognized the importance of being seen talking at people and directing them, and he probably also relished the feeling of importance it gave him.

Gracey waited for a break in his ongoing one-way dialogue to everyone, and then said, "I'm headed to the head for a restroom break."

Aaron opened his mouth to say something flippant, but her glare back at him made him close his mouth and try to feign innocence, as if he hadn't had the thought. She turned and left without a word.

Lucky for her, her quarters were not far away from the canteen on this very ring, so she was going back there, rather than use the public restroom near the canteen. It would give her a few extra minutes away from Aaron.

She made it back to her quarters, took care of business, and was washing up in the sink when the bathroom wall console clicked on to the view of an A-Crew member she recognized from physics class, Yordanos. "Hey there, Gracey, how are you doing over there on F-Ring?"

Gracey was taken aback, but quickly recovered. "I don't have anything to say to you people, and now I get to report up the chain how you gave me a direct line, how about that?"

"Easy, Gracey, I'm not here to cause you any problems, and if you want me to hang up, I will. But right now, I get the feeling that you might want to hear me out, so what'll it be?"

Gracey turned in a huff, a visceral reaction, that did not change the view of her to Yordanos through the wall console view. "Fine, what is it?"

Yordanos spoke. "It doesn't look like you are very happy over there. It also seems like your boss is kind of a loudmouth ass." Gracey was nodding, perhaps she thought imperceptibly.

Yordanos continued. "Is that the only thing, or are you starting to wonder if maybe you joined up with the wrong team?"

Gracey looked up in a flash of anger, but no words came out, and after several seconds, her face softened a little. "Going along with what Zero Crew wants for us is wrong, and even more so without answers. You and your lot don't seem to have any care about who you used to be or who cared about you, and I can't abide by that."

"You're right," was the single response Gracey got from Yordanos, drawing a sharp look up back at her image. Gracey had clearly not been expecting that.

Gracey raised her voice. "So you admit that you were wrong, then why resist us? Why aren't you taking back the ship with the rest of us, and with Corbin too?"

Yordanos kept her earnest look on her face. "Because it won't do any good, Gracey. We are all stuck and the only path out is the path forward, no matter how hard that is to admit to ourselves. Yes, great wrongs were done to us, and while I don't think Zero Crew had anything to do with how we got here, they share in some of the responsibility. There are people back on Earth responsible for us being here, but they are there, and we are here. My point is, Gracey, we are out here in the vastness of space between the stars. There is no going back to what we once were. Our only choice is to get with the program or sit on the sidelines for the rest of our lives, waiting to die out here, no more impactful than the motes of space dust that pass us by. And if there are other options, we sure as hell won't figure them out in open rebellion."

Yordanos stopped there and carefully observed Gracey. She could tell she had made her point, and no more needed to be said. Inside Gracey's mind, Yordanos could tell she had made her decision. In the console view, Gracey looked down and some silent tears left her eyes. She nodded quietly.

Yordanos went on with a lighter tone. "Well the good news is that it's not too late to change your mind. If you want to make a move, now is the time."

Gracey looked up hopeful but still conflicted. "Making a stand, it…it seemed like the right thing to do at first, but now…after the beatings they have been doling out…. After Corbin…" she trailed off looking away, then looked back and spoke more confidently. "After they hurt Corbin and so many others…our fellow crew members. I knew I had made a mistake, but I just didn't see any way back." She looked up, now at Yordanos, now eager. "Are you all up to something?"

Yordanos took on a sterner tone. "I think we have some trust here, so yes, but we need your help."

Gracey's face showed concern, and she nodded and spoke in a quiet voice as if afraid her fellow dissenting crew members could hear her. "What is it you want me to do?"

Yordanos spoke quickly. "You need to dry your eyes, and get yourself cleaned up quickly. Do it while I'm talking, you've already been gone long enough."

Gracey set to her instructions, washing her face with cold water, and fixing her composure as best she could. Yordanos continued. "I need you to check on the A-Crew prisoners, make sure that all of them are conscious, and also that they are holding on to one of the tables or chairs they are bound to. I don't care how you do it, just make sure that they are conscious, and have a grip on something, can you do that?"

Gracey nodded, furrowing her brow. "What are you going…"

Yordanos cut her off. "Once you have done that, I want you to find a reason to leave the canteen alone and go toward the Spine of the ship to the gravity transition zone on corridor eight. Wait there, and you'll receive your next set of instructions. Are we clear on that?"

"Yes, but what—"

"No more questions Gracey, you've been supporting Jessica's side against the rest of the crew the whole time. If you want to come back to us and the crew, then please support us now…can you do that?"

Gracey looked back at Yordanos's image, and said, "Yes, I can do that."

Yordanos nodded urgently. "Good, now get going."

Gracey quickly hustled out of her quarters and jogged lightly back toward the canteen, stopping about ten meters away to catch her breath and ensure that she looked calm and collected.

"Whoa there, Gracey!" Aaron spoke up with a grin, no longer able to help himself. "Were you pinching off a twelve-pounder or what? Took you long enough!" Aaron was already laughing at his own disgusting joke, along with a few others.

"Screw you, Aaron," she said sternly, and his laughter caught, as his humor turned to annoyance at having been insulted in front of everyone, including the prisoners.

Aaron went to retort, but Gracey whirled around to meet the eyes of one of the prisoners staring up at her. She slapped him across the face. "Eyes to the floor, get your face and hands right down there!" she hollered. She then looked over at the other prisoners who were also looking at her wide-eyed at the sudden change in personality. "I SAID FACE ON THE FLOOR!" she roared, and went around smacking the back of some heads. "Grab those table legs, get a fist full of carpet and keep your ugly ass mugs pressed to the ground. First person I see pick their head up or have a hand not occupied is getting curb stomped, you hear me!?"

There were no responses, and when she looked over at Aaron, even he had an astonished look on his face. He swallowed and looked back at her. "Say, Gracey, what's up?"

Gracey darkened her eyes at him, and he winced a bit. She took her rage voice down to a serious tone. "I don't want to talk about it, least of all here. I'm going out on patrol."

Aaron hopped up. "I'll go with you." And she did not object until they were out of earshot and a little way down the corridor out of sight and earshot from the other dissenters and prisoners.

"Look, Aaron, I could use a little solo time. Not long, just need to cool down. Can you take section one through six, and I'll meet you back at the canteen in thirty minutes?"

Aaron started to object, but then visibly thought better of it. "Yeah, okay…umm…yeah, I'll see you in thirty, grab a runner and holler at me if you need anything." He then turned and left.

Gracey felt a little bad at her act, especially for the crew members she had struck, but Yordanos had told her to find a way to make sure they were all conscious and holding on. She had seen that they were.

She was also a little surprised Aaron didn't specifically ask what was wrong with her. Gracey figured he was the type that if you didn't specify, he assumed the worst, probably something with her lady parts or some dumb shit like that from him.

As Aaron's bulky form went in the opposite direction, Gracey did not waste time. She had a nagging feeling she needed to get to the gravity transition zone in corridor eight where Yordanos had instructed quickly. She jogged for the next ten minutes, gradually making her way "up" stairwells and ramps toward the Spine of the *Valor*. She made better time as her weight decreased. As she jogged, she marveled to herself at how massive the *Valor* was and wondered how the hell it got built and up to a fraction of light speed. To her astonishment, she didn't encounter any other patrols, giving her a slight pause to think about how she and Aaron had set them up. *Corbin, Yordanos, and that bunch could have staged just about anything with these gaps in our lines, I wonder wha—*

Her thoughts were interrupted as she neared the gravity transition zone. At a fraction of Earth's gravity, she had to be careful not to bounce each step or she would take many seconds to come back down. The floor was textured to enable maximum friction, but she mused she could have won the long jump back on Earth with this type of low gravity. She truncated her last thought when she rounded the last corridor to corridor number eight and saw a lone HD standing right at the point where people's feet would start to slip, despite the texture of the footwear and flooring, for lack of gravity.

The HD startled her a bit but spoke in a warm and polite tone. "Good evening, Ms. Boggs. Thank you for coming. May I suggest you take hold of my hand, and any other perch you feel comfortable with on my frame or the wall. We are going to experience a small jolt."

Gracey approached tentatively. She had interacted with HDs all the time, but this interaction seemed more personal. Sheepishly she reached for the HD's hand, who took hers gently. She looked along the wall for anything else to hold on to but didn't see anything. She saw the HD looking at her expectantly, so she also sheepishly placed her hand against a metallic version of his collar bone, and then gripped tight.

"Very good," it said again politely. "Please hold on. Gravity change will occur in three.... Two...one." The whole corridor lurched, and Gracey collided halfway with the HD before regaining her composure. As she was recovering, her feet floated off the ground. F-Ring had abruptly slowed, and looked to be slowing further to a complete stop.

From down corridor eight in the direction of the Spine of the ship where the HD had come from, Gracey saw a line of HDs floating in perfect unison and spacing. They went right past her and her HD, propelled by precision bursts of air, and gentle use of the corridor walls, floors, and ceilings.

Gracey looked on in awe. She had seen HDs do this all the time escorting people to and from the Spine of the ship to gravity transition zones across all rings, but to see so many fly into the areas where mostly humans held gravitational reign was new to her.

Her HD began moving down the corridor following his counterparts and gently towing Gracey just like HDs had done in helping people through the Spine of the ship. "Thank you, Ms. Boggs, for your cooperation. At this time, I will escort you to your quarters. My colleagues and I will do the same for all your fellow crew members. Once everyone is safely in a set of quarters, gravity will be restored."

Gracey, ignoring Jessica's protocol snapped her AIMA back on and tried to pull up comms with her F-Ring counterparts who may also be ignoring Jessica's no-AIMA policy, but discovered it was blank. Her HD observed her checking and spoke up. "All Communications between you and your colleagues have been blocked at this time. Please rest assured that everyone is receiving fair treatment during this transition."

Gracey looked at the HD's face. "Transition? What the hell is that supposed to mean?" The HD did not respond, however.

Gracey and her HD effortlessly traversed the multiple corridors on audible puffs of air while in total weightlessness. They arrived a few minutes later at her quarters. The door slid open, and the HD gently pushed her in so that she would eventually reach the back wall in a minute or so. Flailing about would accomplish nothing, this wasn't a swimming pool, so Gracey just watched and waited. "Please try to limit your speed in moving around, Ms. Boggs, I understand your zero-G training is limited at this time."

Gracey responded sarcastically, "Yeah thanks, can you patch me through to Yordanos? I want to talk to that woman." The HD paused for a moment, as if checking, and then responded.

"She is currently engaged in other matters; however, I have alerted her of your wish to speak with her. She will respond when available. I bid you good day." With that, the door slid shut, and Gracey was alone in her quarters.

When Gracey finally reached the back wall, she started to work on maneuvering around using her hands and grabbing onto the furniture. *The HD is right, I am a novice at this, might as well get some practice.* During her moving around and gently pushing from one wall to the other, she realized that most of her things were undisturbed and still in their place. She reached over to nudge her computer console and saw that it slid a few inches away, rose an inch or so and then almost imperceptibly set back into place. She too noticed that her form went back to the floor. *So they didn't stop F-Ring…they just slowed it down, a lot. This gravity has got to be less than 1% of Earth's gravity. Hmm, I wonder if all of the rings can do this.*

Chapter Fifty: Allies?

Corbin, Laura, Yordanos, and their mini command crew in the D-Ring secure space let out another collective cheer as F-Ring turned from red to blue. They watched the HDs retreat from moving all of Jessica's dissenters into quarters and escorted all of the former A-Crew prisoners to the secure space. Some had gone more gently than others. Aaron had tried to bash an approaching HD with a club he had fashioned, but he only served to send himself spinning uncontrollably until another HD had grabbed him and handled him while he kicked and screamed.

"Laura, can you bring up the F-Ring secure space on the main screen?" Laura did as asked, and soon everyone was looking into a view of the F-Ring secure space, where half of the former prisoners were still looking around, marveling at the space having not seen it before, and the other half, immediately took positions at consoles.

Corbin spoke up. "Welcome back to the cause, ladies and gentlemen." They all looked up at Corbin's voice and picture and many broke into smiles. Some were a little teary eyed. Laura also patched in Brittney from A-Ring, and all the other A-Crew feeds from their respective secure space.

"As you can see from what we are sharing, we have managed to take back more than half of the ship; however the Spine, C, our ring D, and E are still occupied by Jessica's team. We have learned that Jessica is on D-Ring, and we—"

Laura interrupted, "Corbin we've received a transmission from the Spine of the ship. We've cut their comms with Jessica, but this one is addressed to you."

Corbin thought about it, and responded, "Put it up on the screen and share with our secure spaces, including F-Ring, please. Laura made the adjustments, and a video feed came to life on the screen.

"Hi Corbin...OH!...uh, and hello A-Crew...umm people. This is Gerald Krenshaw from the Spine. We wish to defect...immediately. About a dozen of our number do not feel the same way, and they have been...restrained." The view from Gerald's AIMA went over to twelve people sitting in three transport cars off to the side. Corbin could see that their bonds were tied tightly, and the people strained uncomfortably against them. Corbin also noticed Gerald had obviously been struck on the eye. It wasn't black, but he had popped a few blood vessels giving his right iris a partial red stain, and a puffy spot was rising on the skin above his right eye. In looking at the prisoners, all three had blood on their faces, but since they were in zero-G, it stuck to their faces in small droplets.

Corbin spoke up. "Okay, Gerald, we appreciate the call. I hope you'll understand if we don't fully trust you just yet, but we will consider your acts after this is all over based on what happens next. Fair enough?" Gerald appeared to harbor no excessive emotion at having heard this, and he nodded. Corbin spoke again, everyone watching. "Good, thanks, Gerald. How many are you?"

"We had ten people watching each ring transition zone, so minus the twelve you see here, our number is at sixty-eight. We stand by for your instruction," Gerald said.

Corbin grinned, recognizing the conundrum and looked around the room to skeptical looks, "Give us a minute here, Gerald." And Corbin gave Laura the hand signal to mute and block his video feed, while leaving everyone else patched in.

"Okay, everyone, we were hoping for this. If this is real and other sections of the ship are willing to break from Jessica, then we might be able to end this thing without any further shenanigans. Since we can't be sure that somehow our communications here aren't being monitored, we are keeping the main execution of our strategy held close to the vest...only a few of us know it. However, if you have ideas about how we may leverage this situation, I would appreciate any suggestions. The objective is regaining control of rings C, D, and E assuming the Spine is now ours based on this development."

About a full minute went by, and Corbin felt he had to speak back up. "Please, speak your mind, if you have any ideas about how best to achieve our objectives, please speak up. I won't say what we will do, or weigh in on it, but we would very much like to hear what you have to say."

"This is Devon Cranston from F-Ring, I suggest you have Gerald break a few bones of each of his supposed prisoners. That way we know they're loyal to our cause."

Gasps went up all around, and people in the secure space with him were already looking at him desperately to see if he would agree. Corbin looked up to see a very attractive brunette who had just made this suggestion. Something in him stirred, like he had been in a situation like this before. Such rash decisions with extreme outcomes had been on his plate before, but a suggestion was just a suggestion, no consequences until it was executed.

Corbin spoke up. "Look I know how some of you must feel, having been beaten and abused by your captors. I myself had to get quite a lot of work after getting my skull cracked, so I feel you about getting some payback. But since we have a bit of a party line here, and you know what we are all about in standing up to the dissenters, you know we can't have any short-sighted goals. We are all going to have more than a century to get to know one another on our way to Gliese 832. We cannot errantly inflict pain and violence for small gains, nor can we put ourselves in a situation where regret will build upon regret, forcing us apart one by one over decades. I appreciate your anger at the dissenters, we all feel it, but one day, these people will be our fellow crew members again. We may depend upon them for our very lives. Jessica's little insurrection here is one of a hundred other dire situations we will face where we are going. She is one more problem to be solved, nothing more. Don't let it get to you, Cranston. And that goes for everyone else thinking the same thing."

There was a bleak pause, and then Corbin assumed a more positive tone. "Okay, what else have we got? Any other ideas if you please?"

"Corbin," Laura said. "Looks like Jessica is addressing the crew."

"Please put it on for all of us to hear, Laura," Corbin said.

Jessica's tone was resolute. "My fellow crew members, I'm afraid we have come to the end of our initial effort here. The lap dogs who want to keep us oppressed have figured out ways to disrupt communications, they somehow control HDs, and none of us appear to have that kind of capability. They must have sided with Zero Crew who have put us here in CHAINS!" She shouted the last word as tears burst from her eyes.

"We are not going to quit, and we are not going to give up. They may take us down, but we are going to take as many of them down with us. If you feel this rage with me, if you are angry that you were taken from where you were from and away from everyone you every loved and who loved you, then rage with me now. Sing out that rage with everything YOU HAVE!" And with that she screamed. It was a high-pitched roar that split everyone's ears via the AIMA and echoed down the corridor from her quarters on D-Ring. Her fellow dissenters picked it up and they all roared in defiance. It went on and on and its sound filled rings C, D, and E and it did not cease.

Chapter Fifty-One: Under Pressure

Corbin looked up at Yordanos, Laura, and the rest of his group, knowing anger and desperation from Jessica and her followers were poor bedfellows.

He rushed over to Laura. "Laura, extend gravity protocol to C, D, and E-Ring and execute" Corbin said.

She turned to look at him aghast as nearly everyone else in the secure space and from the other consoles spoke up concern.

Corbin did not hesitate. "Do it now please, you heard Jessica, she means to drag this out a long as possible, and we need to end this now." Laura did as she was told, and everyone immediately felt a ring-wide lurch, as massive rockets on the tangent of each of the rings fired causing the acceleration of the rings to drastically increase.

Laura spoke up. "Okay, everyone, it will be best if you lie on your back on the ground, with your palms pressed flat on the floor. Use your energy to expand your lungs and try to breathe normally. Don't stress out, pilots used to do this back on Earth all the time with much sharper increases in G's."

The ambient noise increased as if a great strain was affecting the entire ring structure, yet still the gravity increased. Corbin felt like he was hearing from under water.

Corbin called out, "Increase O2 level in the secure spaces to forty percent, I want us conscious when this is over!" he hollered…more croaked, and Laura made the adjustment while lying on her back via her AIMA. She could no longer reach up to her console.

The system obeyed, and everyone felt a cool breeze as pure O2 was pumped into the secure space. Despite peoples' lungs nearly collapsing from the now 7G gravity being applied via the rings being sped up, Corbin and his group began to breathe easier as each short breath yielded more oxygen for their lungs. It wasn't comfortable at all, but they were hanging in there. *This isn't as fun as I thought it would be,* he thought.

"Corbin!" Laura yelled, "I'd say another five minutes, and everyone will be out. We should hold steady right here, no one will be conscious without this much oxygen."

Corbin nodded to Laura and patched in to Jason using his AIMA feed. Jason had moved to the Spine of the *Valor* while the other rings fell with some of the more athletic A-Crew members from his secure space on A-Ring and F-Ring. "Jason, on my mark, deploy to C, D, and E…like we discussed."

Jason's eager, smiling face looked at him and nodded with determination. "You got it, man."

Jason, who floated weightlessly in the Spine of the *Valor*, oblivious to the extra gravity affecting the targeted rings, left his audio feed to Corbin's open. Corbin, though teeth gritted with effort against the additional gravity, could hear Jason call to his hastily assembled teams, many from the Spine defectors. So far, by their compliance and behavior, they seemed to have truly defected back to the A-Crew. Jason spoke. "Okay, teams, gravity is going to be set back to normal in the next ninety seconds. As soon as the gravity near the center of the ring is back at 3G, work with your support HD and enter the transition zone and move to secure everyone from Jessica's group highlighted on your AIMA maps. Use your HD as much as possible. With the extra gravity, I don't want you expending your effort moving through the corridors. Don't be a hard ass; use the tools we have and save all that energy for possible confrontations."

He paused for a breath, and let that sink in before going on. "Each of you has been assigned a different set of people, and they should dazed or outright incapacitated. Keep your heads up though. The more time that goes by, the more time they have to recover and be ready for you. I can guarantee by the time most of you get to the final person on your list, they will be able to resist. Restrain them as you find them with your adjustable bracers, and then secure them in place, but do not. I REPEAT, DO NOT cause bodily harm. If you get into a stand-off where the odds are even or worse, hold or fall back, and call it in via the AIMA feed, and others will be directed to your position to help." He paused for another breath hoping that this set of instructions was digested.

"Are there any questions?" Jason saw that there didn't appear to be any. "Is everyone absolutely clear on the parameters of this action…no bodily harm…yes? Sound off!" A cacophony of yessir, affirmative, yes, and some other expletive filled affirmations filled Jason's ears. The high level of eagerness in some of their voices made him a little nervous about that, but it would have to do.

"Good, get lined up at your respective slipring entrances, and make sure your HDs are ready to move," Jason said. He then took a position near one of the corridor entryways in front of D-Ring. Behind him lined up ten others, each with an HD to assist them rapidly through the slipring as now each ring was spinning much faster, and without an HD assist, a human alone would likely be injured, or worse, cut in half. Also, with the rings about to decelerate, the rate of getting people through each slipring opening would get longer and longer, and a bit harder for a human to time unassisted. However, clever programming allowed the HDs to synch exactly with the ring speed and achieve human transition through the sliprings easily.

Jason looked up to the Spine to see the rest of the breach teams taking up similar positions in the distance, wholly relying on their HDs to suspend themselves in line behind the entryways. To his left and right, it looked like human-HD connectors had blossomed from the center of the Spine.

Jason's focused on his AIMA view of the D-Ring secure space, to see Corbin's image in the top right corner of his view, who was flanked on either side by Yordanos and Laura lying on their backs breathing heavily.

Corbin, who felt like he was in the middle of a set of three hundred burpees, called out with a strained voice. "Jason, you ready man? Twenty seconds to go."

Jason nodded.

"Okay, give 'em hell." Corbin groaned. Before the gravity increase, Laura had adjusted the overhead screen to show a map view of the rings C, D, and E. The map showed the Spine was lined with blue and gray dots, representing each of the breach team members, and their associated HDs. The collective group could see nearly one hundred A-Crew breachers headed into each ring. Now that the Spine had fallen back to A-Crew, Corbin and his team had been able to bring in reinforcements from the other secure areas, and they had picked up a few more willing crew members to join the breach teams along the way. Brittney was leading the C-Ring breach, Jason, D-Ring, and Herbert, who had been able to recover from his vicious beating, led E-Ring.

Still pinned to the floor from the increased gravity, Corbin was nervous. After Jessica's speech, he hadn't wanted to give them any time to coordinate, and thus made the snap decision to apply the increased gravity trick. Yet he still had a nagging feeling of…something.

While the camera views showed the Spine of the *Valor* was clear, he and his team could not see the entryway camera views on C, E, or his own D-Ring. Jessica and her crew had likely obscured or destroyed the cameras. This meant that despite the fact they were all probably just as pinned to the ground as he was, although with substantially less oxygen, they had also likely erected some sort of barrier or impediment to the breach teams. *But what else have they done?*

There was also the possibility that Jessica had come up with something none of them had thought of. Although without access to the *Valor*'s full online resources and intel, there shouldn't be any physical barriers the HDs couldn't overcome. He knew that when someone was cornered, that's when it could get the most dangerous. Thoughts bombarded his mind as the last few seconds ticked down. *Should we have taken more time to prepare the breachers? Should we arm them? Should I call off the breach and try to negotiate? Too late now.*

The external thrusters fired and started to brake the rings' heightened speed. Corbin and his colleagues felt the jolt and could feel the weight on their chests begin to wane slightly. Everyone watched as the gravity indicator began to tick down, breachers in the Spine gripped their HDs tightly, steadying themselves for the push into the rings. Jason spoke up to all breach teams. "Here we go, let's take our ship back!" Everyone let out a cheer.

The gravity counter to 3G's hit zero. "GO, GO, GO," everyone shouted, and the HDs began escorting the breach teams one by one into the entryways. For the people near the back of the line, it was maddeningly slow. Everyone had been envisioning a spirited charge, but the HDs and fast spinning rings would not allow it. One by one, the breachers popped through into the rings, and wasting no time zoomed toward their assigned members of Jessica's group, on the backs of their HDs, who easily navigated to the gravity transition zone and into the rings on loud blasts of air.

Jason was the first through the corridor on D-Ring. He had counterparts on the seven other entryways, but for this corridor, it was just him. "Let's go, move it!" he coaxed his HD, and they both zipped down the hallway. Jason immediately became acutely aware of rapidly rising gravity. Even though he had been at 0G for less than an hour, it felt like he had forgotten what gravity felt like. As hard as he clung to his HD, he started to slip down.

"Hey man, can I get a little help?" The HD, which did not need his hands for any maneuvering, reached back with his hands and pushed Jason up on his back. He was basically piggybacking an HD robot as they made it through the low gravity transition to higher gravity, which continued to decrease from 3G. The HD's feet touched down, and it trotted down the corridor, Jason hanging on. To Jason it felt like the HD was running down a steep ramp, but his eyes showed him that they were running down a corridor, and he knew that he and his friends would need more training to get used to these maneuvers.

"A-Crew, it's easier if you piggy-back your HD, everyone get onto the back and hold tight until your relative gravity is near 1G!" he shouted a little too enthusiastically. By design, his AIMA reduced his volume so it wouldn't sound like he was yelling in everyone's ears.

He chanced a look over his shoulder and saw the next two of his fellow breachers had made it through with their HDs, and he was glad to see them being adjusted onto their HDs backs. Jason and his HD rounded the next hallway from the entryway, and they both pulled up short abruptly. The corridor was blocked with furniture stacked nearly to the ceiling. Jason could see that it had probably been a little higher of a pile, but the extra gravity had pushed the mass down a bit. Two more of his colleagues arrived, and they started to clear the mess by directing their HDs to shove the furniture aside.

Jason glanced at his map view in the AIMA, everywhere across D-Ring, the blue and gray dots were bunched up not far past the entryway corridors with similar blockages. Jason patched into D-Ring secure space. "Corbin, what's going on? My breach teams have been slowed by barriers, we are breaking through, but it will take a few minutes. They must have emptied nearly everyone's quarters of furniture to do this… What a damn mess," he said in disgust.

Corbin responded, "Hang on, Jason, clear a small path through the debris to give you some options, but hold for the time being. I need to check on something."

Jason nodded and transmitted the new directive to his D-Ring breach team while responding to Corbin, "Copy that, standing by, but hurry, I don't like that we are now reacting and not acting on our terms."

Corbin nodded with a grimace. "I'll get back to you in two minutes."

Corbin spoke up. "Laura, what's going on with the other rings?"

Laura nodded toward the other two main screens with Brittney's and Herbert's AIMA view. Both looked like they were advancing without any resistance at all. "They have been expanding across C and E-Ring, where they expected to find members of Jessica's insurrection, but only a few have been found where we thought they would be." Corbin's blood started to turn cold… "How many…what percentage are we finding versus what we expected to find on C and E?" Corbin asked, interrupting her.

Laura did some quick calculations on her console. "I'd say fifteen to twenty percent…and…wait…only a few of these people are actually known dissenters, most of these people are turning out to be regular A-Crew members," she said, astonished. "Where are they?" she asked.

Corbin tried to remain calm, but he could feel his blood beginning to boil and spoke. "I want real-time status at all times with everyone on Jason's D-Ring team. Get back to them and tell them to fall back to the gravity transition entryways, have their HDs form a defensive barrier…on both sides."

Laura and Yordanos both looked at him in alarm. "Just do it, tell them to watch for attacks from either the ring or the Spine…do it quickly," he said urgently, trying not to snap. He had an open AIMA line directly to Jason and spoke to him as he was already obeying the instructions Corbin had just transmitted through Laura. "Jason, how many defectors on the D-Ring breach team?"

Jason spoke back quietly as he and his breachers made their way back to the gravity transition zone on their HDs. "I'd say one in four, and about the same on the other two rings. Why?" he asked.

Corbin responded, "I'm not sure how many, but there are definitely some of Gerard's defectors to our side that are in fact not defecting. Heck, it could be all of them, but it's hard to say. Either they helped to sneak dissenters from C and E-Ring over to D-Ring, or they have something else up their sleeve. Point is, you can't do anything until they make a move, but I want you, and whomever else you trust to keep an eye out for any trouble. I'll reach out to the supposed defectors over AIMA and remind them that every action they take is being monitored and if they step out of line, they'll pay the same price as everyone else supporting Jessica."

Jason nodded. "What price is that?" he asked, partially demanding, yet his tone was calm.

Corbin looked Jason's image in the eye with a little annoyance. "I'm not sure yet. We'll figure that out when we come to it."

Jason nodded, and then looked around him. "Okay, there are twelve of us behind two walls of HDs. Lucky for us these entryway corridors aren't too big. We can block side to side with four HDs, so we have two in reserve on each side."

Corbin looked back at him. "Stand by and stay sharp, we're in the end game now, if we rush in and fall to whatever Jessica has planned, this could drag on and on, or it could get bloody. For now, I don't care what you see. Do not pursue or break formation. If they advance on you, let us know."

Jason gritted his teeth and tried to hold the frustration out of his voice. "You got it, man."

Corbin looked over at Yordanos who was sending out the loyalty reminder correspondence to all of the supposed defectors from the Spine. "Yordanos, ask them if any of them would like to volunteer additional information about how many of Jessica's people have transited between rings in the past few hours…they may have followed Jessica then, but they probably didn't anticipate we would take back as much of the *Valor* as we have, and may be having second thoughts."

Yordanos nodded.

After she had finished, another alert popped up on her console showing archived video footage from a discreet camera far up the

Spine from C, E, and D rings from an hour ago. Yordanos called out urgently, "Corbin! You should redirect Brittney and her C-Ring force as well as Herbert's E-Ring force here to D-Ring now!"

Corbin nodded to Laura, who was already reaching out to Herbert and Brittney. He then followed Yordanos's pointed finger to the screen where an archived video feed from far up the Spine by G-Ring showed Jessica's entire crew leaving C and E -Rings and entering D-Ring.

Yordanos spoke up again. "I'm not sure how she pulled this off without us knowing it, but at least some of those people who supposedly 'defected' smuggled Jessica and her people over the Spine…Now all of her forces are here on D-Ring, with us…some of them embedded with our breach teams."

Corbin cursed quietly. "Pull up the video feeds from the same time window closer to D-Ring. How the hell could we have missed this?!" he said bewildered more than angry. Yordanos called up all of the camera feeds from the Spine and ran the archived footage on the main mission control like screen at the front of the O&M center. She tried to pull up views from the gravity transition zone on C and E rings, but those cameras had either been knocked offline or obscured with tape or other objects by Jessica's people.

Everyone in the O&M center studied the video feeds intensely, not seeing any corroborating videos showing Jessica's people transiting the Spine, until Norton called out, "Look! Pull up video feed D-12." Laura did so, minimizing the other video feeds.

Everyone's mouth hung open as a picture of the serene and unoccupied Spine of the ship hung loosely and gently moving in the artificial ventilation breeze that people often felt in the Spine of the *Valor*. They could see that the misleading image showing no one in the ring had simply become unstuck from its crudely and hastily fashioned harness holding the still picture over the camera's view. In the now unobstructed camera video file, Corbin and his team could all see figures assisting one another "climbing" the Spine wall toward D-Ring.

Chapter Fifty-Two: Trust Your People

Yordanos called Corbin over for a private word. She swiveled in her chair so her back was facing the mission-control-like room and the other A-Crew members, and Corbin pulled up a seat to look at her eye to eye. She began, "Jason's upset. He thought he had command of the D-Ring breach effort, and you stepped in and pulled him back." Corbin's mouth opened in protest, and she held up a hand and continued. "You aren't out on the ring, your ass isn't on the line like his is, and even though you think you need to be the one that has a hand in everything to save the day, that's just not how it is."

Corbin uttered a protest, "They were walking into a trap, they had to pull back."

She jumped in with a smile, not threatening or challenging, but to interrupt him as politely as possible. "There it is, you told him to pull back, you didn't tell him what was happening. Corbin, at this point you are the eyes and ears and connective tissue of getting our ship back. But you can't fight all the battles. Trust your people...our people...they might surprise you in how well they do."

Corbin held her gaze a moment longer, and then closed his eyes, and his shoulders hung, "You're right," he said quietly. He shook his head, sniffed, and smiled. "Keep doing that," he said earnestly. "I need to be held to account, thank you..." He glanced back up at the command screen.

Right then Laura piped in. "Corbin, Jessica's forces are amassing to attack the breach teams in the entryways...our people are outnumbered by over two hundred or so with everyone from A and C rings."

"Shit!" Corbin said aloud. "Run some quick math, based on the numbers are there enough left for a strike team as well hiding somewhere in the Spine?" Laura's hands flew across the console, her mouth muttering commands to her AI in her AIMA, as the operational camera videos and images data was correlated and aggregated.

Laura responded after less than a minute. "I show the possibility of an attack from a Spine team at three people plus or minus two."

Corbin nodded. "That's not enough to take down any of our breach teams…please patch me back in to Jason now."

"Jason, listen to me," Corbin said solemnly. "You guys are about to get hit, and hard. I'm sorry, I should have let you command the minute I ordered you guys in there, but I micromanaged you, and I apologize. You're going to be in the shit, and it's my fault."

Jason made rapid hand motions to his team to tell everyone to be alert and keep an eye out, as he simultaneously keyed in the command via his AIMA alerting the other seven teams in their entryways, and then he focused on Corbin. "I wondered what the hell you were doing, man. So now what?"

Corbin squeezed his eyes shut, knowing he had made a horrible blunder.

Jason spoke up. "Don't go soft on me now, Corbin, tell me what we are looking at and what the hell to do, and we'll get it done!"

Corbin straightened. "With the few cameras remaining, we see assault forces forming up with one hundred yards of each corridor. Looks like they sneaked their people from C and E-Ring over here, and they have about sixty people ready to assault each entryway…it's a lot more than we planned—"

Jason interrupted. "You think!?" he retorted. Corbin winced slightly at the reply and at how he had pissed off his friend. During the exchange, Yordanos sent the coordinates of the suspected dissenter assault teams over to Jason's AIMA. Corbin could see Jason immediately giving orders to the other teams.

"What are you…how can we help?" Corbin asked, correcting his question.

"Aww, hell no, Corbin, you got us into this mess," Jason said seemingly annoyed. And then he smiled his all-knowing confident smile. "My team and I are going to get us out. Stand by on comms and get me some reinforcements as fast as you can."

"Copy that, good luck," Corbin said quietly, guilt plaguing his ability to think logically.

Corbin, working in tandem with his AI Tina, to manage the views and pertinent real-time information, pulled back to the command-and-control view of D-Ring, and was amazed to see Jason's teams re-advancing into the ring, and quickly, with the HDs leading the way at double speed. He saw the blue and gray blips of Jason's team of humans and HDs collide with the barricade icons denoted in orange, obliterating them as if they weren't there. The teams continued to advance out of the low gravity transition zone and onto sure footing toward the center of D-Ring.

Jason and his team tiptoed along the corridor to the coordinates Laura had sent him, indicating where a group of Jessica's followers were amassing. Jason could see that they had chosen a large conference room with two entryways to the main corridors at a right angle from one another. Jason and his colleagues could hear a male voice calling out in motivation and getting a response from all of the others. *Sounds like he's giving a pep talk.*

He keyed his AIMA messaging to his fellow team members, not wanting to make a sound. They each split into teams of six, and each taking six HDs with them. The other group sneaked around to the other entryway. Jason could tell by the tone of the young man's voice that he was nearing the end of his pump-up speech. He had only a few short seconds until they would surge out of the doorways.

Jason went to a control panel outside of the conference room and accessed the screen. To his amazement, he saw that O&M protocol opened a separate menu. He quickly looked at the door options and saw an immobilization procedure. He keyed it, but it spit back an error message, warning him that humans were still in the room. He tried to override but was met with a conditional message about ensuring that the humans to-be confined would have medical attention and access to food and water.

He quickly checked his HD's load-out and saw they all had nourishment bars, water, and medical attention programming. "HDs into the room" he whispered and keyed the instruction to his team on the opposite door. Without hesitation, the HDs entered the other room. Predictably, the shouts went up, and Jason could hear a wild clambering as some must have started to attack, while others probably didn't know what to do.

As soon as the last HD from his team entered the door, it slid closed and locked. Jason sprinted to the other side, just in time to see that door close and the six members of his team's smiling faces looking over at him. "Did we just do that?" one of Jason's team called out.

Jason ran over trailed by his five other colleagues. "Hell yeah, we did. I don't think we should let them out for a year..." He snickered while his team members high-fived.

Jason went back to his AIMA, and at hearing a status update form Laura, he motioned his team closer. "The next team over on corridor six has lost contain against another group of Jessica's people. They are falling back to the Spine entryway," Jason said, and the others piped down.

"What's the play?" one of his team members asked.

Jason checked his AIMA and saw that team leader's status update. Chelsea, the other breach team's lead, keyed back to Jason that they would retreat into the Spine and find another place to re-enter D-Ring where they would have more success. Jason signaled her affirmative, and then got an idea.

He looked over at the barricade, and then he looked at his team. "Let's go and grab that huge couch from the barricade, plus anything you can use that's good for pushing people." He sent an update to Corbin on his status and intent, and then loped off down the corridor with his team.

It took them about four minutes to scurry part of the way around D-Ring over to the next adjoining corridor toward the ramped corridor to the Spine entryway. The lessened gravity made hauling the couch a lot easier than it would have been in Earth gravity.

Jason and his team could hear shouts, yells, and the sound of struggle from around the corner where Chelsea had organized her team and HDs. Some of them were holding the entryway to the Spine against Jessica's attack force, while a few others were evacuating through the slipring back into the Spine.

Jason risked a peek around the corner and saw the full force of about eighty dissenters pressing the small A-Crew team and HDs back toward low gravity, and as their feet began to slip, they were losing control of staying together as a group. It appeared that the dissenters were grabbing for them, trying to drag them back into the ring. They wanted to try to capture his fellow A-Crew members, and probably hold them to force a negotiation.

Jason knew that there could be no negotiation now. The only hope would be to get the dissenters contained without getting anyone killed. So far this had worked, but with actual hand-to-hand fighting, there was bound to be a misstep, Jason knew.

Again, he had to push these thoughts away, and he gathered his team around close. "Okay, there are a lot more of them than there are of us. But if we get a head start and all hit at them at the same time, we'll have a great enough push to get them to low gravity. Remember, all we have to do is get them up the corridor toward the Spine. Their mass will count for less, so our first big push with that big ass couch has to get them to the low gravity transition zone. Once we plow this beast into them, I want everyone to kick off of it on the count of three. Any questions?" There were none. "Ok, wait for my signal, Derrick, Harder, Williams, Kano and Beesberg, you're carrying the couch from the sides, everyone else settle in behind it and get ready to push as if your life depends on it...because it does." Jason made quick eye contact with all of them, and they nodded, determined. Jason then keyed coordination instructions over to Chelsea who keyed back that they were ready to disengage.

Silently, Jason and his team got into formation and started at a run and began to pick up speed. Everyone took aim at the back of the formation of dissenters.

Suddenly Chelsea called out, "Fall back!" Her HDs disengaged from where they had locked themselves into formation, and with preordered instructions, each grabbed one of the A-Crew members and fluidly moved into the low gravity transition zone, blasting air into the faces of the clawing, and grabbing dissenters. Chelsea felt a spike of fear as she saw one of her team members held back by two different dissenters that had vise-like grips on his legs, but an HD casually reached out a robotic arm and pulled her team member back.

From the other side of the dissenter formation, Jason and his team smashed into the backs of the dissenter group. The massive and fast-moving couch first contacted the guy who had been calling out encouragement mid-yell, which cut off in a squelch, as the pressure from the mass drove much of the air out of his lungs. Jason and his team timed the initial surprise push perfectly in unison, and they all collectively flew forward, into one another, and then as a group toward the low gravity transition zone, following in the wake of Chelsea's team's-controlled withdrawal.

"Kick off in three, two…one!" Jason roared. Jason's team jumped up in the reduced gravity, and each placed their feet on the back of the couch. "PUSH!" They all leapt off in approximate unison, and Jason could see the mass of dissenters lurch forward toward the Spine, but after a few seconds, and as the dissent team regained their footing, their progress slowed. Jason could also hear the panicked yells of people at the back of the dissenter formation screaming and panicking as their feet started to slide. Gravity for them was now below the level of controlled upright walking as the slightest push sent them careening.

"AGAIN!" Jason hollered as more and more of the dissenters had picked themselves up and were orienting themselves to resist. The couch was still separating the two groups, so they rallied and ran at it again, leaping to shove the poor piece of furniture and the dissenting group back. Jason looked for the red line on the wall, denoting the spot where humans moving without HDs was forbidden, and saw that they were already well past it. "PUSH!" "AGAIN!" The veins stood out on his neck, and his team members were pouring sweat with effort, but Jason could see them gaining ground as more and more people began to flail and lose purchase with the diminishing gravity. They all shoved the couch barrier again, and three more feet, again, and the distance was lengthening. "ALMOST THERE!…PUSH!" The last rank of dissenters' feet slipped and gave way, and suddenly they were all floating helplessly, their feet and arms failing to make purchase without weight behind friction.

Jason called out, "STOP, STOP, STOP! Okay, pull back." They had been quite overzealous and almost went across the gravity transition zone themselves. They tiptoed back to where they could feel more of the weight on their feet again.

"You guys are such assholes," the young man who Jason had initially mashed with the couch called out.

Jason called back, "Why, because we want our ship back? Trying to take control of what you don't understand is a fool's errand. Why don't you get with the program?"

Jason's team member Derrick put his hand on Jason's shoulder. "Hey, forget that ball sack. Chelsea is going to secure each of them with HDs now that they are floating helpless, and we'll stash them in the Spine until this is over. Now that's two of the corridor teams down, now what?"

Jason spared a few moments to watch the HDs from Chelsea's team grabbing individual dissenters floating in the low gravity, and to much verbal protest, they were being pulled back into the Spine of the ship. Jason figured Laura had somehow switched these HDs into perpetual Spine transit-mode, because they didn't respond at all to the demands of the dissenters to put them down. Jason watched with mild amusement as the loudmouth he had been jawing with tried to strike the HD several times in the face, but the HD calmly blocked each blow and proceeded down the corridor, then pushed the man through the slipring where another HD spirited him away.

Jason opened comms back with Corbin in the D-Ring secure area. "Hey guys, this corridor is secure. Where are the HDs taking this lot?"

Laura smiled. "The HDs are now locked in transit mode. These folks are going to be taking a little bit of a tour of the Spine for the next…say several hours. We can figure out what to do with them later."

Jason nodded. "Corbin, where are my reinforcements?"

Corbin looked up with a bit of a forced smile. "Jason, nice work to you and Chelsea taking out those two entryway teams, but we've lost containment on the rest of the spaces. Almost everyone managed to get back to the Spine, with a few exceptions. We only found a few more dissenter stragglers on A and E-Ring. Brittney and Herbert have locked those few people down into quarters and have left a skeleton team just in case there are any more tricks. However, it looks like we still have about four hundred dissenters left on D-Ring with us. After forcing our people out, they are occupying the main corridors and hallways, apparently no longer splitting up."

Jason nodded grimly and looked back toward the Spine. The last of the dissenters had been removed from the corridor, and Chelsea and her team were being brought back through to the gravity transition zone with their remaining HDs. Jason nodded to her approvingly with a smirk. A few minutes later Brittney and Herbert emerged through the gravity transition zone with their HDs and their teams. The entryway was soon quite crowded.

Jason checked the command-and-control view that showed that no groups of dissenters were near them for the moment, while his numbers swelled to almost two hundred. "Everyone, advance back into D-Ring, to the locations marked on your AIMA," Jason said as his hands flew through open air issuing the commands to everyone's AIMAs. *Corbin must have emptied every secure space on the rest of the rings, except for D-Ring where he and the team are welded in,* he thought, feeling a little guilt about berating him earlier.

Jason synched AIMAs with all the team leaders and the D-Ring secure space. "Okay, what do we do, how do we end this?" Jason asked.

Corbin said, "I have an idea. I'm going to lay it out there, and if someone has a better idea then I definitely want to hear it." No one spoke. "We are going to seal them in."

Corbin manipulated the view on the main screen of the O&M control room and shared that view with all of Jason's team over their AIMAs. The command-and-control view showed that the concentrated dissenters continued to occupy nearly a quarter of D-Ring, across multiple levels from the outer most corridors of the ring, and two of the entryways to the Spine. Everyone saw the problem: the O&M control room was behind "enemy lines." Everyone else could also see from unobscured video and thermal imagery from preventative maintenance bots that Jessica's people were re-building barricades and getting ready to expand their control to other corridors on D-Ring.

Corbin illuminated nearly a dozen points on the shared 3D image of that section of D-Ring, "I want you to get to these entryways and weld them shut. Jessica isn't just going to let you do this, so you will have to block her teams long enough, and without losing people to capture to finish sealing them in."

Corbin expected questions, but the silence stretched out again, so Corbin spoke up again, "Hey maybe Zero Crew will step in and say we can't do this, or who knows. But I do know that if we turn this into a knock-down fight, we risk everything we have been fighting to achieve. I don't like it any more than you do, but after having gone over it time and time again, I think this is best we can do."

Jason spoke up. "What are we waiting for, Corbin, let's get it done. I want the *Valor* back for A-Crew."

Corbin forced a smile and said, "Very well, we will keep the corridor breach team leads as-is, the A and C breach teams are being distributed across the rest of those teams, so reorganize yourselves and get acquainted, but do it quickly. Further detailed assignments for sealing, decoying, or acting in reserve will be sent down to the leads, and the leads will determine the details and direct everyone else."

An alert went off in Corbin's AIMA, and he nodded, and paused his verbal break-down of the plan. He reached out to them directly over AIMA. "Brittney and Herbert, please go to the entryway near Chelsea's team and pick up a few more reinforcements, and then stand by, you have a special assignment."

Corbin extended his AIMA feed with Herbert and Brittney to six other A-Crew members who had just arrived from the Challenge ring. Despite having been beaten by Cadre Paul for days, they seemed to be relatively chipper. Corbin noticed they had been able to shower and get new clothes, including tactical gloves.

"Thanks for coming, how was the challenge?" Corbin said. He quickly caught himself asking the rhetorical question. "Never mind, let's talk about that later," he said with a wince. "Instead, let me ask, are you ready?" They all looked at him with serious determination, each one of them checking the tightness of their tactical gloves, strapped tightly to their hands at the wrist.

"We are ready," one of them said.

"Good, because the eight of you and the HDs coming momentarily, are going to get us the hell out of the control room, we're stuck behind Jessica's people here on D-Ring, and we can't stay around for what happens next."

He looked over at Yordanos. "Have the noncommittal crew members on D-Ring seen reason?" he asked her.

She responded, "All of the ones we are worried about behind Jessica's controlled area appear to moving to the other designated quarters as best they can. We've told them it is just a precaution but haven't given them anything more. Corbin, we probably won't be able to get all of them out."

Corbin nodded. "I know, we've just got to do the best we can. Have the others here work with individuals to guide them around Jessica's checkpoints as best you can. For the rest, get them into quarters near the edge of where we will make the seal, and lock them in."

Yordanos nodded to Laura, and Laura spoke up, steel in her voice.

"Corbin, all teams are in position."

"Execute." Corbin found it a bit nondramatic since all the activity was being done outside across D-Ring, but he knew that was about to change. "Everyone else, switch to AIMA control, and lock out the consoles and anything else operable in here in case this doesn't work. We're leaving," Corbin said.

Chapter Fifty-Three: Extraction

Jason ordered his refreshed rank of HDs to the front and had them start rapidly clearing the barricade Jessica and her people had put up about two hundred meters away from the hold-out D-Ring O&M secure space. The barricade had been lightly manned by only two of Jessica's people, but they took off in a dash, shouting for reinforcements once they saw the advancing HDs.

"Come on, we have to get as far as we can before we make contact!" Jason sprinted through the first opening cleared by the HDs followed by a trickle at first, and then the bulk of the hundred or so people in his ranks. The HDs also shouldered their way forward, having pushed or smashed most of the blocking debris to the sides of the corridor.

Jason shouted over their footfalls as they tore past doors to meeting rooms and other A-Crew members' quarters. "Laura, grab some of the team and get the people in these quarters out and back outside the seal zone," he said into his AIMA, delegating the coordination. He raised his voice to those running with him. "The rest of you come with me!"

Jason and his team rounded the junction to the corridor with the O&M control room at which point, two of his HDs emerged back out on front of the advancing A-Crew force. Jason looked up to see an opposing mob of dissenters, having been alerted by the two runners from the barricade, charging back down in his direction.

Jason shouted instructions over his shoulder, and his team let the other HDs slip through their ranks to the front, just as the mob crashed into them.

"Everyone push!" Jason roared, and he heaved the HD in front of him, followed by hands on his back, and hands on that person's back, all moving in unison. "Push!...Push!...PUSH!" he hollered at the top of his lungs just as he had when he had shoved the last dissenter team into low gravity.

Jason could see the mob followers were disorganized at first, and with the HDs taking the brunt of weight and crude blunt force weapons that Jessica's people had fashioned, his A-Crew and HD team continued to drive them back.

More and more of Jessica's people arrived to join the mob, and threw their weight in against the HD front, and it became a slog. The forward momentum slowed, but they continued pushing and advanced. A moment later Jason was relieved to see the welded mess of the O&M control room door emerge behind his wall of HDs to his left. They had made it to the objective.

He yelled into his AIMA, although everyone inside the O&M secure space had been watching and listening over AIMA and could all hear him just fine. "Corbin, we're here! Let's GO!" No one faulted him for his excitement.

Hank and his other colleague HDs had already begun unsealing the secure space door from the inside. Jason ordered two of his reserve HDs to use their plasma torches, and together the HDs made quick work of the slagged door. They expertly peeled it from its frame as acrid smoke from the metal cutting poured into the corridor and quickly had everyone coughing and grunting in the immediate vicinity.

Jason hollered, "HDs, fan that smoke forward!" The HDs sort of complied, and activated their low gravity navigation fans and pushed the smoke up and forward, doing their best to avoid all A-Crew members, Corbin's and Jessica's people alike. The result was the bulk of any smoke that did get to crew members landed on Jassica's mob, and their pushing slacked momentarily as they continued to cough, eyes watering from the smoke.

Corbin stepped through the smoldering remnants of the door and met Jason in a bear hug. Despite the turmoil around them, Corbin said through the embrace, "I missed you, man!"

Jason embraced him and hollered back, but his smile faltered. "What the hell happened to your head?" Corbin reached up tentatively and felt the thin scar horizontal across his forehead an inch or so above his eyes. "It's a long story man, but first we need to..."

"Hey! Can we get the hell out of here now and talk later?!" Yordanos shouted.

Jason released Corbin and spoke up loudly. "Okay, team, get ready to fall back! HDs stay in formation, everyone else rank up, and maintain your place. We are going to fall back to the seal point."

The two young men looked past the HDs and saw Jessica's initial counterattack finally start to flag. They had pushed at the HDs, but were now exhausted, still sputtering from the smoke, and offered little resistance aside from some ongoing weak pushing and hurled insults.

Corbin grabbed Jason's arm. "Jason, they are going to need your direction to stay in formation. Keep them together. The HDs and I will bring up the rear as we fall back." Jason moved to protest, but an insistent look from Corbin drew a nod. Jason picked four others and weaved his way to the front of the A-Crew extraction team. He started managing their front formation and explained the imminent organized pull-back to the seal point. Here, a separate team of HDs was ready to seal in this section of D-Ring.

Everyone who had been in the D-Ring secure room poured out carrying the hastily built, makeshift shields Norton had worked on with Hank. They had fashioned them from wall materials from the inside of the HD secure room, and while they were merely polymer, they were light and were able to withstand most blunt force hits. Laura and Yordanos had been ready to defend the secure room with those shields, but now they would serve a greater purpose of defending their retreat.

Norton pushed past Corbin along with seven other more athletic A-Crew members who had just been in the D-Ring secure space. They took up positions near the rear of their formation, just behind the wall of HDs. One young woman who looked like she could spit nails was also positioned to the rear of the formation, lining up on the right side just behind the right most HD.

Corbin and Norton shared a glance as they both heard a mass of footfalls increasing in volume. They all looked up to see a mass of reinforcements from Jessica's group surging down the corridor like a tide. Even the exhausted individuals from the previous mob jumped to the side to let them through, and it took everything Corbin had not to let his adrenaline get the better of him.

Instead of panic shouting, Corbion forced calm but firm words to come through. He turned to the formation of neat ranks of A-Crew members, six across the corridor and nearly as many deep. "Okay, we are going to get hit hard; we'll use the HDs to slow them down, but use the shield wall to stop them dead. Don't let them get through. Some of them will try to hit you with weapons. Grab those if you can, and pull them away. Use the shield and anything else to push them back. We fall back, but we stay in control, no matter what happens, do not turn and run, or it will be all of our asses, got it?" There were nods all around. "Good, fill in behind the HDs." He looked over at Hank. "Hank, can you and your fellow HDs join the others and block the corridor?"

Hank nodded, and his team obliged without a word. They stood almost shoulder to shoulder, leaving a small gap, which was filled in by another HD. Right behind the two staggered ranks of HDs, the A-Crew phalanx also formed up. Norton told Corbin, who had wedged himself in the middle of the six ranks to call the shots of the shield wall, while he managed the soon to be coming wounded and exhausted. Corbin selected the middle of the second rank so he would have a good view of the HDs and first shield wall.

"Brace the HDs and hold!" Corbin bellowed. Now fifty feet away, he saw the counter-force flow around a single form, who moved with confidence and terrible grace, with anger and rage clear on her face. Corbin saw Jessica, and he fought down bile and visceral angst at having been almost put down by her hand. Instead of thinking about it, he reached up and gently pressed his own shield to the back of the HD in front of him, and this time he had to shout, "Brace!"

The fastest members of the mob reinforcements crashed into the line of HDs, and Corbin was surprised that they didn't go sprawling back upon impact from the counter force. He looked down to see that the HDs had casually altered their stance to meet the incoming mass of humans.

Corbin saw they had withstood the first massive push from the mob. "STEPS!" he yelled, and they all began to take short steps back in unison, and the HDs matched the pace. Corbin heard a few shouts and curses here and there, as makeshift cudgels and clubs poked through between HD limbs and shields and peppered A-Crew members with glancing blows. The attackers couldn't wind up a full swing with the

HDs blocking, but in seconds Corbin could see that some of his fellow crew members were bleeding from small cuts to their heads, arms, and shoulders.

They fell back past the secure space entrance, and just as Corbin had hoped, a part of the mob mass flowed into the room reducing their forward momentum momentarily. No doubt they were hoping to find some spoils or other A-Crew members, but they would find nothing. Corbin grinned menacingly.

A moment later, he changed out a member of the front rank who was bleeding profusely from a wound just above his eye. He saw that it likely wasn't too serious, but head wounds always seemed to bleed so much. Plus Corbin knew it would embolden the enemy, and scare the defenders who saw the vicious wound and blood. *Best to have him fall back and cover that up.* He guided him with his right arm to Norton while pushing his shield forward to cover the gap.

A shorter and much less muscular young man took his place, but Corbin saw determination in his eyes, and he nodded to him in thanks for shoring up the front rank.

Corbin felt a sharp pain and saw that someone had jabbed his shoulder over the top of the shield with a metal rod in a stabbing motion. He flicked his wrist with great speed and plucked it away from the attacker, quickly spinning it up and over like his baton, and smacked the aggressor on the top of his head. The man let out a howl and fell back into the mass of dissenters pressing them back. It appeared that the secure room was not drawing any additional dissenters in, and the volume and weight of the mob pressed the HDs and the A-Crew Phalanx back farther. "STEPS!" Corbin yelled again, urging his formation back. He slammed the bottom of his recently taken metal rod into the floor of the corridor hard enough that it made a loud metallic clang for all to hear. "Step back in time! Stay together!" He slammed the rod down.

Corbin saw their organized retreat sharpen with the steps moving in unison, and one of the other A-Crew members took the rod from him and continued to bang out the pace of steps like a coxswain commanding the cadence to rowing.

Corbin could hear Jessica shouting over the din and saw her pushing her way toward the front of her formation. He could see two large young men flanking either side of her, and each of them was carrying something heavy and metallic. Their numbers parted and slowed a bit to let them through, giving them a little more space. It relieved pressure on the front of the line, but then all three aggressors moved together and attacked the leftmost HD closest to the corridor. Jessica stabbed another rodlike protrusion toward the HD's face while the other one swung a thicker metal rod at the other side of the HD's head. The HD moved almost casually to grab Jessica's attack, and then quickly halted the metal bar with its other hand. The third attacker brought down a hammer-like chunk of metal, and it smashed the HD's head, which split, sparked, and began to smolder. Its pace faltered, but remarkably it stayed in formation.

Jessica's bruisers, smelling blood in the water, all struck again, and this time the HD only caught one of the blows, but the other two landed, and now the HD began to lose its form. The dissenters quickly grabbed on to it and pulled it into the mass of the pressing crowd. They swarmed over it, bringing makeshift weapons and stomping feet up and down on top of it.

Corbin's mouth hung ajar, along with his fellow defenders. Corbin knew from experience that Jessica and her team had been fairly brutal with the captives on the rings, but many of his fellow crew members had not seen the savagery in person. They all could see that the HD was down, and still tried to move feebly as the attackers piled on blow after blow, pieces of the HD shearing off into the corridor. The sight rattled them, and Corbin glanced around seeing some signs of panic amongst his fellow A-Crew members. "Hank, compensate!" Hank and the HDs fanned out and once again evenly spread across the corridor, but everyone could see the gaps were a little bigger.

"Jason, what's your status? Jason…are you back to the seal point?" Corbin pinged Jason's AIMA, but he didn't respond. Corbin checked the map, and saw they still had over three hundred feet to go to the seal point. He saw they would need to continue moving down their current corridor for two hundred feet and then turn right for another hundred feet to where he and his crew members had set up the seal. He grimaced, knowing that the seal point could only take one person at a time. They would need to maintain this defense all the way back, and then hold as everyone got through. When they got down to single numbers, it was going to be extremely difficult not to have them get captured.

Corbin glanced over his shoulder to see that Jason and about twenty of his original breach team had raced to guard the entrance to the right turn. He and his group got there just as a smaller group of dissenters arrived. They had tried to go around and hit them from behind. Jason and his team met them in a savage clash, and as Corbin jumped up and squinted it looked like Jason and his small team were holding the cross-cutting hallway, but just barely. *They don't have shields,* he realized.

He quickly looked to his own ranks and saw a few people holding shields still behind his first two ranks and shield wall. "You, you, you, and you. Reinforce Jason. Go! Now!" he hollered, touching each of the A-Crew members, so they knew he was addressing them.

Corbin didn't want to make Jason hold for too long, and barked out, "We are going to pull back double time, but stay in control! Only twice as fast, three…two…one!" Hank and the other four HDs essentially created the pace for them, and they all began to fall back faster. The rod hammering increased to double time.

A couple of Corbin's fellow crew members pulled themselves back, holding wounds to their heads and faces, and to some to their hands also. They were replaced with others, but this time more of them were young women. They were still determined as ever, but did not have the sheer mass and brute strength of the leading attackers in Jessica's front ranks. Still Corbin saw them shoulder the shields and kept pressure forward, holding the surging mob around the HDs at bay.

Jessica and her two bodyguards attacked again, striking at the rightmost HD in the same fashion as before. Corbin looked to see how the HD was faring but was further distracted by a shriek as one of the young women in the front rank to his right reached up to her eye, blood pouring through her fingers. She staggered back, Corbin grabbed her and steadied her while Norton took her and handed off her shield to the next one up.

Corbin jumped into the gap she had left in front with rage. He seized one of the clubs from a man that looked younger than him. He jerked it out of his hand and smashed him in the face with it. He swung and hit another in the temple, who didn't see it coming, and both dropped. Corbin roared in anger, He saw another hand grab up onto the guard of one of the HD's faces, and Corbin swung again, connecting with knuckles, emanating a loud crunch followed by a howl. His anger grew, and he looked for another target.

Suddenly he was seized from behind. Small but firm hands pulled him back, and he saw Yordanos, shouting for him to regain control. "Manage and lead! We can't spare you!" She pointed toward the rear and could see that only two ranks of defenders held the cross hallway open. He could see Jason pushing and shoving for all he was worth, and he was battered and bloodied, along with most of them, but they and their few shields held. He also saw that his own front was down another HD, and while the remaining four had filled in shoulder to shoulder, more of his A-Crew front rank was exposed.

"Jason!" Corbin hollered. Jason kicked another young man in the chest, buying him a split second, and he spared Corbin a glance. "We're coming to you, be ready to go back-to-back, and let the HDs in as we fall back down the corridor together!" Corbin couldn't tell if Jason had heard him, but he nodded without a thread of confusion on his face. "Hank, when I give the word, extend the HD line laterally to cover the corridor as we turn right down the final corridor before the seal point!" Hank nodded in affirmation. The HDs slid in formation and began to form a diagonal, Ih was immediately costly.

The two hulking young men with Jessica, seized the now damaged rightmost HD and pulled it out of formation. Many hands jumped in to grab at the HD, and it was brought down with the same savagery of kicks and stomps, destroying the artificial human assistant. Corbin could see there were now only three HDs left, but they held as Jason's front ranks slid in behind them, allowing re-consolidation of shields and ragged ranks of defenders.

Corbin and Jason were now side by side behind the front shield wall. They aided injured defenders to the back and guided fresher A-Crew members to the front, shoring up the shield wall. Corbin also saw with dismay that injured defenders were hopping back in, where they had quickly bound their wounds with rags or torn clothing. Corbin and Jason shared a knowing look. They were running out of able people to hold the line.

Corbin could see that Jason and his line had folded just in time, as now the two groups of dissenters merged and surged down the remaining corridor. If Yordanos hadn't snapped him out of his rage, he might have waited too long to coordinate with Jason to disastrous effect. Corbin had a split second to thank God for Yordanos's lifesaving counsel yet again.

"Keep going!" Corbin shouted, and he jumped up and tried to see Jessica and her two damage-dealing attackers, but could only see one of the larger young men urging the dissenters to the front. "Shit." He looked over at Jason. "Jessica may be angling to hit that last cross-cutting narrow hallway for cleaner bots. You could only fit one or two people through at a time, but if she has a line of attackers with her, we'll be cut off in no time. She also has one of those heavy hitters with her. Run back and pull more of our people from the seal point. You have to hold that hallway!"

Jason responded back through gritted teeth; he was clearly trying to hold his side of the line across the main corridor. "I will, but you need to get everyone down the corridor now. We can't hold another minute." Jason handed off his shield to a much smaller A-Crew member and hollered back over his shoulder as he ran… "Now, Corbin! Move your ass!"

Corbin didn't argue. "Everyone! Hank! Triple time back, we need to fall back to the seal point, three…two…one…NOW!" he shouted over the din of screaming and smashing of makeshift shields and weapons. Hank and the remaining HDs lurched backward, practically pushing the defenders off balance, and it took a second for them to get the shield wall back in order. Corbin urged them on. "Back! Everyone back! Fall back to the seal point!"

Corbin looked over his shoulder and saw that they were almost there. Jason and the A-Crew members were blocking the last cross-cutting hallway when in a violence of movement, it suddenly gave way, and Jessica and her dissenters poured into the breach. Corbin thought he saw Jason drag his people back toward the seal-point, but he couldn't be sure.

He looked at his own formation in horror, as the rear guard of the phalanx was made up of wounded A-Crew members and few fully capable hands. They tried to form up a defense with some who still had shields, but they were too caught off guard, and some of them practically lurched back as grasping hands tried to grab them into the mob. Corbin sprinted through his few rear ranks and grabbed A-Crew members away from them. But looking up he saw that the phalanx had been quickly pinned between the Jessica's two forces. The seal point was less than fifty feet away, but now it was seemingly out of reach.

Corbin's heart dimmed, but he kept shoring people up, and getting a loose shield wall up on both sides as best he could. Corbin looked past Jessica and with relief, could see Jason reestablish his shield wall in front of the seal point with reinforcements, but they could do nothing to help Corbin and his team, now cut off and pinned between vastly superior forces. Sandwiched between the two groups of dissenters, they began to press. Corbin could hear Jessica's shrieks to crush them.

A long pole came over the top and tried to smack Corbin's fellow A-Crew members on their heads. Corbin dodged the pole once but was hit by some thrown debris and it dazed him, bouncing off his forehead. It had had some heft, whatever it was. He called up his AIMA. "Jason, we are getting smashed over here, can you get to us?"

Jason called out, "Stand by, Corbin, help is coming." *Was that a smile he heard in Jason's voice?*

Corbin looked over the dissenter crowd to see Jason's ranks part, and six dark clad figures came dashing out. To Corbin's astonishment, their limbs lashed out to strike the dissenters who had entered from the cross-cutting hall from behind. Jason hollered, and Jason's reserve force surged back through the seal point, and smashed back into the dissenters blocking Corbin's group from the seal point. They started running back into the cross-cutting hallway they had come through. Jessica had seen the sudden surge and was the first to retreat down the small hallway to avoid capture.

Corbin looked in stunned awe as Jessica's remaining hunters became the hunted. They turned to put up a defense, but the six other newly arrived A-Crew members moved with a grace and force that was unbelievable. They ducked and dodged blows and seemingly effortlessly jabbed and punched into ribs, kidneys, necks, and noses. Every blow left a dissenter stunned and bleeding. When one of the dark clad forms went low, a dissenter would quickly be snatched down into a painful grapple, and would not stand back up when the dark form did.

Corbin saw an opening between his formation and the seal point as the dark clad attackers disabled the remaining dissenters who were now down and not able to flee. Corbin shouted, "Fall back! Fold into the last rank for the seal point!" Corbin checked his formations front and noticed it was now down to Hank and only one other of his HDs.

The rest of the wall was made of A-Crew wounded, and a few splintered shields. The agile A-Crew attackers joined Corbin's remaining shield wall at the rear of the formation, their fists and feet flying.

Covered by the A-Crew members who had already dropped dozens of their colleagues, the remaining mob of dissenters stopped pushing and they too flagged. Wasting no time, Hank, the last HD, and the wounded, which now included Laura, Yordanos, Jason, and finally Corbin, were pulled back through the seal point by their fellow A-Crew members.

Awaiting HDs slammed a massive steel slab down, and before anyone on Jessica's side could impact it, the HDs welded it shut. Just as the last slit in the door closed, Corbin caught one last look at Jessica, who was walking in the direction of the seal. She locked eyes with him, teeth gritted in anger, and then she was gone from view. Hank and his sole remaining HD colleague finished welding the slab in place.

No one spoke, and all that could be heard was gasping and weak moans of pain from the wounded. Laura doubled over and bleeding from her forehead looked up and whispered to Corbin and Jason. "It's done, all other corridors have been blocked."

The dissenters were sealed into a section of D-Ring less than one-fifth the full area of the ring.

Chapter Fifty-Four: A Victory

Corbin slumped to the floor, his adrenaline leaving him. He found himself completely exhausted. He quickly became aware of a multitude of pain points as he realized he had been struck all over his body. He found cuts on his face and head, but ignored them, as Jason picked him up off the floor and gave him another bear hug.

"We made it man! It's done! We did it!" Jason shouted. He turned to everyone gathered and roared again, "We did it!" and the A-Crew force let out a shout of triumph despite the pain and bodily damage as more hugs were shared, tears of joy fell, and the more seriously wounded were attended to immediately by other crew members. Medical HDs started to usher in and began administering much needed care.

Corbin used his O&M access and pulled up a channel open to all of A-Crew on his AIMA. No one would be required to watch it, but all of A-Crew would have unrestricted access to his broadcast if they wanted to. He held his AIMA high to show himself, Jason, Yordanos, Laura, and his tireless and bloodied A-Crew members in front of the sealed breach.

"This is Corbin Sterling of A-Crew. The dissenters have been contained and all A-Crew members have been liberated. The *Valor* is ours." A deafening roar of the A-Crew team let out again, cutting off Corbin's attempts to continue talking. Corbin held up his AIMA so everyone could see the weary yet jubilant throng of A-Crew members who had fought for and secured the rest of the ship.

After nearly a minute, Yordanos, Jason, and Laura got people to quiet down, and Corbin continued.

"I know everyone wants to know what will happen next and you don't want to wait for answers, so here is how things are going to play out." He drew in a breath, which hurt. In his AIMA view he could see much of the crew virally tuning in. He measured his tone and words carefully as he and his command team had discussed, should they be victorious.

"For the rest of today and tomorrow you will have time off. You will be free to exit your quarters, see friends, roam about the ship, get some free time and exercise, if you like. You will be completely unhindered by schedule or any other requirements." His group let out another cheer, and Corbin realized he had been a bit too serious, so he cracked a smile, looked back at his friends, who nodded, and with a relaxed and positive look and tone, he resumed his planned remarks.

"Come Thursday morning, however, we are back on our original schedules before all of this conflict began; however, there are going to be some changes. From now on, everything we do is in the best interests of the crew, this ship, which is our home, and our mission. Each one of us needs to rapidly discover their interest areas where they excel and aspirations for who you want to be going forward. Our studies, activities, and training must better reflect this going forward, and that is a journey each of us must discover on their own. With Zero Crew's concurrence, members of A-Crew that have received special training will share the story of how that got started and what is required for all to participate going forward. There will be no further delay in our training to become the crew who oversees every aspect of the *Valor*."

Corbin felt he was on a roll now, and no one in the corridor stirred as he spoke, so he continued. "On about what just happened here. We cannot afford to be pulling in different directions. If we have differences, we need to elevate and discuss them. If we have fears, doubts, and concerns, we must share them with one another and not allow our fellow crew members to feel that they need to be subversive so that their concerns are heard." He paused and adopted a more serious tone. "Every single one of us, A-Crew, dissenter, or neutral is guilty of this, and it has resulted in fracture that from this minute forward, we will begin recovering from. Speaking of that, over the next few weeks, we will be convening with every crew member who is interested in participating in forming a methodology for government of A-Crew while we are aboard the *Valor*. I say that because we won't always be on this ship because we have a destination, even though it is decades into the future. We will have dependencies on Zero Crew, no doubt. But we aren't Zero Crew. We are A-Crew, and we will produce a form of government for ourselves going forward."

Corbin paused again for effect, but began again before attentions wavered. "On the subject of Zero Crew, A-Crew will be forming a list of requests and clarifications. Bottom line, we want to know what happened to us, and whether we can get our memories fully re-instated. We will work toward the full truth and remediation of this each and every day until we have those answers. However, we will do this with diplomatic dialogue, ongoing discussions, and a commitment to a better future for the *Valor* and her respective crews." Corbin felt he had already made his point about staying away from violence, so he left it alone.

"And lastly, I'm sure you are all wondering what will become of the dissenters now trapped into a narrow set of corridors on D-Ring as well as the hundreds of others who have been confined to random quarters. First things first. In the next few hours, dissenters confined to quarters not their own will be relocated to their own quarters, and confined there until further notice. All dissenters locked in D-Ring are welcome to be escorted to their quarters one at a time and to be confined there until further notice as well. For those dissenters wishing to stay in this section of D-Ring for the time being, you will be provided food, water, and medical attention via HD until you decide to return to your quarters or decide to stay put. No one will harm you, and no one is going to force you to do anything you don't want to do, but let's get one thing straight. None of you are going to be put into a position to subvert the safety of this crew and ship. We have six A-crew members in critical condition and many more with serious wounds inflicted by your little uprising. You will no longer be functional members of this crew until it can be determined that you are a trustworthy and willing crew member, and most importantly, no longer a threat. Your deeds have been recorded via AIMA, ship's comms, ship's cameras, and through witnesses, and there is much to account and atone for. All of this information will be collected and collated into a file that will be worked through, adjudicated, and judged on an individual basis via the agreed upon government body to be formed by all of you. The form of punishments is yet to be determined; however, as a dissenter, if you wish to cooperate, review all you have partaken in, and commit to make amends, it will be easier than remaining stubborn and trying to conceal what you have done. In the coming days, details surrounding how all of this will be handled will be forthcoming, subject to change of the pending A-Crew government and Zero Crew dependencies, should there be any."

Corbin had gone on for a long time, and he paused for a few seconds, and then took away the official tone from his voice and went back to his jovial self. "I want to thank every one of you who helped us to take our ship back for ourselves, our crew, and our mission. Many of you have sacrificed much, and some of you risked everything. Your deeds too shall be known and recognized."

Corbin then transitioned the selfie-mode of his AIMA to front facing camera, and directed it over at Jason, who had already adopted that debonair and charming smile he always seemed to be able to summon at a moment's notice. It was a smile that said his heart was connected to his eyes, and it was a smile that had no lie in it.

Jason wrapped his long arms around the people nearest to him and with an even broader smile addressed everyone. "Crew members of the *Valor*, A-Crew would cordially like to invite you to a banquet and celebration tomorrow evening. There will be spirits, delicious food, entertainment, and of course, much merriment. Corbin said everyone has to be back on their schedules the day after, and I agree, but can we make it a 1 p.m. start?" Everyone in the corridor laughed good naturedly. They had spent so much of the past few days being serious and downright fatalistic that the laughter came easily.

Jason went on. "I want to echo Corbin's sentiments, and thank everyone for what you have done to save our crew and save our ship. It is the first of many things we will do together on this journey across the stars. And I am proud to be here with every one of you." Jason misted up at that last bit, but quickly regained his composure. "So, everyone that's busted up, let's get you healed up and ready to party tomorrow night. See you all there!" The corridor erupted again in cheers. Corbin thought the celebration might start here in the corridor and continue straight through to the next day, but everyone quieted as loud banging from behind the sealed barrier began.

Smiles faded as everyone turned to look at the direction of the sound. "Hank, what are we looking at? Any chance they can break out of there?" Over the sound of the banging Hank spoke up. "Negative, there isn't enough material of sufficient strength to create the conditions for a breakthrough of any of the barriers or bulkheads in place. Nor do they have any plasma or torch equipment in this section of D-Ring. They are contained."

Corbin saw visible sighs of relief, and noticed he himself was taking a deep breath. He adjusted the comms on his AIMA to the A-Crew who were holding D-Ring. "Those of you who need medical attention, or those assisting those who need medical attention, get everyone to the medical center here on D-Ring. Everyone else, get with your ring leaders, and begin to escort dissenters back to their quarters. Do it one at a time, and make sure each of them is restrained and under guard from door to door. Everyone else that doesn't have a job yet, get with those who have O&M access—I'm sending the list now—and start to compile the behavioral data from each dissenter. No need to finish it, just get it started and map a plan forward to collect the rest. Regardless of how far you get, I want everyone off duty and relaxing and recovering except for the core O&M team by 2000 hours sharp. Core team, you will receive a message on who you are shortly, and anyone else who would like to volunteer for that duty, message me directly. Thanks again, Corbin out."

Corbin tried to turn to leave, but his fellow A-Crew members wouldn't have it. He was instantly surrounded by every A-Crew member in the immediate vicinity who had shown up to defend D-Ring. He was shaking hands, patting shoulders, and he was maintaining his smile. Although he was starting to feel exhausted to his very bones, he pressed himself harder. This was easy work, but it was so important. Every smile he met, and every hand and shoulder he squeezed was essential in recognizing what everyone had done on this day. He knew he could not have done it without any of the others.

He happened upon one of the six dark clad A-Crew members who somehow had rapidly learned an elite level of hand-to-hand combat. "I'm Corbin, what's your name?" he asked the young man with eyes who seemed much younger than his own despite their comparable age.

"I'm Zach Chambers," he said with a smile, seizing Corbin's

outstretched hand and shaking it vigorously. Corbin tried to match the young man's zeal.

"You and your colleagues really saved our asses back there by the seal point. It appears Paul got my message and was in the mood to help. What did you all do over there on the Challenge ring?"

Zach blushed and looked down at the compliment, but quickly looked up in eagerness to tell of he and his colleagues' exploits.

"Well, some of the dissenters came out to the Challenge ring to bring us to heel, but Paul pretty much beat them senselessly and from there, our challenge training quickly turned into combat training. He told us he was teaching us as quickly as possible and that we would need to go back and learn proper technique and nomenclature, but essentially, he taught us to cause as much pain and suffering to an opponent in the least amount of time." Zach finished with a smile.

Corbin laughed and shook his head. "I can't wait to hear all about it. We've got some stuff to take care of, but let's talk again, sound good?"

Zach nodded. "Hey, can I get in on the core team? I'm a little tired from the Challenge ring, but I want to earn that celebration first. What needs getting done?"

Corbin nodded his thanks. "Get with Brittney and Herbert, they'll need you and your team on security just in case anything else breaks out. Be ready to deter and act swiftly if there is any trouble." Zach nodded and turned away to find Brittney and Herbert.

After what felt like several hours of shaking hands and thanking people, he, Jason, Laura, Yordanos, and Herbert all walked toward the medical center to see how their injured crew members were holding up. As they walked, they organized via AIMA quick reaction forces, making sure to include Zach and his team, should anything else break loose, and got an initial status on the three hundred and seventy-three dissenters locked in D-Ring. Thankfully, there were no serious injuries, but there had been requests for the essentials, and HDs were delivering them via special airlocks, not accessible by humans. Each of the sealed breach points were under HD and A-Crew observation, whose multiple feeds were being monitored by a security detail made up of additional and willing A-Crew members, working from a makeshift O&M room set up in one of the large conference rooms.

After spending a couple of hours making sure the wounded were cared for, comfortable, or resting, Corbin and his friends made their way back over to The Orchard to find Ethan. They didn't bother showering or getting cleaned up; they just wanted to sit and relax with a beverage and spend some time with one another, enjoying the victory.

Chapter Fifty-Five: After the Party

Corbin woke with a start. He was practically hyperventilating and felt some sweat at his brow. He looked around wildly and saw that he was in his quarters and his AIMA beeping loudly as if someone was urgently trying to get ahold of him. He took a deep breath as the severity of a nightmare faded; however, some unknown guilt from his dream tried to stay with him.

"Wake up, Corbin. Commander Sorenson is on the line for you," Tina said.

"Thanks, Tina," he said, and snapped his AIMA on, not having the time to acknowledge Tina's welcomed presence after being on hold for so long. An image of Commander Sorenson popped into his view. He was instantly self-conscious as he had been sleeping in his boxer briefs, but he recalled that the rest of him wasn't visible in that way to the commander.

Before he could speak Commander Sorenson cut in. "Sorry to wake you early after the well-deserved celebration. I also apologize for my crew and I not attending, but we felt that this was A-Crew's moment, and we didn't want to spoil it." Corbin nodded, but didn't say anything. He was clearing the cobwebs and was still curious as to what this was all about.

Commander Sorenson took a deep breath and adopted a more collegial tone. "Not too shabby, Corbin. We had hopes for you, and while you have ruffled some feathers on the Zero Crew's side of the house, I don't see anything we can't work through. As a matter of fact, I think we need to get started a little sooner than you expected on your plan of all of us moving into the future together, and we'll start with an urgent situation that has relevance to our mission, ship, and crew. Are you interested?"

Corbin smiled, but didn't justify the obviousness of his answer with a verbal answer, so she continued, "Good. Gather the thirty people you trust the most and who were instrumental in taking the *Valor* back. Take your group to the Spine at D-Ring at 1200 hours sharp, and an escort of HDs will meet you there. Copy?"

Corbin nodded. Commander Sorenson signed off immediately leaving Corbin and his thoughts to himself. A question had died on his lips. He tried to return her call but received no answer.

He jumped out of bed, and checked on Z, who clearly wanted a food puck, to which Corbin obliged by manually hitting the button. He spoke up to his AI. "Tina, thanks for seeing to Z while I was away."

Tina popped back up in his AIMA, positive and energetic as always. "No sweat, Corbin, I set it on automatic after…" She trailed off, and then restarted. "Say, I heard your last transmission there, might I suggest some outfits for your meeting with the commander today? In fact, these suggestions would go well for all the other core team members you decide to invite." Corbin quickly got over the renewed eavesdropping from his AI and nodded his consent.

While he was in the shower, he called Jason over his waterproof AIMA and gave him the run down. The two of them then called Laura, Yordanos, Herbert, Jeremy, Brittney, and told them to be in an AIMA conference in the next five minutes, giving everyone a few additional minutes to shake off their own respective cobwebs, use the privy, and throw on some clothes. Corbin could tell Jason had not been alone in his quarters, so he and likely the other members of his inner circle would have to politely kick their guests out from the night before out, so they could speak freely.

Corbin hopped out of his shower, quickly drying, and threw a towel on when he noticed the AIMA conference had everyone signed in, so he clipped his AIMA on, while drying his hair, and spoke. "Good, thank you for all making it. I'm sorry to wake you, but Commander Sorenson reached out to me and asked me to assemble the top thirty most capable and trusted people who helped us take back the *Valor*."

Yordanos piped up. "For what?"

Corbin was nodding as he had intended to tell them. "For a meeting at high noon with her today, and nothing more."

"You didn't ask her anything else?" Laura asked.

Corbin was slightly irritated. "No, she hung up on me...look, it doesn't matter. I called all of you because I think you all are the most trusted and capable people who helped to take back the *Valor*, but we still need twenty-one more people, so I was hoping that each of you would pick one or two more people as quickly as you can, and add them to our little conference here, but start by making a shared list first. Once we hit thirty, add a few back-ups, and then reach out to all of them to see if they would like to join this meeting. If they are anything in the shape like we are this morning, then we will need to give them a fair enough heads-up in advance, right?" he said with a smile, less annoyed now.

"Shit, Corbin, if I had known we had almost three hours, I would have gone back to sleep," Jason said, and the others snickered.

Corbin smiled. "All right, all right, fair enough, okay ante up, who is on the list?" Corbin asked, popping up a list view so all of them could see it.

The names popped in, and there were lots of nods, and whispers, as many people knew who they were and what they had done. Corbin could see several people from Navigation and Telemetry, some others from O&M he didn't know, Ethan who ran the bar and grill, and several others. Corbin saw a well-balanced group of people from different levels of experience throughout the ship. Almost all of them had special access or had quickly come into their own, like Ethan. As Corbin and the others leafed through their profiles, he saw that they were a diverse mix of men and women from different ethnicities.

He was sidetracked by the thought that everyone he had met in A-Crew spoke English, but some had accents from clearly speaking another first language, and others had dialect accents. He wondered if everyone on the *Valor* was from one country or from many.

The list hit thirty-five, and Corbin snapped back to focus. "Okay, hold up, that's it for now. Call your top people and report them as "accepted" as soon as they roger up. If they don't answer, give them a few minutes, and then try again. If they still don't answer, on to the next person, we have to keep this moving. Let's all hop back on the conference with the others as soon as the list hits thirty, cool?"

No one had any questions, and he had not offered any names

himself, so he went on hold, and started his morning post-shower grooming routine. In his mind, he went over what he was going to say to everyone when the new core team was back on. He wished he had another day to put more time into the list. The lives of everyone on the list could be affected by what might happen next. They were just going to have to do their best and find out. He also spared an annoying thought at Commander Sorenson. *You guys have been out here for decades, and I have to assemble our first command crew in under three hours. You must not really think it matters whom we pick.*

His mind also drifted back to Blue-Tina. He wanted to celebrate with her, to thank her for all she had done for him and for the help with Hank and the other HDs, but she had not appeared since his hasty surgery by HDs, and he did not know how to summon her.

He didn't try, as he did not want to alert the main AI to her presence on the system. He reached out to her with his mind, trying some wild and goofy telepathy, if there was such a thing, just in case, but he got nothing in return. Regular-Tina's image was all who returned when he called the name "Tina." Disappointed in the result, yet thankful for Blue-Tina's help, he went through the rest of his morning routine to get ready.

Chapter Fifty-Six: This is New

Corbin, his close friends, and the others totaling thirty-seven selectees met the usual HDs who picked them up from the gravity transition zone on D-Ring and brought them into the transit Spine of the *Valor*. Corbin expected them to be placed into cars, but a different set of HDs were waiting in formation, and the regular transit HDs handed each of them carefully over to the larger, more heavily equipped HDs. Corbin couldn't see what all their extra bulk was for, but he felt like there was a lot more beneath the different panels and compartments than welding equipment or simple structural integrity. *Could they be for security…or even combat?*

A shared glance between himself, Jason, Yordanos, and Laura confirmed they were all thinking the same thing. Corbin couldn't help but think about how their level of ongoing discovery since their awakening was just more and more of the same. He wondered about how long it would be until their collective reality would stay stable, for one week, or even just one day. They had been thrown in compounding chaotic scenarios, and had been able to overcome, but now their reality would expand again. Corbin hoped they would be ready for it. *Hell, I hope I'm ready for it,* Corbin thought.

Their escort of seemingly non-verbal HDs brought them all in neat formation up to the "top" of the Spine. They could see the A-Ring transit corridors, but they had already moved past them, right up to the wall, which should have led to the material slug at the front of the *Valor*. From the holographic maps, Corbin had initially figured that the front material slug must be through the wall they now faced, but from his time in storage room with Hank, he knew better. Corbin looked over at his larger HDs shoulder to see a hallway sized entryway appear in the vast wall in front of him.

The HDs and their human passengers were quickly reorganized into single file, and the entryway opened to accommodate. Corbin was near the front of the line and saw that the Spine, in fact, did not end at A-Ring, but continued. He heard a gasp from each of his crew mates as one by one they emerged into a separate transit corridor that accommodated two additional rings. Corbin recalled having seen the updated diagram when Blue-Tina had given him access to an updated ship's view. Looking ahead past the two additional ring entryways, he saw the actual wall to the forward material slug. HDs were coming and going carrying different types of material. The ones entering were bringing unneeded material that had been broken down to its basic form to be filed away in the slug. The ones leaving were bringing the raw material out into the *Valor* to be used for some project, repair, or construction, or something else.

Corbin looked around this shortened and isolated section of Spine and saw additional HDs moving Zero Crew members between the two rings. The human passengers gave their lot passing glances, but they did not linger, and Corbin figured they weren't too surprised to see them here. Their column advanced to the second of the two extra rings and the HDs helped them through the slipring, and down the transit corridor. Corbin took note that this section of the ship seemed different. He noticed that it was not as pristine as the other rings on the vessel. He didn't see dirt or organic accumulation, so the cleaner bots must be working here as well, but everything seemed somehow older and more worn. It also somehow smelled older, but he scoffed at how that wasn't quite right either.

The HDs set everyone down just past the gravity transition zone, where two members of Zero Crew were waiting for them. Combined with his studies of military history, he surmised that these two well-fit, if older, Zero Crew members were part of the military...but he wondered whose. He glanced over at his colleagues and saw they were all looking at the two Zero Crew members wide-eyed. He figured they must all be having the same thoughts. The two Zero Crew members politely gestured, and one of them spoke up. "Form up into two single file lines, and follow us, please." Corbin saw everyone move to obey, and they moved forward.

After a short and uninteresting walk down the transit corridor ramp, they came to a large elevator and were able to file in and maintain their formation. After the gravity increasing ride out to the edge of the ring, they all strode out into a massive corridor spanning what Corbin quietly figured must have been the whole width of the ring. Corbin and everyone else looked on in astonishment, as much of the ring appeared to be an atrium-like space where each of the "floors" were balconied all the way up to the wall of the Spine of the ship. Corbin whispered over to Jason who was in the single file line to his right. "Can you believe this…" His voice trailed off as they all took in the expansive space. Corbin could see planters filled with bright flowers and clematis plants at regular intervals on each floor. In some places, the massive foliage dimmed artificial daylight that emanated from the outer wall of the transit corridor. There was a mild breeze, and the pleasant aroma from the rich plant life wafted down, reminding all of them of the Challenge ring.

A fresh set of Zero Crew members Corbin hadn't seen before met them as they stood gawking. A tall and friendly smiling man spoke. "Welcome to Ring One, A-Crew. If you'll follow us, we'll take you to meet with Commander Sorenson." Corbin and the others nodded to him, and everyone stayed in formation and began to traverse the main Ring One corridor. Every one of the A-Crew members' eyes were wide trying to take in the new sights.

When they moved to follow the two Zero Crew members, through the massive atrium, Corbin and his colleagues noticed that off to the left was a massive flag painted on the wall. It had a blue square filled with ranks of white stars, and then horizontal red and white stripes. Everyone in Corbin's company had their eyes linger on the flag with wonderment.

This means something important, this flag. It has to do with something about home and who we were before this…but I…I can't place it, Corbin thought. Corbin racked his mind and all the history he had studied, but it was all ancient or medieval histories. While he surmised this flag could be an evolution from the many nations and cultures, he had studied, he could not place it, yet he somehow knew he belonged to that nation. They continued through Ring One's main corridor.

Everywhere Corbin looked he saw Zero Crew members moving

from one place to another with purpose and intent. They all had different color uniforms, and many were accompanied by different types of HDs. Their party walked farther, and they were astounded when one section of the corridor wall switched from opaque gray to transparent, and opened up a view into a cavernous space that must have taken nearly a quarter of the ring. Corbin and his party looked over the side, down to the outer wall of Ring One and saw it stretch out into a massive hangar. They looked further and saw multiple spacecraft, some small and others larger. Some were clearly for ship maintenance and repair, but others looked big enough to travel beyond the *Valor*. There were also massive HD-like platforms moving through multi-gravity environment. Some looked to be performing maintenance on spacecraft, and others, Corbin could not tell their function. Cobin saw one of the smaller spacecraft lift off with hot thruster-like engines and disappear into a massive airlock that no doubt assisted the craft in becoming spaceborne without flying off into space or smacking into the spinning rings of the *Valor*.

"If you'll continue to walk with me, please," said one of the other uniformed Zero Crew members, urging them on. Corbin hadn't realized he and everyone had stopped walking to gawk at the gargantuan space hangar.

"Sorry," he stammered, and they all continued to push on, but every one of them wanted to stop and look over and down at what was a massive space port built right into Ring One. Corbin's mind raced. *How do they launch multiple craft? How do they get the bigger craft out? What the hell are all the different craft for?* He wanted to know everything, but he knew he was getting excitable, so he kept focused, took a deep breath, and kept following his Zero Crew escort.

Corbin and his leadership corps eventually branched off from the main corridor, when Jason called from up ahead, "Yo, Corbin, you've got to see this!" Their number broke the loose formation and crowded around what looked to be a large curly-haired dog.

Corbin's mouth dropped open as he explained their reaction to the smiling handler of the dog, "We've all seen pictures of dogs, but we haven't seen any dogs!" Yordanos knelt and the dog approached her wagging its tail. She gently lifted her hand palm down with her finger closed. The dog sniffed, kept wagging its tail, and came closer, accepting a few gentle and then more firm pets from Yordanos.

"How did you know to do that?" asked Jason.

"I dunno, it just seemed like the right thing to do," she said smiling brightly up at him, still petting the animal which had adopted a doggy grin from the attention.

The walker of the giant dog smiled a good-natured smile at the A-Crew onlookers and spoke. "She's a good girl. Her name is Harley." Yordanos scratched Harley behind the ears, which the dog leaned into while she continued wagging her tail.

"Hi, Harley," she said quietly.

The Zero Crew member with the dog spoke again conspiratorially to the A-Crew huddle, "You'd better get on now; your escorts look a bit annoyed to be off schedule."

Corbin's eyes snapped up to see that the escort leads from Zero Crew did look a little annoyed. "Okay, team let's roll," Corbin said, and they all reluctantly fell back in line and followed the two Zero Crew escorts, but most of them spared longing glances back at the sweet fluffy dog sporting a doggy grin, and an equally grinning owner.

They rounded a corner and turned into a large, three-tiered level conference space where there were long tables, like the large classrooms on the other A-Crew rings. The A-Crew members filtered in, and Corbin and his closest friends took seats near the front. The two escorts left, and Corbin was just about to address everyone when Commander Sorenson walked in flanked by several other uniformed members of Zero Crew. One of them brought a box filled with paper folders.

He knew that none of them had seen stacks of paper on the ship as every bit of information was conducted via AIMA or console, except for the optional menus at The Orchard, so this was new. The Zero Crew member began handing out the folders, which had a seal across it marked "Top Secret" in Red. Commander Sorenson leaned over to Corbin and whispered, "I thought I told you thirty people."

Corbin, anticipating her displeasure, looked up at her and smiled politely. "This is the most trusted body of A-Crew who helped us to retake the ship, no more, no less."

Commander Sorenson frowned. "Very well." She then looked up and addressed everyone while the handouts were in process. "The folders you have in front of you contain detailed information, I will soon summarize for you. These documents tell a story, albeit an incomplete one of why the *Valor* was built and how you came to be where you are. After we talk, I will leave you all to study the documents, converse amongst yourselves, and we'll have refreshments brought in. However, none of this material is to leave this room, is that understood?" She looked around meeting eyes and nodded.

"Good, but before we get into all that let's talk about the obvious. You have several hundred A-Crew members locked in their quarters or in the confined space on D-Ring. What are you going to do about that?"

Corbin wasn't entirely shocked at the question but was hoping that Zero Crew may have some options for that instead of an open-ended question. No one answered.

"Corbin," Command Sorenson said, "what are your thoughts on that matter? And don't give me this 'form a coalition government' BS. You all can figure all of that out later, but for now, what is the plan for Jessica and her…umm…followers?"

Everyone looked at Corbin, and he began, "Well, I don't exactly know how to do this, but we need to create a situation where the bulk of the crew members who didn't actively join either side don't decide to follow in Jessica's footsteps. Likewise, we need to create a situation where people who did dissent can somehow work their way back into A-Crew, should they wish it. Lastly, we need to find a way to deal with people who are never going to support this crew or mission, and we need to do it in a way that everyone is going to be okay with morally, or the same situation will creep up again and again or worse. On second thought, it will probably be more violent than what we just went through." He saw a look on Commander Sorenson's face that said, *I agree.* Corbin then looked around. "Does anyone have anything else to add?" he asked his fellow A-Crew members, but they were all satisfied with his answer.

Commander Sorenson seemed pleased by the answer as well. "I'm relieved you all agree with the state of situation, and…for the time being, ambiguous solutions. Between us, I was worried we were going to be here for hours just arguing that aspect, so kudos to you all for at least agreeing on that." She paused, reconsidering. "By everyone else's silence I am assuming you concur with everything that Corbin just said?" Heads nodded all around. "Good, now how are we going to turn these arm waving ideas into real solutions? What are you going to do with those who have taken up arms against your ship and crew?"

Corbin had never thought of it that way, and just when he opened his mouth to speak, Jason jumped in. "Send the violent dissenters back to cryo and redo the memory thing you did to us. We can try again with them after we wake up from our upcoming nap...well the ten-year nap we will lie down for eighteen or so years from now."

He went on. "Then, we set up a ring where the non-acting dissenters can live and do whatever the hell it is they want to do with restricted access from us and the rest of the *Valor*. We also set up a regimented program with training, testing, and metrics that walks them through how to regain crewmember status, and most importantly...regain two-way trust."

Commander Sorenson looked pensive for a few seconds as if further digesting the courses of action. "Not bad ideas, but you would rather sub-divide the crew, and possibly create a multi-class system inside A-Crew? That could be more trouble than it's worth. Better to send all the dissenters back to cryo and then try this again when you wake up the next time, right?"

Laura jumped right in. "But wouldn't that make it a much smaller A-Crew for this tour? Can the ship and planning handle the disparity in crew sizes?"

The commander shrugged. "It has so far, Zero Crew is only one thousand people or so, and we've been able to effectively run the entire ship for decades with the main AI, HDs and elbow grease. I'm sure you can handle everything with sixteen or seventeen hundred, give or take."

Yordanos spoke up. "You have sub-divided the crew already with Zero Crew operating in a bubble while the rest of us duke it out and try to discover what's what with less than half the information. So, what difference does it make if we make yet another division of people who don't align with us? I'm sure B-Crew and C-Crew will add yet more population to the dissenting part of the crews." Corbin could tell Yordanos was struggling to keep anger and frustration out of her voice, but she was understandably having a hard time of it. When she met his eyes, he gave a smile and nodded to her in approval. She had every right to be furious.

Corbin saw Commander Sorenson hesitate for the briefest of

moments at the mention of B and C-Crew, but her face quickly returned to her all-business-like demeanor, and she responded thoughtfully, apparently not feeling insulted. "You have a point, Yordanos. It can be managed, albeit with additional cost in time, energy, and space... If you all are willing to bear it, I believe Zero Crew can approve." She paused again as her face grew a bit more guarded. "This is a good start to the conversation. I wanted to see how far we would get before giving you some more background, and that effort was not in vain...in fact it is more credit to you all...however, with additional information, I believe you can refine your solution." She looked down, collected herself, and sat on the lecturer's table informally and faced the members of A-Crew.

The commander took a deep breath. "I'll try to keep this as conversational as possible, but what I have to say, you will most likely find upsetting, and you will also have many questions. The reason I have those Top-Secret folders in front of you is so that you can dive deep and answer those questions in more detail, so let me try and get the ball rolling before you interject, okay?" Everyone received the question as rhetorical, so no one responded, just a few nods of consent...for now.

"Zero Crew does not know your origin." The words hit Corbin and his crew like a ton of bricks. The anticipation for answers was almost palpable, and yet this one thing would not be answered. Commander Sorenson raised her hands as she could tell she had nearly lost the room in an uproar within five seconds. "What I can tell you is that we do not believe you are here of your own volition, or anyone else who would have vouched for your complicity in being here. When we left Earth, we were told that the three crews were part of a voluntary classified training program and that everyone underwent basic training, health assessments, and the initial gene modification for cryogenic suspension. From there, we were supposed to wake you up and everyone would be ready to get started eagerly, with full acceptance of their situation."

The commander paused to take in the A-Crew members' eyes, and saw they were all stuck to her, practically unblinking. She continued. "For crew training and preparation for your awakening, we sought to verify this by doing additional research into your backgrounds and found the details wanting. When we couldn't get straight answers from the control center on Earth, we pushed harder, and were frustrated again by a narrative that was unchanging and bereft of details on who you were. Where were you from? What was your educational backgrounds? Did you have any work experience in space? None of it was shared with us." She breathed heavy again and went on. "After a long and drawn out...series of events that I will not get into today...we learned part of the truth."

Yordanos's eyes went wide with realization, and she spoke up again. "You knew there would be a fraction of A-Crew that would rise up...you knew what would happen all along!" She raised her voice, but the commander met her with a measured tone while nodding.

"Yes, we suspected that since you were not here by consent, that you would rebel outright...all of you. And then we discovered the memory modification process...Yes, we didn't know about that either until we tried to dig deeper. When we couldn't find anything more about you, we determined that our...Earth side handlers, either didn't think it was relevant or intentionally are withholding that information for an unknown reason. We watched some of your videos that were meant for you when you woke up and did a detailed look into the awakening process. Right then we knew that your memories were either erased or buried." Everyone stared at her in shock, and Commander Sorenson averted her eyes from them.

She stopped and drew her lips into a tight line. "Apologies...this is difficult for me, I have been compartmentalizing information for longer than I can remember, but I will try to be straight with you. Also...someone on Earth...someone who didn't feel right about what happened, leaked the information about the memory modification process to us in the uplink. That happened about ten years ago today, and we have been trying to figure out why. Quite frankly, I don't know what the hell the brass was thinking sending you all up here, but they left it up to all of us to figure it out."

Corbin spoke up to cut off the brewing eruption from his A-Crew colleagues. "Wait, why didn't you just ask them!? Send a message or whatever process it is you follow. Hell, just record a video of yourself saying, 'Hello, it's the commander, just wondering why the hell you sent me twenty-four hundred random people without their memories instead of a well-trained voluntary crew who wanted to actually be here.' Mark it as high priority and hit the 'send' button," he said in exasperation.

"I did," she said, and let the words linger. "It's in your folder, and I did exactly what you just described and the cryptic instructions we received were to bring you out of cryogenic suspension and proceed with command crew training protocol. No other details were provided no matter how many queries we sent, strongly worded or otherwise," she said, taking her turn in being exasperated, but much more in control than Corbin.

She went on. "So that's what we did, we woke you up and got started, hoping for the best, but expecting an eventual revolt. We cannot proceed without A-Crew, we dared not skip over you and wake up B-Crew, so you are who we woke up. And you, this team, everyone in this room, is who we prayed for, and hoped we would get to meet... Eventually."

Yordanos jumped back in. "If you suspected that some or all of us would be at one another's throats, why didn't you do anything to stop us? Why didn't you just tell us all how it is and ask for compliance? Why all of the secrecy and bullshit!?" additional murmurs of dissent perpetuated her question, and the mention of the memory situation was on hold for the moment.

The commander was nodding again, a look of understanding on her face. "Had we...had I done it over again knowing this result, I think that is exactly what I might have done...but I'm still not sure." She paused. "Let me ask you this...how bad do you all want to be here?" No one answered. She spoke again. "Let me rephrase...when Jessica and her team had you against the ropes...tell me, how did that make you feel?" There was near deafening silence.

Laura spoke up with icy calm. "First point, I don't think I am going to be able to forgive you for all of this, and while I'm committed, it doesn't mean I trust you, Commander. Second point, and to answer your question, it made me feel like we were never going to explore the stars...that we would have been given a chance at amazing purpose and then let someone else take that away from us." She finished to many more nods and murmurs of approval on both of her points.

"That's it exactly!" the commander said. "Second point only, would you have arrived at that conclusion on your own if we fed everything to you? Would you still feel as committed?" She stood up and paced before going on. "Or would you have gone along with everything, but kept that seed of doubt alive in your mind, always questioning if this was all for the right purpose?"

Laura shot back, "But look at what happened, and imagine what could have happened?! What if we hadn't been able to retake the ship? And now, at our very best, we have hundreds of people that are committed to not being here, and they are locked in a sub-section of D-Ring. What the hell are we really supposed to do about them, and did that all fall into your contingency plan?" She finished with a raised voice. Corbin looked over at her and saw she had already regretted her outburst, and Corbin nodded with a face that said he understood where she was coming from.

"We'll never know," Corbin said evenly, trying to ease the tension. "But I can see how you had to make the decision, Commander. You made one, these are the consequences…our consequences, and that's that. I think if we had all consciously chosen to be here, that would be much easier to digest, but since we didn't, it's not." Corbin paused to look around, sensing the ragged emotions of his fellow crew members. "Commander, could you give us the room for a few minutes please?"

She controlled the shock on her face as no doubt she wasn't used to being kicked out of her own meeting, albeit politely. She nodded sternly, then softened her face again and left, the door sliding shut automatically behind her.

There was a pause, and Corbin looked around at the rows of A-Crew members in the "lecture hall." Corbin spoke. "The point is, we are here, we now know more of the game, but this universe of ours…this reality is going to keep getting bigger. There are going to be more surprises." He tapped the folder on the table. "And this question of should we be here will come up again, and again, and again. So, with everything the commander has said, the question that each of you has to decide now, right here, in this very room is…do you want to go back to Earth, or back to cryo, or anything other than what we set out to do?" He sighed. "I know it's not fair of me to ask, as I just had my own outburst on the commander, but I can assure you that nothing she said or what we will find out here is going to drastically change our situation or what we have decided to do…unless we can't live with it."

He looked around the room. "All of you were absolutely critical in taking the ship back. Your ingenuity, leadership, and concern for your fellow crew members was exemplary. However, going forward there can be no more doubts, and while we can be angry, we cannot let that distract us from accepting the responsibility of our future. It doesn't really matter what we find in these folders, we'll have to deal with all of it the same way. We either accept this and move forward, or we don't."

There was another pause. "How about this. Everyone stand, take a stroll around the room, converse with your fellow crew members, and discuss anything you want. Get out your worries, your thoughts, and see if you can arrive at some sort of peace about our choices...either way. When you know what you are going to do, take your seat, and then we'll see who wants to continue."

No one said anything, but Laura and a few others stood up immediately. Corbin remained seated, he was committed and that was no secret. Yordanos, Herbert, and Jason never got up either. They looked at one another from their seats, nodded, and smiled. Corbin could hear hushed whispers of conversation, which rose in volume as the standard dynamics of humans talking in an enclosed space rose to a level that was socially acceptable for the topics and circumstances.

One by one the A-Crew members retook their seats. No one wanted to be the last one or two standing so after a few people sat down, everyone else quickly concluded their discussion and sat back down. Corbin spoke again. "I am going forward with the *Valor* and its mission. I value each one of you and will respect your decision either way, but by God, I want you all with us on this"—he sought the right word—"this adventure," he finished with a smile. "You all saw the hangar filled with spacecraft. Imagine what we will get to do, and what we will get to see." He stopped, realizing he was selling.

Jason spoke up to give Corbin a rest. "Everyone who is moving forward with the *Valor* and the mission from here on forward, please stand." Corbin and his friends quickly stood, followed by nearly everyone else. Brittney remained seated looking off in some imaginary distance, deep within thought. She closed her eyes and bowed her head.

Then she took a deep breath and stood. Opened her eyes, where a tear had escaped. She smiled, looked at Corbin, and nodded. Corbin looked around, and no one remained seated. He smiled and did not speak words to cheapen the moment. He calmly strode to the door, where the commander had been waiting, seemingly patiently, and asked her politely to come back in. "Everyone of us is all in, the decision has been made," he whispered to her and then retook his seat.

Commander Sorenson went on as if she had merely taken a bio break, and Corbin appreciated her not making a fuss about what Corbin and his crew had paused to do. The commander picked back up her spot at the front of the room, as well as on the previous topic. "I was talking about the discovery of the memory modification process. Our source of the information indicated that it was part of the cryogenic process, and quite frankly we don't fully understand it. The methodology, however, pushes your long-term memories close enough to the subconscious so that your efforts to reach back to those memories becomes slippery, as if trying to remember a dream, yet it's all still there beneath the surface. When you all awoke, and we witnessed the effects firsthand, our information was confirmed."

"So how do we undo what has been done?" Jason asked calmly. The commander again drew her lips in a thin line. "Unfortunately, it needs to be undone the same way and for the same duration that it was done in the first place. We have the means, but it has to be done in cryo." She waited as everyone digested this. By the facial expression of those around the table, Corbin could tell that it was not sitting well, but he could also tell his people were getting ahold of themselves, and he was impressed when no one had an outburst.

The commander began again, but was interrupted by Herbert. "So our memories are to be slowly reincorporated over the ten-year cycle we go back into cryo? Will that work without changing what we have learned here? What would... Would that change our personality? I mean we have already changed so much since awakening..." he asked, wanting to ask more, but his voice fading.

The commander responded, "I won't lie to you, we have only just become aware of the ability to reverse the memory modification process, and thank God we did. In fact, I'm pretty sure we were never really meant to reverse the process." Everyone continued gawking at her. She went on, elevating the perspective of the conversation. "Look, it hasn't been all fun and games getting ready for you, and then watching you come to blows on your rings of the *Valor*. We have been doing a lot of additional research and tasking on this situation outside of the mission, and not just maintaining this ship's course, speed, and life support. As soon as you are ready to dive into all of it as your own, the better, and then we can work together on the problem."

She relaxed her shoulders, eyed the chair nearest to her at one of the tables next to Brittney. She moved to it and sat, and then swiveled the chair to face everyone. "So, what we are asking you to do, is to work your first tour as-is. The next eight plus years with us, and the ten after that, the way you are now, so you can help B-Crew through the transition you just went through as you see fit. When it's your time to head back to cryo, we'll fix your memory while you're under. When you awaken for tour number two, you'll have some integrating to do, but essentially most of your memoires…ninety-nine percent of it should come back; from your childhood memories, to whatever the hell it is you got into that somehow led you here." Her eyes looked down to the table, a bit of shame on her face, and she waited for an outburst. It didn't come.

Laura, now much more in control of her emotions, asked a question instead. "What are you going to do about B-Crew and C-Crew?"

Commander Sorenson looked up, and Corbin detected that hesitancy again at the mention of B and C-Crew, but she went on. "That will be up to you to decide…together. With the eight plus years B-Crew has left before they awake, we could start the process now and get them back up to seventy-five precent or so of their memories, but we really need that full ten year period to get almost all of it. Would it even be worth it?"

Now there was an outburst as nearly all of the A-Crew selectees cried out, "YES!" Others shouted here and there, "Start the process today! Do it now! 75% is better than nothing!"

The commander looked at Corbin, who nodded and said, "How they are introduced to this new realty will be confusing, and the fact that they too didn't want to be here will be the main factor, just like it was with us." He tried to lock eyes with the commander when he said this, but she would not meet his stern gaze. He could feel the fragility of the room, and Commander Sorenson knew it too. Whatever the issue with B and C-Crew, this group wasn't ready to hear it. He glanced at Yordanos whose eyes were already locked on his. She had seen the same hesitation in Commander Sorenson that he had. At a slight shake of Yordanos's head, Corbin went on, changing the subject. "Just out of curiosity, how is the memory modification process overseen?"

Commander Sorenson responded, "It's a classified subroutine in the main AI which manages the cryogenic storage process. It's nothing we can crack into. If we wanted to learn how to do it ourselves, it would have to be raw R&D…from scratch."

Corbin looked around to see everyone a bit dejected by this. He thought there was no way to know if a small lab somehow figured this out, or if it took thousands of overlapping research projects and subjects to develop and refine the cryogenic management process and subroutine. He inwardly shuddered at the amount of trial and error that had probably occurred to get the capability to the state it was in.

The commander interrupted his thoughts. "There is one other interesting thing. It looks like there are ways to provide education through subliminal suggestion while you are under. It's not all just about obscuring memories."

Yordanos asked, "How do you know that?"

The commander responded, starting with her lips pursed thinly indicating it gave her great discomfort to respond. *No wonder she wrote most of it down,* Corbin thought to himself. "Well…we know that it teaches you American English. We know this because many of your number…do not appear to be Americans."

Everyone went into a collective memory tremor. "Americans?" asked Yordanos.

Corbin spoke up. "The flag on Ring One's main corridor out there. That's an American flag, isn't it?" The commander nodded, and Corbin sat back, exhaling, and recalled his histories of the European powers squabbling over Europe and also lesser developed areas and countries around the world. He surmised a new power must have arose from that history…in the back of his mind he could feel the American identity all there, but consciously he couldn't process it.

Corbin elaborated for his fellow crew members. "So I've been studying Earth's history as part of my warm-up courses. America must be a powerful nation on Earth, that could only have arisen in the past several hundred years…" He jumped his train of thought and went right back to the commander, "Wait, how many of Earth's nations are space faring? Are there more of us out here?" he asked hopefully.

She responded, "It's all in the folder…well, most of it. You'll be given wider access to all the ship's data and information coming in from the link with have with Earth. You'll also get to connect your studies from the fifteen hundreds up until today. You can work out all the details there, but what I'm saying is some of your fellow A-Crew members are not only from different parts of the planet, but as far as we can figure…" She paused and looked down. She continued, "Some of them, well, some of you appear to be from different decades over the last eighty years."

Jason looked over at Corbin down and made a quirky face. Yordanos rolled her eyes, and Laura threw her arms up and then crossed them. The rest of the A-Crew lieutenants had similar variations of the same reactions.

She continued, "Suffice it to say that some of your crew members have not been acquiescing as well as you have. You don't see them because they pretty much confine themselves to their quarters. Many don't accept their companion AIs, nor do they want to engage with their AIMA or consoles. Many of them find solace in the Arboretum and even the Challenge ring, and while they clearly don't want to be here, they are too emotionally broken and too disengaged to have taken up with the dissenters. That is another issue you will have to manage."

Corbin nodded, and sensing that another outburst was imminent, he spoke up. "Thank you, Commander. Is there anything else before we dive into these briefs…umm how long do we have?"

The commander stood quickly, eager to leave, smoothed an imaginary fold on her uniform, and looked around to all of them. "Take as long as you need. Restrooms are through these doors and to the left, and I'll have refreshments brought in to you. Your individual schedules are on hold until you finish here, and have some time to yourselves to digest it all."

Corbin nodded to the commander. "Thank you." She returned the nod curtly and left. Before she could leave the room, the folders' seals being torn through by the eager A-Crew members could be heard throughout the room. From there, the sounds turned to the rustling of paper.

A few minutes after she left, Herbert called out, "Holy shit! Aside from fusion engines, they accelerated the *Valor* using thousands of fission bombs against a giant exploder plate behind the aft material slug!? And that's the same way we have to slow down!?"

Everyone looked at him wild eyed, as he had clearly opened the folder from the middle instead of at the beginning like most everyone else.

Jason spoke. "That must have been a hell of a ride…and will be again," he said with a blank face.

Brittney spoke out next. "The hangar we saw with spacecraft sends out multiple ships a day to explore the space surrounding the *Valor*. Those giant mechanized bot looking things are manned vehicles and are used to perform major construction or repair to the external hull of the *Valor*." And everyone looked over to her.

Before she or anyone else could say any more, Norton spoke up as well. "Did you know there is a huge satellite network around the *Valor* spanning out millions of kilometers!? There's even a set of satellites that have been accelerated way out in front of the *Valor* to track potential bodies which could cause a collision."

Everyone went back to their folders, eager to find something interesting to call out.

Corbin, taking the cue from Herbert, flipped to the back of the folder. His eyes flew across the pages and then he stopped to read in detail. He said in a voice a little above a whisper, "The *Valor* is…heavily armed…"

Chapter Fifty-Seven: A Sleepy Sentence

Corbin and Jason flanked Jessica as they walked through the corridor on D-Ring. It had been two days since they and their other colleagues had read through their briefs from the commander. It had been six hours since Jessica had decided to surrender her walled-off section of D-Ring.

HDs walked in front of and behind their trio. This time, they were programmed to follow Jason's or Corbin's commands, and this time they could restrain Jessica, should she need to be.

Corbin looked over at her and saw none of the fight left in her eyes. As they walked, she had her head slightly down, her eyes tracing several meters in front of her to where the front guard of HDs walked in time with their human counterparts.

Jason inhaled before speaking, but Jessica cut him off. "Save it. This is what I want...and Jason, I would like to speak to Corbin alone." Jason made eye contact with Corbin, and when Corbin nodded, Jason peeled off from their number to head back down the corridor without a word.

The group of HDs and two humans continued down the corridor in silence. Corbin figured she would speak again when she was ready to, so he said nothing. He tried to sneak a glance at her, but since nothing got past her, he decided instead to keep his eyes locked in front of him as well. For the next few seconds, he marveled at how Jessica was still controlling Corbin's actions, even in defeat and surrender. He was sorry to be losing her. She would be an incredible asset to the crew if she was aligned with their cause. He also had to admit to himself, despite his undefined relationship with Sheila that there was also attraction there. Ever since he had first seen her intensely stern gaze at the Briefing, her insane resilience in the Challenge, and followed by her physique in a stunning black dress at the opening formal so many months ago, he felt it.

He felt it even after she had kicked him off the ledge in the Challenge ring, but for a moment there, they really were working together, her broken leg and all. It was a hopeful image of her that included all of what she had the potential to be if things were different... *Well, if she were different.* His verbal thoughts arose to the surface of his consciousness. He immediately felt some shame at this. *People are who they are, not who you want them to be. If you get hung up on who you want them to be, you'll never give them a fair shake in who they are, nor will you appreciate them.* He almost visibly winced at his own thought dialogue, words streaming to him from his own subconscious. He wasn't sure if the words belonged to him or were spoken by someone else. They seemed too wise to be his own.

Snapping out of it, Corbin accidentally snuck another glance at Jessica, trying to see if that image of her he had built up in his mind could somehow match the young woman he was walking next to. In an instant she returned his gaze, albeit fiercely, as if she could detect his thoughts like wandering hands on her. Corbin's face remained impassive, and as she spoke, her tone was not as fierce as that look. "I'm doing you a huge favor, you know." It was a statement, not a question. "The rest of my people should accept that this is the end of it. For what it's worth, I do care about what happens to everyone on this ship...I just..." She trailed off.

Corbin took up her voice track. "Hoped it would have gone down differently," he said knowingly, thinking of everything he and his closest friends had been through.

She paused, giving his word thought, and then nodded silently, looking more tired now than ever. However, that last fierce gaze she had given him showed she still had fight in her. Corbin thought she would always have that. Jessica spoke. "I had hoped for a many great things Corbin...many things..." She trailed off again. "You know, there was one point there on the Challenge ring, where I did like working with you, even though it was through more pain than I have ever imagined. I don't like what you are doing with A-Crew, but I do respect you…well some of what you are, as a man." Neither of them spoke again as they traversed the long hallway.

After several more minutes, they stopped at Jessica's quarters, and the door whisked open. A defiant looking and protesting young man was escorted…more handled…out the door by the lead HDs. He had been locked in there since the re-taking of the *Valor*. Jessica didn't look at him or seem to have any concern that someone had been occupying her quarters. Corbin could see that she was laser focused on the shower room and was thinking about her impending destination of the cryo chamber. He wondered if this is how people looked when they went to the gallows or firing squad.

One of the rear-guard HDs was a medical unit, and it followed Corbin and Jessica into her quarters and then stopped looking at Jessica expectantly. The other HDs left except Corbin could see two of them posted as guards in front of Jessica's quarters as the door slid closed.

"Okay, so what do I do next?" Jessica asked the medical HD, who responded in a polite and compassionate feminine tone. "We can begin the process immediately, or if you prefer, I can wait until you are asleep." Jessica made "eye" contact with the medical HD. "No, let's get this over with, I don't want to brood any longer."

"Very well," said the HD. "I need three minutes to prepare, then please join me in your shower room. You will need to remove your clothing prior to beginning the process." The HD turned and then left them in the main room of her quarters. They could hear the HD's servos whirring and the sound of equipment being set up in the shower room.

Jessica turned to Corbin, and he could see that the iron strong front that she nearly always projected was starting to fracture as her respiration increased and she squeezed her eyes shut, probably trying to force nervous tears away. Corbin stepped over to her carefully and gently folded her into a supporting embrace and made sure to say nothing. She was rigid for several seconds, and Corbin was starting to think he had made a mistake when she relaxed and she let two small sobs through before regaining control, but she stayed in his embrace.

"Can we be adults about this?" she asked him. For once Corbin was on the same page with her thinking. "Absolutely," he responded softly. "Good… Can you stay with me until…" Corbin nodded and turned to face the other way as she disrobed and wrapped herself in a towel. "Okay" she said sheepishly, and he turned around, careful to keep his eyes on hers, as he approached, and they both walked into the shower room together.

The medical HD turned to them, and they could both see that the wall had opened to a large cryogenic chamber, the very same one Jessica had emerged from less than two years prior. The lights dimmed as soft and gentle music began to play at a medium volume. Jessica took a deep breath considering the maw of the chamber. Corbin almost said it wasn't too late to change her mind, but something deep inside of him told him to stay silent, so he did.

The medical HD addressed Jessica. "I am ready for you. When you are ready, please remove your towel and step into the chamber. You can lie back, but you will still need to support yourself for a few moments, so please remain in a standing position. Corbin, you may stay until she is asleep and secured; however, I will ask you to leave as I conduct the final sequence." Corbin nodded.

Jessica let the towel slip from around her, but in a final act of assertion, caught it and handed it to the HD who took it without a word. She stepped into the cryo chamber, and Corbin stood outside of the vertically oblong tub, just to the side. He could see she didn't want to ask, so he took her hand, and she squeezed his in return. The HD moved next to the cryo chamber across from Corbin, and leaned over the tub to talk to Jessica. "I will be administering an intravenous sedative, which will allow you to fall asleep. From there, I will move you through the necessary sequences to prepare you for cryo-sleep. Do you have any other requests before we begin?" Jessica grit her teeth and shook her head.

Corbin was relieved she didn't ask for an explanation. The HD would no doubt get to work on the unconscious form of Jessica as soon as Corbin left. Corbin had recalled his readings from the Top-Secret folder, everything that had to happen for the cryogenic process to begin, and he was glad that Jessica did not know about it. First her digestive system needed to be purged of any food, and there were the additions of other fluids, organic material, to different areas of the body that acted as a cellular reservoir, gradually replacing cells that had been ruptured by the deep freeze process and constant bombardment of cosmic radiation over the years, despite the shielding.

Bottom line is, the process was not entirely gentle, and one would most likely be aghast at watching it happen to another's body.

The HD deftly identified a vein in her left arm, just below the elbow and with grace and precision, inserted an IV which barely drew a wince from Jessica. The HD plugged the other end to the front of its chest, and Corbin could see a watery fluid begin to slowly push toward Jessica's arm. He tracked it until she drew his attention. "Corbin?" He looked at her and saw the fear in her eyes.

"Hey, it's going to be okay. It's just a long nap. When you wake again with the next crew things will be different, you'll see for yourself."

She shook her head and squeezed her eyes shut. "I'm afraid," she said tensely. Corbin looked over and saw the stream of fluid enter her arm, and she visibly relaxed. She loosened her shoulders and opened her eyes, if a little sleepier. "Corbin…did you know that the memory modification process only happened to us in A-Crew and not the other crews?" she asked him.

Corbin's eyes widened. "How do you know that…"

She cut him off getting sleepier. "I got a Zero Crew member to tell me. It…it doesn't really matter. I had planned to use that information later as leverage against Zero Crew, but now…" She shook her head. "Well at least now you know," she finished.

Corbin opened his mouth to speak, but she cut him off again, this time more gently.

"Corbin, please don't wake me up," she asked him, pleading in her eyes.

Corbin's face looked grave. "I can't do that Jessica, no way, that would be a death sentence, and that's not what this is. You don't deserve that."

Her tears returned, although she didn't tense up as she had a few moments before. "I'm so angry Corbin, even now, I can feel it beneath my mind…it bubbles up in almost every thought and emotion… God, I am so enraged…always," she finished in a whisper.

Corbin looked up at the HD prompting it to say, "She'll be under in about thirty seconds."

"Jessica, listen to me," he said, pulling her non-IV arm closer to him, and imploring her to look at him with the intensity of his eyes. "Jessica, we are going to start over, we'll do it right this time, and I'll tell you everything up front, I promise. Jessica, next time we can work together on the same side," he finished looking at her hoping for acknowledgment.

Her eyes gently slipped closed, and Corbin lowered his head, dejected. He felt he was in an impossible situation. *Why did she tell me she intended to stay frozen forever?!* Jessica took one more deep breath, and as she exhaled, she said one barely intelligible word: "Maybe." Then her hand fell from his grasp.

The HD looked at him expectantly, so Corbin turned, and left his lovely, once-arch-nemesis to sleep…for a long time.

Chapter Fifty-Eight: One Month Later

Jason and Corbin sat at their usual table at The Orchard bar and grill. Neither had anything to eat, but they both had been sipping beers, which they enjoyed and relaxed and conversational pace. They relished this time for conversation and introspection, and while the beers were tasty, the flavorful alcohol also did well to simultaneously focus and loosen their minds to the various topics they covered.

Jason spoke. "Hey man, did you ever think about going to church or temple or anything like that?" he asked Corbin.

Corbin looked up at him bemused. "I, ah…you know? I haven't given it much thought, to be honest with you. It's not like we have had a lot of spare time."

"I know man," Jason responded. "But when will there ever be time? Seems to me that a little exploration of faith could do us some good, yeah? I'm just saying, since the insurrection Laura has been going to Christian services, and Jeremy and Herbert have been going to Jewish temple…maybe it's something we want to check out someday."

Corbin furled his brow for a moment, a bit caught off guard at how self-conscious he felt about it. It was like he had missed something important despite him trying to hold what was left of A-Crew together along with his command team.

Corbin sighed and spoke. "You know, I think you are right. We are going to need to subscribe to a higher power if we are ever going to be able to live with ourselves in this messed up state of new memories floating on top of repressed old ones. While talking to the AIs about how I am feeling deep inside is helpful, I think talking to God would be better, and I don't know the first thing about how to do that."

Jason smiled thankfully. "I'm glad you think so. Let's catch one of these masses or services later this week, and we can find out together."

Corbin nodded in agreement, and then thought more on it. "Don't punch me for saying this. Contrary to popular belief I do think about other things than just the future of A-Crew. Anyways, from my history courses, the Jewish faith has been incredible in sustaining their religion and culture for thousands of years, despite incredible persecution and conflict, and I've only covered through 1600s or so. I haven't had the chance to get through all of history up to the present date. Likewise, Christianity showed incredible resilience. Once persecuted by the Roman Empire at its inception with Jesus, the Roman's eventually adopted Christianity within a few centuries."

"And your point, professor?" Jason chided.

"Hey, you brought it up man," Corbin said with his palms up. He went on. "My point is, you're right. If we are going to sustain ourselves out here in the void of space, we could learn a thing or two from the values and faith concepts from Earth. And that goes for the rest too, we need them all; Hinduism, Islam, Buddhism…"

"Nihilists?" Jason interjected.

Corbin sat back and sipped his beer. "Well…no need to get carried away." And they both laughed.

Corbin leaned back, looking at Jason. "Alright now, let's get down to some real business. It seems like you have…what? Three potential love interests here…are you dating all of them at once? How the hell do you even have time for that man? And with this schedule" he asked waving his hand out in space toward where everyone's AIMA would project schedules.

Jason smiled his huge heartwarming smile. "C'mon Corbin, you know I'm not much of a kiss and tell, but let's just say I am figuring things out."

Corbin visually investigated his beer pensively and marveled at how Jason had had enough time to think about all of the intricacies of three different people, and then also wondered how he guarded his heart, as well as how he guarded theirs through his actions. Corbin wasn't entirely sure that his friend was doing that responsibly, but perhaps that was the game in dating. Corbin mused that he couldn't play it the same way Jason could.

"That's it? That's all you are going to give me?" Corbin asked. Jason's grin remained fixed in place, if slightly broader. "Good luck with all of that," Corbin said with a smile, but he was also signaling the desire for a topic change. He finished another sip of his beer, his face turning more serious. He sniffed, set his beer down, rotating the glass idly, and leaned forward.

"Jay, do you think we made the right call on G-Ring? On sending all the dissenters there? I can't stop thinking about it. Our crew is down to sixty percent, and at this point it only looks like a handful of the dissenters even want to work their way back into A-Crew. The rest basically just sit around doing nothing," Corbin finished.

Jason frowned and leaned back dramatically. "Oh they aren't doing nothing Corbin, have you seen the feeds?" He sat up straighter, his face expressive with wide eyes, his grin returning. "Seriously man, you must take a look. The fools have gotten creative in how they spend their time. We've got smash fests that go on non-stop. There is a fight club, where people are learning some fighting techniques, despite us having outlawed it. There are people that sit around all day and just make art. They write, they sing, they sculpt, or paint. We've got folks that essentially just wander around the ring all day, socializing, partaking in some of these activities and not others, and we even have a few that have resumed their coursework and training despite no stated interest in coming back to us and A-Crew." Jason leaned back, taking his beer with him and drew another long sip before continuing. "To tell you the truth Corbin, some of these folks are having a lot more fun than we are. It's a pity we can't pop over and hang out some of the time."

Corbin's face drew stern and grave, but Jason made a conceding gesture by putting his open hands up. "Hey, I'm just saying, Corbin, they are having some fun is all. They might not have been lucky getting picked for this trip, but what they have now…at least for the rest of their wakeful period is essentially a space cruise where they can do whatever they want."

Corbin gestured at him emphatically. "That's exactly my point. We are getting minimum returns on a percentage of them coming back to A-Crew, and in fact we created a place where people may even want to drop to if they get overworked or lose faith in what we are trying to do. On top of that the dissenters now essentially get to live in a lap of luxury for most of their initial twenty years of wakefulness. We've got to figure out a way to get these guys with the program."

Yordanos appeared unannounced and pulled a chair up to their table, and waved over at Ethan, half smiling as a friend, and half beckoning to make an order. Ethan, who had been working on some ingredient's preparation, nodded, happy to see her join their group of friends, and walked over to where Jason and Corbin had temporarily halted their conversation for the newcomer.

Yordanos spoke as Ethan walked up. "Ethan, what's that new drink you were touting to me the other day, the sweet one with the bourbon?"

Ethan smiled with pride. "That's the D-Ring sucker punch." Corbin shot Ethan a furled brow look, recalling how he had taken such a punch a little over a month ago. Jason just narrowed his eyes at him, yet both were still in good humor. Ethan continued. "I'm just saying, now that we have been victorious, we can laugh about it, and laughter is facilitated by a damn good drink. How about I make it a round of three, and you can try grumbling about it then?"

Jason answered quickly, "You have a deal Ethan, we'll take that round, even though they say drinking beer before liquor is a bad idea."

Ethan frowned. "Who the hell ever said that?" he asked.

"Couldn't tell ya buddy, couldn't tell ya. But it was something like, 'liquor before beer, in the clear. Beer before liquor, never been sicker,'" Jason said. And the four of them shared a knowing nod at the untraceable memory pop.

Ethan grinned, rolled his eyes at the saying, and stepped away to get their drink order while Yordanos looked over at Corbin and seemed to read in his mind. "Oh I get it, you aren't pleased with the initial results of the clown show over on G-Ring," she said seemingly all knowing. Corbin had given up on being surprised at Yordanos's incredible power of perception, but Jason still gawked at her.

"How did you know that?" Jason asked.

"Never mind," she said and then went on. "Fellas, I've been thinking about this too. I know we set up H-Ring and moved all of the dissenters over there out of necessity, but now we see how they are getting along, I think some changes and consequences have to be laid down." She went on without much pause. "First of all, these clowns can have all of the fun they want, but we need to motivate them to want to come back so…" She pursed her lips as if worried about the reaction she would get. "We tell them they can stay there and do what they want, but when the go back into cryo, we erase their memories and re-start them fresh, just like we all were two years ago." Corbin and Jason's eyes went wide, but they said nothing, so Yordanos went on, "We set a date, I don't know, something with substantial time for them to do some good…maybe five years left before cryo. If they miss that deadline to fall in line, they get wiped, but if they contribute meaningfully to the crew, they get to keep all their memories they have made here."

Jason raised a hand. "We do that, and everyone is going to dick around until that date. I like where you are coming from, but if it's a cut off time, then maybe we don't announce it, but we do announce the punitive memory reset."

Corbin almost didn't blink, he had wanted to protest, but this was exactly what had been irking him. These people needed consequences other than being banished. His mind raced, but he spoke. "I'm not going to lie, I'm still pretty pissed off at them, but if we make them feel like there is no way out, it could drive desperation that we are not anticipating. In some of these leadership courses they always tell us the carrot is better than the stick…but then we run into the problem of loyal A-Crew people being pissed off that these dissenters are coddled too much, and we can lose productive people as well…what a damn quandary." He took down a large pull of his IPA. Its flavor had soured along with his attitude over the implications of the people exiled to H-Ring.

Yordanos looked down in thought, and then back up at Jason and Corbin. She spoke solemnly. "I think that is what my problem has been, and I didn't want to let go of it until I heard you say it, Corbin."

"Say what? The carrot and stick?" he asked.

"No not that…the part about being pissed off. We've just won the fight, and I'm already not thinking of these people as our fellow crew members. That's a slippery slope, and if I am thinking that we have to be careful that others are thinking that as well."

Corbin nodded gravely. "We must show them what we are doing…share our successes and hell even our challenges with them and let them try and help if they want to. People may choose to ignore us, but if we can help self-actualize people by being a member of A-

Crew, then we need to leave that door open at all times, and not make the road back an unending trek with no hope in sight."

Yordanos was nodding now, and added, "We help them to maintain connections back to A-Crew, support friendships and the like. We need to inspire them…being separate and out of the game is punishment enough."

"This is a good discussion," Jason said, "but whatever we decide here at the bar, we take it up to our council for discussion…hell we could use their ideas on how to deal with this anyways, we don't have to do it all by ourselves now. I guarantee, our first implementation of this plan will need to be tweaked, so we come up with something, try it out with the counsel, look at the unintended consequences, adjust and then put it into place." Both Yordanos and Corbin nodded, suddenly not wanting to talk about it anymore.

Corbin activated his AIMA, and with a few quick strokes of his fingers across the table, he altered the agenda for the upcoming council meeting at the end of the week. Jason and Yordanos saw the alert, and both nodded with approval.

Corbin was halfway through taking another sip of his beverage when a shudder suddenly jostled the glass in his hand. Corbin's eyes went a bit wider. "What was…" Before he could finish the thought, the *Valor* shuddered again." All conversation in The Orchard ceased, and everyone looked at one another, their collective concern growing.

A third shudder, much more powerful, set Corbin jumping to his feet. He snapped on his AIMA. "Tina what's going on?" He tried not to holler too excitedly. Many others were doing the same. Corbin listened for a few seconds as Tina listed yet unknown anomaly impacting the *Valor*, while some additional minor vibrations could be felt by everyone in the vicinity.

Corbin looked at his colleagues. "Dammit, Tina says this is an anomaly, but no further information is being provided."

"What should we do? Where should we go?" asked Jason shrugging.

A pit was beginning to settle into Corbin's stomach. "If no announcement has come yet, this must be something that has not been anticipated. As if to confirm Corbin's assessment, a klaxon began sounding, and now everyone else snapped on their AIMAs, as new information was disseminated to everyone.

"NOW HEAR THIS, NOW HEAR THIS. All A-Crew personnel are to return to quarters immediately and begin prep for emergency cryogenic submersion." The message repeated.

"Damn!" shouted Ethan, "to have to go back into the icebox!?"

Corbin ignored him and raised his voice. "You heard the word, everyone to your quarters, now!" In an instant the seventy or so patrons of The Orchard began scrambling to the main hallways leaving drinks and half-eaten meals where they lay. Corbin grabbed Yordanos's hand, "We need to get to the transit corridor. We have to make it to D-Ring. Jason, give me a hand please."

"Right behind ya, boss," Jason said.

And the three rushed out of The Orchard toward the nearest gravity transition zone and entryway to the transit corridor. Corbin looked over to Yordanos, who was already coordinating an HD via her AIMA to get them at the upcoming junction in the Spine.

A few flights of stairs and a few minutes later they three rounded the hallway to the transition zone to see a mass of A-Crew members already piling up waiting for HDs to navigate them through the slipring and zero gravity Spine.

Corbin leaned over panting and put his hands on his knees. Jason patted him on the head trying to inject a bit of levity. "You out of breath, man? Maybe you need a few more reps on the Challenge ring?" Corbin narrowed his eyes at him, but managed a grimaced grin.

Corbin saw that the HDs were practically chucking A-Crew members through the slipring as it rotated two and sometimes three at a time. He figured that they were counting on the Spine transition HDs to sort them out floating around in zero gravity. Jason barely had time to look back before he, followed by Yordanos, and then Corbin were tossed into the Spine.

Corbin looked around at sheer pandemonium. Hundreds of weightless and flailing A-Crew members were floating or being seized by HDs and whisked off to other rings. No one was taking time with the transit cars.

HDs quickly snared all three of them before they could get to the center of the Spine, and while Corbin saw Jason trying to yell something, nothing could be heard over the deafening roar of hundred or so HDs navigation fans working in high gear to sort out the A-Crew members in the emergency.

A few seconds later they were through back through the slipring and landed with a thud in the gravity transition zone entryway on D-Ring. HDs were not taking crew members directly, but helping them up once they bounced in the low gravity.

Corbin's feet found purchase, and he clumsily pulled up Yordanos, followed by Jason as they began to run down the ramp and to their respective quarters, each of them flanking Yordanos protectively.

"Thanks guys, but you should…" Yordanos was interrupted by Corbin's AIMA, which made a beeping sound no one had ever heard before. They all slowed down and looked at Corbin's AIMA, beeping urgently. "Well, answer it!" Yordanos said.

Corbin saw a way to answer, and his vision switched to looking at a video window where Commander Sorenson's grave face met him. "Commander, I—" He was cut off.

"Shut up and listen, Corbin, drop what you are doing and get to your quarters and prep for cryo right now. Your friends are smart and will take care of themselves, but you have to go! Now! I'll fill you in while you are en route."

Corbin opened his mouth to protest, but Jason caught his hand. In his AIMA, Corbin could see in the periphery around the commander's video window.

Jason whispered while overemphasizing the mouthing of each word. "We got this. You gotta go."

Corbin hesitated, nodded, and with a quick squeeze of Yordanos's hand, he tuned and left them, now traveling upstream against the numbers of A-Crew clamoring to get to the transit corridor, and back their respective ring and quarters. He shifted the AIMA view so that he could see the commander's face in the upper right corner of his view but left his forward-facing view clear to navigate the crowded hallway.

"Okay, Commander, I'm on the way to my quarters, based on what I'm looking at here, AIMA says about 6-7 minutes. I—"

The commander cut him off again. "Push it harder. Corbin, seconds count, move as fast as you can, don't talk, just listen." Corbin then cut her off.

"If seconds count, Commander," he said starting to pant with exertion, "then come up with a more efficient way for A-Crew to get to cryo based on crew location, and available quarters… If everyone jams up the transit corridor, it could take hours!"

The commander's eyes, about to bug out of her head turned to someone just off camera view, "Get it done like he says. Assign A-Crew members to the nearest available quarters based on proximity, have the AI crunch it in real-time and get it out to the AIMAs."

Her sharp gaze snapped back to Corbin. "Now shut up and listen, but keep moving your ass!"

She took a deep breath. "The shudders you felt earlier are from external objects that have impacted the *Valor*'s rear facing material slug. We have detected some damage, and the inner corridor has been breached and decompressed into space. With the explosive decompression several HDs were damaged when they were jumbled up and blasted out through the breach, but we have some video, and I'm sending it to you in a new window now…look, but do not slow your pace."

Corbin listened, kicked his run into a higher gear as the number of A-Crew members in the hallways finally started to decrease. He took note of three people far down the corridor in front of them, entering their respective quarters and disappearing behind the silently whisking doors.

Then the video window popped up. Corbin tried to watch it carefully, however, as instructed he did not slow his pace, so it was difficult. He could see that an HD mounted camera seemed to have taken the video based on the mobile but steady nature of the footage. There was also no sound, as it looked like the atmosphere had already been vacated by the hull breach. The HD increased its lighting, and the camera adjusted, revealing movement down the corridor. At first Corbin thought it might be a jumbled mass of broken HDs trying to untangle themselves from debris, but the movement looked wrong…looked…organic. There also seemed to be a mass of whirring appendages out and behind the mass of the whatever this thing was. *Was that some kind of armor?* The mass of moving limbs suddenly closed the distance between where Corbin first saw it, and the recording HD, and the camera went black.

"What the hell is that, Commander, also why the rear and not the front of the *Valor*? Is that…some kind of foreign entity?" Corbin said breathlessly, a bit shocked at his unprofessional language. He was going to say, "alien."

"We don't know, Corbin. You can take a closer look at the footage when you get to cryo prep and think about it, but for now, this is what is going on," the Commander continued, and Corbin could tell by the tone of her voice, that even though she was delivering her words with the common calm that is required by commanders to deliver instruction in stressful scenarios, masked within her voice, was terror, and something darker. Despair?

"These…things are moving through the aft material slug and destroying anything that moves. Whatever this is, it caught up to us from behind. We have taken some defensive measures, but they appear to be ineffective so far…they are working their way toward the transit corridor." She paused. "In even worse news, we have detected multiple additional inbound signatures behind us. It looks like there are going to be more…a lot more."

Corbin burst into his quarters and threw his AIMA view up on the monitor and switched over the audio. He took off his AIMA and saw the medical HD in the doorway to his shower room. Behind the HD Corbin could already see the cryo unit had been prepped. Commander Sorenson paused in speaking. We think we can stall them for another twenty to twenty-five minutes tops from Zero Crew rings, but that's it."

Corbin stopped in his tracks. "What are you…what are you saying?" he breathed and looked up at the monitor to behold the grim look on his commander's face.

"I'm saying everyone who can is to get into cryo immediately, and the rest of us will hold on for as long as we can."

Corbin looked away in horror, and pinched his eyes closed while also pinching the bridge of his nose. He knew that whatever frustrations he had, they were dwarfed by what Commander Sorenson faced, not to mention her imminent death. He looked back to the monitor where she waited for him patiently.

"Uhh, what can I do?" he said.

The commander went on. "Assuming these things don't rip into every inch of the ship and destroy your cryogenic pods, I'm hoping against hope, that after these things move on, we can reanimate you, and you can find out what happened and…if there is anything more to be done." She paused and took one of her signature deep breaths. "Corbin, I'm assigning you command of the *Valor*, the main AI, all its protocols and HDs. If you are unable to proceed, I'll ripple the command structure down your thirty-six lieutenants...you'll see the details in your AIMA as soon as it boots back up." Another jolt rocked the ship, and Corbin felt it a moment before the commander did.

"Get into cryo, Corbin, and Godspeed. I've got some fighting to do. Commander Sorenson, out."

Without a moment's hesitation, the medical HD was at his elbow. "Please, we must begin the crash cryo prep procedure immediately. You must drink this substance within the next thirty seconds, there is no time to delay."

Corbin downed the small cup of liquid, and the HD spoke again.

"It would be better if you disrobe and follow me to the shower." Corbin was surprised to see the insistent tug on his sleeve, a behavior he had never seen from an HD before. He had just taken off his garb when he felt a slight gurgle in his stomach.

The medical HD, rested its hand on his shoulder, and gently pushed him down to a kneeling position while closing the shower door. "I'm afraid this will be a bit unpleasant."

The HD had barely finished the sentence when both ends of Corbin's digestive track erupted swiftly and violently. Corbin doubled over and quickly curled into a fetal position as the torrents continued. After what felt like an eternity, but could only have been a few seconds, they subsided to a few spasms, and then stopped altogether, but his core muscles were still rigid. Corbin gritted his teeth and wrinkled his nose at the sudden mess he found himself in but was quickly greeted with lukewarm water from the shower, as the medical HD washed his foulness down the drain and sprayed any excess from his skin. The HD then helped him to his feet, and Corbin spared a quick glance in the mirror where he found his eyes bloodshot red, and in one eye he had popped a blood vessel. He felt like some D-Bag after a frat party, but didn't know exactly what that was, and the memory of the words sunk back into oblivion.

"Well, that sucked," he said to no one in particular.

"Please hurry, Corbin, we must continue the procedure. Please get into the cryogenic chamber. I have a few more items you need to imbibe, none of them as unpleasant as the last one, however."

Corbin began slurping down specific liquids, as instructed by the medical HD, who also established an IV and was adding additional liquids to him intravenously. He began to feel a bit more sedated, and the remaining discomfort in his abdominals melted away. He tried to think about his friends, but his mind was getting fuzzier.

"Hey, could you hand me my AIMA please?" The HD reached over and handed it to him without breaking a stride in its cryogenic prep process. Corbin snapped it on and began to manipulate views trying to look at the tactical situation. He was surprised to see a full detailed schematic of the *Valor* including details about both material slugs as well as Ring One and Two. He could see the entire forward material slug flashing red with alerts of hull breach and boarders. As he watched, the transit ring for Ring One also showed a breach, while simultaneously Ring-G at the other end of the ship also began flashing red. "Dammit!"

The medical HD broke in. "Corbin, you have about five minutes until you lose consciousness, please tidy any affairs you have within that time."

He tried to quickly connect to Jason's or Yordanos's AIMAs, but he could not connect. He was relieved to see that the ship's locator showed both of them in their respective cabins. He then panned out his view to check the status of the rest of A-Crew, and his heart sank. It appeared that only thirty percent of A-Crew had begun the cryogenic process. He clicked out a quick model based on the expansion of intruders, and saw that at best, only 40% or so of A-Crew would complete the cryogenic process. He opened a video file, and began recording.

"This is Corbin. Fo whatever it takes to get into cryo and or help others to get into cryo if you are not able to do so yourselves. If we wake up, we will have a lot of work to do. Godspeed." He cut it short, as a sudden wave of dizziness washed over him.

"About two minutes now, Corbin," said the medical HD calmly. He went back into his AIMA, and patched into HD Hank. "Hank! Respond please."

Hank's voice returned almost immediately. "Corbin, I'm here."

"Hank, can you get to my quarters in under two minutes?" he said.

"I'm afraid not, I am several rings away and working on the defense of the *Valor*," Hank responded.

"Override on my authority. I need you in my quarters, we will have a lot of work to do if we survive, and we'll need to work swiftly. I'm also sending you an ordered list of who to go to if you can't get to me." Corbin's hands flew across the outside of his legs, the AIMA interpreting the text and sending it to Hank. Please whatever happens…" he trailed doff.

"Override confirmed, Corbin, on my way," Hank said.

Corbin lay back, and his shrinking consciousness raced with all the things he wished he had more time to do. He typed out a few quick follow-up commands to Hank. He wasn't going to be conscious by the time Hank got there, if he got there at all. Corbin also remembered to send his video file out. He then closed his eyes.

"Corbin! HEY!" a voice piped in insistent.

Corbin, still wearing his AIMA in the cryogenic tub opened his eyes to see Blue-Tina. Corbin tried his voice, but it wouldn't come. It felt like lead was pulling on his eyelids, and the rest of his body felt completely at ease. *Help us!* He tried to say, but all he could do was think 'at' her.

"Corbin, I'm here," she said with that knowing smile that didn't seem to notice that the world was ending around her.

The medical HD suddenly stopped what it was doing and strode into Corbin's quarters. He could hear water sloshing, and then to his amazement, the slimy form of Z was on its hand as it returned to the cryogenic tub. Corbin mentally winced as the HD produced a long needle and jabbed it into the side of Z just above his tentacles, but if there was any pain, Z did not show it. The medical HD reached into the tub and placed Z on Corbin's chest.

Through slit eyes, Corbin saw the medical HD stop his IV and then replaced the fluid bag with something else. Through the AIMA Corbin heard Blue-Tina's voice. "Corbin, snap out of it, we've got to get you up the ladder right now."

Corbin saw the medical HD, engage the sealing procedure for his cryo tub, and the lid slid closed. Darkness enveloped him and everything he was, but in his vision swam the crystal clear and beautiful lattice of the ladder.

The new IV mixture hit him, and his heart rate began to increase just as the epic sound of orchestral music began to fill his ears. The music was slow and impactful at first, and then began to pick up speed. Corbin's mid eye flashed was filled with incredible imagery of racing across mountains, soaring through clouds, and gliding through incredible depths of some vast ocean. As Corbin had trained, although without his body's movements and the baton, Corbin focused his soaring consciousness at the broad base of the shimmering ladder to a node near the bottom.

As before, he forced his entire being into that node, and then reached out in all directions with what he felt was the very fiber of his being. Corbin's consciousness erupted up and through the nodes of the ladder, and as they became smaller they also became more numerous. He pressed harder.

Blue-Tina's voice cut in, a distraction Corbin felt jostle his expanded being. "That's it Corbin, just a little farther….almost…THERE! You got it!" she nearly shrieked with glee.

He felt an ethereal impact while simultaneously feeling his body slam from something hitting the *Valor* hard enough that it shook his cryo-stasis chamber. The boundaries of his consciousness halted abruptly, and suddenly he felt as if he was being pulled. It was gentle at first, but it soon increased drastically. There was nothing to hang onto in this expanded state of consciousness, but Corbin tried and failed to pull away from the rip tide pulling him to…a point?

He felt his expanded consciousness disconnect from the ladder and cascade down as it was pulled into the unknown maw. Just as he returned to the familiar walls of his own mind, everything winked out to black, and some indeterminate amount of time passed.

As his sense of self returned, it felt like he was traveling, or moving through whatever medium held his consciousness. Something that passed for a dim light suddenly appeared, but without sight, it was more feeling than vision.

As he neared, he could "hear" or perceive a soft barely audible word in a language he did not understand. As he neared the light, it got louder, but the word was still not discernible.

The light became so bright it was uncomfortable, but without any anatomy he could not close his eyes or shield himself from the light or sound, which too had become uncomfortably loud. As this continued the word started to take form, and just as the sound and light became too much to bear, he heard the word perfectly, "Rendering…Rendering…Rendering Complete."

Corbin felt himself explode into being, and looked on in sheer awe at what lay before him.

Epilogue: Commander Amanda Sorenson

Commander Sorenson entered the Command Center on Ring One just after hanging up on Corbin. "In case we aren't already there, General Quarters!" she said with stern determination. She looked across the room to the Sensors and Telemetry stations. "S&T, what are we looking at? How many more objects are inbound?"

An ever-nervous man, Daryl Finnegan, in his mid-fifties and wearing glasses spoke up, "Commander, we are tracking seven more objects inbound at high velocity. The second object will impact the aft material slug in just under three minutes. The rest are set to impact at approximately one-to-two-minute intervals."

"How the hell did we miss the first one!?" the commander asked, raising her voice.

Daryl responded shakily, "Unknown, our satellite network is still up and functional, but it appears they did not generate tracks for the targets. Nor did our on board radar and passive sensor array pick these up. We have post-impact spectral analysis factored in from when bogie zero hit the aft material slug. Now that they know what to look for, we have the following track picture."

The man swiped his console and put up the command-and-control picture of space in the vicinity of the aft of the *Valor*'s material slug out to several thousand kilometers. Everyone craned their necks and squinted, although they didn't need to for the high resolution. All could see the red affected area in the aft material slug, and seven more red objects approaching fast from behind the *Valor*. Commander Sorenson wondered how the first bogie had managed to dodge around the aft exploder plate and engines, but she didn't ask…*moot point now.*

Instead, she asked, "Why are these things approaching from Earth's bearing? Is the link still up?"

An elderly gentleman, Randy Henthorn, called out from the Earth link station, "Yes, we are still up and receiving packets…there is a slight degradation due to the objects obscuring part of the comms beam, but we can still transmit and receive."

"Good, patch every shred of sitrep information, as well as log and transmit everything we are seeing from the bogies. Prioritize textual logs before images, and videos…this needs to get out."

Daryl from Sensors and Telemetry spoke back up. "The particle trail behind the bogies indicates our solar system as the origin, but…we can't assume they accelerate like the *Valor* did…if they have different maneuvering and propulsion capabilities, they could be from anywhere."

"How big are they?" Commander Sorenson asked.

"It's tough to get an exact reading due to some interference, but I would say between five hundred and one thousand feet across. I can't get any kind of indication on the shape, but the centroid of the track appears solid, indicating some kind of hull."

The *Valor* security chief spoke up. "Commander! The intruders have nearly reached the central axis of the aft material slug…and all material handling HDs in the vicinity appear to be offline. From the short snippets of video surveillance, we see highly aggressive…breach units with advanced armor of some kind. If they get to the Spine…"

"Got it!" Commander Sorenson said, cutting him off…her mind raced. She called out to her first officer, Leah Charbeneau. "XO, put all HDs within five minutes' proximity to armories and ten minutes within being combat effective into Alamo protocol and post them in the Spine of the ship between the aft material slug and A-Ring. Get some on the outside hull too." She paused, deep in thought. "If they can't get armed and into position within that time frame…send them into the rings. I want an even distribution of HD-types on every ring to the best of your ability but prioritize speed and quantity of HDs over accuracy."

Leah approached Commander Sorenson's console and bent over toward her, gently but firmly grasping her wrist. She whispered to her fiercely, "Amanda…are you—"

Commander Amanda Sorenson cut her off. "It's a precaution, but we need to get the pieces in place, Leah. There won't be time if we wait." She returned her fierce gaze.

Commander Sorenson called out before her XO had the chance to back away. "Ring-One and Ring-Two hangars, I want maintenance vehicles pushed out across all rings. Get all combat effective craft out of the airlocks and headed south to the aft material slug. I want fighter craft ready for fire support if any of these things get outside the hull."

Commander Sorenson and the rest of the command staff looked up to the main screen to see the foreign objects moving closer to the icon of the *Valor*.

She spoke up. "Ladies and gentlemen, we are switching to Aegis protocol. We have trained for this, so every one of you knows what to do. I want all tracks locked in and a firing solution on all objects as soon as possible."

"Commander! We don't know what these things are!" one of the command staff she couldn't see called from a console behind her.

"Noted. We are assuming hostile and are going to defend the ship. Remember why they named this vessel the *Valor*," she said.

She leaned over to the weapons officer, Harry Jager, who was seated to Commander Sorenson's left side. "Weps, Let me know when we have the nearest target in range, and if the track is still good, fire salvos one and two."

The weapons officer nodded, and his hands flew across the console. "Bogie one in firing range…now. Launching salvos one and two."

Everyone looked up to the command-and-control screen to see four small icons appear and begin to accelerate behind the *Valor*. They quickly crossed the dashed line indicating the *Valor*'s momentum envelope, or the point of no return, and sped toward the first target.

The interceptors used rocket fuel and were both endo and exo-atmospheric, able to operate in space, as well as the atmosphere alike, just like the ones used to intercept other missiles in Earth's atmosphere. Unlike the kinetic interceptors that used mass and speed, these interceptors also used mass, but were tipped with nuclear fission weapons, designed to punch into foreign objects and detonate, causing complete destruction. At the speeds the targets and the weapons were maneuvering, pinpoint accuracy was critical, so the *Valor*'s vast sensor network, now locked in on the targets, bathed them in energy to ensure the interceptors would hit.

The initial salvos of interceptors silently screamed through the space between *Valor* and the nearest bogie. The target did not deviate, and all four of the nuclear tipped spears smashed into the target, erupting in an incredible explosion in space that no one on the *Valor* could feel or see.

"Bogie one is down, post-kill assessment shows substantial debris. They are directed away from our momentum envelope...no chance of impact to the *Valor*. Bogies two through seven are still inbound. They are in a loose string formation, and course and speed remain unchanged. Bogie two will enter firing range in twenty seconds."

Commander Sorenson got a gut feeling. "Hold fire on bogie two. Sensors, can we get all seven targets within firing range before bogie two impacts the material slug?"

The Sensors lead spoke back up, the initial nervousness now having left his voice. "Negative, Commander, our best firing solution has bogie seven entering firing range after bogie two is within danger-close of the *Valor*."

"How close?" asked the commander.

He responded, "Potential structural damage to the aft material slug and exploder plate and an off-access acceleration...the AI can't tell me by how much."

Commander Sorenson thought for a moment. "Okay, okay...okay...proceed with that firing solution, I want an even spread of penetrators and proximity bursts for the interceptors...get me six interceptors per target...and have the penetrators out in front of the proximity bursts."

Her first officer, Leah, who hadn't strayed far from her side again whispered fiercely at her so no one else could hear. "Commander, that is nearly all of our interceptors. Whether this works or not, we'll only have a few left."

Commander Sorenson spoke back, keeping her voice low. "None of this will matter if we can't repel those things, whatever the hell they are." She looked past him to the security team, which were hard at work directing HDs and other Zero-Crew defenders toward the aft portion of the Spine. She looked over to Jim Wainwright, her lead Security officer. She could tell by the grim look on his face that he did not know how to contain the attack.

The weapons officer continued to work on his console, followed by several others assisting with the multiple targets. They broke down the extremely complex problem set into target-by-target solutions. Harry, the weapons officer, or Weps, spoke up. "Commander, I need to begin launching within thirty seconds to make this firing solution work with the time we need to reload the launchers."

Commander Sorenson made eye contact with her first officer, Leah, again. "Do it, and put the status up on the main command and controls displays."

Everyone looked up to see interceptors streaming out of the *Valor*'s Spine, clearing the rings, and then moving on thrusters to various positions away from the *Valor* to set up slightly different strike angles on the targets. The kinetic strike interceptors moved aft of the *Valor*, and the proximity blast interceptors held position. The loitering interceptors waited until all forty-two interceptors were in position, and then, all at once, their tail engines roared to life. From the *Valor*'s perspective, the missiles tore away to attack the inbound objects approaching the *Valor* from the stern.

All eyes in the Command Center went back up to the command-and-control screen. They didn't have long to wait.

"Commander!" the S&T lead called out. "Bogie two has taken evasive maneuvers, first three interceptors will miss."

Weps called out in short succession, "I'm re-directing the blast fragmentation interceptors…now."

Everyone saw the first three blips fly past the icon for bogie two, and the next three interceptor blips disappear in red starburst icons around bogie two. Everyone's hearts sank when bogie two's trajectory remained unchanged.

Commander Sorenson issued a flurry of orders. "Weps, try to re-target those first three interceptors before they leave the envelope. Update all remaining interceptors for simultaneous arrival and orient the blast fragmentation interceptors to try and drive the bogies to evade out of the momentum envelope."

She hoped that they would not be so agile as to be able to turn around once they flew past…at the speeds they were moving, a solid redirect would take months or years to catch back up to the *Valor*.

And then in a louder voice, "Launch remaining interceptors on bogie two—"

The sensors lead raised his voice and drowned her out. "Too late! Brace for impact!"

The bulk of the *Valor* jolted beneath everyone's feet as the foreign mass of bogie two collided with the aft material slug. Like bogie one, it had bypassed the rear engines and exploder plate.

The security lead's voice could be heard first. "Commander, additional intruders are entering the aft material slug. Combined with the initial force from bogie one, they will breach the Spine near A-Ring in about three minutes."

A different tactical picture came up next to the main screen, showing hundreds of red icons pouring through the detailed map of corridors, and storage areas of the aft material slug. Screen-in-screen video footage from corridor cameras showed fast armored insect-like creatures racing through corridors, and somehow were not troubled by the varying gravities depending on their proximity to the non-spinning Spine of the *Valor*. Where they had traversed, deep gouges could be seen in the steel of the corridors, and everyone could see that the airlocks and sealed doors were torn through. Those barriers were holding up little more than a few seconds to slow down the advancing horde of hostile intruders.

The commander observed the video feeds knowingly. She could see they seemed to rush ahead bi-pedally, but at times went down on all six of their limbs. The rear two were more like legs, as they were larger and more powerful, but seemed to lack dexterity. The front pair of arms emanated from where the torso or thorax was located. They were longer than human arms, and had two "elbows," and the appendages ended in blade shaped hands, that could split into an unknown number of what passed for fingers. Their skin was light brown, and was dry, it almost looked powdery if one were to get close enough to touch. Every large contact surface on their bodies was covered with a dark matte armor that also encased their heads, so no one could see their faces.

As the video images were viewed by everyone in the Command Center, Commander Sorenson felt her heart sink. She heard someone throw up, and in taking a quick look around, she could see frozen shock, hands held over mouths, and one person simply got up and shuffled out into the corridor.

Jim spoke up from the security stations. "Commander, the hostiles have advanced outside of the hull of the material slug, and are pushing toward the Spine, I have external HDs and fighters in position."

"Attack," she said, trusting them to do their best, and returned her eyes to the command-and-control screen, where the interceptors were nearing the additional bogies.

The interceptors streaked through space and approached the evading bogies, whose icons were shifting erratically. The screen indicated the interceptors' hulls had erupted with some sort of thruster pulses to drastically change their direction in an effort to stay on their targets. Two interceptors whiffed on bogie three when suddenly there was another plume of red, and bogie three disappeared into a shower of unorganized debris.

The weapons officer re-targeted the remaining proximity interceptors meant for bogie three, and the space battle continued. Bogies four through seven suddenly accelerated, and some of the penetrating interceptor packages missed, far behind their targets from one moment to the next. The weapons officer salvaged what he could from the remaining missiles, but some of those missiles that missed were out of the envelope, and the battle. They would travel on through the galaxy and perhaps never hit another solid object until the end of time.

Commander Sorenson saw that all remaining missiles were converging on the remaining bogies, four, five, six, and seven. Bogie four suddenly jumped as three proximity interceptors detonated in rapid succession. The trajectory arrows leapt onto the main screen and showed that the bogie had been pushed into evading out of the momentum envelope…it disappeared from the command-and-control picture. Bogies five and six disappeared in red starbursts, as penetrator interceptors slammed into them and vaporized in a mass of released energy.

With nearly twenty inbound interceptors remaining, bogie seven began to move again, and this time interceptors began disappearing from the main screen at an alarming rate. One blast fragmentation warhead erupted near bogie seven causing a sharp evasion, but its trajectory remained unchanged. A few seconds later, the remaining interceptors streaked by missing bogie seven and disappearing from the screen as they left the envelope. Bogie seven began to accelerate when three blips reappeared on the screen. They were the ones that had missed on bogie two and had somehow remained in the momentum envelope. They slammed into the side of bogie seven, and it disappeared from the screen, leaving the *Valor* and external fighter craft from Ring One and Two the only spaceborne objects remaining on the command-and-control screen.

The Command Center erupted in a cheer, and everyone began to re-orient to shift to the security team as the primary function. Commander Sorenson spoke. "Security Report."

Jim spoke. "Our external HDs and fighter craft have opened with missiles and guns to minimal effect. The projectiles seem to bounce off the armor of the intruders…but…fast moving debris from the ricochets is blasting many of the external attackers off the hull and into space. They do not appear to have a method for getting back into the *Valor* as no grappling or individual propulsion devices have been detected; however, the intruders appear to have realized their vulnerability and have moved back into the aft material slug. Our external craft and HDs can't get to them, and I have lost three fighter craft to intruders leaping onto them from the *Valor*…they left the envelope before we could help them."

Everyone in the Command Center felt the loss of Zero-Crew life. Once out of the momentum envelope, there was no way to get back to the *Valor*, and the *Valor* could not slow down, nor spare momentum to assist. The fighter craft occupants would either be killed by these creatures, or drift until they ran out of life support functions.

The security lead continued grimly, noting the performance of the Valor's armored mechanized combatants or MCs. "From what we have seen, the armored MCs have the only ordnance to push any of these things back, but any HD with a Gatling gun or anything lower than a .50 caliber is not going to get the job done… Commander, it is the AI's, as well as my assessment, that we will not be able to hold the Spine if these things get in."

Both Commander Sorenson and her first officer met the knowing eyes of the security lead, and Commander Sorenson spoke much more calmly than she felt. "Broken Spear Protocol."

The Command Center erupted in panicked flurry of activity, verbal objections and cries of despair as a large thirty-second countdown took over the main screen. Everyone raced around to strap themselves into chairs, deploying hidden harnesses and cinching them down. Others poured tablets, coffee cups, anything that wasn't nailed down into secure compartments before sprinting toward chairs of their own.

The HDs abandoned the Spine and left the larger MCs behind as they would not fit through the sliprings. The Zero Crew MC occupants, grim with determination, left their massive projectile weapons trained on the aft material slug connector corridor, which began to deform from repeated blunt force impacts from something much bigger than the original intruders they had all seen from the video feeds.

In the Command Center, suddenly everyone became deathly silent as the counter counted down, five…four…

The MCs, manned by brave Zero Crew members saw the door to the aft material slug split and then blast outward sending steel debris flying through the Spine of the *Valor*. They opened up with five-inch guns fit for Navy ships at sea, and fired their lesser caliber weapons as well. The Spine became a hornet's hive of racing hot metal projectiles, and as they smashed into the intruders confined to the small space of the aft material slug entryway, they were blasted back into the material slug.

Encouraged by the progress the MCs began to advance, when a massive shape emerged from the remnants of the aft material slug corridor. The creature looked to be nearly twenty feet tall, stood on four legs, had four arms, and a mass of whirring protrusions on its back and sides whipped around in a torrent of movement.

The massive being shot down the Spine, before the MCs could open fire. It flew past the lettered rings toward Ring One at incredible speed.

The counter in the Command Center hit zero, and everyone's world turned into vibrating exploding chaos.

Explosive bolts throughout the *Valor* detonated simultaneously. The slipring shredded apart almost instantly, and each of the lettered rings fractured down preset fault lines and were blasted apart by additional explosives. The rings sheared apart, and with no anchor to the Spine of the ship, they flew off into space in different directions based on their rotation, trailing debris, gases, broken HDs and the bodies of A-Crew members who had not made it back to their cryogenic chambers.

The bulk of the force of intruders erupted into the Spine just as pre-laid fission warheads detonated vaporizing the Spine and everyone left in it. The aft material slug along with any remaining intruders were sent spinning away from the expanding field of fractured rings and showers of debris.

Ring One remained intact and connected to the forward material slug. Commander Sorenson called out, "Report!" The command crew was still recovering from the jolting explosions. She didn't want to think about those who were not strapped down or in cryogenic suspension. She and her team had been strapped in, and she could tell many were concussed or had internal injuries from the massive and powerful jolts.

The security lead spoke back up in a ragged voice, "Broken Spear confirmed. The Spine has been destroyed along with any intruders and…others present. All rings have been ejected, and before you ask, I can't tell if any intruders were able to make it aboard any of the ring remnants. Their telemetry is still coming up so I can't even tell if they are…um…intact." He breathed, struggling. He went on. "As for intruders making it aboard, I don't think so. But since we see these things can survive in hard vacuum, I'm not sure if any of them managed to jump to the rings as they were breaking up or not," he finished.

"Understood," Commander Sorenson said. She pushed some buttons in her console and brought up the Hangar lead, "Hangar One, are you up and running?"

A voice could be heard over the console. "About half of the external craft are down with damage, but we have enough to get started.

"Good, deploy when ready and—"

She was interrupted by a small jolt as something impacted A-Ring.

"Security…Jim, what was that? Debris impact?" she asked.

"Stand by," Jim said as he conferred with his team and his hands flew across his own console. "Commander we have another intruder…it's on Ring One and…dear God it's…"

He was then interrupted by the sound of gunfire from down the corridor as a sentinel HD must have seen it and opened fire. Commander Sorenson looked at the video feed of the massive creature that was nearly as large as the main corridor. It pressed itself through the corridor leaving shreds of steel, and the high velocity rounds fired by now several sentinel HDs. The rounds impacted the creature's armor, and either bounced off, or split into fragments and fell away. They left small dents and scratches in the armor, but nothing more.

The beast ripped through any HDs and Zero Crew members in its path, and advanced toward the Command Center.

Commander Sorenson privately interacted with the ship's main AI, racing to run a few quick simulations on her console. Her brow furled at the result, and she began issuing a few more commands by typing. She didn't have time to look up at any of her fellow crew members she had served with for years. She didn't have time to tell them she was sorry. She didn't have time to think about the incredible experience of encountering extraterrestrial life no matter what their intent. And she didn't have time to think about what would happen to Earth and everyone else if these creatures arrived there.

The wall of the Command Center was ripped open, and everyone in their horror turned to see the gargantuan armored being. It moved on massive but lithe legs that reminded the commander of a dinosaur, and it had two sets of powerful clawed arms that seemed to come directly out in front of a huge torso. Its head was discernible beneath a huge helmet that was clearly technological in origin. Its brightly lit eyes, a set of four on the front of the helmet illuminated the now dark control room as power throughout Ring One began to fail.

The giant and violent being approached Commander Sorenson and then seemed to hesitate and look around. At that instant, Ring One's reactor went critical. Commander Sorenson took in her arch nemesis, and nodded in its direction, a wry smile on her lips. She breathed her last word, "Checkmate."

Ring One erupted in a massive explosion, bigger than all the other explosions from the engagement combined. The shock wave washed across the floating pieces of the other lettered rings, damaging, and jostling them further. A cloud of debris and exotic particles showered outward in every direction, and the extremely bright space borne battlefield quickly returned to silence and darkness as the embers of released energy faded.

The fragments of the rings continued to expand away from the vector the *Valor* had been traveling, and on one of the fragments of D-Ring, Corbin's cryo pod remained undisturbed.

Information

Corbin, and the crews of the Valor will continue their adventures in Book 2 of the Eartherians Series.

Stay up to date on the Eartherians Series, read author blogs, and sign up for the e-mail list at https://www.mccavanaugh.com

A little about the Author:

Matt Cavanaugh, a.k.a. "Cavi", is a new American science fiction author and the author of the Eartherians Series. He is a science fiction and fantasy novel aficionado and is an avid podcast listener and reader on all things UFO, space, defense, astrophysics, the ethereal, and mysterious esoteric topics. Other interests include grilling & tailgating, watching college football, skiing, and spending time with great friends and family. Cavi has a bachelor's degree from the University of Michigan in Industrial Operations Engineering, and an MBA from Syracuse University Whitman School of Business. He is married with three children, and lives in Southeast Michigan.

The cover art has been masterfully done by Justen Dippel.

Made in the USA
Monee, IL
15 April 2024

5aac4fb3-caa3-4488-95ab-77fba07d5134R01